LETTING GO WITH DR RODRIGUEZ

BY
FIONA LOWE

DR TALL, DARK... AND DANGEROUS?

BY
LYNNE MARSHALL

MILLS & BOON

Always an avid reader, **Fiona Lowe** decided to combine her love of romance with her interest in all things medical, so writing Medical™ Romance was an obvious choice! She lives in a seaside town in southern Australia, where she juggles writing, reading, working and raising two gorgeous sons with the support of her own real-life hero!

Recent titles by this author:

SYDNEY HARBOUR HOSPITAL: TOM'S REDEMPTION*
CAREER GIRL IN THE COUNTRY
SINGLE DAD'S TRIPLE TROUBLE
THE MOST MAGICAL GIFT OF ALL
HER BROODING ITALIAN SURGEON
MIRACLE: TWIN BABIES

Sydney Harbour Hospital

Lynne Marshall has been a Registered Nurse in a large California hospital for over twenty-five years. She has now taken the leap to writing full-time, but still volunteers at her local community hospital. After writing the book of her heart in 2000, she discovered the wonderful world of Mills & Boon® Medical™ Romance, where she feels the freedom to write the stories she loves. She is happily married, has two fantastic grown children, and a socially challenged rescued dog. Besides her passion for writing Medical Romance, she loves to travel and read. Thanks to the family dog, she takes long walks every day! To find out more about Lynne, please visit her website www.lynnemarshall.com

Recent titles by this author:

THE CHRISTMAS BABY BUMP
THE HEART DOCTOR AND THE BABY
THE BOSS AND NURSE ALBRIGHT
TEMPORARY DOCTOR, SURPRISE FATHER

LETTING GO WITH DR RODRIGUEZ

BY
FIONA LOWE

MILLS
BOON

First published in Great Britain 2012
by Mills & Boon, an imprint of Harlequin (UK) Limited.
Harlequin (UK) Limited, Eton House, 18-24 Paradise Road,
Richmond, Surrey TW9 1SR

© Fiona Lowe 2012

ISBN: 978 0 263 89790 6

Harlequin (UK) policy is to use papers that are natural, renewable and recyclable products and made from wood grown in sustainable forests. The logging and manufacturing process conform to the legal environmental regulations of the country of origin.

Printed and bound in Spain
by Blackprint CPI, Barcelona

Dear Reader

A couple of years ago I was fortunate enough to attend a polo match. Watching those nuggety polo ponies strut their stuff was awe-inspiring. With their hogged (roached) manes and braided tails, they have amazing agility and can turn on the spot. Polo players will tell you that their game is eighty percent horse and twenty percent their own skill.

Ever since that sunny Saturday afternoon I have wanted to have a polo match in a book but each story ended up on a different trajectory and the polo match didn't fit. Until now. I mean how could I have a gorgeous Argentine hero and *not* have a polo match?

However, I didn't realise how important this polo match would be to my characters until I wrote the book and the polo match became another character in the story.

Marco is from Argentina and living in Outback Australia. He answered the call to come to Australia to help fill the doctor shortage, and now he is there his greatest wish is to stay and carve out a life for himself and his young son, who has mild cerebral palsy.

Lucy Patterson grew up in Bulla Creek, Western Australia, the much-loved only child of the local doctor. In keeping with family tradition Lucy became a doctor, and had plans to join her father—until her mother died and her world was turned upside down.

I'll let the book tell their story. Meanwhile, if you want to see the pictures and videos that inspired the book head to www.fionalowe.com I love to hear from my readers, and you can find me on Facebook, Twitter and Goodreads.

Happy Reading!

Love

Fiona xx

For Monica, with thanks for giving my eldest son
an amazing time in France, and for all her help
with Marco's Spanish.

Special thanks to Alan,
who cheerfully answered my e-mail
and gave me a rundown on the intricacies of visas.

CHAPTER ONE

'LUCE, wait.'

Dr Lucy Patterson heard the call and with a smile, she thrust her hand against the fast-closing elevator doors at Perth City Hospital. They bounced open.

A moment later, Daniel Edgerton, radiographer and her boyfriend, strode over the silver threshold. 'Thanks.' His smile for her wasn't quite as broad as it had been in the past, but if he was as weary as she was, she totally understood.

He slapped the large 'G' button with the heel of his hand. 'You finishing up for the day?'

She bit her lip, knowing he wasn't going to be thrilled with her reply. 'Not quite. I have to admit a late addition to the prof's surgical list and re-site an IV.'

His sigh reverberated around the boxed space, settling over her with cloying disapproval. He worked a roster with a definite start and end time, and he didn't always understand that her day finished when the work was finally complete. With forced brightness and a wide smile, she quickly added, 'But then I'll be done and yours for the night.'

Daniel opened his mouth but an ominous grinding sound drowned out his reply and the smooth descent of the elevator suddenly jerked, throwing Lucy sideways.

She gripped the support rail and righted herself. 'Please, no, not again. I got stuck here last week for twenty minutes.'

'It's not a total disaster.' Daniel reached his arm around her waist, pulling her in close and nuzzling her neck as he ran his hand up her back, his fingers reaching for her bra strap. 'We can do a lot with twenty minutes.'

She laughed, but splayed her fingers against his chest, leaning back and putting some distance between them. 'True, but I'm not risking my senior registrar's application by being caught "in flagrante" in an elevator.'

His blue eyes hardened as he dropped his arms to his sides. 'Jess didn't have a problem with it.'

She blinked at him in surprise. Jess was her housemate of four years and they got along well, sharing not only a house but gossip, clothes and after a tough day, a glass of wine. 'There's no way Jess would have sex in an elevator.'

He shrugged—the action a total disregard of her reply. 'There's every way and she did.'

A jab of indignation caught Lucy under the ribs and she crossed her arms. 'If Jess had sex in an elevator she'd have told me.'

Daniel's brows rose as his mouth flattened. 'She doesn't have to tell you everything, Luce, and let's face it, just lately you've hardly been around.'

Lucy stifled a flicker of unease that Jess may have confided in Dan rather than her. 'Why are you so certain she did?'

This time Daniel crossed his arms. 'Because I was there.'

'You were there?' Confusion drove the words across her lips and for the briefest moment she thought Daniel meant he'd walked in on Jess and her lover when the elevator doors had opened. Suddenly, her sluggish brain decoded his body language—stiff and defiant—and a chill raced through her so hard and fast that she trembled. '*You* had sex with Jess?' Her voice rose and cracked. 'Here?'

He met her shocked gaze with a combative glare. 'Yeah.'

Her friend. Her hand flew to her mouth as nausea spun her stomach and threatened to return the chocolate muffin she'd just eaten. Stepping back, she flattened herself against the wall and tried to put as much distance between them as possible. 'When?'

Dan sucked in his lips and finally said, 'Last week.'

She thought back to the sex they'd had last Wednesday after she'd cooked his favourite dinner—the night she'd been the one making all the moves. At the time it had surprised her because usually Dan initiated sex, but it hadn't taken long before he'd got on board. Her stomach pitched again. Desperately trying to keep her composure, she spoke softly but with an edge of steel. '*When* last week?'

For the first time, he dropped his gaze. 'It doesn't matter.'

She gripped the support rail as her knees turned to jelly. 'Yes, it bloody matters.'

He ran his hand over his short-cropped hair. 'Look, Luce, there's no point—'

'Tell me!' She heard her tears in the shout as she lost the battle to hold herself together.

'Wednesday afternoon.'

It was as if the cable of the elevator snapped right there and then, releasing the silver box into free-fall. Only it was her life that was tumbling and crashing down around her, and taking all the supporting pillars with it. Pillars she'd barely shored up after they'd spectacularly collapsed in on her six months ago, making her question everything she'd ever believed in.

Every part of her was numb—her lungs refused to move and tears blurred her eyes. How could this be happening? Why now when everything else in her life, including her career, was so unsettled? A shot of righteous anger suddenly pierced through the numbness giving rise to blessed pain. 'You bastard.'

His head snapped up. 'Oh, that's rich. I'm the bastard, but you've been the one who's been closed off for months. You might be standing next to me, but you're never really here. Jess at least understands me. Jess gives me something. You've given me nothing for way too long, Lucy.'

Her anger swelled, propelled by a hammering heart and utter devastation. 'You're not just a bastard, Dan, you're a selfish bastard. You know what's been going on with me and Da—' She stopped herself, not able to finish that particular word. She swallowed and pushed on. 'With William. You know what I've been going through, but that doesn't count for anything, does it? Nothing matters if it's not all about you.'

His mouth tightened giving his boyish face a hard edge. 'It's been all about you for months, Luce, and I've had enough.'

She'd known in her heart things weren't good between them, but she'd never expected such a bitter betrayal. 'Then why didn't you just leave? Why take my friend with you?'

A light came into his eyes. 'I think I love her.'

The simple words plunged into her heart making her double up in pain. Words he'd never voiced to her in all their time together. Her chest rose and fell way too fast and she put her hands around her mouth so she didn't hyperventilate.

Daniel slammed his hands against the 'door open' button. 'Come on.' He hit every other button too, wanting out of this box of torrid emotions as much as she did.

Lucy dug deep and found her voice. 'You say you love Jess and yet you still had sex with me? Oh, that's classy, Dan, really classy.' The combined infidelity of her friends burned through her soul. 'You both deserve each other.'

A trace of contrition played across his cheeks. 'Look, Luce, I'm sorry it ended this way, but it's not *all* my fault.'

Utter wretchedness dragged at her and she nodded mutely, not because she agreed with him, but because she couldn't voice even a tenth of her feelings at the utter disloyalty of the two people she'd drawn on for support over most of the year.

A whirring noise sounded, followed by the elevator moving slowly down. Finally the doors opened with a ping and Daniel muttered, 'Thank God,' before stepping out and walking away without a backwards glance.

The doors slid shut and Lucy sank to the floor, closing her eyes. Even in her darkest moments she'd never imagined she would have been part of the conversation that had just taken place. She lurched from one memory to another, searching for clues, hints—anything at all that might have prepared her for Daniel's bombshell. Things had been strained, but there'd been no hint of him and Jess.

None that you noticed. But then again, you haven't noticed much lately, have you?

Her head pounded and resentment burned through her. She felt her smart-phone vibrate and she pulled it out of the deep pocket in her white coat, expecting a message from the ward asking where she was and how much longer she'd be, because her patient was overdue for IV antibiotics. The message wasn't from the ward, but an email from an unfamiliar name.

She squinted through her headache to make the words come into focus.

Ms Patterson,
As you know, your father, Dr William Patterson, has fractured his tibia. He is not a man to ask for help so I, as his doctor and the second medical practitioner in Bulla Creek, am asking for you to visit at your earliest convenience.
Marco Rodriguez (Dr)

She stared at the email, reading it three times before the words finally sank in. *Fractured tibia?* She bit her lip as guilt spun around worry. Of course she hadn't known about William's leg. She hadn't communicated with him in months and the emails he'd sent had dealt only with the information she'd requested. None had mentioned his health. Neither had he mentioned a doctor with a Spanish name and a formal writing style, which indicated that English wasn't his native language. What was a Spaniard doing in outback Bulla Creek?

At your earliest convenience. She instinctively shook her head and then, from the tangled mess that was currently her life, she stared up at the ceiling of the elevator absolutely certain about one thing. No way was she going back to Bulla Creek.

You mean home.

'No, I mean Bulla Creek.' Her emphatic voice sounded strident in the confines of the otherwise empty elevator.

Right, so you're ignoring duty, staying in Perth where your boyfriend's just dumped you, and your housemate has utterly betrayed you. That's gonna be cosy. Kinda makes Bulla Creek almost attractive, doesn't it?

Lucy dropped her head in her hands and wished she could wind back the clock one year—back to a time when she knew who she was, knew where she belonged and where she was headed. Instead she now faced a road that stretched way out in front of her that was filled with a pea-soup fog.

Every part of her railed against the idea of going back to Bulla Creek, but the news about William tore at the box she'd shoved all her feelings about him into—feelings she didn't want to revisit. They came back anyway in unsettling waves. No matter what had happened between them and no matter how much she didn't want to see him, she couldn't just ignore the fact he'd broken his leg. Not at his age. The doctor in her knew that only too well. Acknowledging it smoothed out her tangled thoughts.

'I'll take some annual leave, fly up to Bulla Creek for a quick visit and check that William's receiving the correct medical care. Then I'll come back here, find a new place to live and sort out the rest of my life, which won't include disloyal friends and cheating, bastard men.'

You do realise there isn't anyone here listening except me and I don't need to hear you talk to know exactly what you're thinking.

'Shut-up.' The yell propelled Lucy to her feet and she brushed down her white coat. Her life was in tatters, but at least she had a plan. One she was clinging to like a floating log in a choppy sea.

The red dust of Bulla Creek was covered in a layer of green, courtesy of a record-setting wet winter followed by a sunny spring. The sheep wore thick fleeces, lambs gambolled on fat legs and the farmers smiled, which was almost as uncommon as the weather. Dr Marco Rodriguez returned a farmer's hat tip and grin as he strode down the main street toward the Bulla Creek Medical Centre. It wasn't the first time he'd reflected on the fact that, in general, farmers in Western Australia shared a taciturn approach to life that was very similar to that of the farmers of his homeland of Argentina. Life on the land was tough and a good season was cause for celebration.

He turned left at the rust-and-sand-coloured church, which stood diagonally opposite the pub. Both buildings had been built over a hundred years ago from local rocks quarried when veins of lead in the nearby hills had guaranteed prosperity. Bulla Creek today was not as affluent as it had been back then, but the legacy of heritage buildings not only reminded residents of its wealthy past, but more importantly it brought in tourists with money to spend. People paid a lot to step back in time and spend a weekend or longer imagining simpler times.

Marco knew it was just an illusion. There'd been nothing simple about living without running water and basic hygiene in a time when a broken leg had often resulted in amputation, when the birth of a child could easily take the life of a mother and a secondary infection after a common cold could kill. Even today, childbirth had its risks and he was far too intimate with the dangers.

Pulling open the door of the modern medical clinic, which also fronted a small hospital annexe of five acute-care beds and ten nursing-home beds, he walked into a packed waiting room. Just as he'd done every day for the last few weeks since his medical partner had fallen ill. He was worried about William who'd been adamant he didn't want his daughter told about his accident, although when he spoke of her his eyes lit up before sadness filled them.

William was not his usual, upbeat self and he was taking longer to return to work than expected. With the death of his wife earlier in the year and now the fracture, Marco believed he needed cheering up.

He pressed down on the ripple of unease that had been trickling through him ever since he'd overridden the other doctor's request and written to William's daughter. He'd needed to do something because he really believed William needed time with family so he could re-find his spark. With one doctor down, Marco's days ran together in a long blur of work with snatches of fatherhood wedged in between. This wasn't what he'd envisaged when he'd made the decision to come to Bulla Creek. It was supposed to have meant more time for Ignacio, not less. He needed William back at work yesterday.

He swallowed a sigh and mustered up a smile for his waiting patients because his problems were not theirs and they deserved his complete attention. '*Buenos días*. Good morning, everyone. I am at your service in just a few moments.'

'We have an empty waiting room and I'm off home. You should go too while you can.'

Marco looked up from reading pathology reports to see Sue Hogarth, practice nurse, farmer's wife and soon-to-be grandmother, standing in the doorway of his office. 'Ten minutes more.'

She nodded slowly. 'I'll lock up the front doors then

and all you have to do is go out the back and make sure it's locked behind you.'

'Sure. Thank you for your help today.'

'Ah, Marco, that all Australian men could be so polite. See you tomorrow when we get to do it all again.' She grinned and pushed off the architrave preparing to leave, but turned back suddenly. 'Oh, Ignacio's appointment's been changed to Tuesday. I've put it directly into your electronic calendar. Night.'

'Goodnight.' He heard her fading footsteps and the door slam shut. He waited a moment and then smiled as he soaked up the peace of a closed clinic—silent phones, still rooms and the blissful quiet of absolutely no interruptions. He finished reading the reports, methodically listing the names of the patients that Sue needed to call tomorrow to schedule review appointments, and as he reached the last one he let out a breath. Thankfully there were no sinister results in this batch and he was spared the need to make the hard phone call and give someone seriously bad news. He hated doing that as it reminded him of the time he'd received it and the powerlessness that came with it.

He texted Heather—his housekeeper and Ignacio's afterschool caregiver—telling her he'd be home in ten minutes and then he packed up his desk. Grabbing his bag, he entered the corridor and headed toward the back door, flicking off the hall lights as he reached the switch. The expected darkness didn't come. With a sigh, he realised that Sue had left the office light on and he spun on his heel, walking the length of the corridor to turn it off.

As he slid his hand up the doorway to reach the switch, something made him glance into the room. A round and pert, jeans-clad bottom stared straight at him.

'*Querido Dios.*' Shocked surprise sent his English scurrying and it took a moment for him to find the correct words. 'What are you *doing*?'

A young woman turned abruptly from the computer, her chin-length, chestnut-red hair swinging wildly around her guilt-streaked face. Round eyes, the colour of an Argentine summer sky just before the descent of a storm, stared at him, brimming with a thousand emotions. A heartbeat later they cleared as if she was practised in forcing her feelings to retreat until only defiance remained. She stood less than tall despite the boost of high wedge heels and then her chin tilted up, her shoulders rolled back and her breasts rose, straining against the free-flowing pink halter top that draped itself around her curves and ended by softly caressing her hips.

A jolt of heat whipped him—heat that hadn't flared in his veins for a long time—and for the briefest of moments his eyes followed the tantalising fall of the soft material as if they hoped to glimpse what nestled behind it. Thankfully, common sense shot in to rescue him and he quickly hauled his gaze back to her face.

At that precise moment he knew the words he should have spoken were 'Who are you?'

As if reading his mind she stepped forward, extending her hand. 'You must be Marco Rodriguez. I'm Lucy.'

The overly wide smile gave her away. From the age of fourteen girls had flirted with him, and it had taken him almost as long to learn that the flirting wasn't always about wanting him. Often it was about wanting something else entirely—a bitter lesson that Bianca had taught him too well. Now at thirty-three, his radar was pretty well tuned. She spoke as if he should recognise her, using his name as a bridge to connect them with a familiarity that didn't exist. He had an excellent memory and he knew they'd not met before.

You would have remembered those breasts.

He shrugged away the inconvenient awakening of his libido and focused on the facts. He might not know her but he did know that whoever she was, she shouldn't be here in an office that didn't belong to her. Neither should she be viewing a computer that contained the confidential files of all of the patients of Bulla Creek and the surrounding district.

A fizz of anger shook him and for the first time in a long, long time his inherent good manners deserted him. He didn't greet her and instead left her extended hand hovering between them.

Damn it. Lucy's plan of coming unobserved into the clinic after hours was unravelling faster than a skein of wool in the claws of a cat. It had taken all day to drive from Perth and she'd only arrived half an hour ago. During that time she'd been parked outside in her new car with a cap pulled low on her head so she wouldn't be recognised. She didn't want to talk to anyone in town before she'd seen William and she wanted to read his medical file before she spoke to him.

When Sue had finished her methodical locking-up routine and had double checked everything, Lucy had been certain the clinic was empty and that she was good to go. Even then, she'd held back, checking the immediate area for other cars parked in the clinic car park or nearby. Only then had she been convinced the building was empty.

You got that wrong.

She had to fight hard not to bite her lip. That the man in front of her could grace the runway of a fashion show and make every woman in the crowd swoon was a given, but considering an average-looking guy had just tossed her aside, treating fidelity as if it was completely expendable, she was now giving all men a wide berth. No matter how handsome or how thick, dark and wavy was the hair which fell over the top of tanned ears and teased fingers to brush it back, she would not be tempted. She was especially impervious to square, broad shoulders that despite her being in her highest heels were at perfect head-resting height. She'd been fooled by the promise of a safe haven more than once.

No, the effort required not to bite her lip came from the derisive look that scoured his high cheek bones and burned from his rich-cocoa-coloured eyes. The look that said, I wouldn't touch your hand if you were the last woman on earth.

He crossed his toned arms with their dark hairs almost standing on end over his wide chest and completely ignored her hand. 'I do not know you.' His accent thickened. 'You should not be here.'

You know he's correct.

She gritted her teeth against her conscience and told herself she had the right to be here. Mustering up a smile, the winning one she'd used a lot as a child to get her own way, she forced her hand to stay hovering between them despite wanting to whip it back by her side and dry the sweat on her jeans. All she needed to do was explain who she was and her plan would be safe. 'I'm Lucy Patterson. You emailed me about William.'

'You're William's daughter?' Chocolate brows shot halfway up an intelligent forehead and his gaze raked her from head to toe as disbelief momentarily pushed his anger aside.

She was used to this reaction, having experienced it

often from the age of sixteen when it had become obvious she was never going to grow any taller. Once it had made her laugh and she'd had a steady stream of jokes at the ready about her and William's excessive height differences. Only that had been before everything had changed and a lifetime lie had been exposed. 'Like I said, I'm Lucy Patterson.' She tilted her extended hand slightly.

He slowly uncrossed his folded arms and slid his right palm against hers, his long fingers curving around her hand like a splash of dark paint against a white canvas. The heat burned her, shooting up her arm before diving deep and leaving behind a trail of addictive tingles and shivers.

Oh, no. Not now and not here. Shocked at her body's reaction, she abruptly pulled her hand away to the safety of her side. After the debacle that had been her relationship with Daniel, she didn't want or need any type of attraction to any man. Especially one in Bulla Creek where she wouldn't live again even if they paid her.

Marco didn't seem to have noticed her hasty end to their handshake. 'Lucy Patterson, why are you here?'

Lucy wondered if perhaps his English wasn't as good as she'd assumed. She smiled again. 'You wrote to me and asked me to come, so here I am.'

Two deep lines etched into the bridge of his nose. 'I asked you to come and visit your father, not the computer in this office.'

The muscles in her cheeks ached from the continual bright smile. A smile that didn't seem to be having any effect on its intended target. She went for chatty. 'I'm not sure what doctors are like where you come from, but in Australia the combination of being male and a doctor makes the worst type of patient.'

Marco tilted his head in thought and a curl fell forward. 'This may be.'

Yes, she was getting somewhere. 'So it makes sense for me to read his medical history before I see him.'

So now you're lying to other people and not just yourself.

Again, she silenced her conscience. *Let me do things my way.*

Marco continued to stare at her with a questioning look. 'But you are not William's doctor.'

'No, but I *am* a doctor.'

Again his gaze censored her. 'Then you should know better.'

She tossed her head, overriding the sliver of guilt that pierced her and instead converted it into righteous indignation. 'William hasn't mentioned to me that he broke his leg and at his age a fall can be a sign of other things so it makes sense for me to read his file.'

'Your father is not so ill that he can't speak. William is very capable of telling you the information.' A look of realisation suddenly shone brightly in his enigmatic eyes. 'Have you spoken to him?'

She shrugged so as not to squirm and held onto her bravado. 'Thank you for emailing me, but I've got it all under control.' She moved back toward the computer.

In two long strides he was by her side with his hands on her upper arms and suddenly her feet left the floor.

Abject offence roared through her. 'Hey! Put me down.'

A moment later, she was back on terra firma with Marco, feet wide apart, standing solidly between her and the computer and blocking her path.

His glare matched hers—incensed and scowling.

'As William's doctor and partner in this practice, I will not allow you to read his file without his permission.'

She held onto her dignity by a thread. 'I'm his next of kin.'

'*Sí*, so you know that does not give you the right to read his file.' His hand shot out. 'You have a key to the clinic?'

Her arms shot over her chest as guilt and anger hammered her. 'I'm not giving it to you.'

'You do not work here and I do not trust you.'

'I grew up here.' Words spluttered in her throat, chained by a rush of conflicting emotions that made her sway. 'God, I spent so many Saturday mornings playing in the waiting room that it was my second home. You're the stranger here, buddy, not me.'

He didn't even flinch. If anything he seemed more implacable than ever and the quietness of his voice didn't hide for a moment his firm intent. 'Go and talk with your father.'

The prospect of talking to William had anxiety and heartache making her feet twitch in readiness to run far from Bulla Creek. 'I *will* read that file.'

He shook his head. 'Not without William's permission.'

'Fine, I'll ask Sue.'

His jaw stiffened. 'I think that Sue is disappointed that you have not been to see your father in a long time. She will side with me.'

She swallowed hard, hating that the town might have turned on her without knowing the full story. Her hands shot out in bitter aggravation. 'This isn't how we do things in the country.'

This time one brow rose sardonically. 'So, you would

let *anyone* read your patients' files where you work? If this is so, I would not want to be under your care.'

The shot against her professionalism jolted her hard.

You know he's right. From before he caught you trying to read the file you've known he was right.

My situation is different. She harnessed all her frustration, using it to push away the other emotions that threatened to swamp her the way they had on and off over the last six months. She fisted her hands by her sides. 'You know nothing about me, Dr Rodriguez, and therefore not enough to judge me.'

Before he could reply, she pushed past him, stalking out into the fading light and back to her car, homeless in a town she'd once called home. Only then did she allow herself to cry.

CHAPTER TWO

'*Papá?*'

Marco lay on his son's bed as part of their 'good-night' ritual. 'Yes.'

'No boys…' Ignacio spoke slowly, each word an effort to form perfectly. He breathed in '…have crutches.'

Marco tried to keep the tension out of his voice. 'Lots of boys use crutches.'

'Not at school. Not in town. I looked.'

Marco swallowed a familiar sigh. 'You are right. No other boys in Bulla Creek use crutches, but you're special.'

'No. I'm not.' Ignacio's voice rose and his small body spasmed, making it even more rigid than its usual state. 'I'm different. I don't like it.'

Each word pierced Marco's heart. A part of him knew that one day his wonderful son would make the connection that he didn't have the same free and easy control of his body as most other boys his age. Marco had hoped however that the realisation would come much later than at a mere five years of age. The irony of it all was that inside a body that failed Ignacio daily on so many levels was a mind that was sharp and fiercely intelligent.

'*Querido*, your crutches are your friend when your

legs are tired. Now you must sleep so your legs are rested in the morning.'

He slid the soft-toy koala, the one Ignacio had chosen on their arrival at Sydney airport, into his arms and then tucked in the sheet and light blanket around him. Pressing a kiss to his forehead, he whispered, 'I love you. Sleep well.'

'I love you, too, *Papá.*'

Marco closed the door behind him and walked directly to the kitchen. Heather had prepared a plate of cold chicken and salad for him and as he poured himself a glass of wine to accompany the food, he wished he was eating a thick steak straight off the barbecue instead of yet another cold meal. Of course, he could fire up the grill and cook one, but he lacked the energy. Bulla Creek, the place he'd come to as a sanctuary and for a new start, was wearing him out.

As he ate, he glanced at the calendar, mentally calculating how long William had been out of action. It felt disloyal to wish his colleague and mentor back at his desk when he clearly didn't feel up to it and yet if William could give just two hours a day to see the straightforward cases it would ease Marco's load considerably.

Lucy Patterson is a doctor. You could ask her to help.

No. He pushed his plate away and took a long gulp of his wine as the combined image of wild, grey eyes and pale cheeks stained with pink hit him. It was instantly followed up with the backhander of a lush-red, pouting and highly kissable mouth. His blood pounded more than a fraction faster.

He quickly stood up and stowed his plate in the dishwasher as if movement would empty his mind of her. It galled him that his body had decided to come alive in the presence of a woman who looked like a fragile porcelain doll, but in personality was the exact opposite. Plus, she came with questionable professional ethics. A lesser man would have melted under the incensed fire blazing from those eyes, which had flared when he'd denied her access to the computer.

His palms suddenly glowed hot, reliving the soft warmth of her skin where he'd touched her arms. Skin that covered surprisingly taut muscles that had hinted at some weight-work. That he'd lifted her out of the way still shocked him, but he'd acted out of loyalty to William. William was his patient and he knew nothing of Lucy.

William didn't speak of her and Sue had sighed when she'd reluctantly handed over the email address saying, 'He won't be happy about this and she should know better.' At the time, he'd been intent on getting some help for William and by default for himself so Marco hadn't given Sue's statement much thought. However, now he'd met Lucy Patterson, he wondered if it was her conduct as a doctor that was the issue that lay between her and her father. William was one of the most principled and professional doctors Marco had ever worked with and he couldn't imagine him condoning any behaviour that went against his code of practice.

No, it was enough that William would resent his intrusion in summoning his daughter without Marco adding to it by asking her to work in the clinic. He couldn't in all conscience have someone in the practice who ignored protocol. No, Lucy Patterson wasn't the answer to his problems.

Decision made, he took his wine out onto the back deck which overlooked the surrounding rocky hills and breathed in the sweet, cool evening air that slid in over the fading heat. Out here, he could usually shed some of the pressures that plagued him, but not tonight. As he watched the night star rise in the darkening sky, his thoughts spun out to Argentina and to his parents who were anxious to join him in Bulla Creek the moment he was granted permanent residency and he could legally sponsor them. They missed their grandson. His thoughts bounced back to Ignacio's heartbreak. He let his head fall back on that grief, feeling it moving through him again, just like it had years before, and then suddenly, without any bidding, an image of Lucy Patterson's curvaceous behind swooped in sending all other thoughts scattering.

Swearing in Spanish, he stood up and walked inside.

Lucy repaired her makeup in the car using the tiny mirror on the visor and then ran a brush through her hair. The yellow light gave her a jaundiced look and she pinched her cheeks trying to infuse some colour. She should have checked into the motel, but she really didn't want to meet anyone she knew until she'd spoken to William. She stared at her pale face. 'Lucy Jane whoever-you-are, it's time.'

Stepping out onto the sweeping, circular driveway outside Haven, the gravel crunched under her feet and she stared up at the house. The stone and iron cottage with its whitewashed window sills and decorative wooden veranda rails stood as it had for the last one hundred and thirty years. It had been her home from the age of one when her parents had moved with her to Bulla Creek, and right up until she'd left for university. After that it had been her haven when life in Perth pressed in on her, and she'd run home for some rest, relaxation and general cosseting.

All that had changed and now it was a house associated with heartache. Part of her wanted to knock on the front door to emphasise her visitor status, but it was a long walk from the back of the house and no matter how furious she was with William, he would be on crutches. She didn't want him to walk further than necessary so she walked around the side of the house, opened the squeaky gate and entered the cottage garden. The scent of lavender hit her nostrils and she breathed in deeply, trying to use its calming properties. To her left, an enormous grapevine grew over a frame, providing shade to what William had always called 'their outdoor living room'.

Her gaze extended beyond the deck, through the large, glass doors and into the kitchen. She saw William sitting at the long, Baltic pine table, with crutches resting on one end as well as a cane. A book lay in front of him, and he held a glass in his hand. Her heart rolled over despite itself. When had he got old? The last time she'd seen him his hair had had flecks of silver streaking through the black. Now all his hair was silver grey.

Go in, talk to him, and make sure he's okay.

She tossed her head as she grumbled quietly to herself. 'Yes, I'm going inside but after that, I'm checking into the motel.'

Blowing out a breath, she tried to capture a semblance of composure because everything to do with William always generated a mass of contradictory feelings. She rolled her shoulders back, raised her hand, knocked and walked in.

'Hello, William.'

The man she'd called her father for twenty-six years looked up from his book, shock draining his face of colour. 'Lucy.' He stared at her and blinked, as if he didn't believe his eyes, and then slowly his mouth curved up into a wide and familiar smile. 'What a wonderful surprise.'

She bit her lip, not knowing what to say because 'Just passing through, thought I'd drop in' didn't allow for the seven hundred kilometre journey from Perth. She tilted her head toward the crutches. 'You've been in the wars.'

He raised his leg, the cast white against the dark material of his trousers, and gave a self-deprecating grimace. 'Came off my bike dodging a kangaroo. Big red hopped away and now I'm hopping too.'

His humour circled her like it always had—warm and loving—but she refused to give in to it because being a doctor was so much easier than the minefield of being his daughter. 'So I see. Any other damage besides a fractured tibia?'

His smile faded slightly. 'How do you know I have a fractured tibia? I haven't mentioned what bones I broke.'

Busted. But she had no qualms telling him the truth because she had no need to protect the source, especially given what had happened. 'Your Spanish doctor emailed me.'

For some reason her face felt suddenly hot, which was crazy because she hadn't even said the man's name. However, since she'd stormed out of the clinic, each time she'd thought about the raven-haired, accented doctor, this heat-fest flared inside her. She wanted it to stop.

'He's not Spanish. He's from Argentina.' William's face sagged, making him look more haggard than ever. 'So, the *only* reason you're in Bulla Creek is because Marco asked you to come?'

She shrugged trying not to let his palpable hurt touch her. She was hurting too, only her reason was much bigger and more life-altering than his. 'I'm here to make sure you're getting the right medical care.'

This time William shrugged and when he spoke his voice held the well-modulated tone of a country GP giving a report to a colleague. 'You can set your mind at ease immediately. Marco is more than competent and the break wasn't complicated, but even so he insisted on me going to Geraldton to see Jeremy Lucas, the orthopod. As you can see, I'm doing well and I've graduated to a walking stick.'

She wanted to believe him, but evidence to the contrary was in front of them. 'So why the crutches?'

'I was tired tonight after more walking more than usual so I've been using crutches. If you don't believe me about the break, you can look at the X-rays if you wish.'

'Dr Rodriguez wouldn't let me look at anything.'

He frowned again. 'You've been to the clinic?'

She shifted on her feet realising there was absolutely nothing wrong with her father's lightning-quick brain. It was a good thing except when it pertained to her. 'I had to drive past the clinic to get here so it made sense to call in first.'

You're big on self-delusion today.

She kept talking to silence her conscience. 'But like I said, he wouldn't give me any information and he told me in no uncertain terms...' she found herself gently stroking the tops of her arms and dropped her hands away fast '...that I had to talk to you.'

'As it should be.' His lips twitched. 'Still, I imagine that would have been very frustrating for you.' The words held the type of understanding that only came from knowing someone for a very long time, and they held a slight hint of censure.

'It was.' She braced herself, expecting him to say something about the fact she hadn't spoken to him in months.

He cleared his throat. 'As you can see I'm doing fine and the cast comes off in a few days. Sharon comes in each day to cook and clean just as she has all year, and Sue calls in as well. There's absolutely nothing for you to worry about.'

William rose to his feet and ignoring the crutches used his cane to rest against. 'Cup of tea?'

She hesitated, rationalising that he sounded fine and he seemed to have everything organised without her help so she didn't have to stay.

He doesn't look fine. He looks tired, old and sad.

She didn't want to think about that because it tempted her to question the decision she'd made months ago. 'Um…thanks, but it's been a long day and…um…I still need to check into the motel.'

'The motel?' William's movement stalled and his face paled. 'Lucy, you know you *always* have a room here if you want or need it.' He stared at her silently, not asking her to stay in words but with his hazel eyes which filled with quiet hope.

She swallowed, trying to hold herself together as the long drive, her horrible last two days and the fracas in the clinic slammed into the comforting scent of bergamot, fresh mint and leather-bound books—some of the many fragrances that defined her childhood. Despite the catastrophic disclosure that had changed everything, despite her anger and confusion regarding William and Bulla Creek, the aromas of yesteryear pulled at her strongly, upending her plan of a quick, clinical visit.

Fatigue clawed at her like sticky mud on boots and the thought of having to deal with the questioning looks of Loretta, the gossipy motel owner, was more than she could bear. She was a grown-up, not a child, and surely she could get through *one* night in this house with all its ghosts. One night of duty to really make sure William was doing as well as he said.

She sank into the comforting depths of the chesterfield before she could talk herself out of it and said, 'Tea would be lovely, thank you.'

Lucy squinted against the bright sunlight which poured into her bedroom through the now thin and faded pink curtains. She flipped onto her side, pulling the pillow over her head, but then the raucous screech of the white cockatoos greeting the dawn shocked her fully awake. As her heart rate slowed, she remembered she was lying in her childhood bed in Haven, back at Bulla Creek.

This time her heart rate stayed normal, but her stomach squirted acid. At this rate, her stress levels were going to seriously injure her. She threw back the covers. Shower first and then food.

Twenty minutes later she padded into the kitchen, totally starving and on the search for breakfast.

She found a note on the pantry door scrawled in William's trademark black ink and squinted, trying to decipher it. No nib, however fine, had ever improved his doctor's handwriting. Seeing it drew her back in time to when she'd been a fourteen-year-old girl watching the man she hero-worshipped writing at the old oak desk in the study and telling her that the fountain pen, which had been his father's, would belong to her one day.

Just think, Lucy, there could be three generations of doctors in the family writing prescriptions with the same pen. Wouldn't that be special?

At the time she'd thought it would be amazingly special because it meant the need to care and heal ran so strongly in the Pattersons' veins it couldn't be denied, and she was part of that destiny.

Lucy gave herself a shake and centred her thoughts on the prosaic present. William no longer wrote prescriptions with the fountain pen because they were computer generated and printed, and she wasn't certain the pen represented anything any more other than being part of the elaborate fake facade of her life.

She read the note.

I hope you'll stay for lunch. My treat at the Shearer's Arms at noon? Either way, please don't go without a goodbye. Dad x

Last time she'd left Haven she'd run through a veil of tears propelled by anger and the devastating cost of a lifelong lie. Ironically, she was back here not only to check up on William, but because of another lie. Only the loss of Daniel didn't hurt anywhere near as much as the loss of Jess.

She ran her hands through her hair, missing her friend who she'd always turned to for advice, especially after the death of Ruth when everything had gone so pear-shaped. Now she had no one to talk to.

I give good advice. Not that you listen much.

She ignored her own unsolicited advice and glanced at the huge station-style clock in the kitchen, its black hands showing that it wasn't even seven. Five long hours until lunch.

Facing William alone over lunch.

She knew he would have booked the alcove table, the one tucked away from prying eyes and flapping ears so they could 'talk'. She pressed her temples with her fingers. She didn't want to do that, but then again she really didn't want to leave abruptly again either. Putting

the invitation into the 'too hard basket', she filled the
kettle and set it to boil before opening the pantry door.
She stepped inside its cool walls. The usually groaning shelves were under-stocked and as she reached for
a box of breakfast cereal, her gaze landed on a blister
pack of tablets that were slid in next to the breakfast
condiments. She picked them up, turned them over and
read the name. *Anti-hypertensive tablets*. She frowned.
How long had William been taking blood pressure medication?

The doctor in her wanted to ask him right now, but
waking him up to do that wasn't the best idea. She
picked up the cereal and noticed the box was almost
empty. She checked the fridge, which had no yoghurt
and only a small amount of milk. She pulled open the
freezer and apart from a sports pack and a bag of peas
and one casserole, it was predominantly filled with ice.
Grabbing a pen, she wrote a shopping list, and then she
pulled six grocery bags from the pantry and picked up
her keys. Before she left Bulla Creek, she'd make sure
William had a full pantry and a few more frozen meals.

The supermarket manager was just opening the doors
when Lucy arrived in town. She didn't know him, but
she gave him a nod as she passed through and wrestled with a trolley which didn't want to leave its pack.
Welcoming the chance to focus on groceries, which
were delightfully simple compared with everything else
in her life, she started collecting the ingredients for a variety of casseroles. The radio blared loudly and she sang
along with the music right up to when she presented
her load to the checkout. She'd just started placing her
items on the black conveyer belt when she jumped at
the blast of an air horn and dropped a can of tomatoes.

'Loud, eh?' The heavily made-up teenager grinned. 'That's Jason saying "G'day". He always does that when he's taking a load of sheep to Perth. He does it when he comes back too so Kylie knows he's safe.'

'And no one's ever asked him not to?' Lucy's adrenaline surge was fading, leaving her jittery and slightly on edge.

The girl looked at her as if she had two heads. 'No. You get used to it when you—'

The gut-wrenching sound of the long screech of rubber against asphalt deafened all other noise, followed immediately by the chilling crunch of metal against metal.

Lucy ran. As her feet hit the pavement she looked left, but could only see heat haze shimmering on the road. Then she looked right and gagged. A jack-knifed truck lay on its side along with a four-deck trailer full of sheep. Sheep were everywhere—some standing, some bloodied and bleeding, but Lucy's eyes passed over them as she saw the driver climbing out of the cabin. She ran to her car, picked up her medical bag and kept running.

When she reached the driver, he was walking in circles, his hands pulling at his hair and blood pouring down his face. 'Jason? You need to sit down.' Lucy took his arm and shepherded him toward the kerb, wanting to check his pupils for a concussion.

His unfocused gaze settled on her face. 'She came from nowhere.'

Lucy didn't know what he meant. 'Who's she?'

'The other car.'

The other car? She spun around, her eyes searching beyond the truck and the bleating sheep.

'Lucy!' Deb, an off-duty nurse from the hospital,

ran up to her breathless. 'Geraldine Carter's in the other car.'

Oh, God, she couldn't even see another car and a thousand thoughts ran through her head. 'Get Dr Rodriguez, ring the police, find someone to stay with Jason and then come and help me.'

As she ran, she heard the scream of sirens in the distance and gave thanks, knowing the police and local volunteer fire brigade would block off the road and sort out the sheep. She rounded the truck and braced herself for what she imagined would be horrific.

She breathed in hard to keep from retching.

What had once been a small hatch-back car was now smashed almost beyond recognition. The impact of the crash had flattened the passenger side of the car before pushing it off the road into the low stone fence of the community park. A woman was slumped forward over the steering wheel, deathly still.

Checking there were no power lines touching the car, Lucy gripped the car door handle and prayed it would open without needing the cutting skill of the 'jaws of life'. She gave an almighty pull and felt some give so tugged again. Grudgingly, the door opened just enough for her to squeeze in. She put her hand on the woman's shoulder. 'Can you hear me?'

The woman didn't move. What had Deb said her name was? 'Geraldine, can you hear me?' She heard a moan. 'I'm Lucy and a doctor and I'm going to help you.'

Airway, breathing, circulation. Lucy pressed her fingers against the woman's neck, feeling for the carotid pulse. *Thready.* Carefully, using her hands as a brace, she brought Geraldine's head into a neutral line. She needed to apply a cervical collar, but to do that she needed to sit her upright. Ideally, it was a two-person job.

Hurry up, Marco.

Airway comes first. She knew she didn't have time to wait, especially when she had no clue how far away help was from arriving. 'Geraldine, I'm going to move—'

'What's her condition?'

Thank you. Lucy had never been so pleased to hear a Spanish accent in her life and she swivelled her head around in relief. Intelligent, dark brown eyes filled with a host of medical questions gazed at her, backlit with care and concern.

A odd, fleeting half-thought amidst the chaos of the moment made her wonder how it might feel to be the focus of that sort of caring.

She brushed it aside as completely irrelevant. 'She's conscious, although only just, and given her pulse rate, probably bleeding somewhere. We need to treat her as a possible spinal injury.'

Marco nodded and tugged on the door which shifted, giving them a bit more room, but they'd need a lot more to get Geraldine out of the car. He turned and yelled to the police sergeant, 'Graham, we need this door off.'

'On it.'

Lucy heard Graham on his two-way radio to the fire brigade and then Marco moved in next to her, filling the cramped space with his clean, fresh citrus scent and the welcome support of professional reinforcement. 'Geraldine, this is Marco. We're going to carefully sit you up and protect your neck.'

The woman groaned without forming any words.

Lucy continued in triage mode. 'Marco, you support her mid-thorax and I'll support her neck. On my count. One, two, three.'

They sat Geraldine up and then without being asked, Marco passed Lucy the cervical collar.

'This will support your neck, Geraldine.' She quickly wrapped it into position.

'Lucy, take this.'

She turned and Marco held out the equipment she needed to attach Geraldine to the Propaq so they could monitor her vital signs. 'Thanks.'

He nodded. 'I'll insert the IV.'

'Sorry, Geraldine, but I have to rip your shirt.' The woman's eyes flickered open and shut again. Lucy tugged at the buttons on the blouse and they came open and she applied the patches to the woman's skin. A moment later, the machine beeped into life. 'BP's low. Two lines would be good.'

'Oxygen too.' He shoved the green mask and plastic tubing into her hands and then he returned to his task, his forehead scored deep with worry lines. He quietly reassured a barely conscious Geraldine while his fingers moved up and down her arm seeking a viable vein. He tightened the tourniquet and tried again.

Lucy wanted to watch, wanted to will a vein to appear but she knew it wouldn't help. Her job was to check Geraldine's pupils' reaction to light and hopefully rule out a head injury. They each did their job, working as a team and pooling their body of knowledge as they scrambled to stabilise their patient. They spoke few words, but the ones they voiced locked together to build a synchronicity that flowed between them.

'IV is in.'

'Great. Push fluids.'

Marco pumped in a litre of Hartmann's through the hard-won IV line in a furious attempt to bring up Geraldine's blood pressure.

Blocking out the bleating of sheep and all other extraneous noises, Lucy moved her stethoscope around Geraldine's chest. The woman was taking short, shallow breaths and her pulse-ox numbers stayed low despite the help of the oxygen. 'I think she's got a tension pneumothorax.'

Marco's frown deepened. He handed the bag of Hartmann's to a bystander saying, 'Hold it high.'

The young man nodded and did as he was asked while Marco passed gloves, antiseptic and a large bore needle to Lucy. 'Needle decompression.'

Lucy snapped on the gloves and sloshed the brown antiseptic onto Geraldine's skin. 'Second intercostal space at the level of the angle of Louis.'

'*Sí*. Then gentle traction on the plunger and checking for air bubbles.'

Lucy knew it all, but saying it out loud to a colleague and hearing confirmation always helped. 'And then an immediate relief of symptoms.'

I hope. Her fingers located the position and she pressed the needle into place, praying the needle wouldn't block. The beeping of the monitor faded.

'*Beuno,* you're in. Pulse-ox is rising now.' The relief in Marco's deep voice vibrated around them, matching her own. 'Leave the needle open.'

'Yep, had planned to.' The rush of a good save flowed through her. Although Geraldine wasn't out of the woods yet, at least they'd sorted out one big problem.

The sensation lasted ninety seconds.

The sharp and incessant beeping of the Propaq rose again, screaming at them as their patient's heart rate soared and her blood pressure plummeted. For the briefest moment, Marco's gaze met hers and she had an overwhelming moment of connection, unlike anything she'd ever experienced with a colleague.

Their words collided as they both yelled out in unison, 'Jaws of life now!'

CHAPTER THREE

THE emergency helicopter banked and quickly headed south towards Perth, taking the deafening noise of the rotors with it, and exposing the continual bleating of injured and scared sheep. Marco ran his hand through his hair and glanced at Lucy. They'd worked side by side for over an hour and he still had the alluring scent of her perfume in his nostrils. Call him overtired, but he'd swear it was a combination of vanilla and liquorice. At first he'd breathed in deeply, using the scent as a shield when the smell of blood and fear had threatened to choke him. After that, he'd just wanted her scent—wanted it badly, like a smoker needed his next cigarette.

Lucy was staring down at her feet and her smooth and sleek hair fell forward across her cheeks like a curtain, masking her face and masking her emotions. Not that it mattered—even when he could see her expressions, he couldn't work her out. Today, she'd been a totally different person from yesterday, running the emergency expertly and efficiently, and without any of the high drama and emotion that had been on display in the practice. She knew her medicine and he'd been grudgingly impressed. Given the difficult conditions, they'd worked together well, anticipating each other's needs as if they'd worked together for years. All he had to do now was think of her in terms of a doctor rather than a woman and his life could return to normal. How hard could that be?

As if she could sense his gaze on her, she raised her head, tucked her hair behind her ears and attempted a smile, only the accompanying tension thwarted it. 'It's going to be touch and go, isn't it?'

He nodded, sharing the exact same concerns for Geraldine. 'It is, but together we've given her a chance. Thank goodness the accident happened in the town because otherwise…'

'Yeah.' She nodded. 'She'd be dead like so many of these poor sheep.'

A team of farmers had arrived to tend to the injured sheep and a shot fired out, the first of many. Lucy flinched before giving a self-deprecating laugh. 'Obviously I've been living the city-girl life for too long.'

He smiled wryly. 'No one likes to see animals injured. Even the farmers are going to find this tough.'

'True.' She tilted her head as if she was sending some sort of non-verbal message to him.

He turned and saw small groups of people gathering, all edging towards them looking slightly stunned and shocked, and needing to talk about what had happened so they could absorb it and put it into perspective. His day, already late starting due to the emergency, just got even busier.

You've got a competent doctor standing in front of you so use her.

The thought of how he'd warned her off yesterday loomed large in his mind, but he could no longer deny the fact that he was exhausted and with this disaster he absolutely needed help.

'Lucy.' The rest of the sentence stuck in his throat.

'Yes?' She shoved her hands into the pockets of her cargo pants and rocked back and forth on the balls of her feet as if she wanted to move away and move fast.

He swallowed and forced up the words. 'Can you examine the driver of the truck for me, please, while I get started on the day's work?'

Her chestnut brows rose to her hairline. 'Are you sure you trust me in the clinic?'

He sighed, knowing he should have seen that coming. 'Based on how you treated Geraldine, I trust your clinical skills implicitly. I appeal to your conscience and ethical standards that you respect the rules regarding confidentiality, and unless you have William's written permission, you do not look at his file.'

He held his breath, half expecting her to hit him with an Australian expression that said he could damn well work on his own.

Her grey eyes flickered. 'Fair enough.'

He blinked. 'Excuse me?'

It was her turn to sigh. 'Yesterday…' She tugged at her bottom lip with her teeth.

Mesmerised, his gaze dropped, glued to her plump mouth and the flash of white against ruby-red. Heat socked him, rushing into every crevice and he instantly wondered if the visual lushness they promised would be matched by the touch of his lips against hers.

Now isn't the best time for this.

Horrified that he was lusting after a colleague—especially after he'd just given a speech on professionalism—he dragged his eyes to her face and tried to remember what they were talking about. 'You were saying?'

She cleared her throat. 'Yesterday, I was a little bit...
strung out. I haven't seen William in a long time and...'

He thought about his ex-wife, about his parents and
siblings and had a moment of understanding. 'Family
can make you crazy sometimes.'

'You have no idea.' She lifted her chin sharply in an
increasingly familiar action and her hair fell back from
her cheeks. 'As much as I hate to admit it, yesterday
you had a point.'

He couldn't stop the triumphant smile racing across
his face. 'So, you are saying I was right?'

She crossed her arms, but a twitch of her lips softened the rebellious stance and her voice held a teasing air. 'I could agree with you or I could help you out.
You choose.'

An unexpected sense of lightness streaked in under
the stress of the last hour, which was layered on top
of the permanent tension of his life and his fears for
Ignacio. He grinned, enjoying the banter and the fact
that she'd made him laugh. His days were divided into
being a doctor and being a father, but right now, in
this moment he was Marco and that didn't happen very
often. 'For now, I will take your help.'

'Done.' Lucy shielded her eyes and squinted up the
street. 'Looks like Deb's got the driver in the ambulance
so I'll go with them to the hospital.' With a quick wave
she walked away, dodging stray sheep.

He should have turned and headed towards his car,
but he stood watching the seductive swing of her hips
and the way the material of her pants caressed the sweet
curve of her behind. His fingers flexed into the same
shape and his blood descended with a rush to his groin.

'Marco. Dr Rodriguez?'

Through a fog of lust, he somehow recognised his

name and he jerked his head around so hard that he heard a crunch. Emily Blair, a young mother from the primary school, stood staring at him with a slight frown on her face and a disposable coffee cup in her hand. She'd been very kind to him and Ignacio since their arrival, often bringing around food and inviting Ignacio on play dates. Marco knew Emily wanted more out of their friendship, but he didn't want to offer her more. He didn't want to offer any woman more because it was easier that way. No one got hurt.

'Are you okay, Marco? You look a bit...'

Aroused. Turned on. Marco uttered a silent oath and tried to think cold and chilling thoughts. What was it about Lucy Patterson that had him acting like a teenage boy? He mentally started listing off all the bones in the body until his blood returned to his brain and common sense resumed.

Emily pushed the coffee toward him. 'You don't look your normal self, but it was a pretty horrible accident. I thought you might need some coffee.'

'*Gracias.* This is very thoughtful of you.' He accepted the cup being careful not to brush her hand with his.

'Do you need to talk about it?'

Her hopeful expression made him feel like a jerk. 'I am sorry, but I cannot stay and talk. I need to get back to the clinic because I have patients waiting.' He started to back away and raised the coffee in a salute. 'Thank you again, Emily.'

He turned before he saw disappointment line her face.

Three hours later, Marco couldn't quite believe that he was standing in an empty waiting room. He leaned against the counter and spoke to Lisa, the clinic's friendly receptionist. 'I thought there must be something wrong with the computer. There must be more people to see me, no?'

Lisa shook her head with a smile. 'Not until afternoon clinic starts at two. Don't look so worried. For once you get a lunch break.'

Yet, based on his patient load over the last few weeks, none of this made sense. 'But I started late and—'

'Didn't Sue tell you?'

'Tell me what?'

'Lucy Patterson's been seeing patients all morning.'

As if on cue, he heard Lucy's musical voice drifting down the corridor saying, 'Make an appointment with Dr Rodriguez for Friday and by then your blood test results will be back. Meanwhile, David, the most important thing for you is to get some rest.'

A moment later David Saunders appeared at the desk and Marco turned, walking directly to William's consulting room. Lucy was reaching over the examination table, stripping it of linen and his gaze immediately zeroed in on her bottom. 'You—' His voice cracked and he cleared his throat. 'You stayed?'

She straightened up, tossing the sheet into the skip. 'I did.' She flicked out a clean sheet and shot him a smile. 'I had to hang around for Jason's head injury checks so I had the choice of catching up on all the celebrity gossip from last year's magazines or helping you out with your morning list. Didn't Sue tell you?'

Her smile was doing odd things to his breathing and his pulse. He swallowed before managing to say, 'No.'

A single line appeared between her brows. 'Was it the wrong thing to do? I thought you wanted my help?'

He realised between his confusion at learning she

was still here and his body's lust-fest with her cute behind, he was frowning at her. He made himself smile. '*Sí*, I did want your help for the truck driver, but I did not expect you to do more. Thank you. It was very generous of you to stay.'

She shrugged as she smoothed down the paper-protector over the sheet. 'Not really.'

This woman was a mass of contradictions and just like yesterday evening, he was immediately back to not understanding her. 'But you came to Bulla Creek to spend your time with William, not to work here.'

She briskly tucked her hair behind her ear, the action defensive. '*Really*, it's not a problem. I was happy to help.'

And he was very appreciative of it. Appreciative of her. Remembering Lisa's words about a real lunch break, he said, 'Can I buy you lunch to thank you?'

'Oh, God, lunch.' Her pupils dilated so wide they almost obliterated the grey, and her hand flew to her mouth as if he'd just suggested something completely inappropriate.

Hell, had she noticed him staring at her behind?

No, she had her back to you.

He ran his hand through his hair, wondering if being off the dating scene for seven years and only having one night stands had affected his judgement. 'Inviting you to lunch, this was the wrong thing to say?'

'No. It was totally the right thing to say.' She picked up her bag, grabbed his arm, and started pulling him toward the door. 'I'm starving. Let's eat right now.'

The delicious warmth of her hand seeped into him and immediately combined with her enthralling scent. He knew he should resist the tug of that intoxicating pleasure which pooled inside him and that he should press his feet to the floor and refuse to follow her. He knew without a doubt he should pause and question her on why one minute she was horrified by a simple lunch invitation and the next minute she was crazily overenthusiastic.

Knowing and doing were two separate things and he ignored common sense, letting the river of desire that burned in him rule. He allowed himself be led out of the clinic and marched up the street like a teenage boy in lust for the very first time.

The Shearer's Arms was the oldest building in town, pre-dating the church by a good ten years. A large, rectangular, whitewashed building, it stood at the top end of Main Street with its distinctive red corrugated-iron veranda. Large tables sat under its shade and the regulars could sit and catch the passing breeze while keeping their eye on the activities of the town.

By the time they reached the door, Marco had regained his composure and was determined to reclaim control as the host of the lunch. As he reached for the door handle ahead of Lucy so he could usher her inside, she stopped abruptly and stood staring at the door. 'Are you okay?' She looked as if her thoughts were miles away and she didn't respond. 'Lucy?'

A slight tremor flicked across her shoulders and she gave him a brittle smile. 'Let's go in, shall we?'

He tilted his head and smiled. 'That was my plan.'

He'd expected a laugh, but if anything she seemed even tenser as she ducked under his arm and walked straight past the sign that said, 'Please wait to be seated.'

This wasn't going quite as he'd planned. 'Lucy.'

She didn't slow or turn.

'Dr Patterson.'

Not even the use of her professional name made her

pause. Irritation rolled through him like the prickle of a burr. Silently rebuking himself on letting his body over-rule his brain, and regretting having issued the lunch invitation, he reluctantly followed her to the furthest corner of the dining room, feeling like a consort trailing behind a queen.

She disappeared behind a partition and he heard her say, 'Sorry we're late.'

Late? He rounded the faux-wood panel and came face to face with William.

The elder doctor leaned against his stick and for the briefest moment confusion flitted across his face, followed by regret. Both were instantly replaced by a polite smile, which looked like it needed the muscles to haul really hard to raise the corners of his mouth. He extended his hand and in a voice that was neither friendly nor unfriendly said, 'Marco.'

'William.' He gripped the GP's hand for the first time since he'd emailed Lucy without William's permission.

'What a pleasant surprise.' William finished the firm handshake and dropped his arm by his side.

Marco was left with the overwhelming sensation that not only was William displeased with his interference, he wasn't happy that Marco was standing at his lunch table. 'I don't want to impose.'

'You're not.' Lucy's hand wrapped itself around his forearm again, but this time with a grip stronger than super-glue. 'Is he, William?'

The pressure of her fingers dug in toward the bone. Marco caught the unambiguous challenge in her eyes as she fixed her stare on her father and he heard its match in her voice. His gaze flicked between father and daughter, not understanding at all and wondering what was going on. Why was Lucy addressing her father by his first name?

'It's not an imposition, Marco.' The well-mannered William didn't skip a beat. 'Have a seat and I'll ask Felicity to set an extra place.'

'The steak here's always good, isn't it, William?' Lucy's hand stayed in place on his arm as she sat down, almost dragging Marco with her.

William hung his walking stick on the edge of the table with a sad smile. 'I'm glad you remember that.'

With a trembling hand, Lucy picked up a glass of water and lifted it to her mouth, downing it in one, large gulp.

What is going on? Torn between wanting to do the right thing by William but at the same time experiencing an unexpected need to protect Lucy, Marco reluctantly sat down next to her. Suffocating tension hung over the table encasing the Pattersons and by default, oozing out to include him. It completely blocked any feelings of relaxation that should have come from his first real lunch break in weeks. The irony of it all hit hard. Bringing Lucy back to Bulla Creek to help cheer up William might not be the quick fix he was hoping for.

Lucy's skin tingled as she felt Marco's questioning gaze on her, but she kept her head down as if the pattern on the placemat was the most fascinating thing she'd ever seen. Hot and cold chills zipped through her— heat from the touch of those inky eyes and cold from the fact she'd shanghaied him into lunch to use him as a brick wall to William's anticipated lunch for two. Although, given that a different person from the restaurant or bar was walking over to the table every couple of minutes to ask if they had an update on Geraldine and to thank them for their efforts earlier in the day, she probably needn't have dragged him here.

In between interruptions, they gave their orders to the waitress but even the arrival of the food didn't stop the townsfolk. As they ate, they answered questions and finally everyone drifted away. The uncomfortable silence shot back into place.

'It was fortunate Lucy was in town this morning.' Marcos's lilting accent elongated the syllables of each word. 'It would have been very hard on my own.'

'It was fortunate.' William ran his index finger around the edge of a coaster.

Lucy flicked a quick look at Marco to see if he'd detected the soft accusation in William's voice that she'd left Haven before he'd got up, just as he'd expected her to. This time it was Marco who had his head down. She noticed his hair fell over his collar and kicked up around his ears in a mass of curls. On most people it would have screamed, overdue for a haircut, but with Marco it seemed to fit. An image of a gaucho—the famous Argentine cowboys of the pampas—flitted into her mind and she immediately imagined him well seated on a horse, galloping across the grasslands with the wind tearing through his hair.

A flush of heat started at her toes and finished at her scalp. The urge to pant was strong and she gulped more water.

William continued, 'Why were you up and out so early?'

'To stock up your pantry.' She refilled her glass and changed the topic. The only way she could deal with William was to put some professional distance between them and be a doctor. 'Given Geraldine's injuries, I suspect she'll be in an induced coma for at least twenty-four hours and possibly longer. It's odd to think that if I hadn't have been in Bulla Creek treating her, she'd probably have been my patient at Perth City.'

'In Emergency, the operating theatre or ICU?' Marco put his knife and fork together on his now-empty plate and smiled at the waitress who quickly removed it.

His smile fascinated Lucy. It started with a lop-sided grin before evening out with both sides of his wide and full mouth pulled up into a broad curve. That action set up dimples twirling into his cheeks before the smile spun out into deep crinkles around darkly delicious and enigmatic eyes.

The traitorous warmth stirred inside her again.

'Lucy's currently torn between Surgery and Emergency.'

William's voice shocked her attention back to the fact she hadn't answered Marco's question and her cheeks burned.

Stop gazing at him. Focus. Remember Daniel and what he did to you?

She immediately justified her actions as window-shopping. After all, where was the harm in that?

Smoothing her napkin against her lap, she looked directly at William. 'Actually, I've just applied for a third year position in Emergency, but I'm thinking of pulling it and applying for a similar job in London.'

William's sharp intake of breath and subsequent cough had Marco quickly refilling his water glass. 'Are you all right?'

William nodded and took a drink. 'Fine. Never better.'

Marco didn't look convinced.

The waitress arrived with coffee orders and three large slabs of chocolate cake. William thanked her and picked up his cake fork. 'Marco, given that you weren't very happy with Lucy yesterday, and justifiably so, how did you find working with my daughter today?'

This time Marco spluttered and shot her a look that traded entrapment with stunned surprise. She returned it, having never heard William—who was known for his mildness—to be quite so direct.

She answered for Marco, feeling slightly guilty she'd put him in this position and because she'd been out of line the day before. 'He told me he doesn't have any problems with my clinical skills.'

William ignored her. 'Marco?'

A faint line creased his brow and he took a moment to reply. 'Lucy knows her emergency medicine. I didn't see her with any other patients so I cannot comment on that.'

'Excuse me,' her voice rose, 'but this is lunch, not an assessment of me. I helped out today, end of story.' She shovelled a huge piece of cake onto her fork, needing the sugar hit.

'Actually, it *is* an assessment of you. I need to know if Marco would be happy to have you work in the practice until I'm back on my feet.'

Her cake-laden fork clattered to the plate. 'Shouldn't the first question be to me, asking if *I'm* happy to work in the practice?'

William shook his head and spoke quietly. 'No. Marco is a practice partner and you're not.'

Practice partner. It was like an open-handed hit to the face and a torrent of emotions flooded her, confusing her even more. Anger quickly dominated over heartache. 'I have a job, Da—William. In Perth, remember.'

'I'm fully aware of that, Lucy.' His voice was quiet

but firm. 'However, until recently you always said you
wanted to work here.'

She wanted to yell, *That was before everything
changed*, but she stopped herself in time. She wasn't
about to share private information with Marco that belonged between herself and William. Furious with him,
she said, 'Marco has concerns about me and patient
confidentiality.'

'Marco contacted you without my permission so
you're both as bad as each other. However I'm taking
it as a compliment that you both care about me.' A determined glint lit up William's hazel eyes. 'Lucy, this
is your chance to see if your decision to give up on taking over the Bulla Creek practice was the right one.'

The double meaning—'giving up on me'—wasn't
lost on her, and she felt herself being backed fast into
a corner. As she started to formulate a reply—one that
couldn't be argued away—Marco joined in with, 'Your
father's cast is off in three days. I'm sure you planned
to visit for at least this long, yes?'

Her chest tightened. Oh, God. If she said 'No' she
looked like the daughter from hell and despite everything that had happened she didn't want that tag, especially as she really hadn't done anything to earn it.
She glanced at William, stunned by his strong-arm tac-
tics which she'd never seen before, and then she looked
back at Marco.

His tanned face showed signs of deeply entrenched
fatigue and the quiet sort of desperation that stemmed
from that. 'I could use your help.'

She didn't owe Marco anything and she tried to resist the pull of his words. Hell, she'd only just met the
man, but she knew enough about men to know they
hated asking for help. The fact he had meant he must

really need it and it prompted the question of why. But helping Marco meant complying with William's request and the fall-out from that was staying at Haven. Sharing the house with William.

'It's only three days.'

William's well-modulated Australian accent melded with Marco's Spanish one, circling her, entreating her, but with two very different reasons.

Feeling trapped, she bit her lip. *Three days.* She wasn't thrilled about the idea at all and yet, she supposed if she was honest with herself, she'd always known she'd probably have to spend at least two days in Bulla Creek anyway. Work would keep her busy, making the time pass quickly.

You'll be working with eye-candy, Marco.

She gritted her teeth and reminded herself that she was only window-shopping. Subverting her treacherous body's adolescent rips of desire wouldn't be hard. Hell, she'd only just broken up with Daniel so no way was she ready to jump feet first into a new relationship. Given the mess her life was currently in, that would be the icing on a cake of insanity. No, the hard part would be staying with William, but given the emergency this morning, she hadn't even completed her plan of filling his freezer or asking him about the medication in the pantry. She might not consider herself his daughter any more, but the doctor in her wouldn't let her walk away until she was certain he was as well as he could be.

Determined not to appear to be a woman easily manipulated or a push-over, she tossed her head and jutted her chin. 'Three days, but that's all.'

The two men at the table smiled.

CHAPTER FOUR

SWEAT poured off Lucy as she stood inside a tin shack thirty kilometres out of Bulla Creek trying to convince Iva Labowski that he needed to come into town and spend a night in one of the hospital beds. It was the absolute opposite of the state-of-the-art hospital she worked at in Perth, but then again she didn't do home visits in Perth.

She'd deliberately left this visit until last, because according to a tight-lipped Sue at the morning practice meeting, the old Polish prospector wouldn't be happy about leaving. The practice nurse had been correct.

Lucy gambled on medical grounds. 'Your blood sugar's too high and the ulcer on your leg's looking nasty.'

Iva wore a mulish expression. 'Send the nurse.'

'She's the one who sent me.' Lucy tried appealing to the old bachelor through his stomach. 'Just think, you won't have to cook for a couple of nights.'

'I cook good food here.'

Lucy attempted not to recoil at the sight of the fly-infested food which sat uncovered on the sagging bench. 'I'm sure you do, but Rachel cooks the best roast lamb in the district, not to mention her crispy golden roast potatoes.'

He reached down and fondled the ears of his aging red cattle dog. 'I no leave Rusty.'

Lucy mopped the back of her neck with an alcohol-impregnated wipe and wondered how Iva had survived fifty summers in this shack, when she was melting on a balmy spring day of only thirty-three degrees Celsius outside. She was worried about his leg and the ever-increasing risk of gangrene. She sighed, feeling defeated. 'Rusty can stay with me.'

Iva's rheumy eyes narrowed as if he was looking at her for the first time and in his heavy accent said, 'You like your mother.'

The words stabbed into Lucy's heart like a blunt knife and she swallowed against a wave of pain. 'I don't look anything like Ruth.'

He shook his head and put a gnarly hand on his heart. 'She look after Rusty when I go to Perth for heart operation. You right. You no look like her, but you have her heart.'

I don't. Lucy didn't want to talk about the woman she'd loved and trusted. 'So it's settled. You're both coming to Bulla Creek. Let's pack a bag.'

'I think I'm in love with air-conditioning,' Lucy said two hours later as she filled out the blood slip before handing it to Deb, the hospital duty nurse.

'I know what you mean. I'm getting more love at the moment from technology than I am from any man,' Deb quipped as she selected the appropriate blood tubes.

Lucy laughed. 'And all you need are rechargeable batteries. Still, with the ratio of men to women in Bulla Creek, technically you should be fighting them off with a stick.'

'True, but it's the ones you want that are always the ones you can't have.'

'Ohh, now I'm intrigued. Who doesn't want to be got?'

Deb picked up the kidney dish with all the venipuncture equipment. 'I need to take Iva's blood.'

'Remember, I know just about everyone in town,' Lucy teased, 'so I'll work it out eventually.'

'Hello.' Marco walked up to the desk with a polite smile that included both of them, but his gaze quickly slid away from Lucy until it was entirely focused on the nurse. 'Debra, I am changing Mrs Luxton's medication. Please can you give her the first dose of the antibiotics now?'

Two bright pink dots stained Deb's cheeks. 'Sure thing, Marco.'

'*Gracias*. Flucloxacillan. I wrote it on the chart.'

Lucy watched Deb hurry off.

So bachelor Marco's the man who doesn't want to be got. Good thing I don't want him then.

Her skin suddenly tingled and she swung around to see Marco's dark chocolate eyes watching her with a burning intensity that sucked the breath from her lungs. Her heart tripped and a ribbon of unexpected longing tore through her making her legs weak. She was thankful she was still sitting down.

Marco blinked and a second later he was looking at her the way he always did—with no interest in her other than as a colleague.

Her cheeks burned as her desire-flooded body got hammered by appalled embarrassment. *Oh, God, I just imagined attraction.* It was one thing to objectify Marco and enjoy watching him as gorgeous eye-candy. It was something else entirely to invent non-verbal signals and imagine he was attracted to her.

Damn it. That went beyond crazy and tipped right into scary.

She knew she wasn't crazy—at least she was fairly certain she wasn't—so she put her inappropriate reaction down to the shock of being dumped by Daniel. That had to be it. Pop psychology would say that her body was reacting to rejection and compensating by wanting to be seen as attractive.

Seriously?

It's all I've got.

To prove to herself that she really was in charge of her body, she jumped to her feet, determined to rescue the uncomfortable moment. 'I was just on my way to see you about Iva. Can you walk and talk?'

'Of course.' He stretched his arm out, the action saying, *After you,* and her body quivered again.

Get over yourself. Plenty of men have good manners. Name one you know other than William.

But she didn't want to play that game and she didn't want to think about the fact that she'd always used the way William's manners had always made her feel special as a benchmark to measure potential boyfriends against.

Lucy outlined her treatment plan for Iva, and Marco listened, nodding occasionally. 'And now Iva's settled in bed, I have to go and look after Rusty.'

'Excuse me?' His accent rose as he tilted his head and a curl fell onto his forehead making him look like a confused boy rather than a square-jawed, über-professional, doctor-in-charge.

She laughed, but at the same time had to restrain

her hand from reaching out and flicking back his hair. 'Iva's dog.'

'He needs the veterinarian?'

'No. I'm looking after him. He just needs some company.'

'Ah, so, this Rusty, is he well-behaved?'

She thought of the aging dog who loved nothing more than having his belly scratched. 'He's a total sweetie, why? Are you worried about me?'

The moment the flirty words tripped unbidden out of her mouth, she wanted to pull them back. She groaned silently, aghast that her body was no longer just content with non-verbal lusting. She kept walking.

He pulled open the door for her, the one that separated the hospital annexe from the main clinic area, and the babbling noise of children's voices rolled towards them. They were happy sounds rather than the crying of sick kids.

Lucy turned back in surprise asking, 'What's going on?' and in the process brushed up against Marco's arm and bumped hard into his chest. His hand shot out to steady her and she suddenly found her fingers splayed against his chest and her forehead resting against his sternum. He smelled of sunshine, leather and a slight hint of antiseptic.

A childhood memory stirred—one of being protected and safe from the world. It was a feeling she hadn't experienced in six, long months and she'd wondered if she'd ever know it again. She breathed in, this time a long, slow, delicious breath, which not only absorbed his scent, but also the firmness of his chest, the warmth of his skin, and the loud and solid sound of his beating heart. She wanted to stay lost in the memory forever, trapped in a time when life had been so much simpler.

His fingers, which had gently held her with perfect stillness, started moving against her skin with feather-soft touches.

The memory scattered.

Heat built.

This was nothing like the sanctuary of a father's arms. This was the touch of one consenting adult to another and the caresses ignited her blood, making her heart leap. Hot and addictive need pumped through her.

She gasped as his heart jumped to match hers, sending vibrations of unambiguous wanting—his wanting—into every cell of her body. His body called to hers, urging a response, but the call was unnecessary. Her body was already throbbing to the beat of his. Under her palm, his nipple rose, pressing against his shirt. Pressing against her palm. She automatically brushed her thumb over the fine cotton, wishing she was touching skin. His skin.

His soft, guttural groan echoed her heady need, acknowledging it, and a wondrous and teasing ache burned at the apex of her thighs. His heat plundered her body like a wave breaking hard against sand, flattening every shaky defence she'd attempted to build and rendering her legs utterly boneless.

In a blissed-out state, she sank against him, her tingling breasts pressed against his chest, her legs lining his legs, and she tilted her head back, needing to touch his lips.

A new tension in his body pressed hard against her.

Reality ripped into the lust-filled fog that had taken control of her brain.

What are you doing?

With a gut-dropping shock, she realised exactly what she was doing. *Oh, God.* Not only weren't his arms a place of safety and protection—they had danger written all over them. Her head didn't belong on his chest no matter how firm or broad it was or how amazing he felt and smelt, and her hand didn't belong on so intimate an area of the body of a man she barely knew, let alone that they were standing in a very public place. Horrified, she stepped back quickly and her hair fell forward, masking her face. 'Sorry.'

'No problem.'

Hoarseness clung to his words, drawing her gaze to his face like a magnet. Buried in the depths of his chocolate eyes were the not-quite extinguished embers of a raw desire she knew was mirrored in her own. It had hit them both with the velocity of a two tonne truck and he looked as stunned and as shocked as she felt.

If she had a choice, she'd wish herself gone from this uncomfortable situation, but she didn't have magic powers so she was stuck here. *Just deal with it.* She was an adult who had to work with Marco for another few days.

She rolled back her shoulders and faced her embarrassment. 'Seems I'm clumsy today.'

He gave a wry smile which seemed to say, I know what you're doing and thank you. When he finally spoke he said, 'I think your shoes should come with an "unstable" warning.'

She grabbed onto the humour like it was a lifeline and harnessed some faux indignation. 'Hey, my shoes are an occupational necessity. I can't reach the top shelf of the medical supplies room without them.'

He laughed. 'That's what the step-ladder is for. I think you just like pretty shoes and you use your height as an excuse.'

'Tall people never understand.' She tossed her head to hide the zip of surprise which spun in with some discomfort at the fact he'd just read her perfectly. Shoes were her weakness and the source of many burn marks on her credit card.

Keep the focus on work. It's safer.

She walked through the doorway. 'So why all the kid noise?'

Marco kept a firm distance between them. 'Therapy day.'

'Therapy day?' She couldn't recall ever hearing about that from William.

'*Sí*. We host the paediatric clinic once a month and physiotherapy, occupational therapy and speech therapy come to us. It gives the families in the district some relaxation from driving to Geraldton.'

'What a great idea.' Genuine delight rolled through her at his thoughtfulness. 'These families have enough to contend with without adding long-distance travel to the mix.'

'Thank you.'

This time his smile was wide, wreathing his entire face and spilling from his eyes. It was like she'd just bestowed a great compliment on him. Her heart did an odd hiccough-thing. The rest of her wanton body stayed relatively normal.

Thank you! It's about time you started behaving yourself.

'So this Rusty,' Marco said, 'if he is good with children I think they would love to see him.'

She grinned, liking his train of thought. So often, kids with disabilities missed out on the everyday things that able-bodied kids took for granted. 'I'll go and get him and bring him into the waiting room.'

When she reached the truck, Rusty's ears pricked up and he was instantly on his feet, looking at her from over the top of the tray sides. 'Hey, boy.' She rubbed him under his chin. 'Come with me because there's more love like this inside.'

The old dog enthusiastically wagged his tail and with a vigour that belied his age, jumped down from the truck. Trotting by her side, he seemed to smile up at her as they entered the front door of the clinic.

Sue's face stiffened. 'Cattle dogs belong outside.'

Lucy over-smiled in response. She could no longer kid herself that Sue's cool manner toward her was because the nurse was busy or preoccupied—it had been the same each time they'd met. Sue avoided her when she could and when she couldn't, she used a tone filled with condemnation. 'Marco thought the kids might enjoy a dog visit.'

'If he makes a mess, you clean it up.' Sue picked up a ringing telephone, effectively cutting off any reply Lucy might have wanted to make.

She sighed, patted Rusty's head and whispered, 'We're both in the doghouse, mate. Come on, let's go see some kids.'

Given the amount of noise she'd heard ten minutes ago, she was surprised to find only two children waiting and she realised the others must now be in with their therapists having treatment.

Both of the kids were boys. One appeared to be about eight and he was intensely focused on connecting together magnetic sticks in colour-coordinated order. Despite the click-click sound of Rusty's nails on lino, he didn't look up from his task. The other boy was younger with dark hair, and dark eyes which lit up the moment he saw the dog. He stood up and promptly fell backwards onto the chair, as if his legs lacked the strength to hold him.

Lucy took Rusty over and the obliging dog laid his head on the little boy's lap, gazing at him with liquid eyes.

'I'm Lucy and this is Rusty. He loves having his ears scratched.'

Before the child could reply, Sue bustled in and said, 'It's your turn now, Iggie.' She shooed Rusty out of the way and handed the little boy his elbow crutches.

Disappointment burned on the child's face and Lucy moved to reassure him. 'We'll be here when you get back.'

He gave her a shy smile before following Sue, his crutches tapping on the floor.

Lucy watched them leave and turned toward the other child, whose mother had just entered the room. Lucy didn't recognise her and assumed they must live on one of the sheep stations in the district.

The woman bent down next to the child. 'It's time to go, Rob. I'll help you pack up.'

'No.' Rob kept working on his project.

'You can do this with your set as soon as we get home,' his mother beguiled.

'No.' The boy bumped his mother to move her out of the way.

The woman wobbled and shot her hand out to support herself. She looked up at Lucy with a tight and worn-out smile. 'Just once, I'd like him to say, "Yes." I can push it and risk a full-on tantrum or I can sit it out until he's finished.' She sighed. 'It's hard, you know.'

'I'm sure it is.' Lucy really felt for the woman. Based on the child's behaviour, she guessed he might have autism spectrum disorder. She glanced in the large box of magnetic sticks and realised the mother could be in for a bit of a sit if she was going to wait until the box was empty. 'Can I get you a cup of tea and a magazine while you wait for him to finish? You can catch up on the latest celebrity gossip.'

'Thank you. That would be lovely. I'm Janet, by the way.'

'Lucy.' She smiled and then checked how Janet took her tea. Taking Rusty, she walked directly to the kitchen and told the dog to sit by the doorway. As she was searching for the elusive sugar, Marco walked in and immediately dropped down on his haunches, greeting Rusty at eye level. The dog tried to lick him.

Lucy laughed, ignoring the unwanted trill of sensation in the pit of her stomach, and instead concentrated on keeping things light, given what had happened between them twenty minutes ago and what might have happened if she hadn't come to her senses. 'I don't know who's happier to see whom. I'm guessing you have a dog waiting to lavish love on you at home.'

He rubbed noses with the dog. 'Not yet.'

She finally found the sugar in a sealed container in the fridge, having remembered the constant battle Bulla Creek residents waged against ants. 'Why not?'

'I am waiting for the official email from the Department of Immigration telling me I have been granted permanent residency. *That* is the day I get a dog.'

She was intrigued. 'A commitment to Australia?'

'*Sí.* A celebration. The interviews are over and now I wait.'

He rose to his feet and looked at her for the first time since entering the room. A question dominated his warm, brown eyes and she resisted the huge temp-

tation to look beyond it and see if there was any sign of
the fire that had burned so brightly earlier.

Marco gave Rusty a final pat. 'I thought you were
taking the dog to the children?'

'I am but one of the mums needs some TLC so I'm
making her a drink.' She thought about Janet as she
stirred the sugar into the tea. 'It must be *so* hard having a kid with a disability. I mean, it's your basic nightmare, really.'

His relaxed demeanour vanished and his jaw tightened, making the end-of-day stubble appear even darker
and sexier. He moved abruptly, striding directly to the
sink, flicking on the taps with a jerk and tugging overly
hard on the liquid soap dispenser. 'All children deserve
love.'

The thickly accented words whipped her with unexpected condemnation and she felt the sting all over.
'Of course they do and that's *not* what I meant,' she de-
fended herself. Taking in a deep breath, she pitched for
a conciliatory tone. 'But let's be realistic. No expect-
ant parents with their day-dreams of a perfect family
would ever put up their hand up for a sick kid. All I'm
saying is that it's a basic human desire to have a child
who is healthy and normal.'

His large hands yanked on the paper-towels with a
vicious pull and about five tumbled out. 'Do you mean
disability-free?'

His tone could have cut glass and his animosity hit
her hard in the chest. She arced up, cross at being deliberately misconstrued again. 'You can give things politi-
cally correct labels but it doesn't change the emotions.'

'Is this our dog?'

Lucy turned toward the young voice and saw the cute,
little dark-haired boy on crutches who'd she'd briefly

met in the waiting room. He dropped his crutches and
threw his arms around a jubilant Rusty. She immediately glanced beyond him, through the doorway and
out into the hall, looking for his mother. She couldn't
see anyone.

The boy gazed across at Marco, his face alive with
animation and with adoration in his eyes. 'Is he?'

Dark, brown eyes the colour of treacle.

Marco's eyes. Marco's curls.

She was staring at Marco's son.

The spoon she was holding fell out of her shocked
and numb fingers, clattering loudly onto the stainless
steel sink.

Without a glance in her direction, Marco crossed
the kitchen and knelt down next to the little boy, tou-
sling his hair. 'No, Ignacio. This dog is just visiting.'
He reached for his son's hands. 'We have to go home.'

'But that lady said.' He took in a breath and immense
concentration lined his face as he slowly formed each
word 'He likes to have. His ears scratched.' Iggie gave
her a conspirator's smile. 'Didn't you?'

Before she could reply, Marco had picked up the
crutches with one hand and his son with the other. With
his shoulders rigid, he turned and walked into the corridor and out of view.

Iggie's loud objections floated back to Lucy.

Marco has a son.

She realised she was now leaning against the sink
for support and her brain, usually so quick to grasp information, was lurching and stumbling like a drunk
in the dark.

Marco's a father.

She couldn't quite believe it. She thought back to
Deb who'd said, 'It's the ones you want that are always

the ones you can't have.' Lucy had assumed that was because he was a commitment-phobic bachelor, not because he was married.

No. She shook the thought away, recalling him saying, *he* was waiting to hear from immigration, and there was no way Deb would be after a married man.

Not to mention the two of you almost made out in the corridor.

She thought of Daniel. Being in a relationship didn't stop all men from straying and yet there was something integral about Marco—him being a stickler for rules perhaps—that told her he wouldn't cheat on his wife.

Did all of these titbits of information point to him being a single dad? One thing snagged her—if he was a single dad, why was he doing it alone and so far from his family in Argentina? Especially when his cute-looking son appeared to have cerebral palsy.

It must be so hard having a kid with a disability. I mean, it's your basic nightmare.

She gasped, her hand slapping her mouth as her stomach cramped. Her words, driven by empathy for Janet and spoken so freely a few moments ago, now spread through her like a toxic spill, tainting everything in their path. She'd unwittingly reduced Marco's life and love for his son down to a nightmare.

She wished for all the world she could take those words back.

CHAPTER FIVE

MARCO lay flat on his back on the outdoor table, struggling to find his daily dose of peace that he usually gained from staring up at the night sky. It wasn't working for him. Tonight should have been a fun evening spent with Ignacio, the first early night he'd had in a long time, but Ignacio had been grumpy and difficult all evening, punishing him for the presumptive way he'd picked him up and taken him home without letting him play with the dog. The evening had gone steadily downhill from that point until Ignacio, who was overly tired after his therapy as well as cross with him, had gone to bed. His little boy had even turned his back on his goodnight kiss. Marco had kissed him anyway.

He didn't want to consider that perhaps he'd overreacted to Lucy. His emotions, usually so ordered and controlled, had been see-sawing erratically from the moment he'd discovered Lucy Patterson in the office two days ago. Since that moment he'd run the full gauntlet of everything from anger to appreciation, loathing to lust, and a thousand other feelings in between, although if he was honest, he'd let go of his first impression of her after the accident and then when she'd made him laugh. Her blend of strength and fragility fascinated him, drawing him in despite himself. But of all the con-

flicting emotions that had surged and retreated, none
of them had discomposed him more than the moment
she'd barrelled into his chest and his arms had insisted
on holding her there.

Not since Bianca had he experienced such a strong
reaction and even then, those past feelings paled in
comparison to what had happened with Lucy. He'd
never lost control of himself with a woman, but when
she'd sagged against him in that doorway, all soft and
small as if she needed protection and yet smelling of
hot need and unsatisfied hunger, he'd wanted to lift her
up against the wall, wrap her legs around his hips and
bury himself in her until they were both senseless with
greedy satiation.

He ran his hands through his hair, pulling at the
roots. Why now? Why with this particular woman had
his body decided to re-find its sex drive? The last time
he'd had sex had been just before he'd come to Bulla
Creek. He'd been at a conference in Perth and the combination of a wave of unexpected loneliness combined
with one glass of wine too many had met with a pretty
nurse's flirting and they'd gone up to her room. Even
then, his heart hadn't been in it and he'd left soon after,
knowing he didn't want any emotional entanglements
with any woman. Bianca had burned him for that.

No, his priority was Ignacio and then to the community of Bulla Creek, just like it had been for months.

Yesterday, when William had asked him if he could
work with Lucy in the practice, he'd seen her help as
a way of claiming back his time for Ignacio and helping William. He'd easily dismissed his zips of attraction to that small, lithe body as momentary aberrations
without substance because in the past he'd successfully
controlled himself. Today in the corridor those zips had

laughed in his face and all previous rafts of desire for her had quadrupled in a heartbeat.

Thankfully, the moments with Lucy in the clinic kitchen had given him an abrupt reprieve from his lust-shaken body. No matter how much he'd thought about having Lucy naked and underneath him, no matter how much she fascinated him, all desire for her had frozen the moment she'd called his beautiful son and his life 'a nightmare'. That bite of reality was enough to restore his equilibrium and he knew it would protect him over the next two days. After that, Lucy Patterson would leave Bulla Creek, William would return to work, the long-awaited email from the Department of Immigration would arrive and he could arrange for his parents to move to Australia. When that happened, then he could really settle into his life in Bulla Creek.

A shooting star whizzed across the sky and he took it as a sign that all would be well and everything would go according to plan. Finally, the calm he'd been seeking descended over him like a cloak and he picked up his phone. He consulted the star guide app and then lifted his binoculars to his eyes, trying to locate another constellation that was new to him despite the light pollution from a full moon.

As he stared at a cluster that was trillions of miles away, he heard a click-click noise and belatedly realised it was the sound of heels tapping on the path that ran along the side of the house.

He'd only just sat up when Rusty appeared, followed by Lucy, who held a large carrier bag. When she saw him on the table, surprise made her brows draw down for a fraction of a second, making her look vulnerable and ill at ease. 'Hello, Marco.'

He jumped on the tiny sparks that tried to flare in response to her mellow voice. 'What are you doing here?'

She bit her lip but held his gaze. 'I came to apologise. I obviously upset you very much and that wasn't my intention at all.'

He stayed seated with his hands pressed against his thighs, trying to keep his composure. He spoke through a stiff jaw. 'My life is *not* a nightmare and neither is my son.'

'No. True. Sorry.' Her mouth pulled down on one side. 'It was a poor choice of words.'

An image of Bianca with a matching sound track played across his mind and he flinched. 'We don't want yours or anyone's pity.'

She stood perfectly still, her knuckles gleaming white in the dark as she gripped the handles of the bag. 'Good, because I wasn't giving it.'

'To me it sounded like you were.'

He tried not to let himself be drawn in by the fall of her hair as it brushed the slight jut of her chin. In the last forty-eight hours he'd noticed far too much about her, including the way she tilted her head back slightly when she was convinced she was right.

She held up the bag and a bottle of wine peeked out of it. 'I bought a peace-offering. Would you be prepared to share a glass with me while I attempt to explain?'

No! Experience had taught him that explanations only gave credence to prejudice and yet despite all that, part of him wanted to hear her talk. He argued out the points in his mind getting nowhere.

Her shoulders slumped slightly at his silence and eventually she put the bag down next to the seat his feet rested on. Rusty sat next to it. She gave the dog a pat and then straightened up. 'I'll just leave the wine here then. I hope you can enjoy it at some other time.'

She cleared her throat while her right hand gripped her left. 'I thought seeing as your son was upset, he might like to wake up to Rusty in the morning. I've got his rug in the bag if you're happy to have him for the night.'

He'd been able to withstand her attempt at an apology and the wine, but the ice around Marco's heart softened slightly at this unanticipated thoughtfulness. 'Ignacio would like that very much.'

Say goodbye now. He reached down and picked up the bag and glass clinked against glass, surprising him. 'You brought glasses?'

She shrugged but again she didn't shy away from his gaze. 'Glasses, wine, cheese and grapes. The full apology.'

He read real regret in her eyes and he found himself over-ruling his previous decision. 'It would be ill-mannered of me then not to share it with you.'

Without moving from the table, he opened the bottle and poured the wine before holding out a glass. As she accepted it, her fingers brushed his lightly and the touch streaked through him like a hot wind, flaming the embers of his barely banked desire.

Hold fast to what she said.

She raised her glass in his direction. 'Marco, when you came in yesterday I was making tea for a completely stressed out mother who'd just told me how hard things are for her. My comments to you were driven by empathy for her. Her life is harder because of her son's disability.'

He shook his head. 'Her life is different from what

it might have been but that does not make it the night-mare you believe.'

She sighed and tucked her hair behind her left ear. 'The expression "your basic nightmare" isn't literal. It means something you don't really want to have happen. I doubt that Janet's experience of parenthood is what she would have expected before Rob was born.'

He thought of his marriage to Bianca and immediately took a gulp of wine. '*Sí*, but everyone's reaction to that experience is different.'

'Absolutely. On that we agree.'

Only that still didn't tell him where she stood on the prejudice scale for people with disabilities or if she even did. Had he misunderstood an Australian colloquialism? He was trying to work it all out when she swung up next to him on the table. Her scent eddied around him in the cooler night air and was even more alluring than in the heat of the day. He steeled himself—on guard against his body's reaction of an addictive surge of primal need.

A ripple ran through him, calling him to follow.

Lucy set down her glass next to her and handed him a small bunch of grapes before helping herself to some. 'I didn't know you were a father until your son appeared in the kitchen. Is he your only child?'

'My one and only.'

'Tell me about him.'

He pulled the grapes off the now-brittle vine and thought about his little boy who slept only metres away in a bedroom decorated with posters of action heroes. 'Ignacio is five and in his first year at school.'

'Sue called him Iggie. Do you?'

Her question surprised him. After their earlier conversation he'd expected her to go straight to, 'Is his diagnosis cerebral palsy?' 'I call him Ignacio, but everyone else in town calls him Iggie. It is the Australian way I think, to shorten a name.'

She laughed a husky rough-throated sound which was at complete odds with her petite frame and feminine curves. It rolled through him, overtaking the previous ripple and bringing with it visions of tangled sheets and hot, sweaty bodies. He slammed grapes into his mouth, trying to concentrate exclusively on chewing.

She stared straight ahead. 'You're right. We shorten a long name and lengthen a short one. Does Ignacio like being called Iggie?'

'He does.' He thought about how desperate his son was to fit in. 'He likes anything that makes him feel like he's the same as the other kids in his class.'

She tilted her head back and dropped a grape into her mouth. His gaze zeroed in on her slender alabaster neck, pulled there by a force greater than his resistance. When she swallowed, his groin tightened.

None of this is wise.

He made himself look away.

She twirled her glass and the moonlight danced in the reflections. 'I remember when I was in my first year at Bulla Creek Primary and everyone was asked to bring in a picture of their brother or sister for show and tell. I'd been asking for a baby brother or sister for a year so the request really hit me because I was the only child in the class of thirty without a sibling. I didn't want to be singled out by not having a photo so I took a picture of our dog. It back-fired and I still get teased by people who were in that class.'

He felt himself smile. 'It is not such a bad thing to be an only child. I have two brothers and all I wanted was a room to myself.'

She turned to look at him, her grey eyes huge in her face and filled with an understanding that had nothing to do with either of their unmet wants about siblings. She spoke softly. 'At that age we hate anything that marks us as different.'

He nodded. 'Right now Ignacio hates his crutches.'

He heard himself speaking the words, stunned he was telling her because he hadn't shared this thought with anyone, not even Ignacio's therapists who he occasionally confided in.

She gazed up at the sky. 'Of course he does, but it's better that he hates his crutches rather than his legs.'

He mulled over her words as the complex flavours of the merlot rolled over his tongue and he realised with a jolt that he hadn't thought about Ignacio and his crutches in those terms. The words made it sound like a subtle difference, but in fact it was the complete opposite. It momentarily eased the permanent ache in his heart for the struggle his son faced every day of his life.

Lucy stared up at the night sky, idly thinking it had been far too long since she'd stargazed. Marco sat next to her, silent and brooding, and although she had no clue what he was thinking, she'd sensed a shift in his attitude toward her. At least he was no longer furious and he'd listened to her try and dig herself out of an off-the-cuff comment. She must remember that despite his excellent English, some expressions might confuse him and she didn't want or need another misunderstanding like this one. She had no emotional energy left to deal with situations like this when she still had all the stuff with William hanging about like a massive elephant in the room.

Granted, she hadn't spent much time at Haven, although she'd cooked a meal for him tonight but had left soon after to come here. Over dinner, William's conversation had been centred on the food, the weather and the arrangements for the removal of his cast. Was he waiting for her to talk to him? Just thinking about it gave her a tight throat and wet eyes and she wasn't ready to say anything.

Lucy broke the silence. 'I'd forgotten how amazing the stars are up here.'

Marco lifted his head and his smile lacked the tightness that had clung to his lips when she'd arrived. 'I was lying down looking at them when you arrived.'

'Ah! So that's why you're sitting on the table?'

'*Sí*. It's much easier on the neck. Try it.'

The idea appealed and she set her glass down on the seat out of harm's way and then lay down. Unbidden, a sigh rolled out of her as she lost herself in the world of space. 'A purist would say the moon's too bright and it isn't worth looking tonight, but I disagree. What's that?'

Marco's dark head followed the direction of her arm. 'Let me check.' He held his phone up in the direction she was pointing and then lay down next to her, his movements very controlled as if he was determined not to touch her.

She hated the disappointment that scudded through her.

'That is Betelgeuse.' He touched the information button and all the technical details appeared. 'It's a red supergiant.'

'That's a totally awesome app. I'll have to tell Da—' She stopped herself, not wanting to think about the times she'd used William's telescope. 'Can I try it?'

'Sure.'

She held it up in the direction she'd been looking

and kept moving the phone but the screen spun unable to settle on anything. 'I can't find it.'

'You need to go more slowly.'

She kept trying but without success and eventually Marco slid his palm over the back of her hand and his arm entwined with hers. His touch spread through her like caramel sauce—hot, sweet and never enough—and with gentle pressure, he moved her hand slowly and steadily until the name of the star cluster appeared.

She struggled to concentrate on the stars as his warmth slowly stripped her brain of cognitive thought. 'So if I do this—' She moved the phone carefully and his hand stayed with hers.

'You are now looking at Sirius in Canis Major. It looks like a big dog.'

'This is so cool.' She lowered her arm and his came down with it. Their hands rested on top of each other in the space between them. The touch was completely passive; no linking of fingers, no movement, just the back of her hand sitting against his palm and yet it burned into every part of her with a fiery grip as if his fingers were actually crushing hers.

She turned her head and her hair brushed against his shoulder. 'Thank you for showing me that.'

He met her gaze, his eyes as dark as the night. 'You're welcome.'

Time to look back at the stars.

But his eyes held hers with hypnotic control. Silence enveloped them, except she could hear the erratic thumping of her heart as loud as an amplified bass-beat.

His breath fanned her face and all she had to do was move her head a fraction and her lips would brush his. God, she wanted to move. She wanted to know if his full lips would cushion hers in softness or press firmly against them before his tongue entered her mouth with coaxing need. She wanted to learn if he tasted of the fire she'd seen bright in his eyes earlier and experience the moment it lit through her and merged with her own in an explosion of sheer tingling and wondrous bliss. But mostly she wanted to feel his arms tight around her again so she could lose herself in them and forget everything.

Instant gratification comes with regrets. His lips might be cool, he might taste of rejection and his arms might not want you.

But her body throbbed in time to the beat of an internal drum that called her to risk it all.

He swallowed.

A low moan left her lips.

She didn't know who moved first. Their lips met in a clash of unleashed need which seared her to her core. His taste of mulberry and mocha filled her mouth followed by a fireball of desire that rocked her to her toes. His left hand roamed over her and his right hand cupped her neck, pulling her closer.

She buried her hand into his thick hair, needing to touch him, and his phone dug into her leg. She didn't care. All she knew was that she wanted to line his body with hers and feel him pressing against every part of her. Her breasts flattened against his chest and her nipples—grazed by the confines of her bra—ached so hard to touch his skin they hurt.

His knee nudged between her legs and she slid hers over his, welcoming the weight of his thigh firm against her hot, wet and throbbing place that was now calling all the shots, and controlling her with a strength she'd never experienced before.

She willingly surrendered to it.

His tongue plundered her mouth, meeting hers, and together they duelled, fighting to dominate and lay claim to their equal need. She couldn't get enough of his taste, his touch, his pressure and her head spun so fast she risked blacking out.

At the same moment they broke away to breathe, their chests heaving and gasping for breath.

They stared at each other, stunned.

The moment extended beyond a long breath. Beyond two. Her body sobbed, demanding she kiss him again, kiss him right now, but something held her back from slamming her mouth against his where it so wanted to be.

His fingers trailed a deliciously slow path from the back of her neck and along her jaw until his thumb gently brushed her swollen lips. As the touch—so calm and controlled compared to the frenzy of a moment ago—spiralled through her, his eyelids lowered, shutting her out. Distancing himself from her.

A chill washed through her.

'*Papá!* I'm thirsty.' Ignacio's sleepy voice called out from inside the house.

'I have to go.'

Marco's hoarse words said it all but when his hand fell away from her and he sat up, their separation was complete.

She sat up as well and somewhere through the thickness of the heady need that made her limbs heavy and her mind slow, she managed to find her voice. 'Yeah, of course.'

'I'm sorry, Lucy. This is…' He ran his hand through his hair and let out a ragged breath. 'My priority is my son.'

'Of course he is. Don't be sorry.' She managed a

dry laugh as she fingered her rumbled hair back into place. 'I just broke up with someone so this is all way too fast and too soon. Besides, I'm heading back to Perth in a couple of days and I won't be back.' A tug of something she didn't want to name made her add, 'Not often anyway.'

He picked up his phone and then slid to his feet, his demeanour now professional and distant. 'So I will see you at the clinic in the morning?'

She stood up, shaking her head slowly as her unease about tomorrow curdled in her gut. 'No, I'm taking William to Geraldton to have his cast removed, unless of course you want to take him and I'll run the clinic? You might enjoy a change of pace.'

He frowned. 'You're family so it is best that you go. I don't know what has gone wrong between you two but perhaps the time together in the car will help?'

'*Nothing* is going to help.' She crossed her arms to stop the tremble that threatened to roll through her and spill tears. 'I'll be back by late afternoon so you can get home earlier and I'll be on call for any evening emergencies.'

'Thank you. I appreciate that.'

A moment ago they'd been about to tear each other's clothes off and now they were being so polite she thought she'd crack from the strain. 'Not a problem at all.'

She expected him to leave. She *needed* him to leave, but he stood there watching her and she grew hot under his gaze.

'*Papá!*'

She glanced toward the house. 'He's sounding upset. You should go and take Rusty with you.'

His whole body jerked. '*Sí. Buenas noches.* Goodnight, Lucy.'

Goodnight, Marco. She nodded, watching him leave, hearing the crash of the wire door closing behind him and the dog, and then her wobbly legs gave way and she sat down on the hard seat.

Well done. You're both being sensible.

So why did it feel like she'd just severed a limb?

CHAPTER SIX

'Does it feel odd?' Lucy's hands gripped the steering wheel as she took a quick glance at William's leg, which was now devoid of a cast and muscle wasting was obvious.

'It feels a lot lighter.' William's voice sounded tired. 'The physio put me through my paces and it's aching a bit now.'

'Do you want some ibuprofen? You could take it with the leftover salad roll?'

'No, I can wait until dinner.'

They were close to home. She'd treated the day as being a carer for William because it gave her the detachment she needed to cope. They'd discussed articles they'd both read in medical journals, her surgery rotation in Perth and William's perspective on the future health needs of Bulla Creek. They'd finally lapsed into silence and let music fill the space. 'I won't be home for dinner. Seeing I've been AWOL most of the day, I'm going to finish up for Marco.'

'I'm glad the two of you get along.'

Sadness tinged his words and the unspoken message was, *We used to get along.*

She blocked it, refusing to go there and thought instead of Marco. The memory of being pressed hard against him with her tongue deep in his mouth, greedily tasting, slammed through her making her cheeks burn.

Bad move.

She cleared her throat. 'We do okay.' *Change the topic.* 'You didn't mention he had a little boy.'

'You didn't ask.' The words carried a quiet note of condemnation, one that said, *You don't talk to me any more.* 'Iggie's a delight. He can out-race me on his crutches, but that's not unexpected. I'm slowing down.'

William had always been a powerhouse of energy and she shrugged off his words. 'Now the cast's off, you'll progress quickly.'

'You were sitting next to me when Jeremy Lucas said not to overdo things. I've decided to take another couple of weeks off so I can return at full power.'

His decision surprised her but it also gave her a perfect opportunity. 'Is this anything to do with the blood pressure medication you're taking?'

William sucked in a sharp breath. 'There's nothing wrong with my blood pressure.'

She slowed as a kangaroo hopped across the road. 'I saw the tablets in the pantry.'

'They're not mine.'

She didn't believe him. 'Then what are they doing in the pantry?'

'I can't quite bring myself to throw them out just yet.'

This time grief threaded through his words and tried to catch her, but she wouldn't allow it. Relief that he wasn't sick got tangled up with her own grief and ever-present anger with Ruth. 'I didn't realise she'd been taking medication. I'm glad you don't have hypertension but is taking more time off fair to Marco?'

'It is if you stay, unless of course Daniel can't bear to be without you?'

'We broke up.' The words slipped out automatically, breaking the self-imposed rule she'd made the day of Ruth's funeral to no longer share any of her life with William. Stealing her get-out-of-Bulla-Creek card.

'Good.' William sounded the happiest she'd heard him since she'd arrived. 'He was too smooth by half and he lacked heart. So with no real ties in Perth you *can* stay longer.'

She stared straight ahead hating that 'no ties' pretty much summed up her situation. She didn't belong anywhere. Her roots had been unceremoniously ripped up and were yet to be replanted. Gritting her teeth she said, 'I wasn't planning on a working holiday.'

'But you enjoy the work?'

Lucy saw the two kilometre sign flash past, heralding how close they were to Bulla Creek. So close in distance and yet so far in seconds. She swallowed against the acid that burned the back of her throat. 'There was never any doubt I'd enjoy the work but *you* know why I can't stay here.'

'What if I said this was the last thing I'll ever ask of you?'

His quietly spoken words packed a punch. She'd avoided William for months and now he was giving her the perfect out. Do time and then cut her ties for good. It should have brought relief but instead she felt desperately sad.

William continued quietly. 'If not for me, Lucy, then do it for Marco. He's a good bloke working hard at being a sole parent with the added strain of Iggie's CP. He's a damn fine doctor and Bulla Creek needs him.'

And utterly sexy and totally unavailable.

Her fingers had been gripping the steering wheel so hard they cramped. She was torn. Neither staying nor

leaving was palatable as each option came with its own
set of demons. In Perth she was alone. It wasn't going
to take three weeks to move house and did she really
want to return to work early just to deal with hospital
gossip and faces filled with curiosity and pity? No, that
wasn't tempting in the least, but the other choice was
staying in Bulla Creek. Two more weeks going hot, cold
and tingly, and lusting after a man she shouldn't want
and couldn't have.

Things in her life just kept getting better and better.

A surge of bitterness burned her. 'I thought I knew
you, William, but now I realise I never did. You have
the soul of a blackmailer.'

He flinched. 'Is that a "yes"?'

*You can continue to work huge days with no time
to think.*

'I'll stay two more weeks but I'm only doing it to
give Marco time with his son.'

William didn't reply and the music rolled out between them filling the pain-filled space.

As she slowed to turn off the main road, William
asked, 'Have you heard from your mother, Lucy?'

His question sliced through her, ripping away any
scabs that had tried to form over the weeping wound
that was her heart. 'Not yet.'

'I hope for your sake that you do.'

Her neck jerked around so fast and hard it hurt, but
if she'd heard understanding in his voice, his profile
was taut with tension. 'You told me trying to contact
her was a betrayal of Ruth.'

Sadness ringed him. 'We've both said things we regret, Lucy.'

'You can only speak for yourself, not for me.' She
pulled up outside Haven, his duplicity still gripping her

as strong as ever. Her need to flee made her heart beat faster. She jumped out of the car, strode around to the boot, grabbed William's walking stick and got to his door just as he stood up.

He swayed slightly and gripped the top of the door to steady himself.

She shoved the aid into his hand as the doctor in her came to the fore. 'Here. You need this to help with your balance. I've left your dinner in the fridge and remember to take some analgesia with it.'

William took a few steps, his hazel eyes dark with shadows. 'Is it always going to be like this?'

She refused to let him draw her into that conversation so instead moved ahead of him and slid her key into the old lock on the front door. As he walked through the doorway she said, 'If you do your physio you should be off the stick within six weeks.'

He stamped the cane on the old hardwood floors. 'Damn it. You're my daughter, Lucy, not my doctor.'

She tilted her chin, keeping her tears at bay. 'Right now being your doctor is the *only* thing I can be.'

Before he could reply she stepped back onto the veranda and closed the door behind her.

Marco was on his way back from his last appointment, a home visit to an elderly patient where he'd been held up waiting for the ambulance. It was the worst night for it to happen because Heather had a family birthday and wasn't available to collect Ignacio. After-school care had rung to say they were closing and they'd arranged for Ignacio to go to the clinic. Marco knew Sue would have him set up doing jigsaw puzzles or listening to talking books and that he'd be fine, but it made it a long day for a little boy who was always physically exhausted even after a normal day.

As he approached the clinic, he slowed, driving past the oval where the Bulla Creek junior footballers were working hard at their training session. He was still trying to get used to the Australian Rules Football code and accept the fact that what he called 'football', Australians called 'soccer'. Soccer wasn't big in Bulla Creek although a few parents at the primary school—mostly mothers—were trying to generate interest and field a team because it was a game that generally came with fewer injuries. Emily, who had one son who played football and another who played soccer, had asked him to give a talk about it at a parent evening. He'd accepted the invitation and pushed down his heartache that Ignacio wouldn't be playing either sport.

The soccer nets were adjacent to the oval and not often used so he was surprised to see in the distance what looked like a mother and her child. The kid stood in front of the goal and the woman was doing a fair job of kicking the ball to him while a dog charged around them both. He squinted against the setting sun, trying to work out who it was.

His foot hit the brake.

He looked again and shook his head at the silhouettes. *You are imagining things.*

For six long days he'd been imagining things—things he and Lucy Patterson could do dressed and naked, in a bed, on a desk, almost anywhere, and it left him feeling permanently strung out and frazzled. When he'd taken William's phone call telling him that Lucy was working at the clinic for two more weeks he'd almost said no.

Help like that was no help at all, not when it slammed up against his sanity every moment of the day and night.

If he was honest, the only thing testing his sanity right now was his imagination because he'd hardly seen Lucy since the night in his garden. It was as if by mutual agreement they were giving each other a wide berth. A very wide berth. Only right now he was certain he was looking straight at her. And Ignacio. It made no sense at all.

He parked and jogged around the dusty edge of the oval. As he approached, the orange light of the setting sun lit up Lucy's hair like a beacon as well as illuminating the sweet curves of her breasts and behind. Shocks of pleasure detonated and he tingled with the memory of her body pressed hard against his.

Surprise collided with it. He didn't recognise her shoes. Instead of her usual platform wedges or high-heeled stilettos, she wore flat, white, sports shoes. He hadn't thought such utilitarian footwear existed in her collection.

Beyond her, at the edge of the goal net was the familiar sight of his little boy who stood with a slight lean to the left. His face was fierce with concentration and his eyes were fixed on the black and white ball at Lucy's feet.

She kicked the ball and Ignacio blocked it with his crutch. A wide grin wreathed the little boy's face as he punched the air with his right hand.

A lump formed in Marco's throat.

Lucy cheered as she moved forward to pick up the ball.

Ignacio suddenly saw him. *'Papá!'*

Lucy spun around as Marco closed the gap between them and he saw the moment she locked down the need—desire generated by the exact same memory that had just rolled through him.

He concentrated his gaze on his son, hugging him close. '*Querido* that was a good block.'

Ignacio squirmed out of his arms and said, 'I've done it. Five times. Haven't I, Lucy?'

'You have.' Her smile for Ignacio shone as bright as the setting sun.

'That is a great job. Like I told you…' he tousled his Ignacio's curls '…your crutches are your friend.'

The little boy pouted. 'I want to kick the ball.'

Lucy handed the ball to Marco who set it down in front of Ignacio wondering how this would go and if he could coordinate the kick to hit the ball, let alone the centre. 'Give it your best shot.'

'You and Lucy need…' Ignacio pointed as he took a breath '…to stand over there.'

Marco hesitated but Lucy walked about ten metres away. He frowned. There was no way Ignacio would be able to kick the ball that far.

'Marco,' Lucy called out to him and beckoned with her hand.

'Go, *Papá*.'

He unhappily crossed the short distance and as he reached Lucy, he turned to see Ignacio's gaze fixed intently on the boys playing football.

His son dropped his crutches.

'Ignacio.' Marco heard the sternness in his voice as he moved forward.

Lucy's hand touched his arm, pulling him back. 'Let him try.'

He shook her hand away. 'He will fall over.'

'Is that a bad thing?'

He stared at her, stunned. 'You want him to fail?'

'I want him to *try*.'

Apprehension for his beautiful son morphed with love and protection. 'Ignacio, use your crutches.'

Black curls bounced in defiance and his small shoulders moved forward as he drew his leg back, the toe of his shoe dragging in the dirt. With huge effort, he moved his leg forward toward the ball but his left leg crumpled underneath him, bringing him down in a heap before his right foot could connect.

'*Querido Dios.*' Marco moved quickly. 'Are you hurt?' He ran his hands over Ignacio's legs.

'I'm okay. *Papá*, Stop it.' He batted Marco's hands away. 'I want to. Try again.'

'It's getting late, Iggie.' Lucy's voice was both calm and firm as she pointed to the oval. 'The other boys are stopping too because it's almost dark and it's time for dinner. Rusty and I are starving but we can do this again another day.'

Iggie's face lit up with hope. 'Tomorrow, Lucy? Please.'

Lucy kept her gaze fixed on Ignacio. 'Your dad's free tomorrow afternoon so he can bring you here.'

'*Papá* doesn't know...' he breathed in '...how to kick a ball.'

'What?' Marco heard the defensiveness in his voice. 'Of course I can kick a ball. Why would you say that?'

Dark eyes as familiar to him as his own met his. 'You never kick. A ball with me. Not like Lucy.'

Because you fall over. Marco's heart twisted, only the pain wasn't solely the etched-in heartache for his son's constant battle with his limitations. With a shock, he realised he was jealous. Jealous that Ignacio was looking beyond him for experiences and finding him lacking.

'Come on, mate. On your feet.' Lucy bent down and picked up the crutches.

I am his father. A surge of irritation scratched him inside and out. Marco scooped Ignacio into his arms and swung him up and onto his shoulders, holding him firmly by the waist. 'He's tired and it's a long walk to the car.'

His son laughed the way he always did when he rode up high on his shoulders and Marco's world levelled out again. He knew Ignacio. Only he knew what he needed and he definitely knew what was best for him. Lucy had no clue. 'Sue usually does jigsaws with him.'

Lucy heard the disapproval in Marco's voice which matched the deep scowl on his face, one that could summon thunder. Last time she'd seen it he'd accused her of prejudice against people with disabilities. That accusation could no longer be levelled at her and yet he was upset with her again. Everyone in town said he was easy-going, but with her he was all over the place; polite one minute, cross the next, laughing with her or kissing her senseless.

He's struggling with this crazy attraction as much as you are.

Poor guy. I know how he feels.

The thought was somehow gratifying and despite almost getting a crick in her neck, she made herself meet his eyes from her flat-shoed stance. She refused to apologise for choosing the ball activity to entertain Iggie. 'Sadly, Sue couldn't stay late tonight and as I'd cleared the waiting room of patients, I offered to help out. It's too nice an evening to be indoors and with the summer heat arriving soon, it seemed a shame to waste it.'

'Thank you for minding him.' The polite response seemed to be wrung out of him, as if he wasn't thankful at all.

She swallowed a sigh and held out the ball. 'Here you go. You guys will need this for tomorrow.'

Marco's mouth firmed into a grim line as his eyes rolled upwards to indicate the fact that he was gripping his son firmly, supporting the little boy's core muscles so he could remain upright, and that Iggie was holding on tightly to Marco's neck.

There were no extra hands to hold a ball.

She felt stupid for not realising but at the same time resentful that Marco seemed to be making her out to be the bad guy. It was beyond obvious he thought she'd overstepped the mark by choosing a ball-game activity but she knew Iggie had enjoyed it right up until Marco had wanted to control the game. Granted, trying to kick a ball at the end of the day wasn't the best timing, but the kid had guts and determination which counted for a lot. Did Marco recognise that?

It was clear as the outback sky that he loved his son dearly, but she couldn't help but wonder if he was overprotecting the little boy.

'Marco! Lucy!' Emily ran over panting. 'James Audrey's hurt.'

'I'll go,' Lucy offered.

Marco shook his head. 'I have my bag in the car which will save five minutes.'

'Both of you go,' Emily said, 'and I'll mind Iggie.' She held out her arms out for Ignacio with a proprietary air, as if she'd done it many times before.

Lucy experienced an odd sensation that she couldn't

name, but she had no time to second-guess it. She started running.

'Excuse me, boys.' Lucy moved through the circle of people who'd gathered around the twelve-year-old boy. James lay on the ground, his face ashen and tight, and despite his heroic efforts, a tear rolled down his cheek. His left hand held his right arm slightly away from his side as if he was guarding it. 'Are his parents here?'

The coach held a mobile phone. 'I'm trying to contact them now.'

'Thanks.' She knelt down beside the boy. 'James, my name's Lucy and I'm a doctor. In a minute another doctor, Marco, will be here with his medical bag. Tell me, where does it hurt?'

'My arm.'

'Does it hurt worse in one place than another?'

His finger's crawled to his shoulder and he flinched. 'It's really bad here but it hurts everywhere,' he sobbed.

'Do you remember which part of your body hit the ground first?'

'No. It really hurts.'

'Did you hit your head? Black out?'

James shook his head and flinched again. 'No.'

'Okay, then let's see what you've done to yourself.' She had her suspicions but her time in emergency medicine had taught her that a thorough examination meant she didn't miss something important by jumping feet first to a diagnosis. Carefully running her hand along his lower arm, she felt for a break in the radius and ulna. Nothing. She gently continued up the arm but couldn't feel the distinctive lump of a break on the humerus either.

James moaned.

'Does this hurt more than the lower part of your arm?'

'Yes and your fingers feel fuzzy.'

'Is your arm numb?'

'Sorta.'

Radiating pain and numbness matched her initial suspicions and things firmed up the moment she examined his shoulder. Instead of looking round, it looked square with a bump under the skin. The head of the humerus was no longer in the glenoid fossa and instead was lying anteriorly. At twelve, dislocated shoulders were not that common and the tenderness along the humerus worried her.

She glanced up to greet Marco's arrival. 'Dislocated shoulder and possible fracture of the humerus.'

'Poor kid.' He did a set of observations and then handed the boy the 'green whistle', the emergency painkiller of choice for haemodynamically stable patients. 'James, I want you to suck on this and it will help you with the pain. Take a couple of deep breaths to start with.'

The boy accepted the whistle and sucked in a long breath, happy to do anything that might help. Lucy ran through their treatment options. 'He's got severe pain and I'm not convinced that there isn't damage to the head of the humerus, so I want an X-ray before I try to pop his shoulder back.'

Marco looked thoughtful. 'By the time you move him to the clinic and do the X-ray, the muscle spasm will mean he'll need a light anaesthetic for the reduction.'

'I know but it will be a lot less painful for James all round.' Lucy scanned the oval looking for running parents but they hadn't arrived. 'We need his parents' permission for the procedure so we keep him as comfortable as we can until they arrive.'

'Of course.' Marco suddenly sighed and his expression tensed.

'Problem? You're not comfortable doing the anaesthetic?'

He shook his head. 'The medicine isn't the problem. It's the timing. Why does everything happen when Heather is unavailable?' He ran his hands through his hair. 'I suppose I could ask Emily to take Ignacio to her place.'

He didn't sound keen on the idea and despite the fact he'd been so disapproving of the way she'd entertained his son, she found herself saying, 'William's a five minute drive away and he not only loves kids, he's great with them. Take Iggie to Haven and they can keep each other company.'

His deep forehead creased in thought. 'But that leaves you here with James.'

She laughed. 'I'm a big girl, Marco, and all I'm doing is observations and waiting for the ambulance. You'll probably get back at much the same time as James arrives at the hospital.'

He had the grace to look slightly sheepish. 'I'm not sure I'm totally deserving of your help.'

She grinned. 'Probably not, but it's William who's doing the helping and right now he's not kicking any balls.'

'This is true.'

His wry smile washed over her like a sunbeam and her blood instantly heated, pumping through her hard and fast, carrying with it the addictive need that refused to fade no matter the instructions she gave herself.

James groaned. Lucy's attention snapped toward her patient, thankful she had a reason to look away from those dark, dark eyes that always called to her to abandon all common sense. 'You okay, mate?'

'I think I'm gonna throw up.'

And he did.

CHAPTER SEVEN

MARCO found Lucy in the clinic kitchen. 'James is awake and his parents are with him.'

'Great. And almost as good is that I've just finished up his report.' She shot Marco a smile filled with the companionship of a job shared and done well.

Something inside him shifted and he found himself needing to clear his throat. 'All that pain and the poor boy does not even get the status symbol of wearing a cast.'

'I'll make sure he goes home tomorrow with a permanent marker so his mates can sign his cuff and collar sling.'

The more he worked with Lucy, the more he realised she did little things like this all the time. Thoughtful things like caring for an old man's dog.

Bringing the dog around so Ignacio could spend time with him.

He held up a mug. 'Drink?'

Astonishment flared in her eyes. 'You're not heading straight to Haven?'

He shook his head, having learned the drill of single parenthood years ago. 'William texted to say Ignacio fell asleep on the couch so I am eating first and collecting Ignacio second or it will be another hour before I get anything to eat.'

Understanding crossed her face. 'Good idea. The few friends I have with children tell me that you use the time they're asleep wisely.' She pushed up from the chair. 'I'm starving too so I'll join you.'

It was his turn to be surprised. 'I thought you would be going to Haven?'

'And risk waking Ignacio before you arrive?' The tension that often ringed her shot back in and she gave him a tight smile. 'I wouldn't do that to you. Tell you what, after all that drama I need chocolate. If you make me a hot chocolate I'll cook.'

He had a very strong feeling that her not going home had nothing to do with waking his son. Ever since that first lunch with William and Lucy, he'd been hoping they could sort out whatever it was that had put them at odds. It didn't appear to be working. Neither William nor Lucy had spoken to him about the problem and as much as he wondered about it, he hadn't asked because it wasn't strictly his business. He'd got the help he needed and the less he knew about Lucy, the more protection he had in trying to keep his distance from her. It fortified his defences, preventing him from succumbing to the ever-present urge to haul her hard against his chest and kiss her senseless.

He rolled his eyes and said, 'Reheating a frozen meal in the microwave is hardly cooking.'

She laughed and her whole body seemed to relax as she opened the freezer to the stack of healthy meals that Susan and Felicity kept stocked. 'And yet all too often it's as close to cooking as I get.'

He remembered his early years of being a doctor. 'Residency is a crazy life.'

The beep of the microwave buttons echoed around the kitchen. 'So it's like that in Argentina too?'

'*Sí*. Hard years of long hours.'

He made the drinks and she accepted the steaming mug of chocolate, breathing in the rich scent. A look of bliss washed over her face.

The image of her naked and sprawled across his bed, with an even better expression on her face slammed into him, making him hard. He gulped his tea. *Dios.* The hot drink burned his mouth as much as his blood burned with his need. He flicked on the tap, filled a glass with water and downed it fast, trying to cool his body.

'You okay?'

Her breathy voice matched his heat-filled body and did nothing to help him wrestle back some control, but he managed to grind out, 'Fine.'

She bit her lip and centred her gaze at a point somewhere over his shoulder. 'I sometimes think that instant hot water isn't a good idea and we should go back to tea and coffee out of a pot.'

He grabbed onto her throwaway line, happy to have a safe and boring conversation during which he could re-find his equilibrium. 'I will buy a coffee machine.'

'Great idea.'

He opened the cutlery drawer, picked up the knives and forks and set the table. When he glanced up, she was staring at him, her warm, grey eyes filled with questions.

'We were talking about medicine in Argentina.'

'Ah, yes, we were.' He smiled. Talking about work was safe. 'What do you want to know?'

'Why you've made a permanent move to Australia?'

The unexpected question reverberated through him and he watched the meals going around and around in

the microwave while he carefully formulated his reply.
'It was necessary.'

She diced some salad. 'Necessary how?'

The microwave conveniently beeped, thankfully diverting Lucy's attention. She carefully spooned out generous portions of beef in red wine casserole into pasta bowls and Marco sliced some ciabatta loaf, adding it to a plate in the centre of the table.

He sat opposite her, needing the width of the table between them to avoid any unintentional touching because it wouldn't take much for him to push all his reasons aside and pull her into his arms. The serving of the meal had broken the conversation he didn't want to have and he was determined to start a new topic. A topic that had nothing to do with him.

He took a mouthful of the food. 'This tastes okay but you haven't lived until you've tasted Argentine beef cooked to succulent perfection on the barbeque.'

She dunked a piece of bread in the jus. 'So you were saying that leaving Argentina was necessary. As you're practising medicine I assume you weren't run out of the country for criminal activity.' The smile in her voice was underpinned by an edge of determination.

He swore silently. She had no intention of talking about food. 'I am sorry to disappoint you but it was nothing so interesting.'

Curiosity flared in her pretty eyes. 'Try me.'

He shrugged, trying to keep things very casual. 'Bulla Creek is a fresh start for Ignacio and me.'

'And?'

'And nothing. I think Bulla Creek is a good place…' he smiled at her '…but I don't need to tell you that because you grew up here. Ignacio loves the library and the pool. What did you like most about the town when you were a kid?'

Frustration played around her kissable mouth. 'Marco, why did you need a fresh start?'

He gripped his fork tightly, feeling the same surge of anger and betrayal that flared every time he thought about his marriage to Bianca. Feelings he badly wanted to banish but he couldn't seem to manage just yet. 'I am divorced.'

Her eyes widened. 'Oh. I...'

His jaw ached with tightness. 'Thought I would be a widower?'

'I did. Sorry.'

The fury inside deposited there by Bianca burned brightly. 'Sorry for what? That my wife is not dead?' The unjust words left his mouth before he could pull them back.

She blinked, but kept her gaze steady. 'There's no right way to answer that question, Marco, and I don't want to pick a fight with you.' She gave him a quiet smile and opened her palms. 'I'm sorry you're hurting and I'm sorry your marriage failed. Not that I've been married but I can't imagine anyone ever enters into it wanting it to fail.'

His fury faded under her empathy and he sighed. 'I'm sorry. What I said was unfair and you're right. I didn't want my marriage to fail.'

She twirled her fork around the bowl. 'So you got divorced after you arrived in Australia?'

He picked up his empty plate and stood up needing to move as memories crowded in on him. 'No, I got divorced in Argentina.'

Her forehead creased. 'So where's your ex-wife living?'

He stowed the bowl in the dishwasher. 'Bianca remains in Buenos Aires specialising in infectious diseases and affairs.' He slammed the dishwasher shut. 'She was very good at that.'

The sympathy in her eyes suddenly cooled and her chin rose as did her voice. 'So your fresh start is separating Ignacio from his mother to punish her?'

Bitterness burned the back of his throat. 'This is nothing about punishment. Ignacio is better off without her in his life.'

Lucy's face twisted in pain. 'Adults might think they're acting in the best interest of the child by denying access but, believe me, a child needs to have contact with his parents. *Both* his parents.'

His chest burned at the unfairness of life and he stared down at her, peppering her with words. 'Not if *one* of the parents doesn't want him in their life.'

Lucy swayed in her seat as her face blanched to a waxy alabaster.

He moved quickly, instinctively pulling out her chair and pushing her head between her knees. 'Take deep breaths.'

A slither of guilt caught him under his ribs that he'd yelled at her and had caused this, but common sense won over. Lucy wasn't a timid or frail woman and it wasn't the 1800s where tight corsets made women faint if they got upset. She was more than capable of standing up for herself and she did it all the time. So what exactly had upset her? That Ignacio didn't have contact with his mother?

He thought about what had been said just before she'd almost fainted. *Contact with both his parents.* Lucy wasn't a child of divorce. She'd grown up in a stable family with both of her parents. None of it was making much sense.

'Marco.' Her voice was muffled by her lap. 'Let me sit up.'

His hand fell from her silky hair, immediately missing the softness on his palm, and she sat up slowly. He handed her a glass of water. 'Are you dizzy?'

'No.' She gave herself a small shake. 'I'll be fine. Obviously a long day's caught up with me.'

He supposed that could be true. 'I will drive you home.'

She shook her head. 'Thanks for the offer but that would mean in the morning I'm stuck at Haven without my car.'

'No problem. William can drive you in. He'd be happy to do it.'

Her mouth thinned. 'He would but I'm not going to ask him.'

And there it was again. This issue with William. 'Your father's a good man, Lucy. I think it is sad that you're not closer.'

She stood up with a jerk and pulled her jacket off the back of the chair. 'I think it's sad you're divorced but that doesn't change the situation, does it?'

She had him there. 'True, but with blood relatives things are different. There is a special bond that is worth keeping.'

'I wouldn't know about that,' she muttered. 'I'll see you at Haven.'

She walked out the door without a backward glance and despite all his promises to himself he found himself wanting to know what made her tick.

Lucy pulled into the empty clinic car park at six p.m. It had been her day to do the 'rural loop' and she'd enjoyed the long drive and the solitude, although the number of times that thoughts of Marco had intruded, she'd hardly been alone. Yesterday's bombshell of his divorce kept coming back to her as did his words about Ignacio's mother.

She hated how profoundly it had affected her. Hell, she never fainted, but his words had rammed home all the uncertainties about her own life. She'd been waiting months for a phone call, hoping it would solve everything by telling her who she really was and where she belonged. She craved to feel settled and secure again rather than having this constant feeling that gnawed away at her, making her feel hollow. She was living in the detritus of a massive lie and everything she'd ever believed in had vanished. All she wanted was some facts so she could rebuild her life on them.

After gathering up her gear, she walked into the building just as Sue was closing up. 'Hey, Sue.'

'Lucy.' The practice nurse gave her a curt nod as she pressed 'cancel' on the security system. 'I'll leave you to lock up, but before you do, there's a stack of results on your desk that need your signature. I've put the concerning ones on the top including Nyanath Gil's pap test result. I'd appreciate it if you called her tonight.'

'Will do.' Lucy smiled in an attempt to get Sue to thaw but the woman's mouth stayed in a firm line. It was the first time they'd been totally alone since she'd arrived and there were some things she needed to say to Sue, overdue things, despite the waves of animosity that were rolling off her.

Lucy sucked in a fortifying breath. 'William says you took great care of him over the last few weeks and I really appreciate it. Thank you.'

Sue's eyes flashed. 'Someone had to do it.'

She swallowed the hit, telling herself that no one on the outside ever knew the full story of what went on inside a family. Hell, she was *in* the family and she'd had no clue. 'I wasn't here earlier because he didn't tell me.'

Sue folded her arms across her chest. 'Did you ask?'

Ouch! She wanted to yell, *All of this is William's fault not mine*, but there was no point so she fell back on country pleasantries. 'Enjoy your evening, Sue, and please pass on my best wishes to George, Chloe and Liam.'

Sue's mouth lost its tart line. 'Chloe's pregnant. She and Liam decided there was no point in waiting and the baby's due next month.'

'That's lovely news, Sue.' Lucy was genuinely pleased although oddly a tiny part of her ached and she didn't know why. It wasn't like she wanted to marry a sheep farmer like Chloe had, and being a mother should be the last thing on her mind given she had so many unanswered questions about her own life.

Feeling oddly discomfited by the unexpected sensations, she said, 'Goodnight,' and walked down the corridor to William's office.

Working her way through the pathology reports, she made a few phone calls leaving Nyanath to last because she knew her conversation with the Sudanese woman would take a long time. It was never easy trying to explain the need for a repeat pap test due to pre-cancerous cells and yet allay anxiety that it wasn't actually cancer. People always jumped to the worst conclusions first. When she'd hung up the phone, she absently flicked through the mail stack, pulling the medical journals and any mail specifically for William. At the very bottom was a packet addressed to her in Jess's bold script.

Her mouth dried and she picked up the envelope,

turning it over slowly. She hadn't spoken to Jess since she'd found out about her and Daniel. Running a paperknife across the seam, she tipped the envelope upside down and half a dozen letters fell out along with an accompanying note from Jess.

Luce, I'm soooo sorry I hurt you. I honestly never meant to, but this thing with Dan, it was bigger than both of us, you know, and it just was always there. I know things weren't great between you, and I should have waited until it was over. What I did was so wrong and I regret it and if I could turn back time I would. Can you ever forgive me? Jess x

Did an apology for sleeping with a friend's boyfriend make any difference to the feelings of betrayal, even though the relationship was floundering? Could a friendship ever survive something like that?

She conceded the fact that Jess had admitted fault did help a little bit, and she knew in her heart that she and Daniel had been all but over but everything was still too raw for her to begin repairing the friendship just yet. Her shaky fingers sorted the envelopes and she recognised her bank statement, her health insurance renewal and a newsletter from her favourite shoe shop. There was only one real letter and it was in a small envelope. It was addressed to her by hand with no return address and it had been franked in Sydney.

She slid William's silver paperknife carefully through the top of the envelope and pulled out a piece of blue-lined paper. It was covered in neat writing.

Dear Lucy—Jade as I've always thought of you.

Her fingers trembled. This was the contact she'd

waited so long for. She'd expected a phone call, but she didn't care that it was a letter. It was contact. From her birth mother. The urge to rush through the letter— to find the part where her mother wanted to meet her— was so strong that she made herself read it out loud to slow herself down.

'I got your letter. You're a doctor. That's an achievement that can never be taken away from you. I clean houses which isn't quite as important but I get satisfaction from closing the door on a house that is neat, clean and tidy and at peace for a moment.'

Lucy smiled. She'd always enjoyed the feeling of a tidy room and a neat workspace.

'I'm married now with two teenage sons and my life is finally settled after years of uncertainty. I've found a form of happiness that I never thought I could.'

Happiness flooded her. She had brothers! After all these years she had an instant family and the siblings she'd longed for.

'Getting your letter was a shock and it's taken me this long to face answering it because it sucked me back twenty-six years to a bad place for me. Part of me always wondered if you'd make contact and when you were a teenager I sort of expected it. When I didn't hear from you then I finally let you go. I needed to let you go. I gave you up because

at sixteen I couldn't be the mother you needed.
Nothing has changed.'

Lucy's throat tightened so much she stopped reading
out loud because she couldn't form words. Frantically,
her eyes scanned the next paragraph.

I've never told my husband or my children about
you and I never will. It's taken me a long time to
find some peace in my life and I can't risk losing it. Not now. I'm so sorry your mother passed
away but you have your father and your life as a
doctor. Please respect my wishes and don't try
and contact me again.
Allison

Lucy could barely breathe as she re-read the last
paragraph, hoping against hope that she'd read the
words wrong.

Don't try and contact me again.

Hot tears scalded her cheeks as her long-held hopes
of the last six months shattered into painful shards
with jagged edges. She bled eviscerating pain and her
hands shook so much that the letter fluttered to the desk.
Everything she'd spent six months hoping for had just
turned to dust.

Her mother didn't want her.

Had never wanted her.

Her breaths came in short, jerky bursts and her brain
was stuck on a repetitive track of, *She doesn't want
me.* She put her hands over her ears but it didn't stop
the voice in her head. An overwhelming need to flee
swamped her and she stood up fast, sending the office
chair skating back across the room. Plucking her bag

from the floor, she ran down the corridor and with numb fingers somehow managed the complicated locking up process. Through a veil of tears, she got into her car, started the ignition, threw it into gear and drove. When she reached the main road she knew she couldn't go to Haven. She couldn't face William this upset or hear him say, 'I told you so.'

She pulled the steering wheel to the left, taking the opposite direction but without a clue where to go. There wasn't anyone in Bulla Creek she could confide in because no one knew the secret that the Pattersons had held so close for so long. Despite her anger with William and Ruth over everything that had happened, she didn't want their story to be the butt of gossiping groups. She turned a corner and another, driving aimlessly until she found herself outside a familiar house and the one person she could face talking to. The one person who might just understand.

She let her head fall onto the steering wheel and wept.

Marco couldn't settle. He'd been looking forward to having an evening to himself as Ignacio, having had so much fun with William the night before, had invited himself to Haven for a 'real sleep over'. William had been enthusiastic about the idea, Ignacio was very excited, and because it was Friday night, Marco had agreed. Right now he should be kicking back on the couch and reading the novel he hadn't had time to pick up for weeks, but unwisely he'd checked his emails prior to sitting down. That had blown apart all his plans of relaxing.

In disbelief, he'd printed out the offending email, hoping that reading it in hard copy would somehow change the words.

Dear Dr Rodriguez,
As per the Migration Act of 1994, if you or a member of your family has a condition where the provision of health care or community services would be likely to result in a *significant* cost to the Australian community, then the visa application is rejected. Your son Ignacio Rodriguez's condition of cerebral palsy fails to meet the health requirement and permanent residency is denied.
Your temporary 457 Visa is valid for 180 days.

Incandescent with rage, he balled the paper and threw it across the room. This privileged country, so desperate for doctors to work in far flung places, had fallen over itself to have him come and work in the outback. Now, when he wanted to stay and commit to this community, spend his life and his money here, they rejected his son and in doing so denied Bulla Creek the second doctor it so badly needed.

His fury dimmed slightly as fatigue clawed at him. It wasn't physical tiredness, though, but an emotional weariness that was now as much a part of him as his curly hair. From the moment Ignacio had been born and had looked up at him with his bright eyes, Marco had been fighting for him. At first it was fighting for his mother's love and he'd failed miserably so now he was mother and father. He'd had more success with access to therapy but none of it had come without diligence and constancy of effort.

His most recent battle had been to get an aide at school so his physical limitations didn't impede his learning. He fought to create opportunities so Ignacio had the same chances to excel academically as his able-bodied peers and he fought prejudices all the time. *Dios,* he would fight this visa ruling too.

First he needed a drink. Then he needed a lawyer who was an expert in immigration law. As he crossed the living room on his way to the kitchen, his front door-bell pealed incessantly. The two previous times this had happened he'd opened the door to find someone in urgent need of a doctor. 'You see!' He shook his fist in the air as if the bureaucrat who'd ruled against him could see and hear him. 'This town needs me.'

Grabbing his medical bag, he opened the door. 'How can I help—? *Querido Dios.* Lucy?' Shocked, he stood perfectly still, staring at her. Then fear tore through his heart. 'What's happened? Is it Ignacio? William?'

She rushed past him into the house and then hesitated for a moment as if she wasn't sure why she was there. She raised her face to his and looked at him from blank eyes in a red and blotchy face. 'I... They're fine, I think, I...' Her shoulders sagged and her body seemed to crumple. 'It's me.'

The pain in her voice lanced him, pushing his own concerns sideways. Instinctively, he held out his arms, wanting to protect and shelter her from whatever it was that was distressing her so much.

She stepped straight into them, pressing her head onto his chest and resting it under his shoulder. Her body shuddered, racked with sobs that seemed to come up all the way from her soul.

He gently held her apart from him and stared down into her traumatised face. 'What's wrong? Tell me.'

But she couldn't form any words so he let her rest back against him, stroking her hair and waiting until she was calmer. He dropped his head close to hers, breathing in the vanilla scent of her shampoo, and his body stirred.

He swallowed hard, hating it that he was aroused when he should be concentrating on giving her comfort. '*Está bien.* It's okay, you are safe here.'

Slowly, her breathing steadied and her fingers which had clamped around the front of his shirt relaxed. She looked up at him, her eyes the colour of snow-filled clouds made even more luminous from the tears. 'I'm sorry. I've made your shirt all wet.'

'No problem.' The huskiness in his voice betrayed him totally. Every part of him roared to kiss her.

Comfort only. Treat her as you would a child.

He pulled a handkerchief from his pocket and dabbed at the wet trail of tears that snaked down her cheeks, and then he wiped her nose.

She hiccoughed. 'You've done this before.'

'I am a father and used to tears.'

'Yours or Ignacio's?'

He slowly stroked some damp strands of hair behind her ear and thought about his battles for his son in the past and the fights that were still to come. 'Sometimes both.'

She kept her gaze fixed on his and raised her hand to his cheek. 'God, life can totally suck.'

'*Sí*, it can.' Her heat burned into him and he wanted to forget everything—the unfairness of life, the promises he'd made to himself—and just bend his head, capture her lips and lose himself in her hot, lush mouth.

She sighed. 'How do you deal with it?'

'One day at a time.'

'Right now, I'm down to one hour at a time.' Rising

on her toes, she slid her hand into his hair and with her fingers pressing into his scalp she pulled his face down to hers and kissed him.

Her wet lips met his dry ones, firing desperate and frantic need into his blood, which instantly became part of him.

One hour at a time.

He knew exactly what she meant. Life could change in a heartbeat. He had no clue what had sent her here so distraught, but he knew he needed her now as much as she needed him. They were using each other to forget but he didn't need regrets. Her regrets.

With superhuman effort he broke the kiss, his breath coming fast. 'Are you sure?'

'That I want to have sex with you right now?'

'Yes.'

Shadows scudded through her eyes. 'Do you want to have sex with me right now?'

'*Dios,* yes, but—'

'It's just sex, Marco.' Her smile said, *Don't panic. I'm not moving in.* 'We're just two people giving in to the lust that's been pulling at us from the moment we met. Don't overthink it. Accept it. No past, no future, just now.'

Just now. He'd wanted her for days. *No past, no future.* God help him, after that email he wanted her more than ever, if only to give temporary ease to his permanent heartache.

Marco's lips captured Lucy's with a force so strong it sent days of restrained passion tearing through her so fast she forgot to breathe. His arms pulled her off her feet, holding her tightly, and her body instantly melded against his—grateful and seeking. He felt solid, hard and hot, but most importantly, he wanted her.

Right now she needed to be wanted and needed to feel safe—needed it badly.

He broke the kiss for breath. 'Bed.'

'Really?' She eyed the generous sized couch. She didn't want to slow things down in case he changed his mind so she started walking backwards toward it while she undid the buttons on his shirt. Her fingertips brushed the smooth skin of his chest, skin she knew hid toned and tight muscles.

His large hand closed over hers, trapping her fingers. 'Really.' His index finger trailed down her cheek and his dark eyes shimmered as they hooked hers. 'I do my best work in bed. I assume you want my best work?'

Her legs lost all power to hold her up.

As he held her steady, his laugh said it all and then he kissed her again, this time his tongue flicking into her mouth in a tantalising display of what was to come.

They ran to the bedroom.

As she kicked off her shoes, she took in the made bed and general tidiness. 'You're neat.'

'I have a cleaning woman who comes on Fridays.' He pulled off his shirt, letting it fall to the floor.

She watched mesmerised as sinew and muscles and tendons worked together in one fluid and rippling motion. 'You're absolutely stunning.'

'I think I am supposed to say that to you.'

She shrugged. 'I get told I'm more cute and wholesome than gorgeous.'

He stepped in close, his hands easing her sundress over her head until she stood before him in a black and white lace demi-bra with matching bikini briefs. She'd always loved shoes *and* underwear. His gaze burned a trail of longing through her as it flicked across the lace line of her left breast before dipping at her décolletage and rising again.

He lowered his head until his lips brushed her ear and when he spoke his voice was raspy and low. 'Cute and wholesome does not wear underwear like this.'

A shiver of delight tingled between her legs and she pressed her hand flat over his nipple. Remembering the moment in the corridor at the hospital, she caressed it with her thumb. 'I want to explore every inch of your body.'

This time he shuddered and it rolled off him and directly into her. She closed her mouth around his other nipple. His guttural groan vibrated into her mouth and the next minute her feet were off the floor, her back was pressed into the mattress and she was staring up into dark chocolate eyes alight with heady need.

She grinned and traced the dark hair on his belly that arrowed down toward his waistband. 'So, this best work of yours…'

He caught her hands with his, pinning them lightly by her sides. 'It happens when you let me pleasure you.'

His voice caressed her like the touch of a feather, but when his mouth closed over the lace of her bra, suckling her through the flimsy material, pure pleasure poured through her. Her body immediately begged for so much more. 'Take my bra off.'

'Shh.' He shook his head. 'I do my best work without instructions.'

'In that case, I'll stop talk—'

He swallowed her words with his kiss, and she gave

herself over to the wondrous pressure of his mouth on hers, and the explorations of his hands as they skimmed over her thighs. His fingers moved tantalisingly slowly from thigh to hip to waist—a pleasure pathway that built on the desire that had simmered inside her for days and days, until she thought she'd combust from joy.

With an expert flick, he unclasped her bra and her breasts tumbled from their flimsy, lacy prison. She hugged his sigh of delight to herself.

With an almost reverent touch, he traced everdecreasing circles on her soft flesh until her nipples stood tall—seeking and aching for his touch. Then his tongue licked their base and she heard herself moan.

'If you like that, *mi amor*, perhaps you will enjoy this.' He ran his teeth across the tip of her nipple before taking her into his mouth.

Jagged sensations of agony and ecstasy whipped through her until deep down inside her everything throbbed and called out for more. Her head thrashed against the pillow as her hands plunged into his hair. Oh, God, she never wanted him to stop. He trailed his mouth down her belly—kissing, licking and branding her, whipping her body into a frenzy of craving that was ramped up notch by notch with every addictive touch. Caresses that gave so much and yet always taunted that there might be more.

His mouth reached her panties and while he pressed kisses along the line of elastic, his fingers toyed with the edges of her crotch. Sometimes they stroked the material, sometimes they flicked underneath to touch her. She was wet, slick and throbbing and her muscles screamed to close around him.

In an agony of unending pleasure, she writhed, pushing against his hand, desperate for the pressure of his palm cupping her. Nothing existed except this feeling of bliss and her urge for it to carry her along with it. His thumb brushed her clitoris and she cried out his name. Then his finger slid inside her and she shattered instantly, drowning in liquid pleasure.

He rolled away from her and as cool air rushed over her she heard the slide of a bedside drawer. Her hand shot out, closing tightly around his forearm.

'I am not leaving, Lucy.'

She gasped and dropped her hand. It was like he was inside her head, reading her thoughts and seeing through all her protective layers right down to her bruised and abandoned heart. She forced out a laugh. 'Of course you're not. Especially when I'm about to give you the best sex you've ever had.'

'Is that a promise?' He quickly shucked his pants and put on a condom. Now he sat back on his haunches, his hands resting gently on her ankles and his erection tall and proud.

She gazed at him in his full glory of manhood and a tiny concern that she wouldn't quite match up taunted her. She lifted her arms above her head, knowing that her breasts would rise. 'Absolutely.'

With a raw groan, he pulled her up until they were at eye-level. She linked her arms around his neck, wrapped her legs around his waist, and let his hands knead her buttocks.

He kissed her slowly and deeply as he raised her up.

Kissing him back, she lowered herself down onto him, her body ripe and ready to accept him, instantly moulding around his strength as if he'd been designed for her. With a cry of delight, she gave in to the power of the beat, tuning into the rhythm of life and she let it take them higher and higher until they spun out together, soaring high above themselves and where for a precious moment time stood still and all earthly ties fell away. Nothing existed but the bliss.

Then, spent, they fell back on the bed.

CHAPTER EIGHT

MARCO fired up the barbeque, turning it up high so the grill would be the perfect temperature to sear the meat. He couldn't remember the last time he'd felt quite this relaxed and loose-limbed, but he had no desire to examine the feeling too closely. He just…was. He turned at the sound of heels on the deck and smiled.

Lucy's hair was still damp from the shower and instead of falling in its usual smooth wave, the strands clumped together. She gave him a wide smile, one he knew she always used when she was nervous or wanted something. 'Thanks for the shower.'

'Are you hungry?'

She blushed and then laughed at herself. 'After that work-out, I think we both deserve to be.'

He grinned and dropped a kiss on her nose. 'So that is a "yes"?'

Her expression sobered. 'Please don't think you have to feed me, Marco. I'm happy to leave now and next time I see you we'll be back to being Dr Patterson and Dr Rodriguez.'

It was a gift he should take but as he stared down at the scoop neck of her top, taking in the curve of creamy-white skin that he knew ended up around rose-bud pink nipples, he didn't want her to leave. Not just yet. 'Stay for a glass of wine and I'll cook you a steak. If you go now, Ignacio will expect you to play his new favourite game that William taught him.'

'Go Fish.' Her voice sounded flat and weary.

'*Sí*, you know it?'

'It was the first game I remember William teaching me.' Her throat convulsed and she quickly poured herself a glass of wine, sculling the contents in two long gulps.

'And it drove you to drink?' He'd meant it as a joke but he saw familiar shadows scudding across her eyes and given the state she'd been in when she'd arrived earlier, it was time to pry.

She set down the glass. 'I think I should just leave.'

He shook his head. 'Stay. You just drank a glass of wine on an empty stomach so you cannot drive.' He stroked her cheek. 'Lucy, your father is a generous and good man who clearly loves you. Why does a happy childhood memory have you guzzling merlot?'

She bit her lip. 'Because—' her voice was so soft he had to strain to hear '—William isn't my father.'

He frowned thinking he must have misheard her. '*Qué?*'

'Exactly.' She poured two glasses of wine and handed him one before sitting down. 'Try magnifying your surprise a million times and you still won't come close to how I felt when I found out that after twenty-six years the man I idolised wasn't my father. How it stuns me still.'

'I can't even imagine.' As much as he felt for Lucy's sense of betrayal, he now understood the sadness that ringed William. 'When did you find out?'

'Earlier this year. Not long after the woman I'd always thought was my mother died.'

He picked up her hand, cradling it in his. 'William's wife? Ruth?'

'Yes. Neither of them are my biological parents.' She took a small sip of wine. 'When I was a little girl I used to watch Ruth sitting at her dressing table putting on her jewellery before she and—before they went out to the Bulla Creek races, or the polo matches and the community dances. I loved a particular pair of her earrings she always wore to parties and each time she put them on I'd say to her, "When can I wear those?" She'd always say, "The day my feet stop dancing."'

Lucy closed her eyes for a moment before blowing out a long breath. 'When she died so unexpectedly, I was bereft and I thought that if I wore the earrings I'd always have a part of her with me. After the funeral I asked William about them and he told me to take them back to Perth with me so I went into their bedroom to get them. She'd always kept them in a box in the small drawer next to the mirror, but when I looked they weren't there. So I started clearing things out, hoping to find them, only I found a lot more than earrings.' Her knuckles whitened on the stem of the wineglass. 'My adoption papers were at the very back of the drawer.'

He held her close and pressed a kiss into her damp hair, trying to absorb some of her pain. 'And you'd never suspected?'

'I didn't have a clue. Maybe it was because I didn't have any siblings to feel different from, I don't know. But suddenly everything I understood about my life was false and I'd lost my history. I wasn't me and my life was a lie. I was so angry.' She stood up abruptly and threw the steaks onto the grill, watching the flare of the flames searing the meat. 'I'm still angry. How could they hide the truth from me?'

That was a question he could answer. 'Because they love you.'

Lucy couldn't believe her ears and she spun around to face him. The night she'd found out, the *only* thing William could say to her was, 'We love you so much.'

She fought the tightness in her chest. 'You sound just like William and it's a cop-out, not a reason.'

He opened his hands. 'I am not saying it was the right thing to do but they probably thought they were protecting you.'

She hugged herself to try and stop the surge of emotions that always took her back to that dark, dark moment when she'd opened up the yellowed pages to see the word 'adopted'. She didn't want to keep going back there because it always left her so drained and worn out. 'Believe me, the only people they were protecting were themselves.'

He stood up and walked over to her, resting his hand gently on her shoulder, and gazed down at her with a knowing look. 'I know it's hard but when you're a parent yourself, perhaps you'll understand.'

'Don't patronise me.' She shrugged away his touch, not even able to visualise herself as a mother.

His eyes darkened. 'I am not patronising you but when you hold your baby in your arms there is such a surge of love and protection that it changes you.'

She started shaking. 'I don't believe that for a moment. You told me that your ex-wife didn't want to be part of Ignacio's life and my—' She swallowed, trying to keep calm, but her chest cramped and her throat tightened. 'My birth mother gave me away and now she has the chance to know me as an adult, she writes and says she doesn't want me.'

He scooped her in close, cradling her like a child.

'Some women are not meant to be mothers. Bianca is one and perhaps your birth mother is another.'

She shook her head. 'She was sixteen and I understand at that age, back then, perhaps she couldn't keep me but now she's a mother of two boys. My half-brothers.' She heard her voice rising and she wiped her face with the back of her hand. 'She doesn't want them to know about me. I'm just a dirty secret from her past that she wants to forget.'

'No. You are never that.' He tilted her chin. 'You are a talented doctor and a beautiful woman with a shoe addiction.'

She mustered up a watery smile, appreciating his kindness, but it didn't stop the voice deep inside her from repeating what it had been saying for months. *You have no clue who you are.* 'You forgot the decadent underwear.'

His dark eyes shimmered. 'That I will never forget.' Still holding her hand, he flipped the steaks. 'Biology is just a starting point, Lucy.'

As ridiculous as she knew it was, her heart ached for what she'd never known and the person she might have been if her biological parents had raised her. 'Is that what you're going to tell Ignacio when he asks about his mother?'

He dropped her hand and picked up a plate. 'I will tell him that his mother is the one who missed out on the joy of knowing him.'

She drank more wine. 'He'll still feel empty.'

'I know.' Marco pulled the steaks off the grill with a sigh. 'And it's my fault.'

She sat back down at the table confused. 'How do you figure that exactly?'

He put the succulent steak down in front of her and

passed the salad before sitting down. She watched him fork lettuce onto his plate, slice off a piece of meat and chew it slowly, letting the silence ride.

Finally, he met her gaze. 'I had always wanted children so when Bianca told me she was pregnant three years earlier than we planned, I was thrilled. Bianca was not. She is a perfectionist and she saw the pregnancy as slowing down her career. She wanted to have a termination. I convinced her not to because I believed the regrets we'd both have if she did would ruin our marriage.'

He bit into another piece of meat, chewing with a tight jaw. 'I think our relationship was beyond repair then but I didn't recognise it.'

Lucy thought of Daniel. 'There are times in our life when we need to believe things are better than they really are and relationship-blindness can serve a purpose.'

He raised a brow. 'This boyfriend you just broke up with?'

'He broke up with me, actually.' She rubbed her temples. 'I should have seen it coming but I didn't want to open my eyes or my mind to the possibility because I needed him as an anchor. My mother had just died, only she wasn't my mother, and my father was no longer my father and I had no clue if I was coming or going. As it turned out, he wasn't anchor material and I probably shouldn't have expected him to be.'

'I am sorry to hear that.' He linked his fingers with hers and gave her a half-smile. 'You are right, I needed that blindness. I was going to be a father and I needed to believe it would all work out. Bianca had no interest in the pregnancy and I found myself defending her behaviour to my family. They were horrified that I had chosen all the nursery furniture and purchased all the baby clothes. So many times I heard myself saying, "Bianca is too tired, too busy, too…"'

Lucy watched his richly tanned fingers against her whiter hand and waited. The outcome was known but she wanted to hear how it had played out. She rationalised her fascination with Marco, telling herself that by knowing she could perhaps understand his almost self-contained relationship with his son.

And then what? Help? You need to sort out your own life first.

Marco let out a long sigh. 'Ignacio was born eight weeks premature and Bianca returned to work at the hospital when he was seven days old. I thought it was her way of coping and a way to be near the baby. I visited him in the nursery three to four times a day but I never saw her there. When I arranged to meet her to share a feeding time, she would often be late.'

'Did you know about his CP then?'

He shook his head. 'We thought he was a just a premature baby with normal delay and that by his first birthday he would have caught up. We brought him home when he was term plus two weeks but not a lot changed with Bianca. She was always at work and I didn't question her long hours because I knew Ignacio's arrival had come at a bad time for her career plans. I wanted to support her but I also knew her baby needed her.'

She wondered about post-natal depression. 'It sounds tough.'

He shrugged. 'Between me, my mother and a nanny, we got through each day. I don't remember much of it. I was worried about Bianca, worried about Ignacio and I was living in a fog of exhaustion…' His eyes clouded as if he was back in the past.

She finally prompted him. 'Until?'

He grimaced. 'When Ignacio was nine months old, we got the official diagnosis of cerebral palsy. It sounds strange but I was relieved that we finally knew what I had suspected for months. Now we could plan and get the help Ignacio needed. Bianca refused to discuss anything with the doctor and when we got home from the paediatrician's office, she packed a bag and said she was leaving. She told me she'd never wanted a child and she did not want one that was damaged.' His voice turned harsh. 'I am *never* telling Ignacio those words.'

Her delicious meal turned to stone in her stomach not just because a mother had rejected her child but because she knew exactly what that was like. 'You won't ever have to tell him. He's an intelligent boy and he'll work it out all by himself.'

Marco's fist hit the table, making the plates rattle. 'He is surrounded by love and that is what is important. The people who raise you, walk the floors at night patting your back, march you out of underage parties and stay up late helping with homework, they are the parents. I always tell Ignacio that I love him. His grandparents love him and they will arrive here soon, and William loves him. Just like William loves you. You need to accept his love.'

She pushed her plate away. 'It's not that straightforward, Marco.'

'It can be. You came back to see him.'

'I came back because he was sick and I'm not totally heartless. Don't read more into it than that.'

She gazed at his handsome face and knew he didn't really understand. How could he? He could look around his family and see who he inherited his curly hair from, recognise his mannerisms in his parents and brothers, and share a blood bond that she never could. Suddenly she felt unbelievably tired. 'I should go.' She stood up and the world swayed. She sat down again. 'Sorry, I think I need you to drive me back to Haven.'

'I have had as much wine as you. Neither of us is going anywhere.'

She dropped her head into her hands. 'Oh, God, this is embarrassing.'

He laughed, his eyes dancing with fun as he stroked her hair. 'I have a guest room and it will not take long to make up the bed.'

Part of her wanted to call his bluff and spend the night in the guest room but her traitorous body leapt into life at his touch. 'I wouldn't want to put you to any trouble.'

He leaned in, his lips brushing her ear. 'You are a very obliging guest.'

Tingling need made her voice breathy. 'That's me. I'll do anything to help. All you just have to ask.'

He whispered his detailed request into her ear.

With her body alight with heady desire she pulled him into her arms and did exactly as he'd asked.

'Marco's coming over,' William announced a moment after his phone pinged with an incoming text.

It was Sunday night and a familiar shot of excitement pulsed through Lucy. Thankfully William was still looking down at his phone and she had a moment to suck in some deep breaths and cool her cheeks. She hadn't seen Marco since very early Saturday morning, but every time she thought of him her body tingled with a craving that both thrilled and worried her. Sex with Marco was supposed to get him out of her system, not inculcate him.

She turned the page of the weekend magazine she'd been reading, hoping to look casual and only moderately interested. 'Does he usually just pop in?'

William frowned. 'He and Ignacio often drop by but he never usually texts me to announce it. I can't imagine why he's coming this late in the day.'

The click of the back gate and the crunch of gravel had Lucy up and on her feet. 'We're about to find out.'

Marco opened the door, his face lined with strain which was in stark contrast to the last time she'd seen him in his bed and given him a deep kiss goodbye.

'Hey, buddy.' William's face lit up when Iggie entered the room. Using his walking stick, he did a complicated hockey-stick-like cross against one of Ignacio's crutches.

Laughing, the boy returned the action as if it was a secret handshake between the two of them and a lump formed in Lucy's throat. Growing up, she and William always had in-jokes and secrets, so much so that Ruth had often joked, 'Just as well I know you love me because you're such a daddy's girl.'

But she wasn't daddy's girl any more. All that closeness had imploded, leaving her empty and adrift.

You miss it.

She bit her lip against her permanent heartache and then her protective anger rose again. *His* lie had stolen their relationship and there was no going back. Now when she looked at William, all she could do was wonder who her biological father was and lament that she'd never know.

'Are you okay?' Marco asked quietly, his eyes far too perceptive.

She tossed her head and concentrated on the here and now. 'Fine. Are you and Iggie staying for dinner?'

'That's a good idea, Lucy.' William limped towards Marco with his hand extended.

'I don't want to impose, but I do need to speak with you privately.'

William looked thoughtful. 'If it's about the practice, Lucy should hear it too. We can do it over a meal.'

Marco tilted his head toward Ignacio and Lucy realised that whatever Marco wanted to talk about he didn't want his son to hear.

'Iggie, do you want to watch some TV?' Lucy asked. 'It's going to be more fun than listening to us talk about work.'

The little boy looked at his father who nodded his approval. 'Yes, please.'

Lucy set Iggie up in the den with a drink, some chips and the children's channel, and came back into the room to hear William saying, 'That's outrageous.'

'What is?' Lucy joined both men at the table.

Marco's hands fisted tightly. 'I have been denied permanent residency because Ignacio failed the health test. He is considered a risk to the public purse.'

His pain sliced into her heart and without thinking she laid her hand over the top of his. 'That's just wrong.'

William shot her a look that combined surprise and a tiny flash of hope. 'In six months Bulla Creek might be back to one doctor and it needs two.'

She shook her head slowly against his veiled request. She wasn't ever returning to live in Bulla Creek. Looking back at Marco, she said, 'We have to fight this.'

This time Marco shook his head. '*I* have to fight this. It is my battle.'

With a jolt, she realised from the moment Ignacio had been born, Marco had been fighting for him on his own. That wasn't how things happened in Bulla

Creek. 'No, it isn't just your battle. Hell, the government needed you enough to bring you here. Iggie's settled and goes to the local school, he's integrated and bright and we have to prove to the faceless bean-counters that they're wrong. You came here to start a new life, you want to be here and the town needs you. It's their fight too.' She squeezed her fingers around his fist as she leaned forward. 'What can we do?'

'We're here to support you and Ignacio in any way we can, Marco,' William said.

Marco felt William and Lucy's gazes boring into him, waiting for him to tell them what he needed. It set up the strangest sensation in his chest—a pull of belonging and the equal push of his own rejection. *Dios*, he'd got so used to doing things on his own because that way he could control his life. Protect Ignacio's. How was this battle different?

Only he knew it was because the lawyer hadn't sounded very positive. Could he ask for help?

He was struck by the irony that in Lucy's offer to help, she'd unintentionally agreed to work with William. His visa problem was a common bond for them, a connection, which was something they needed badly if they were ever to close the massive fissure in their relationship. He wanted that for both of them. Lucy's grey eyes were fixed on him, filled with empathy and the light of indignation born from injustice. Something inside him softened. 'I spent yesterday on the phone to a lawyer and—'

'But yesterday was Saturday. When did you hear from the department of immigration?'

Marco could see her mind connecting the dots. 'Friday evening.'

She blinked. Twice. A wry smile wove across her lips

as understanding dawned in her eyes. They'd both had a reason to reach out to each other that night.

'The day is irrelevant, Lucy,' William said, getting the conversation back on track with his usual sharp-minded style. 'What did the lawyer say?'

Marco ran his hand through his hair. 'He is going to lodge an appeal but it could take months.'

'You need more than an appeal. We need some noisy rural outrage.' Lucy jumped up, opened a drawer in the large dresser and pulled out a notepad. 'William, do you know anyone in the media?'

'No.'

'Oh.' She sat down drumming her pen against the paper. 'What about you, Marco?'

'I spoke to a reporter once after I delivered a baby in a motor home.'

'Do you remember who he was or where he worked?' Lucy's expression urged him to think and think hard.

He recalled the reporter with her blonde-streaked hair and immaculate nails urging him to accept her business card, and saying that if he was ever in Perth he should call her for a drink. He wasn't fool enough to tell Lucy that. 'I think her business card is somewhere in my office.'

'It's a start.' She jotted it down on the pad.

'Bulla Creek is hosting the polo the weekend after next,' William added.

Lucy frowned. 'So?'

William smiled. 'The Perth press always attends because the sponsor hosts a generous marquee where the drinks flow. Occasionally a politician attends.'

The permanent tension that ringed Lucy whenever she was with her father relaxed slightly and she gave him a genuine smile—the first one Marco had ever seen her give him. 'I think you're onto something, William.' Her attention shot back to Marco. 'Can you ride a horse?'

He was momentarily affronted. 'What sort of a question is that to ask an Argentine? I grew up on a polo horse.'

'Sensational.' Her eyes sparkled at him. 'You'll be picture-perfect on a horse and a media darling. Oh, do you have a horse?'

William laughed. 'David Henderson was so desperate to have Marco join the polo club, he offered him the use of one of his ponies until Marco bought his own.'

Stunned surprise flitted across her face. 'Wow, you must be good. David Henderson's very fussy about his horses.' Her looping writing started to cover the page. 'For this to work we need a town meeting. I can organise that and we'll prime everyone so no matter who talks to the press the message will be the same. I can get a—'

'You do realise, Lucy, if you get involved in this you need to extend your time in Bulla Creek,' William said quietly, hope lining his face.

Lucy's mouth tightened as her father's words sank in. Maybe this was what she needed—a chance to heal the wounds of the past.

Marco saw a glimmer of hope and immediately justified his idea, telling himself he was doing this to help Lucy and William. The more time the two of them spent together, the more chance they had to work through the hard emotions. Of course that meant they had to start talking and so far he hadn't seen any evidence of that. Asking Lucy to stay was all about her and William and nothing to do with keeping her in his bed a little bit longer.

Under the table and safely out of William's sight, he

ran his foot along the back of her leg. 'If you can find the time to stay...'

Her eyes widened at the unspoken suggestion and she stared straight at him, her grey eyes flickering with desire. She licked her lips. 'I...' She didn't look at her father. 'I suppose I can delay moving house another week.'

William grunted, '"Outback Australians deserve health care." Write it down, Lucy. "Bulla Creek deserves to have its dedicated and well-respected doctor remain in Australia, living in the community he values and loves."'

Marco glimpsed a spark of the old William. Was that a good sign?

Lucy chewed her pen. 'That's pretty good, but if we add in...'

Marco listened intently as Lucy and William batted ideas around, extending thoughts, tweaking them and using their years of local knowledge and their understanding of politics to create a first draft of a press release.

He let their energy and enthusiasm envelop him and felt a tiny release in some of the anxiety that had been spinning inside him from the moment he'd read the email. A small seed of hope sprouted that this plan to get some media coverage might just work. If it didn't, at least his problem had put Lucy and William on a shared path.

Lucy's mind was on fire, not just because of the unambiguous desire in Marco's eyes but by the invigorating debate with William. Only she didn't want to think about how good it had felt because she was still so hurt by what he'd done. What Ruth had done and how it had derailed her so badly.

She pulled her mind back from the mess and concentrated on writing down her ideas for how to put some pressure on the department of immigration.

William rose to his feet and rested his hand for a moment on the table as if to steady himself. 'You two start throwing dinner together and I'll make some phone calls now so we make sure we have the district's most influential families at this meeting tomorrow.' He disappeared down the hall.

'Will Ignacio eat cold chicken and salad?' Lucy asked, wondering if he didn't, what else she could offer.

Marco smiled at her. 'He will enjoy that.'

'Great.' She stood up, her stomach doing somersaults from his smile, and she extended her hand. 'Come on then, you're up too.'

Marco grabbed her hand but instead of rising, he pulled her into his lap, pressed his lips to hers and gave her a long and smouldering kiss. A kiss so similar to all his others with its play of heat and need that turned her limbs liquid, and yet so very different with its lingering touch of something that seemed to stretch out between them like a piece of fine wire.

Connecting them in some vague way.

Sex was all you and he agreed to. It's all you can give at the moment.

I know that. I'm not stupid.

And yet the feeling remained.

Shocked and confused, she slid off his lap. 'You know what would be great? If you and Ignacio had your photos taken together.'

He flinched and the familiar shields of protection for Ignacio slotted into place. 'Is it really necessary?'

She chose her words carefully, remembering how he'd reacted at the soccer nets. 'The message will be a lot more powerful with him.'

He stood up but he didn't look convinced. 'He does not need pity.'

'He won't get it.' She rested her hand on his forearm. 'Iggie's a gregarious and delightful child who wins hearts easily. Pictures of the two of you together would be really powerful. Emotion is the best strategy to use to fight this unemotional ruling.'

'I can win this without putting him in the spotlight.'

She linked her arms around his neck wondering if he could win this fight without using every weapon in his arsenal. 'Bulla Creek needs you.'

She closed her ears to the echo of, 'So do I.'

CHAPTER NINE

MARCO stood on the red-dirt cliffs and gazed down onto the white-sand beach and smiled. The colours always astounded him. How did the desert stop so abruptly? It was as if nature had built a barrier that prevented the red sand going any further and insisting the white sand take over. If he shut out the red sand of the dunes, the beach reminded him of the beautiful beaches of Argentina but without the crowds.

A picnic rug and hamper sat on the sand, along with scattered beach toys and a pair of crutches. Lucy and Ignacio sat in the clear, blue-green waters of the Indian Ocean and Ignacio had a bucket and was pouring water over Lucy. She was holding her hands up and laughing and then she wrestled the bucket from him and did the same back.

He laughed, feeling the stress of the day start to ebb away. He'd come to Point Henry to run the weekly clinic, and the previous evening Lucy had said, 'The Bulla Creek clinic is closed tomorrow afternoon. Why don't I pick Iggie up from school and drive him over to the Point? It's only forty minutes and you can do the whole father and son swimming thing. I'll bring a picnic.'

Marco had been worried it would tire his son too

much and had said no, but Lucy had countered with the fact it was a pupil-free day the next day and she'd pack his pyjamas so he could sleep on the way home. Then she'd stepped in close and kissed him, her tongue both cajoling and giving all at the same time, and his reservations had slipped away. Later, after she'd once again shared his bed, Marco had suggested she invite William to come to the beach as well. At the time she'd been snuggled up to him with her head on his chest and her hair tickling his nose. Her reply had consisted of 'Hmm' followed by another kiss.

Now as he glanced along the beach he couldn't see any other people so she obviously hadn't taken his suggestion on board. He rubbed his chin, feeling the end of day stubble on his palm, and wondered what it would take to cut through Lucy's hurt so she realised she was losing too much by freezing William out of her life.

The water looked inviting after a long day at work and with a roar of delight, he ran down the beach and scooped up Ignacio, swinging him around and around over the water. His son's squeals of delight filled him with joy and as he sat down in the shallows with him, something made him look at Lucy.

Her gaze was transfixed on the two of them and yet she seemed to be looking straight through them, her expression both happy and desperately sad all at the same time. Deep down inside him a dull pain throbbed for her. 'Lucy?'

She blinked as if she was returning to him after being somewhere else. 'That looks like awesome fun.'

'*Papá*,' Ignacio panted, still breathless from the game. 'Swing Lucy.'

Lucy laughed. 'I think I'm a bit too heavy for your daddy to do that.'

'Never.' He pulled her to her feet, loving the look and the feel of her in a royal blue bikini, and wishing he could lower her into the water and make love to her. But in front of Ignacio, everything had to be PG rated. Swinging her was the perfect excuse to touch her. 'I can swing you but I need deeper water. Ignacio, you must stay here to watch and not come into the water without me.'

'Okay.'

'*Gracias.*' After Ignacio's recent spate of pushing against Marco's instructions, it was a pleasant surprise to find him so co-operative.

Wrapping his arms around Lucy's bare waist and with her back pressed hard against him, he carried her out a small way and then swung her around and around. Her laughter vibrated through him and he deliberately fell backwards into the water, pulling her with him. His hand cupped her breasts and she turned in his arms, wrapping her legs around his waist before they broke the surface, panting for breath.

He watched the salt water bead and linger on the tips of her eyelashes. 'You know I want to kiss you.'

'I know.' She gave him a wicked grin and wriggled against him.

Despite the coolness of the water he instantly hardened.

'*Papá*, come.' Ignacio waved a shell he'd found.

He groaned quietly.

'That was your intention, right?' Lucy laughed.

'*Papá!* What shell. Is it?'

He shook his head, spraying her with water. 'You re-alise that you are destroying my credibility as a father.'

She flicked water back at him. 'Seeing you need a moment, I'll go and name the shell.'

'Okay.' But just before she moved away, he tenderly kissed her and she jerked against him, her eyes dilating into large inky discs. This time he laughed. 'Finding it hard to stand up?'

'Lucy. *Papá.* I'm hungry.'

Lucy gave him a thoughtful look. 'So this is what being a parent is like?'

He thought of how much fun he was having and how normal it all felt to be sharing what in essence was a family picnic. 'This is the easy part.'

She squeezed his hand and then they ran the short distance back to the shore together.

Lucy pulled on her running clothes, knowing she was cutting things very fine. 'Seeing Iggie's at Haven, will I bring him to the polo and meet you there?'

'Pardon?' Marco appeared in the doorway of the en suite, a white towel slung low on his hips and his torso with its dips and crevices on full display.

She dropped the shoe she was holding.

He winked at her and with a knowing look, he leaned his arm up against the wall, the movement flowing through toned muscles. He was the complete package—handsome, thoughtful, loving and caring—and she adored spending time with him and Iggie. Her heart hitched in her chest. She didn't want to think about how it was going to feel when she left Bulla Creek, left Marco and Iggie, but she knew she had to leave soon.

You could stay and join the practice.

The thought floated around her like a bubble of warmth and security and then it popped and reality dumped all over her. She didn't belong in Bulla Creek any more.

She didn't know where she belonged, which was why

she'd put in an application to the UK. Surely it would
be easier to be a stranger in a strange land rather than
feeling like a stranger in a place where everybody knew
her and considered she belonged. But even the idea of
the UK didn't seem quite right and the thought gave
her headache.

She picked up the shoe. 'You're so not playing fair.
You know I don't have time to stay and take advantage of you.'

He pushed off the door and gathered her in his arms.
'You do realise that arriving at Haven all hot and sweaty
having run from here pretending you were out for a
morning jog is not fooling him. William knows.'

'No, he doesn't.' Her vehement words echoed around
the room.

'He does.' Marco kissed her lightly on the lips. 'He
has given me "the look".'

'What do you mean by that?'

'The look fathers give to the men their daughters
date. The look that says, *Tread carefully and if you hurt
her I will kill you.*'

She stooped down and tugged hard on her shoelaces,
trying to get rid of the uncomfortable feeling that eddied inside her that William might know about her and
Marco. She shrugged it away because William no longer
had a say in her life, even if deep down she knew she
wanted him to. He'd forfeited the right. 'You don't have
to worry because I'm not his daughter or his concern.'

His hand stroked the top of her head. 'Lucy, for your
own peace of mind you need to forgive him.'

His quietly spoken words packed the punch of an
exploding grenade and she shot to her feet. 'Oh, you
mean just like you need to forgive Bianca?'

'This is not at all the same thing.' He pulled on his

jodhpurs with a stiff jerk. 'Bianca does not love me or Ignacio. She does not belong in our lives but William loves you and belongs in yours. You grew up feeling loved, yes?'

Guilt, confusion and shame tangoed inside her as they often did. Yes, she'd had a loving and happy childhood and she knew she should be grateful but it was so hard to be when it turned out everything about her life had been predicated on huge, unspoken lies. 'I did but—'

'Trust the feeling.'

'I can't.'

Two lines appeared on the bridge of his nose. 'You have to. It is your lifeline through all of this.'

Was it? No. If the last six months had taught her anything, it was that thinking about being adopted just made her miserable. People told her, 'You should be grateful you got great parents.' Did children raised by birth parents feel grateful? No one understood the emotional roller-coaster.

She took in a deep breath and shifted her focus to today and everything that hung on it being a success. Picking up his black and gold polo shirt, she threw it at him. 'Make sure you look as sexy as hell on that horse and strut your polo-playing skills. We need every reporter at the ground to notice you and Bulla Creek will do the rest.'

The tone of her voice and the jut of her chin told Marco he'd pushed her too far about William and he knew he'd chosen the wrong time to do it. Their picnic on the beach seemed a lifetime ago and the last five days in the run-up to the polo tournament had been huge, leaving them both strung out. Between his work as a doctor, his role as a father, the planning of the 'change the visa campaign' and being creative in finding convenient times when Ignacio was out of the house so he could make love to Lucy, he felt like he was four different people.

'Lucy.'

She jammed her cap on her head. 'What?'

He wasn't going to apologise but he didn't want her to leave angry either. Wrapping his arms around her rigid body, he pressed his lips to her ear and whispered, 'I promise to look as sexy as hell, but while I am doing it, I will be thinking of you.'

'Damn straight you will.' She lightly thumped his chest with her fist, and a smile creased her face. 'Iggie and I will be on the sidelines cheering you on.'

The thought of the two of them together made him smile.

'I don't think I can watch,' Lucy muttered as the fifth chukka came to an end with the score tied.

The weather couldn't have been more perfect if they'd been able to control it and the polo carnival was in full swing under a vivid blue sky. Black director's chairs with the sponsor's name stencilled in gold lined the edge of the field and behind them a large white marquee with its distinctive four 'steeples' served a never-ending supply of food, champagne and beer. The crowd was a mix of locals and people from Perth, and women in their fashionable best promenaded along the course, happy to have their photos taken for the social pages of the Perth papers. For the first time since arriving in Bulla Creek, Lucy was outclassed in footwear.

'*Papá* will get...' Ignacio took in a breath '...another goal.'

'I hope so.' Lucy tousled his hair as bitter longing rolled through her. She remembered having that sort of hero-worship for William and she hadn't lost it as a teenager like many children did. She'd lost it now though and she was struggling with the gaping hole its absence left in her life. Marco said, 'forgive' but it wasn't that straightforward. His life hadn't been stripped of history and connectedness. He still had family even though he'd chosen to live in Australia. He knew who he was.

She didn't.

William had been the reason she'd become a doctor because that's what the Pattersons had done down the generations. Only now she kept wondering what other career paths she might have taken if the expectation of medicine hadn't been held up to her for as long as she could remember. If she'd grown up with her real parents. The idea that her life could have been so very different, making her a different person completely, both taunted and perplexed her.

'Where is. William?' Ignacio turned in his chair, looking around at the crowd.

'He's meeting a friend.' Actually, he was having a beer with the local Member of Parliament, who he'd always had a good relationship with, and was trying to get some action happening to help Marco.

The thud of hooves against turf made Lucy look up and the pack of ponies thundered past, throwing up divots of grass as the sixth and final chukka commenced. As a child she'd belonged to the pony club but she'd never gained the skill of these horsemen who could control their mounts at the same time as leaning out sideways from the saddle and hitting a ball with a mallet. A polo pony needed heart, speed, stamina and the ability to turn on a penny. A good pony was eighty percent of the game.

The other twenty percent came from the player and Marco had that in spades. As expected, his dark, Latino presence on a thoroughbred horse made heads turn and cameras had been flashing all afternoon. They saw the way his muscular thighs gripped the saddle, how his tight behind rose and fell in perfect sync with the horse's movement and the power with which he hit the ball. She saw all that too, but she also saw a grace, determination and humility which flowed from the inside out and made her heart quiver in a way it never had before.

You love him.

No, I do not!

She gave herself a determined shake. No way was she falling in love. She couldn't. It wasn't her time. Not now with her own life in a total mess. Even though she hated the way Daniel had broken up with her, she now realised he had a point when he'd said she'd was emotionally cut off. She wasn't able to give enough so involving someone else wasn't a good idea. Especially a man with a child. With so many unanswered questions about her own mother, she could hardly be one herself. No, she was just in lust with Marco and it was all a temporary escape—from William, from the shambles of her life in Perth and the fog of her future. From everything.

As the final moments of the match counted down, sweat foamed on the coats of the hard-working horses and their tiring riders made some rookie mistakes. Supporters on both sides were biting their nails as the match stayed tied.

'If no one scores, they have to play another chukka,' she told Iggie. She'd expected him to lose interest in the match a long time ago, but he loved watching the horses and his father.

He stood up, leaving his crutches hanging on the chair. 'Go, *Papá*.' He waved his arms as Marco rode past and then he promptly listed sideways.

Lucy slipped her hand into his to steady him and his small fingers immediately closed around her palm. He grinned at her, his excitement palpable.

A rush of happiness so simple and pure poured through her and she grinned back. Raising their arms together, she yelled, 'Come on, Marco. Come on, Bulla Creek, you can do it.'

Marco wheeled his horse around and charged back down the field, his shirt billowing behind him as he chased down the white ball. He swung his arm out in a wide arc and his mallet hit it with a loud clack, sending it careening straight at goal. The number four player from the Perth team lunged from his saddle and blocked the ball.

Groans of despair mixed in with cheers of delight as the crowd revelled in the closeness of the game. Lucy didn't think her body could cope with much more adrenaline.

David Henderson was playing number three position and working hard to turn the play. Leaning from the near side of his pony, he shot the ball back toward his fellow Bulla Creek players. Marco saw the shot and urged his pony on, reaching the ball unopposed but at a sharp angle to goal. Reaching down and gripping the flexible bamboo shaft, he placed the mallet head behind the ball.

It was a tough shot and Lucy held her breath as the goal defence manoeuvred his horse into position.

Whack! Marco connected with the ball, sending it

into a tight curve that shot straight through the goal posts.

'Yes!' Lucy screamed and punched the air and Iggie copied her, his face bright with delight.

Dizzy with excitement, she picked him up, kissed him on the cheek and hugged him. 'We won, we won, we won.'

Iggie rested his head on her shoulder for a moment, his small, warm body relaxing against hers, and her heart cramped. Allison would have held her sons like this but never her.

She swallowed against the lump in her throat. If she ever had a child, she'd never let him go.

'Too tight.' Iggie wriggled in her arms.

With a start, she realised she was gripping the poor child so hard he could barely breathe. She put him down and patted his shoulder. 'Sorry, mate.'

The Bulla Creek crowd roared around them as the umpire blew his whistle, signalling the end of the match. The players rode off toward the saddling area and Lucy rose on her toes, craning her neck to see, but Marco had vanished into an appreciative crowd. She wanted to rush over to him and throw her arms around his neck in a congratulatory hug, but she didn't want to get in the way of the plan. Besides, Iggie couldn't 'rush' anywhere.

'Lucy?'

She squatted down so she was at Iggie's eye level. 'Yes, mate?'

'Can I.' He seemed to be concentrating harder than ever to get the words out. 'Ride a horse?'

'Ah…sure. I can't see why not.'

'Awesome.' His small body quivered with excitement. 'Can I do. It now?'

'Um.' She almost said 'no', because a polo pony was

not the steed Iggie needed and then she saw David's wife, Tilly Henderson, and remembered that earlier in the day she'd seen her leading her three-year-old around on an old pony. 'Tilly.' She waved. 'Have you got a minute?'

Ten minutes later with a helmet on his head, Iggie was sitting on Betsy, with a grin on his face as wide as the world. Tilly led the pony and Lucy had her hand on Iggie's waist, supporting him like she'd seen Marco do when Iggie rode on his shoulders.

His legs which were so often tight because of spasming muscles relaxed and she didn't know if that was from the warmth of the horse or the movement or both. With each step the horse took, his hips tilted and Iggie sat up straighter. 'I want to try on my own.'

Lucy bit her lip, torn between wanting him to try and worried he might fall. 'Okay, but I'm going to have my hands just here, ready.'

'I won't need them.' His hands gripped the reins with a determination that seemed to hold him even straighter.

'I'm sure you won't but that's the deal.' She stayed close and he was remarkably steady as the movement of the horse flowed through him. His laughter and joy was infectious.

'I want to go faster.'

'One thing at a time, Iggie.'

Tilly turned around. 'Bets at a trot is still pretty slow, Lucy. You could jog next to him with your hand on him and then if he's steady move it to the back of the saddle.'

'Please, Lucy. I want to. Try.'

'I start all my riders on Bets,' Tilly said, 'and I haven't lost a customer yet. He's looking really comfortable and considering his unsteady legs, his rhythm is good. I have a friend down in Perth who provides the horses for therapy with kids—' she dropped her voice and mouthed '—worse than Iggie.'

A light bulb exploded in Lucy's head. 'Of course. Hippotherapy.' Going by the expression on Iggie's face, it would be worth investigating for him. Gripping the back of the saddle, she said, 'Hold on tight, Iggie.'

Marco was hot and sweaty, smelt like horse and his mouth ached from smiling. He'd been thumped on the back by most of the men of Bulla Creek, kissed on the cheek by women he'd never met, but most importantly, he'd been able to tell his story to William's parliamentary friend. Now he was speaking with a television reporter. He knew this was important, but even so, he was drawing on all his patience to be charming and obliging and answering her questions fully about Ignacio and his own life when he was used to keeping things like that private. All he really wanted to do was find Lucy and kiss her hard and ask Ignacio what he thought of his *papá*'s winning goal.

'So your son?' The reporter asked with a smile. 'How old is he again?'

'Five. He is in first year of primary school.'

Her eyes lit up. 'Oh, cute age. Is he here today?'

Marco nodded. '*Sí*, he was watching the game with my—' *Your what? Lover? Girlfriend?* 'A colleague and friend.'

The reporter flipped her notebook closed. 'Thanks, Marco, I think I've got all the information I need.'

A river of relief flowed through him that the interview was finally over. '*Gracias,* Patty.'

'All we need now is some footage of you and Ignacio together.'

His chest tightened. 'Is that necessary?'

'A picture tells a thousand words,' Patty quipped.

'I am happy to be filmed. You could—' Familiar laughter made him look beyond the reporter and his blood swooped to his feet. *'Querido Dios.'*

The reporter swung around to see what he was looking at. 'Is that your little boy on the horse?'

'Sí.' He strode directly to Ignacio with fear for his son and anger at Lucy burning in his veins.

He was only vaguely aware of Patty behind him saying, 'Come on,' and the ratting sound of equipment.

Ignacio's small hands gripped the reins as the horse moved briskly toward them. *'Papá,* I'm just. Like you!'

'Be careful,' Marco yelled. 'Grip with your legs.' The moment the words left his mouth he knew how useless they were. His son didn't have the strength to do that. 'Stay still.'

Lucy's face was pink from her jog and she gave him a huge smile. 'Doesn't he look fantastic?'

He dropped his head close to hers and it took every ounce of control to keep his voice low. 'Did you lose your brain? He could have fallen and broken his neck.'

Incredulity shone stark on Lucy's face and her grey eyes flashed with the hurt of being misconstrued. 'You think I'd allow that? I would never put him in danger.'

He didn't want to listen to the voice inside him which agreed because he had evidence to the contrary in front of him.

She turned and spoke directly to Patty who'd arrived with a cameraman. 'Have you asked Dr Rodriguez about the benefits of hippotherapy for children with cerebral palsy? The movement of the horse flows though the child and it mimics the feel of walking. This adds to their physiotherapy with improved balance and gait.'

Her words ramped up his ire. He couldn't believe she

had no clue she'd done something so inherently wrong. 'It is important that the parents give the permission for hippotherapy.'

Lucy's jaw shot up. 'Some parents are too scared to allow their children to take the therapy and by doing so hold their child back.'

His jaw locked with anger. 'Parents have rights.'

Lucy's faced blanched. 'So do children.'

Patty frowned, glancing between them, clearly confused. 'I'm sure this is all very interesting but right now this is the perfect picture we've been looking for. Pete needs to start filming if it's going to make the six o'clock news.'

The situation roared around him, growing into its own identity, totally disregarding his opinions and piling on top of the unease that he was losing control of his son and his life to other people.

This was *his* fight to stay in Australia and as much as he appreciated the support of the town and the power of the media, Ignacio shouldn't be part of it. 'Patty, I don't want—'

'Will I be. On TV?' Ignacio's eyes were wide with wonder as he watched the fluffy boom microphone being positioned.

Lucy laid her hand on his arm. 'It's a *good* idea, Marco.'

He couldn't believe she'd just said that.

'Dad, if you stand next to the kid.' Pete started setting up the scene.

'I don't want Ignacio to be filmed.' The terse words exploded out of him making everyone stare at him in shocked surprise.

'I want to be. On television.' Ignacio's sweet voice sounded loud in the sudden silence. 'With you, *Papá*.'

Marco opened his mouth to say 'I'm not going to be on television' but Pete got in first.

'You don't want to disappoint the little guy especially as we've already got footage of you playing polo.' The cameraman grinned, knowing he'd just trumped the argument.

Bile rose in Marco's throat as the situation closed in on him. He could oblige or risk Ignacio having a tantrum, which they'd probably film anyway and that wouldn't paint him in a good light as a parent or a future citizen. In less than two minutes it would undo all the work of the previous week. He hated it that he'd been put in this position and he was furious with Lucy for siding with the press. Fathers were supposed to shield and protect their children, not sell them out by putting them on public display. *Dios*, he was pictorialising Ignacio's disability which was something he'd never wanted to do.

The cameraman said, 'Put your hand on the back of the saddle just like—'

'Lucy,' Ignacio offered up happily. 'Lucy found me. The horse. She's fun.'

A flash of green joined the rising bile. Ignacio needed an adult who knew what was best for him, not someone who acted first and thought second.

'Lucy, right.' Pete nodded. 'You don't mind stepping aside for a moment, do you?'

'Not at all.'

'An excellent idea.' Marco stepped in close to the pony.

'Just like hippotherapy.' Lucy moved sideways but her expression said she regretted nothing.

Marco swallowed a curse. She always had to have the last word but this time she'd gone too far. She had no right to be making decisions about Ignacio. He gripped his son's waist.

'Ouch. *Papá*.' Ignacio wriggled away from his touch. 'Put your hand. On the saddle. Like Lucy.'

The green flare intensified. 'Lucy should have held onto you.'

His terse tone only made Ignacio more resolute. 'No. I can do it. On my own.'

'Smile, mate,' the cameraman said.

Knowing what was at stake, Marco got his lips to curve while he inwardly cursed the government and Lucy in that order.

CHAPTER TEN

LUCY had been called into the hospital to treat a horse handler who'd been kicked as he'd tried to load one of the polo ponies into a float. She'd been worried about the risk of cardiac tamponade, but thankfully it was only bruising of the chest wall. Even so, neither horse nor handler would be making the trip back to Perth tonight.

For the last two hours, she'd been trying to leave the hospital, but each time she picked up her bag someone else arrived who needed treatment, including two children sick with asthma. Now she'd finally got away and had driven straight to Marco's. She hadn't seen him since the television camera had stopped rolling and he'd taken Ignacio home without a backward glance.

That had been hours ago and they'd both had time to calm down. She'd been furious and hurt that he could think for a moment she'd put Ignacio in danger, but she now realised that his reaction had probably stemmed from the stress of the day and all the uncertainty around his future in Australia. She regretted the bitchy way she'd tried to involve the reporter in the argument and she planned to apologise. In fact, she was looking forward to spending an hour alone with Marco. It meant it would be past midnight by the time she got back to

Haven, which was a good thing as William would be in bed.

Marco was outside, lying on the table with his hands behind his head, and she smiled, thinking how she could watch him for hours. A crazy feeling that almost resembled sadness came out of nowhere, curling through her, shocking her with its intensity. He looked so alone.

He needs someone to share the load.

An answering thought fluttered through her which she immediately scotched. They only shared sex. That was what they both wanted.

She bent down, brushing his lips with hers. 'So, are we going to add make-up sex to our repertoire?'

Instead of kissing her back, he sat up stiffly. 'You had no right to put Ignacio on a horse. I did not want him photographed and you knew that but you didn't care and you disregarded my opinion.'

She jerked back, totally blindsided by the intensity of his anger—an anger she'd assumed would have faded now he'd had time to think things through rationally. 'Hang on just a minute, those two things are not remotely connected.'

Despite trying to find calm, she couldn't keep the incredulity out of her voice. 'You think I put Ignacio on the horse for a PR stunt?'

His stony expression didn't flicker. 'Yes.'

Did he really have such a small amount of regard for her?

Why not?

The traitorous voice of doubt that had plagued her since she'd found out she was adopted boomed in her head. *Allison didn't want you and William didn't think you deserved your own life story.* The tremble of rejection started at her toes and like wildfire driven by a hot wind, it whipped through her, consuming all of her in a second. 'It was sheer coincidence that Iggie arrived on a horse.'

Rejection morphed into fury. 'But you know what? You should be thanking me because it was the ultimate PR coup and we couldn't have hoped for better. Iggie was as cute as a button sitting astride that old pony looking like every other five-year-old, and *not* a drain on the public health system. It got you on the news, giving you the coverage you need. It's all about exposure.'

His hand slapped the table. 'Using my son is not what I wanted and now I have more reporters wanting to intrude on his life.'

'Good. It will only help your cause. Let's hope the immigration minister saw the news too.' Her anger deflated as fast as it had come and she sighed. 'Marco, you're not using Iggie. If it helps, think about it this way. He loved being on TV and he's a natural in front of the camera so you haven't scarred him for life. He wanted to do it. I understand you want to shelter him from a media circus, but this isn't one so stop being so hard on yourself.'

She traced his cheek with her finger, aching for him and the fact he'd had to parent Ignacio on his own for so long and deal with all the extra things that a child with a disability brought into the mix. She wanted to lighten his load. 'Think of it as broadening his experiences. He loved watching you play polo and he wanted to share part of the experience. At least I think that's why he asked me if he could ride a horse. He was desperate to try it.'

He cupped her wrist and brought her hand down from his face. 'And if he asked to play on the road would you say "yes"?'

'Oh, come on, Marco.' She slapped her hands against her hips. 'That is a ridiculous thing to say. I was next to him the whole time just like a therapist would be if he rode each week. Can you honestly tell me that if he'd asked you if he could ride a horse you would have said no?'

His face remained intransigent. 'He's seen me play polo many times and he's never once asked me if he could ride a horse. If he did I would have told him he needed to be older.'

But Ignacio getting older wouldn't change anything. It was like pieces in a puzzle suddenly slotting together to show the full picture and it looked like fear. 'This is just like the soccer ball.'

Marco's shoulders stiffened. 'If you mean you should not be making decisions for Ignacio then, yes.'

'Actually, that's not what I meant at all.' She let his comment roll over her and sat down next to him, wanting to touch him, wanting to make him understand. 'Marco, like I told you earlier, I'd never put Iggie in danger, but he needs experiences. I don't think you wrapping him in cotton wool is healthy.'

He frowned. 'What do you mean by cotton wool?'

'Over-protecting.'

'You don't know what you are talking about.' The words came out tight and guarded. 'I provide him with therapy so he can improve, so how is that over-protecting him?'

She stroked his arm with her hand. 'I don't think you *mean* to do it.'

'I don't need to know what you think, Lucy.'

His accent usually caressed her name, but this time it came out as a warning growl. The hair on the back of her neck stood up.

Back off now before you get hurt.

But she couldn't because every part of her said, *Open his eyes and help him understand. Fight for Ignacio.*

It's not your fight.

Yes, it is. I love them both too much to let this ride. Her breath solidified in her lungs. Oh, God, she loved them. *No, no, please, no.* It was too soon, it was the wrong place and the wrong time, but her heart was deaf to it all.

Love propelled her onward. 'Marco, if Ignacio didn't have CP you'd be pushing him harder, but fear is making you play it safe. What if safety is the worst thing for him? What if you keep him so safe he never achieves his potential? What if you're so busy protecting him you don't give him the opportunity to strive and try harder?' She gulped in a quick breath and slid her hand into his. 'Hippotherapy is wonderful for helping with balance. It improves all movement and as Iggie adored being on the horse so much he'd get even more out of it.'

He withdrew his hand. 'I think I know what is best for *my* son.'

'I'm not sure that you do.' She rushed on, trying to get through to him. 'I'm only saying this because I love you both and if Iggie was my son, I'd be signing him up for a weekly session and watching him blossom.'

Oh, God, what did you just say?

Marco's eyes widened in shock. 'You do *not* love us.'

She wrung her hands, horrified that the words had slipped out. 'I do and believe me, it's as much of a shock to me as it is to you.'

'I don't want to be loved, Lucy. Not that way and you're so confused about your life that I think you are confused about loving us. I know you're upset that your birth mother and her family don't want you in their lives, but you have a family with William who loves you.' He ran his hand through his hair. 'Ignacio and I can't be your family.'

We can't be your family.

His words sliced deep into her naive and unsuspecting heart, the one she should have protected, and she bit her lip against the wave of pain. The metallic taste of blood hit her tongue.

She should have known better. She should have been more alert, more on guard. Now she'd just allowed more pain to pile up on the cairn that was currently her life. She scrambled to her feet. 'You've made yourself very clear, Marco.'

Tension held him captive but anguish flared in his eyes. 'I needed to.'

She tilted her chin, trying to hold back bitter tears. 'I think we're way past the point of make-up sex, don't you? This is the end of our road.'

'*Sí*, it is.'

Her heart wept and she walked to the gate. When she reached it, she turned back slowly, determined to leave with some dignity intact. 'Most of it's been fun. This last bit not so much.'

His face twisted. 'Lucy, be kind to yourself. Take some time to answer all the questions that are plaguing you so you can live your life without regrets.'

She didn't want to hear that. 'Goodbye, Marco.' She closed the gate behind her.

Lucy sat at the kitchen table with a throw rug over her shoulders, her knees pulled up to her chin and her hands wrapped around a coffee mug. She was watching the dawn break and the golden fingers of sunlight spreading across the sky. She hadn't gone to bed, there'd have been no point. Awake or asleep her mind was reliving every heart-breaking moment of her conversation with Marco from the instant she'd realised she loved him to the second he'd shut her out of his life.

Shut out like her birth mother had shut her out.

'Problem, possum?'

Her heart, already wrung out to the point of dryness, managed to bleed a little more. She hadn't heard William call her by her pet name since the morning of Ruth's funeral and with a jolt of shock she realised she'd missed it.

She gulped coffee, not having expected to feel that way. Why did everything to do with William have to be bitter-sweet? It was exhausting and nothing would induce her to talk to him about Marco. She didn't confide in him any more.

'It's nothing. Why are you up so early?'

'Couldn't sleep.' He limped over to her and sat down, his face drawn like it had been when she'd first arrived. It was in stark contrast to his healthier glow of the last two weeks and she felt a twinge of concern.

'I've known you all your life, Lucy, and it doesn't look like nothing.' He poured himself a coffee from the pot and took a sip. 'You sitting there all curled up reminds me of the time you and Phoebe Henderson took the car and crashed it into McCurdy's ditch.'

She remembered that. Phoebe's then boyfriend had been throwing a party on a nearby property but Phoebe hadn't been allowed to attend. Phoebe had turned up at Haven in tears and had convinced Lucy she should drive her, levering the fact that a boy Lucy had liked at the time would be there and if she didn't go to the party he would end up with Chloe Hogarth. The sixteen-year-old logic had seemed flawless right up until the car had hit gravel and spun out of control.

God, she'd been so scared—scared she'd hurt herself and Phoebe, and then scared to tell William because she didn't want to see his disappointment of her shining bright in his eyes. The memory stirred up a question that had played on her mind ever since she'd discovered her adoption papers. Maybe it was the quiet of the dawn or her ragged emotions, but she thought things couldn't get any worse. 'Were there times like that when you regretted adopting me?'

William gasped, his face twisting with sorrow. 'Never. Not one single moment. Your mother and I loved you from the moment we laid eyes on you and you've always been, and always will be, my pride and joy. Why would you doubt that?'

'Because of the lie.' Her voice broke. 'Can't you see it casts doubt on everything? I trusted you implicitly. You were always the person I took my problems to and yet you did this to me.' A rogue tear escaped, rolling down her cheek. 'Why? I can't get around it. I can't forgive you for that.'

William shuddered. 'You're right, it's unforgiveable. What we did was wrong and I've known it was wrong from the moment I reluctantly agreed not to tell you.'

Startled, she thought she must have misheard. 'You agreed not to tell me? Agreed with who?'

Despite the cool of the early morning, sweat beaded on William's brow. 'Your mother.'

She almost said, 'Which one?', but the question was futile because to William she'd only ever had one mother and that was Ruth. Truth be told, Ruth *was* the only mother she would ever have. Bitter pain twisted through her and she heard herself say, 'My birth mother sent a letter and it turns out you were right all along. She asked me not to contact her again.'

'Oh, Lucy.' His hand reached out and hovered above hers as if he was wondering how his touch would be received and then he briefly squeezed it. His grief flowed into her, melding with her own. 'I'm so sorry. I know how much you wanted a connection with her and with Ruth gone it was even more—'

His shoulders slumped but then he seemed to gather himself. 'Ruth and I had always dreamed of a large family but as you know, she had several miscarriages due to her diabetes. When we had the opportunity to adopt you, we were in seventh heaven. From the moment she held you in her arms and you wrapped your tiny hand around her finger she was your mother.'

Marco's voice drifted across her mind. *When you hold your baby in your arms there is such a surge of love and protection that it changes you.* 'But that doesn't explain why she didn't want to tell me I was adopted.'

'She was scared.' The simple words hung in the air. 'Perhaps because she'd lost so many babies she couldn't quite believe you were hers to keep and her biggest fear was losing you. She was a tigress in her protection of you. She begged me to support her in keeping your adoption a secret.'

William loves you and you need to forgive him. Lucy sat back in her chair, fighting to reconcile love with secrecy and trust with misguided loyalty. 'Did you ever question it?'

His eyes filled with distress. 'I loved you both too much to risk making either of you unhappy and I justified it as protection, but it's a decision that's eaten at me for years. The way you found out haunts me every day.'

'You sound just like Marco.' The words slipped out

on a sea of heartache. 'What is it about parents and mis-guided protection?'

Astonishment flooded William's face quickly fol-lowed by understanding. 'So this is why you're huddled up here? You and Marco had a lovers' tiff?'

Tiff so seriously understated what had gone down between them that her stomach cramped. 'We're not lovers.'

'I have eyes, Lucy.'

She sighed, knowing she'd rarely ever got anything past him. 'Put it this way then. We're no longer lovers or even friends. He told me in no uncertain terms I'm not part of his life and he's furious with me for suggesting he's over-protecting Iggie. Having been over-protected, I think I know what I'm talking about.'

His normally mild hazel eyes flashed in his pale face as he momentarily rubbed his chest. 'Did I ever hold you back from what you wanted to do?'

Her instant response of 'You lied to me' rose to her lips, but something in his gaze made her set that aside and she thought about all the opportunities she'd been given. 'No.' She bit her lip as everything rushed back. 'Did you ever plan to tell me I was adopted after Ruth died?'

'Yes.' He nodded slowly. 'I was going to tell you the day after the funeral. I know this isn't any consolation, but please know that your mother only ever wanted you to feel loved. She *never* wanted you to feel the way I can only imagine you've been feeling since she died.'

Long held-back tears spilled over. 'I love you both but I hate how all of this has made me feel. I have this great, big empty hole inside me like I'm not good enough and that my life isn't mine.'

'We failed you.' Utter desolation lined his face and

he suddenly gasped. His already pale face went from white to ashen grey as one hand gripped his chest and the other reached out to her.

Fright tore through her. Had she just reached a point where they might be able to move forward only to have him die? 'Dad? Do you have pain down your arm?'

He could barely speak. 'Can't. Breathe. SVT.'

'What?' Incredulously, she pressed her fingers against his neck. Stress could cause it but she didn't trust self-diagnosis especially with such a sudden and unexpected onset. How would he even know he had super ventricular tachycardia?

His pulse pounded so hard it was almost too fast to count but after ten seconds she rapidly multiplied. 'Two hundred beats per minute. I'm going to try vagus nerve massage.'

William barely nodded as her fingers started massaging his neck near his trachea. The plan was to stimulate the release of chemicals and break the abnormal electrical circuit in the heart which had triggered the SVT. A minute later his heart was still galloping out of control.

'Don't move.' She shot to her feet and tore down the hall to his study where he kept his medical bag.

When she got back William was leaning back in his chair gulping in short, shallow breaths.

Oh, God, no. Lucy's fear for William—fear for herself—escalated. If she didn't slow his heart down fast, his blood pressure would plummet and he'd be at a risk of cardiac failure and anoxia of the brain. 'I'm going to give you adenosine.'

Hardly able to speak, William closed his eyes as if saying yes. The drug had to be given intravenously and she wrapped a tourniquet around his arm, pulling it tight and then started tapping for the feel of a vein.

Her fingers begged for the worm-like rise as her eyes scanned for the trademark blue wiggle.

Nothing. *Stay calm.* 'I'll try your other arm.'

Whipping the tourniquet off, she tried his left arm but she could see tiny scars on his inner elbow as if others before her had tried and failed to find a decent vein when he wasn't peripherally shut down. She checked his pulse again. Two hundred and twenty.

She had to act fast. 'Stay with me, Dad. I've got one more idea.'

She raced into the kitchen and with the crash of baking pans and wire cake coolers tumbling out onto floor, she hauled out the huge stainless steel basin Ruth had always used when she made the Christmas cake. Filling it with ice and cold water, she carried it quickly back to the table, sloshing water everywhere.

William's frantic gaze met hers. She bit her lip, put her hand on the back of his head and said, 'Okay, you know the drill. Hold your breath.' She pushed his head down to the freezing water.

He jerked as the cold hit him and she kept her hand firmly on his head, keeping him in place and she counted to four. *Please let this work.*

She pulled at his hair and William sat up gasping and coughing, and Lucy wished she had a towel to give him but the most important thing was to take his pulse. Her fingers pressed against neck and his pulse thundered under her fingers still fast but stronger. Her legs trembled as relief flowed through her. 'One hundred and hopefully dropping. Thank goodness for the diving reflex. Are you feeling a bit better?'

His hand found hers. 'I can get my breath and my heart no longer feels like it's going to bounce out of my chest. Thank you, sweetheart.'

She gave him a weak smile and checked his pulse again. 'Eighty. I think we've won for now. I'll get you some dry clothes to warm you up and then I'm inserting a butterfly so we have an open vein. Then you're going to the hospital and as soon as I can arrange it, you're going to Perth attached to a cardiac monitor.'

'You're my daughter. Tell Marco and he can arrange it.'

Her heart cramped. Her plan had been to leave for Perth this morning and never see or talk to Marco again. 'Surely I can refer you to a cardiologist in Perth.'

William looked sheepish. 'I already have one.'

Betrayal mixed in with indignation. 'And Marco knows and neither of you told me?'

William sighed. 'Marco doesn't know and I didn't tell you because I didn't want you to come to Bulla Creek out of duty. I wanted you to come back because you *wanted* to see me. But Marco contacted you and duty brought you back.'

'And you kept extending my stay.' She thought about how tired he'd often looked, how he'd been slow to return to work and how he'd self-diagnosed, only it hadn't been self-diagnosis after all. 'Those anti-hypertensive tablets are yours, aren't they?'

He grimaced. 'Yes.'

'If you've known you have SVT for a while, I don't understand why the cardiologist hasn't inserted a pacemaker already?'

'I haven't seen the cardiologist.'

She slapped her forehead with the palm of her hand thinking that doctors—male doctors—made the worst patients. 'Why on earth not?'

'Up until today, the episodes have only lasted a couple of minutes and I put the dizziness, anxiety and occasional runs of palpitations down to stress.' He started to shiver. 'Given the year we've had, that wasn't such an outrageous assumption.'

'Oh, Dad, I'm sorry. I've been so caught up with how I've been feeling that I pinned all my feelings of anger onto you. That wasn't fair and I totally missed that this whole mess has been as tough on you as it has been on me.'

'I love you, Lucy. You're my sun, moon and stars and I'm just glad you're here.'

She hugged him hard, feeling his arms tight around her just as they'd always been when she'd been a child and one hand patting her back. A shiver rocked through her and she realised that water had seeped through her T-shirt and onto her skin. 'We need to get you dry.'

She organised towels and clothes and while William changed, she rang the ambulance and Deb at the hospital. The nurse offered to contact Marco and Lucy accepted, not having the energy to face him.

As she slid the tourniquet onto William's arm, he put his other hand on her hair, just like he had when she'd been a little girl. 'Always know that you're a wonderful doctor, Lucy, and a true Patterson.'

'Only we both know that's not strictly true.' She wiped his arm with an alcohol swab. 'If at eighteen I'd said I wanted to be an artist, what would you have said?'

Surprise lit across William's face. 'You have many talents, darling, but drawing isn't one of them. Besides, you always said you wanted to be a doctor.'

She expertly slid the butterfly needle into his arm. 'I know, but that's because I thought medicine ran in my veins. Now I'm not so sure and I keep wondering what I might have done, who I might have been, if you were not my father.'

A tremor ran through him. 'Then go and find out.'

Stunned, she looked up from taping the needle. 'Really?'

A look of utter defeat crossed his face. 'The truth is that I've always hoped and dreamed you'd join the Bulla Creek practice, and when I saw you falling in love with Marco, I hoped against hope you'd stay.'

'He doesn't love me.'

'Well, he's a fool, but we're often fools when it comes to love.'

'I'm so confused, Dad.'

He sighed and squeezed her hand. 'Your mother's and my secret has caused you so much anguish and as much as I want you to stay, I don't want you here out of duty. If this feeling of "Who am I?" is tormenting you so much then go and find out. I only want you to be happy.'

Take some time to answer all the questions that are plaguing you so you can live your life without regrets.

The image of Marco and Iggie loomed in her mind and on a surge of pain, she shut them out. They didn't figure in her future and even if they did, both Marco and William were right. Before she could move forward, she had to find out who she really was.

CHAPTER ELEVEN

THE clock chimed three and Marco's stomach grumbled reminding him he hadn't had lunch. It had been a hellish few days. William was in Perth recovering from having a pacemaker inserted and Lucy had gone south with him. He'd spoken to William on the phone in Perth. The elder doctor had told him he'd be home in two days, back at work in two weeks.

William had also added that he was sorry but Marco would have to cope without a locum during that time. This meant Lucy wasn't returning to Bulla Creek. He grabbed a handful of sugar-coated chocolates he kept in a jar on his desk to encourage uncooperative children into thinking that he wasn't a bad guy.

An image of Lucy's grey eyes filled with hurt and pain seared him. He shovelled more candy into his mouth. He'd never wanted to cause her any anguish or suffering, but how could he not when she'd broken their self-imposed rules by thinking she'd fallen in love with him? He didn't want to be loved—not in a way that meant marriage and a partnership. He and Ignacio were fine on their own and that was why he'd spent years keeping women at bay.

Regret that he'd inflicted pain surged again, just as it had every day since Lucy had walked out and his gate had thudded shut behind her. He should have known better than to get involved with her when she was so emotionally vulnerable, but she'd got under his skin like no one else ever had. She made him laugh, she made him hungry for life, but at the same time she had no hesitation in getting involved in things that didn't concern her—like Ignacio—and telling him in no uncertain terms when she disagreed with him. Not even Bianca had done that.

Bianca didn't care though.

The thought rattled him just like all thoughts of Lucy and he squared his shoulders. It was time to stop thinking about her and get on with his life. He had a visa battle to win and he couldn't afford more days of feeling spun out and emotionally shell-shocked. Whatever it was that had swirled between the two of them, creating an irresistible force which pulled them together with the strength of a magnet, it had come to an end. He was back to being alone again which was how he liked it and how he needed it to be. He and Ignacio against the world and his heart safely intact.

He stood up in preparation to call his next patient but as he reached the door his phone rang. He doubled back to answer it. 'Marco Rodriguez.'

'Hi, Marco, it's Pippa Martin, Ignacio's physiotherapist.'

He'd put Ignacio on the bus earlier with Heather and the other children as it was a Geraldton therapy day. 'Yes, Pippa. Is something wrong?'

She laughed. 'Why do parents always go there first? Nothing's wrong and Iggie's doing great. His walking in today's session was the best I've ever seen it and I was wondering if you'd tried something new since I saw him last week?'

Last week had been beyond busy, full of town meet-ings, preparing for the polo match, a normal clinic load and Ignacio's parent-teacher night. *And making love to Lucy.*

He disregarded the last thought. 'It was an unusual week and to tell you the truth I did not have time to do the extra—' A thought exploded in his head, sucking the words from his mouth.

'Marco?' Pippa sounded concerned. 'Is it an okay time to talk?'

Her voice was just a faint echo because his mind had been whipped back to the polo, seeing Ignacio sit-ting on the horse, feeling fear making his heart leap in his chest and hearing Lucy say, 'The movement of the horse mimics the feel of walking and improves balance and gait.' He swallowed and tried to relax his throat. 'Ignacio rode a horse on Saturday.'

'Awesome. Keep it up.' Pippa's enthusiasm poured down the phone. 'You know I've been trying to start hippotherapy but we need horses and funding. I saw you on the news playing polo so you've obviously got horse contacts and I'd love it if you'd join a committee to help get this project off the ground.'

His head spun. 'I may not be in Australia much lon-ger.'

She laughed. 'Marco, you've been all over the media for five days talking up the need for rural GPs and how Ignacio is a valued member of the community. The Bulla Creek district has deluged the immigration department with emails and petitions, and this morn-ing on the radio I heard the health minister saying the ruling against you was "a disgrace" and that Australia needs doctors of your calibre.'

He'd heard it too and hope had risen but reality had

immediately levelled it. 'She is not the immigration minister and he is the one that makes the final decision.'

'True, but she's one heck of a strong-minded woman and I can just picture her stomping across the pale green carpet at Parliament House and storming into the minister's office to give him a piece of her mind.'

Lucy's earnest face rose in his mind. *If Iggie was my son, I'd be signing him up for a weekly session and watching him blossom.*

'I'll let you go, Marco, but if you can get Ignacio on a horse for half an hour each week, that's really going to help him. The moment your visa's approved, I'm co-opting you onto the "Freedom Riders" committee.'

The phone went dead and he sat down abruptly, his legs suddenly unsteady. *Dios.* Lucy had been right all along. He'd been so furious at her for what he saw as her undermining his rights as Ignacio's father and scared for his son that he hadn't wanted to hear her, but he'd been doing the exact thing she'd accused him of. He was letting fear get in the way of what was best for his son. He ploughed both hands through his hair. How long had he been doing that? From the beginning? *No.* That couldn't be.

I provide him with therapy so he can improve, so how is that over-protecting him?

His self-righteous words to Lucy boomed in his head with horrifying clarity and he knew he could no longer ignore them. For too long he'd used those words to justify the fact he always chose the safest path for Ignacio. He challenged him academically but he always shied away from extra physical activities beyond his therapy.

I'd never put him in any danger. I love him.

His chest tightened. Lucy had been the brave one. She'd taken the fight for Ignacio to the next level, recognising he was growing up and needing that sort of stimulation. No wonder Ignacio had been getting cross with him and railing against his cosseting. Lucy hadn't let fear get in the way and as a result she'd opened up Ignacio's world. He'd thrived under that sort of love.

You thrived too.

He dropped his head into his hands as the truth was laid out bare. He hadn't wanted to admit it to himself but he could no longer deny it. He'd hidden behind his anger since she'd left, but he knew it was because accepting that he missed her would rupture the bubble he'd locked his heart in since Bianca's betrayal. That had scared the hell out of him.

But thrived he had and he thought of how well they'd worked together, exchanging ideas, learning from each other and growing as doctors. He couldn't deny the caring way she'd rallied the town behind him to help him fight the visa decision, but with her sense of social justice, he knew she would have done that for anyone in his position. What he treasured most were the picnics, the shared meals, the conversations in his bed when she'd rested her head on his chest and her hair tickled his nose—the everyday things—that had given him moments of peace unlike he'd ever known.

That's love.

Every part of him stalled in shock. *Love is too risky. Lucy is everything that Bianca is not.*

He knew that as well as he knew that the sky was blue and the earth was round. His breath rushed out and the years of being alone rolled away.

He loved Lucy.

You told her you didn't want her in your life.

He'd admit to stupidity, apologise and hold her

tight. He wanted her in his life, wanted her to be part of Ignacio's life and he wanted it all to start now.

He just had to find her.

Lucy stared at the twelve boxes that were sealed up with brown packing tape and represented the end of an era of her living in Perth, and sharing a house with the woman who'd been her friend. 'Jess, the removal van will be here in an hour and...' she wound a key off her key ring '...this is yours.'

Jess twisted her hands. 'I hate what I did to our friendship, Luce.'

'Yeah, I know.' Lucy rubbed her dust-covered forehead, feeling grimy and tired after a day of packing. 'Dan and I had hit the wall, but it still hurt. It hurt a lot.'

'Do you think you can ever forgive me?' Jess asked in a small voice.

'I think just recently I've learned that forgiveness isn't so much about wiping the slate clean and going back to the way things were, but about moving forward and forging a new way of doing things.'

Relief flooded Jess's face. 'So you're going to be okay about Dan and me?'

'Yes, I am. That said, I'm not quite ready to have dinner with the two of you, but you never know. Maybe after I get back from India.'

'Thanks.' Jess moved in and hugged her. 'I can't believe you've pulled all your registrar applications and you're just taking off. I just hope you find what you're looking for.'

Lucy didn't want to try and explain that it wasn't about finding any more but about learning, so she just hugged her back.

The doorbell rang and Lucy checked her watch. 'Wow, removalists who are actually early.'

Jess gave her a quick kiss goodbye, slung her bag onto her shoulder and said, 'I'll leave you to it.'

Lucy started marking the boxes with a black felt pen and she heard the murmur of voices and Jess saying, 'Go straight down the hall.'

As the tread of footsteps got louder, she straightened up saying, 'You can start with—' The pen slipped from her fingers, rolling across the floor to stop at Marco's dusty boots.

'*Hola, Lucy.*'

He stood in front of her wearing dark blue slim-fit jeans that emphasised his long legs, and a pale blue casual shirt with the sleeves rolled up, exposing tanned skin and the veins and tendons of his powerful forearms. Her heart flipped in her chest before she could wrap it up safely in protective foil. 'You're a long way from Bulla Creek.'

Tension held his cheeks hostage but his eyes sought hers. 'I came to see you.'

She swallowed against the traitorous pull of her body which craved to feel the security of his length lining hers and she resisted the urge to step into his arms. She knew that until she was able to stand alone and feel whole she couldn't seek him out. It wouldn't be fair to him and Ignacio. Besides, he didn't want her. The memory of his unyielding stance the last time she'd seen him, combined with his transparent words, were impossible to misinterpret.

Crossing her arms to steady herself, she tilted her chin. 'Why? Need some more help with the visa problem, do we?'

He flinched as if her words had inflicted a wound of their own. 'I came here to apologise. I was wrong.'

Stay strong. 'You were wrong about a lot of things. Which one in particular?'

'About Ignacio. You were right. I have been sheltering him too much from his life.'

She sat down abruptly on a box before her legs gave way and deposited her unceremoniously on the floor at his feet. She hadn't expected that confession and confusion got tangled up with all her other feelings. Crossing her legs, she bounced a gladiator-sandal-clad foot up and down to help her think.

His hungry gaze followed the movement and she quickly uncrossed her legs, pressing both feet firmly against the floor. Desire had no place between them. Not any more. 'Well, it's good that you've finally worked it out but you didn't need to come seven hundred kilometres to tell me.'

'*Sí*, I did.'

'And why is that?'

He moved toward her but she pushed out her hands like two red stop signs. It was hard enough to think with him in the room without him being so close that his vibrant scent of pure soap and citrus eddied around her, reminding her of everything she'd lost.

He paused unhappily a few feet away from her. 'Because you're the one person who pushed me and opened my eyes to what I was doing. I have been letting fear get in the way of Ignacio becoming the best person he can be.' His fingers ran though his hair as if he was pulling the words out one by one. 'His mother didn't love him and I didn't want him to feel he isn't enough for me as he is.'

Her heart twisted for Ignacio and herself. Both of

them had birth mothers who couldn't love them, but at least Marco had worked out how damaging over-protection was while Ignacio was young enough to forget the pain it caused. She wished her adopted mother had. 'He's a lucky boy.'

His gaze searched her face. 'He is because of you.'

Waves of pain radiated through her and she rose to her feet not wanting to think about his beautiful little boy because it hurt too much. 'I'm glad I could help and now you've got that off your chest, you need to go. I have to finish writing on these boxes.' She bent down to pick up the felt pen and as she rose, his long, lean fingers closed gently around her wrist.

'I *love* you, Lucy.'

Her grey eyes filled with shock, quickly followed by something Marco couldn't exactly name. It sent a chill scudding through him.

Glancing down at his hand on her arm, she then looked back at him. 'What happened to "I don't want to be loved"?'

Honesty was all he had to offer. 'I was wrong about that too.'

She stared at him coolly as if his words hadn't penetrated at all. 'So what are you actually saying?'

On the flight down to Perth, he'd run a variety of scenarios through his head and all of them had pictured Lucy being initially upset with him, but falling into his arms the moment he told her he loved her. Right now she looked as far away from doing that as Bulla Creek was from Perth. A tremor of panic started to build.

Catching her hands with his, he said, 'Come back to Bulla Creek with me.'

She stared at him wordlessly, her face contorted with

suffering and then she spun out of his reach and disappeared into another room.

His heart paused—suspended in mid-beat for a long, pain-filled moment—and then it thundered hard and fast, sending desperation scudding through him. He strode in the same direction and found her leaning against the kitchen sink, gulping down a glass of water.

'Lucy, I do not understand. Less than a week ago you told me you loved me.'

She slowly raised her head and the agony in her eyes pierced him. 'I do love you. And Ignacio. I love you both more than I can say.'

'Gracias a Dios.' Relief poured through him and he closed the gap between them, sweeping her into his arms.

She leaned in against him, resting her head under his shoulder the way she always did but then she dragged in a shuddering breath. 'I can't come back to Bulla Creek with you, Marco. Like you said, it's all happened too early and too fast.'

'So we will go slowly and take our time.' He gently gripped her upper arms and moved her slightly away from him so he could see her face. He needed her to see his, to read his regret and now his hope.

'I was a fool and I was wrong. Your love for me and Ignacio was like the force of a tornado, swooping in and knocking us off our feet, and at first I was terrified of letting myself love you back. But life with you is so much better than without you. You have woken my heart from hibernation.'

She stared at his shoulder. 'Bianca hurt you and Iggie very much and I don't want you rushing into a relationship worried that I'll leave like she did.'

'That isn't going to happen. You're nothing like

Bianca. You wear your heart on your sleeve and are one of the most giving persons I've ever met.' He believed that with every fibre of his being and he pulled her back close, stroking her hair. 'I've been letting the past be my present, but sharing the last few weeks with you and Ignacio have been the happiest times in my life and my heart is yours. I want to share my life with you.'

She bit her lip and he held his breath, thinking, hoping, that by reminding her of what they'd experienced together she'd change her mind.

She stepped back from him and drank more water. Slowly, she put the glass down on the bench as if she was carefully formulating her reply. 'I've had almost a week to think and something you said to me, about me looking for a family—'

'I promise you that Ignacio and I are your family. You are his mother.' Words tumbled urgently from his mouth to both stop her from speaking and to force her to change her mind. 'William is your family and my parents, when they arrive, they too are your family. Bulla Creek is your family. Everyone who loves and cares for you is there.'

She shook her head. 'I've spent the last six months wondering who I am and as much as I love you I've realised that if I don't work through this, it will eventually destroy us. *I* will destroy us. It's why I'm going to India.'

India. His blood plummeted to his feet as he remembered the boxes in the other room. 'For how long?'

Tears shone in her eyes. 'For as long as it takes.'

No. 'We will come with you.'

Her face filled with a tortured understanding. 'Like you've always said, this is something I have to do on my own and even if it wasn't, with all this visa stuff, you can't leave Australia at the moment. Besides, Ignacio doesn't belong in the foothills of the Himalayas and I wouldn't do that to him. I love him too much.'

'Then stay. Don't do this to us. To me.' He heard the anguish in his voice coming straight from his heart. 'I need you.'

'Do you think—?' Her voice broke and she reached out, touching his arm. 'Do you think I'd be leaving you and Ignacio if I had a choice?'

Desperation drove him on. 'Of course you have a choice. You say, "Marco, I am not going to India, I am coming home to Bulla Creek with you where I belong".'

She tugged at her hair as tears fell. 'I was taking my love for you with me to India to learn how to deal with it. You weren't supposed to turn up here telling me you loved me and making everything harder. This wasn't part of the plan.'

He saw a chink in her resolution and hope surged. Wiping away her tears, he said, 'There is nothing to deal with. I love you. I'm sorry it took me so long to realise that, but I am here now. We have a life together. *This* is the moment you change your plans.'

Sobbing, she shook her head. 'I want to but I can't. You told me that if I didn't forgive William it would haunt me. You also said I should take some time to answer all the questions that are plaguing me so I can live my life without regrets. I can't do it here. I have to go away and India offers me the place to still my churning mind so I can start the search of who I am. I'm sorry but I *have* to do this.'

The memory of his well-meant words taunted him, and he couldn't believe he'd been the architect of her plan that was now taking her away from him. The resolve in her voice left him without a single doubt that she was going to India and dread made him beg.

Hugging her tightly as if he thought she might vanish immediately, he said, 'I don't want you to go. Please stay.'

'It's not that simple, Marco.' She hiccoughed, wiping her face against his shirt. 'I keep asking myself am I the person I'm supposed to be? How can I be part of your life, part of Ignacio's if I don't know that?'

Tears built behind his eyes as he struggled to fight something that towered over him like a fire-breathing dragon protecting the treasure he desperately wanted and he had no sword strong enough to slay it. 'Stay here and try new things. If you don't want to work as a doctor any more so be it. Take a course, sell houses, I don't mind. Just know that whatever you do, you are the woman I love. It is enough.'

She cupped his cheek gently and her grey eyes swam with pleading. 'If I don't go, it will fester and damage us and I won't allow that. Please understand that I'm doing this not just for me but for us. For Ignacio. I never want to put the two of you through the pain of us failing because I was emotionally distant wondering who I am. I have to do this or we'll regret it for the rest of our lives.'

He gripped her hand as if the pressure would change her mind. 'You going to India is abandoning us.'

'No, it's saving us. Short term pain for long term gain. *Please* understand.'

The irony that he'd been the one to push her to deal with her adoption lay at his feet and defeat licked at his heels. He finally knew that if he wanted her in his life forever, he had to let her go to India, but he hated the idea. 'I will phone you every day.'

She shook her head. 'I'm on retreat, Marco. I'm out of contact with everything familiar. It's the only way.'

His already pulverised heart whimpered. He sud-

denly pictured her far away from home, lonely and iso-
lated, and falling in love with someone else. He couldn't
bear the thought so instead of asking the question that
burned him, he made it into a statement. 'You *will* come
back.'

She rose on her toes and kissed him—a kiss filled
with love and longing but devoid of a solid answer.

What was left of his heart splintered into a thousand
pieces as she walked away.

Sweat poured off Marco as he lowered another fence
post into position. He'd been out at Haven, repairing the yard in front of the old stables in preparation
for the arrival of Ignacio's pony. Since Lucy had left
he'd found that life went on and yet in so many ways
it seemed to stop. For months he'd always thought the
day he was granted permanent residency would be the
day he started the next phase of his life. He would buy
a dog, he would buy a property and polo horses. He now
had official confirmation, but without Lucy everything
seemed a pale imitation of itself and he'd done none of
those things. He was living in limbo.

'Tea break.' William handed him a steaming mug.

He wiped his forehead with a bandana and accepted
the tea. 'Beer would be better.'

'It's chilling for when we've earned it.' William
raised his mug to him and surveyed their work. 'Another
ten posts and we're done. Lucy won't believe it when
she sees how well we've spruced it all up.'

Marco sighed. William always spoke of Lucy as if
she was about to arrive any moment, but as each day
passed, Marco found it harder to believe and he wanted
more and more to jump on a plane, find her and bring

her home. 'Why are you so convinced she is coming back?'

'I have to believe it. And so do you.' William clapped a hand on his shoulder. 'I'm sorry you're both suffering because of my mistake, but hold onto the fact she loves you. Loving someone is the easiest and hardest thing you'll ever do.'

'That I know.' He thought of his love for Ignacio which alternated between utter pride and heartache for his struggles. He remembered the exhilarating high of the moment he'd realised he loved Lucy and of the heartbreaking despair when she'd said she loved him but she had had to leave him. He was lonely with each long day that stretched out without her and the number of days she'd been absent were carved into his heart.

'Your love will bring her home.'

He put down his now empty mug. 'I am not so sure. She left because of me.'

'Exactly.'

'Qué?' He had no idea what William meant.

'I've never thanked you for writing to Lucy asking her to come to Bulla Creek. Duty brought her home but we both know we want her here with us because she wants to be here more than any other place. She needed to leave us for a while and as hard as it is, you did the right thing letting her go.'

William's hazel eyes urged him to keep the faith. 'She'll come back to Bulla Creek because of you as well.'

He thumped a fist into his palm. 'The moment she is back I am marrying her and *never* letting her leave again.'

The words tumbled out of him and with a brain-shuddering jolt he realised the idea of marriage no longer scared him. In fact, he'd never wanted anything more in his life than to be Lucy's husband.

William grinned at him. 'I'm glad you plan to marry her, but if she comes home she won't need a legal document to stay.' He cleared his throat. '*When* she comes home it will be for good.'

Marco had to believe that William was right.

CHAPTER TWELVE

LUCY purposely slipped on the plain, flat leather sandals she'd worn every day for three months and set out on the walk to the nearby tiny village. She hoped to buy some more paper—this time with lines on it because as it turned out, William had been correct. She couldn't draw to save herself, but she'd found she had a knack for words, something that she'd never really explored because she'd taken the science stream in high school.

During her first month in India, she hadn't ventured far from her self-imposed isolation. From the veranda outside her small room she was surrounded by towering, craggy mountains which made her feel almost insignificant and the rushing sound of racing water from the river relaxed her. Slowly, she'd managed to still her churning mind of the constant recriminations and regrets, the biggest one leaving Marco. It had taken a very long time for the question *Was coming here too much to ask of him?* to be silenced.

By the second month she'd found the calmness to try new things without any preconceived ideas or learned behaviours. She was an empty slate and she soaked up all her experiences. Now she had a sense of being herself rather than having been moulded into someone else. She hadn't worked as a doctor, or even thought of herself as one in weeks, which had freed her up and that had been when she'd realised she could write. Words had poured out of her and she'd written poetry, descriptive prose, short stories and letters. Lots of letters, although they remained tucked up in her satchel not posted and that was where they would remain. For the first time since she'd discovered she was adopted, she felt almost at peace with herself. The 'almost' was her stumbling block. She hadn't been able to make the final leap she'd expected to by now—the leap she'd watched others make.

She arrived at the village and stopped at the rough-hewn stall that made the best chai tea. She knew it was fresh because she could hear the ping of the milk being squeezed directly from the goat into the tin. She gave her order and sat down to wait.

The life of the village went on around her as she imagined it had for hundreds of years with cows wandering along the dusty street. A pedal-powered sewing machine whirred and brightly coloured material flashed in the sunlight. Lucy recognised 'wedding red' and smiled. Weddings were a multi-day affair where the actual marriage was just one part of the many ceremonies including the *mehndi* where the women decorated the bride and then each other with delicate henna designs.

Children dressed in very little were squatting down playing by the side of the road, looking for treasures that might have fallen off passing trucks. They called out to her and she waved back. A little boy crutched past toward the group, one of his legs withered and deformed, and unable to provide any support to him. Instantly, she thought of Ignacio. She'd worked hard on keeping all thoughts of home out of her mind but once she'd thought of him, he seemed to move right on in, snuggling down as if to say, *I've been waiting for you*.

She found herself comparing Iggie with the Indian child. Even though his prematurity had caused his CP and his mother hadn't wanted him, he'd been lucky to be born to a father who could support him and love him.

Just like you.

Just like me.

She knew that now. Ruth and William loved her and even though Allison couldn't, their love was enough.

You didn't have to come to India to learn that. Marco told it to you weeks ago.

Her heart lurched as she thought about him. He'd been right but at the time she'd been unable to trust herself enough to know.

Her tea arrived as a truck rumbled past, throwing up dust to add to the millions of layers that preceded it. She automatically shielded the glass with her hand, wanting to enjoy the flavours of the chai spices not the dust. As she raised the drink to her lips, a child's pain-filled scream rent the air.

Terror froze her blood and the glass clattered against the table as she shot to her feet. After a rotation in paediatric emergency, she knew that harrowing sound too well, and nothing good ever came from it. She ran, following the gut-wrenching sound of women wailing and men yelling, and the first thing she saw was a broken crutch on the side of the road.

She lifted her gaze and just ahead of her she saw the little boy. He lay on the dirt and gravel of the road, his deformed leg in its normal alignment, but she could clearly see a white bone on his good leg protruding through the skin. The doctor inside her rushed back as she ran forward. Using her limited local language and hand actions, she explained who she was and started examining the child. She ruled out internal injuries and breathed more easily.

Compound fracture of the femur. Possible complications hypovolemic shock, fat embolism, osteomyleitis, bone shortening, avascular necrosis…

The diagnostic reel in her head ran on and her breath turned solid. In Australia this would be a serious injury but in rural India it was life-threatening. She ripped up the sarong she always carried in her bag and as she started bandaging, she sent up a prayer she could save this little boy and save his leg.

Twenty-four hours later Lucy was in a Delhi hospital having moved heaven and earth to get transport from the northern medical centre to bring him south, and then she'd done it all again to get him into surgery. That had been yesterday and now Arun lay between white sheets looking vulnerable and scared, but alive with a good chance of diminished complications. Today, she'd spoken to the surgeon and arranged for payment along with making sure Arun's mother had money so she could stay with him. Worried about the woman being alone in such a big city and so far from home, she'd contacted an Australian NGO and begged for follow-up for the family.

'We'll take it from here, Dr Patterson.' Jerry Tansy, from Aussies in India, smiled at her. 'You've done an amazing job.'

'Thank you, but it was just what anyone would have done.'

He didn't look so convinced. 'We could really do with someone like you on our team so if you're looking for a job in India…?'

She didn't have to think about the question. She'd spent hours fighting for her patient's life and for his ongoing care, and at four a.m., when Arun had finally gone into surgery, she'd known without a shadow of a doubt that she was a doctor. Not because she'd been raised by William but because it was her passion and her vocation.

She was Lucy Patterson, doctor, and medicine ran in her veins.

Ran in her veins back in Bulla Creek where she belonged with the man and child she loved. India had given her space to work things out, but only Marco could fill the one gap in her quest for peace. Marco, Iggie and her loving father who'd given her so much—all of them had been with her in spirit the entire time she'd been in India, giving her love and support. Last night when she'd been saving Arun, it had been Marco's voice she'd heard guiding her and answering any clinical doubts.

It was time to go home.

What if he hasn't waited?

Time to find that out too.

She gave Jerry a weary smile. 'Thanks for the offer, but I've got a job and people I love and need back home.'

He pulled a business card out of his wallet. 'If you change your mind or if there's anything I can do to help just yell.'

'Do you have a phone I can use right now?'

'Sure.'

She accepted the mobile and moved into a quiet alcove. With trembling fingers, she punched in the number she knew off by heart. As she waited for the connection, she could smell the clean scent of eucalyptus, taste the strong flavours of kangaroo and feel the wondrous feel of Marco's arms around her as he buried his face in her hair.

The sound of the rings hummed in her ears for nine long rings. *Please answer.*

The ringing stopped.

'Marco Rodriguez.'

His deep, accented voice came down the line and her heart stuttered, and her throat tightened as reality hit her that her future hung on this call.

Gripping the phone, she lifted her chin and said, 'Marco, it's me.'

Lucy ran down the steps of the Fokker F50 and straight into Marco's outstretched arms. Wrapping her arms around his neck, she kissed him long and deep, as if he were the sole provider of desperately needed oxygen.

He broke the kiss and held her so tightly she could barely breathe and then he ran his hands over her hair and caressed her face with his fingers. 'I can't believe you're here.'

She half laughed and half cried. 'Believe it. I'm here and I'm never leaving again. At least not without you.'

He gazed at her, his eyes twinkling along with a myriad emotions. 'So it was worth it. You have learned something while you've been away.'

Her fingers curled into the placket of his shirt. 'I learned that you were right all along. Everything I need, want and love is right here in Bulla Creek. You...' She turned her head toward the low cyclone fence. 'Where are Ignacio and Dad?'

'Back at Haven. William suggested I meet you alone.'

A slow realisation washed over her. William had given them precious time together before they shared themselves with him and Ignacio. She smiled. 'I've also learned that my father is a very wise man.'

Marco smiled knowingly. 'He is. I don't think I would have got through these three months without him, but he kept telling me to keep the faith and that you would come home to me and he was right.'

She bit her lip. 'Did you ever think loving me was too hard?'

'All the time and never.' He pressed a kiss to her forehead. 'Loving you is the joy of my life. You and Ignacio.'

'Oh, Marco.' Tears she'd long held back poured down her cheeks. 'I'm sorry I put us through all this but—'

'Shh.' He pressed a finger against her lips. 'There is no need to be sorry, I understand. Waiting was hard but it was important for you to go, and it has made us strong.' He stroked the tears away with the pad of his thumb. 'Lucy?'

She hiccoughed. 'Yes?'

Dark eyes stared down at her filled with love. 'Marry me.'

Joy surged and she threw her arms around his neck. 'Oh, Marco, you have no idea how I've longed to hear those words.'

He grinned. 'Is that a "yes"?'

'*Sí*, my darling Argentine, that is an emphatic and categorical "yes". I will marry you and proudly be your wife and Iggie's mother.'

This time Marco's eyes seemed moist. 'You will be a wonderful mother to Ignacio because only you can truly understand the questions he will eventually ask about his mother.'

The thought of being a mum glowed deep down

SAVE UP TO 25%

Subscribe to Medical today and get 5 stories a month delivered to your door for 3, 6 or 12 months and gain up to 25% OFF! That's a fantastic saving of over £40!

MONTHS	FULL PRICE	YOUR PRICE	SAVINGS
3	£43.41	£36.90	15%
6	£86.82	£69.48	20%
12	£173.64	£130.20	25%

As a welcome gift we will also send you a FREE L'Occitane gift set worth £10

PLUS, by becoming a member you will also receive these additional benefits:

- FREE Home Delivery
- Receive new titles TWO MONTHS AHEAD of the shops
- Exclusive Special Offers & Monthly Newsletter
- Special Rewards Programme

No Obligation - You can cancel your subscription at any time by writing to us at Mills & Boon Book Club, PO Box 676, Richmond. TW9 1WU.

To subscribe, visit
millsandboon.co.uk/subscriptions

MILLS & BOON

M261

inside her. 'We'll be honest with him and help him through it together.'

He nodded his agreement. 'As his parents and as partners we will face whatever life throws at us. All that matters now is that you are home.'

She slid her arm around his waist as they walked to the car. 'So where is home?'

'William has offered to sell us Haven.'

Shocked surprise stilled her feet. 'Where would Dad go?'

Marco stroked her hair. 'He's talking about semi-retirement. Haven comes with twenty-five acres so if you are happy with the idea, he will build a house on the east side of the property and my parents will build on the west.'

'A family compound?' The idea circled around her, taking hold and reinforcing her feelings of true belonging. 'I like the idea.'

'So do I. We will fill it with children.'

'Fill?' She laughed. 'How about two or three brothers and sisters for Ignacio?'

'That sounds perfect.'

Holding her hand, he drove the short distance to his house and as he opened her door on the four-wheel-drive, she held out her arms. He stepped in and she gloried in the love and desire that burned so hot and strong in his eyes. With a wicked grin, she slowly slid down his body until her feet hit the ground. His heat and love seeped into her, bringing her body alive in a way it hadn't been in months, and it merged with his need and love until she thought she'd melt on the spot.

Groaning, he buried his face in her hair and then he cupped her buttocks and lifted her. She matched his groan with one of her own and wrapped her legs around his waist. 'God, I've missed you. Please take me home.'

'It will be my pleasure.' And he carried her inside to his bed.

A while later they lay under the soft touch of cotton sheets, nose to nose with their arms around each other.

Lucy gently pushed at Marco's shoulder until he was on his back and then she straddled him, staring down into his eyes. 'You know you've got me for forever, right?'

'I do.' He pulled her down against him, kissing her long and hard, and infusing her with his love and everlasting commitment.

EPILOGUE

'MUM, I like it when you're *this* pregnant.'

Startled, Lucy pushed herself up slowly from the vegetable crisper and closed the fridge door, not even trying to second-guess what made her very bright ten-year-old son say that.

At eight and a half months pregnant, Lucy was thinking that as much as she enjoyed being pregnant, she was ready to hold this baby in her arms. 'That makes one of us, Iggie. Why?'

He grinned. 'Because for a little while. I'm not the slowest walker in the family. Even when you go fast. You waddle.'

Laughing, she threw a carrot at him and he caught it with an even bigger grin. Her heart swelled at how much his hand-eye co-ordination and balance had improved over the years and at how hard he worked at it.

'Take that and some apples, and go feed Hoola and Hooper before I waddle after you and make you dry the dishes. Take your sister with you, please.'

'Okay. Come on, Ruthie, let's go feed the horseys.' He held out his hand to his four-year-old sister who happily took it and skipped along next to his loping gait.

Two minutes after they'd left, the wire door banged open and William walked in first, holding flowers and wine, immediately followed by Ana and Carlos, Marco's parents. They immediately started fussing.

'Lucy, why are you on your feet?' William asked, looking concerned. 'You worked this morning so you're supposed to be taking it easy. Any twinges?'

'We stay and we cook the dinner. It is ready at seven,' Ana added, strapping on an apron.

Carlos tapped the cooler he'd carried in. 'Steak. Is good for the *bebé*.'

Lucy held up her hands in mock surrender. 'I was making a salad, but I can easily stop and go and sit on the veranda, and catch the breeze.'

'You do that,' her father instructed. 'Leave the kids and the dinner to us. All you have to do is be at the table in an hour.'

'Iggie and Ruth are feeding the horses and then the dogs. Dad, can you check on them?'

'Sure. I know the drill and I'll bath Ruthie. Now go.'

She let herself be shooed outside and just as she was about to sit down she heard the crunch of gravel under car tyres. She met Marco at the bottom of the steps. With some flecks of silver nestling in his jet-black hair, she thought he was even more handsome than when she'd met him five years ago.

The most rewarding and wonderful five years of her life. Not that there hadn't been challenges, but Marco's prediction had been correct. They both knew the pain of being apart which made them work even harder at being together and making their family a happy one.

He slipped his arms around her waist and bent in to kiss her before dropping a kiss on her swollen belly.

She kissed him back. 'It's Friday night and everyone's here. The grandparents are busy being helpful.'

A hopeful expression lit across his face. 'That means steak for dinner?'

'It does. It also means you get a glass of wine because William's on call and no dishes for either of us. We're being very spoiled.'

She felt spoiled all of the time. Marco adored her, William took his role as a grandfather very seriously and Marco's parents, who spent half the year in Australia and other half in Argentina, had reorganised their schedule to be here for the birth of their third grandchild. For someone who'd once thought she had no family, she now had it in spades.

She ran her fingers along Marco's chest, loving the feel of him under her fingers, a feeling that had only grown over time. 'Iggie says I waddle.'

He smiled down at her. '*Sí*, you do.'

She gave him a gentle punch. 'That's not helping. I'm feeling fat and frumpy and I'm sick of patients saying, "I thought you'd have had the baby by now".'

'Come.' He held out his hand and walked her to veranda swing and they sat down. 'You are beautiful.'

She dropped her head on his shoulder, snuggling in. 'Go on.'

His hand caressed her shoulder. 'You glow with an aura of fecundity that is very sexy.'

She wriggled her nose. 'Really?'

'Yes.' He gave her a long, open-mouthed kiss and her body immediately went slack.

'Hmm, you'll have to kiss me like that again after dinner.'

His eyes darkened with a wicked glint. 'Didn't you say the grandparents were on duty?'

'I did. But you're a boring, old married man so you can't possibly be suggesting—'

'You cannot call the Bulla Creek Polo champion old.' He pulled her to her feet and started walking softly around the veranda toward the front of the house and their room.

She grinned. 'I can if you say I waddle.'

He opened the French doors and tugged her into their bedroom, closing the curtains behind him. Pressing his lips to her neck, he started a delicious trail of kisses. 'You glide like a swan.'

She let her head fall back. 'Now you're talking.'

Only he'd stopped talking and she didn't mind one little bit.

* * * * *

DR TALL, DARK…
AND DANGEROUS?

BY
LYNNE MARSHALL

MILLS
BOON

First published in Great Britain 2012
by Mills & Boon, an imprint of Harlequin (UK) Limited.
Harlequin (UK) Limited, Eton House, 18-24 Paradise Road,
Richmond, Surrey TW9 1SR

© Janet Maarschalk 2012

ISBN: 978 0 263 89790 6

Harlequin (UK) policy is to use papers that are natural, renewable and recyclable products and made from wood grown in sustainable forests. The logging and manufacturing process conform to the legal environmental regulations of the country of origin.

Printed and bound in Spain
by Blackprint CPI, Barcelona

Dear Reader

It's wonderful to have another Medical Romance out, and DR TALL, DARK…AND DANGEROUS? is very special to me. I got the story idea while visiting my daughter in Boston, so I decided to use the lovely New England town as my setting.

I've often heard that our attitudes are the single most important influence in our lives, so I set out to prove it by giving Kasey one huge hardship with which to grapple. At first she feels defeated when she learns devastating news, but lying down and giving up isn't her style. Instead, she decides to take another path—a more active approach, if you will—one that involves a certain aloof plastic surgeon.

Kasey is a savvy Nurse Practitioner who runs the small Everett Community Clinic. She is well aware of the phenomenon of cause and effect, or in her case actions and consequences, yet under her new circumstances she casts her cares to the wind and makes a play for that plastic surgeon anyway. Little does she know that she is precisely what Jared needs at the perfect time in his life.

I've heard other sayings throughout my life—that good often comes from bad circumstances, or difficulties can enlighten us and make us stronger individuals—and, well, I'll let you read the book and decide if you agree with me about that or not…

I hope you enjoy Kasey and Jared's book—a story about two people who really deserve each other!

All the best

Lynne

Visit Lynne Marshall's website here: www.lynnemarshall.com and watch out for her weekly blog.

Or friend her on Facebook! She loves to hear from readers from all over the world.

DEDICATION

Heartfelt thanks to Sally, for keeping in touch and
encouraging me, and to Sheila for welcoming me back.

Also, special thanks to my daughter Emily,
for being my first reader on this book,
and for her input regarding Boston.

CHAPTER ONE

KASEY waved toward Vincent Clark in the clinic hall-way. A baby cried in the background. "Room three," she said. "Mrs. Gardner needs the second shot in her hepatitis B series."

Nine in the morning and already the small clinic's waiting room was full. A newborn needed his six-week examination; a toddler's allergies were flaring up with spring and the coming grass season; a teenage mother needed counseling on diet; a senior citizen's diabetes wasn't under control. On and on went the list, making Kasey wish she had forty-eight hours in her day.

Although today she welcomed the non-stop regimen and distractions.

"I'll get right on it," Vincent said, grabbing his lap-top, flashing his killer smile.

She forced a phony grin, since smiling was the last thing she felt like doing. He deserved no less, and she didn't believe in dumping her foul mood on others. Charming, bright and sensitive, not to mention well groomed and fit, Vincent was everything Kasey looked for in a man, or used to, anyway. The catch was *she* wasn't her RN and assistant clinic administrator's type, because he was gay.

Besides, she'd given up on finding Mr. Right. Her

last big love had told her he loved her one weekend and the next said that whatever he'd said last week he didn't feel any more. What was a girl supposed to do with that? In reality, men had never stuck around for her or her mother. Since good old Arnie had broken her heart two years ago, her motto had been to keep it superficial all the way—no investment; no pain. It wasn't everything she'd hoped for in life, but it would have to do.

Vincent patted her shoulder as he passed. They adored each other in a strictly platonic way, the perfect working situation, and he was a good friend, one she could depend on. Since she'd put so much time and energy into her job over the last few years, she could count her friends on two fingers, sad but factual. As an RN, she believed in facts.

Besides, she wasn't in the market for a partner, and had given up looking, especially now, since she'd gotten the horrible news about her birth father. What would be the point of getting involved with anyone for the long haul?

She dashed to her desk to look for the notes on the toddler she'd seen last week, and found six more patient messages.

What would Vincent think if he knew her prognosis? Maybe, if things ever slowed down today, she'd tell him. No. Not here. Not quickly over a cup of coffee in the lunch room. She'd need an entire night over drinks and dinner to work up the nerve to say what frightened her more than anything on earth. But she needed to tell somebody, and soon, or she'd explode, and she needed to build her support system. She definitely needed more than two friends, especially as one lived out of state.

She let out a quiet breath and picked up a note from her receptionist and read, "*Facial laceration*", then grabbed her laptop and strode toward room one. As long as she was married to the community clinic, there'd be no chance of making new friends.

Laurette Meranvil was a name she hadn't seen before. After knocking, she opened the door and found a petite, brightly dressed woman sitting on the examination table, holding a cloth to her cheek. Kasey put her computer on the stand then reached for and shook the lady's free hand.

"I'm Kasey McGowan, the nurse practitioner. What seems to be the problem?"

"I cut my cheek on glass," the woman said with what Kasey had come to recognize as a Haitian accent.

Gingerly removing the cloth, Kasey discovered a jagged cut dangerously close to the woman's eye and extending out over her cheek. Fresh blood oozed with the release of pressure. She donned gloves and checked for obvious glass slivers in the wound but didn't find any.

"How did this happen?"

Kasey read the hesitation in the patient's eyes before the woman glanced at the floor. So often the truth went untold at the clinic. "I fell into a glass door."

Kasey ground her molars and hid her disbelief. Not that it couldn't happen, but… It was more important to treat the wound, knowing she might never get to the truth.

Though she was trained to suture, this facial laceration would leave an ugly scar if not expertly handled. Kasey knew her limitations, and the woman deserved the best treatment possible.

"Ms. Meranvil, would you be able to stay at the clinic a bit longer while I have one of the plastic surgeons from the Mass General hospital stitch your wound?" She was aware that keloids could develop at the site of the scar, and because it was on the patient's face Kasey didn't want to take any chances of disfiguring the patient even more, so she wanted to bring in an expert.

Laurette drew her eyebrows together. "I cannot pay for special treatment."

"This is the community clinic, remember? There won't be an extra charge."

After a moment's thought, Laurette gave a serious-faced nod.

"Great. We'll take you to the treatment room and get the RN to clean your wound while we wait." Kasey carefully pressed the skin flap closed and put a sterile four-by-four over it to catch the slow flow of blood then discarded her gloves and entered a quick note into the computer. "The nurse will be right with you, but in the meantime keep light pressure on it," she said, signing off and grabbing the laptop on her way out.

Once back at her desk, she found her co-worker sorting another stack of patient messages.

"Vincent, can you clean the wound in room one, give her a tetanus shot, and move her to the procedure room? I've got to make a call to see who's taking plastics call this month." As a nearby training hospital, Tufts regularly sent medical students to volunteer at the clinic, but this wound called for extra special care.

She went straight to her desk and dialed the long-memorized number of the massive teaching hospital. It supported the Everett neighborhood community clinic by supplying residents on call in various specialties as needed. After going through the usual chain of command, Kasey reached the department of surgery and was promised a second-year plastics fellowship doctor would be at the clinic within the hour. Just when she'd gotten used to last month's doctor, a bubbly young woman, May rolled around and she'd have to readjust to yet another face and name and, most importantly, personality. But that was the name of the game when operating a community clinic with a limited budget that got scrutinized with a magnifying glass each month by the trustees. She took what she was given and smiled gratefully. Fortunately, the hospital thrived on the extra experience for their interns, residents and doctor specialists in training.

After hanging up the phone and on her way to see another patient, Kasey peeked in on Laurette, noting Vincent had done a fine job of cleaning and dressing the wound. The patient rested on the gurney, staring at the ceiling, the head of the bed partially elevated.

"Can I get you some water?" Kasey asked.

The woman nodded. "Yes, thank you."

If only Kasey were a mind reader, a skill not taught in the Master's in Nursing program, maybe she could find out how the accident had really happened. Once the young woman took the water and sipped, she closed her eyes, sending the message loud and clear: I'm not talking about it. So Kasey quietly left the procedure room.

As the other examination rooms filled up, Kasey became involved with patient care, physicals and treatments, and an hour and a half later she glanced at her watch and stole a moment to get back to the nursing station.

Just about to call again, a shadow covered her desk.

She glanced up to find deep blue masculine eyes staring at her from beneath brown brows, and the hair on her neck prickled. The strikingly serious eyes studied her as if she'd come from another planet. Dark brown hair swept back from a high forehead and curled just beneath his earlobes suggesting a professional haircut hadn't found a date on his calendar in a couple of months. A day's growth of red-tinged beard covered the man's sharp jaw.

"You have a patient for me?" The quiet baritone voice sent more chills down her arms, throwing her off track and making her a little ticked off as he hadn't bothered to introduce himself yet.

Needing to look away, Kasey glanced over the man's shoulder at Vincent who, in his usual playful way, watched wide-eyed, biting his knuckle over the hunk, and she tried not to roll her eyes. Vincent was a sucker for a handsome face, and with this man Vincent's assessment was right on target. Too bad the doctor's impatient expression ruined the effect.

"Oh, um, yes, I do have a patient for you. That is if you're the resident from Plastic Surgery."

To be honest, she'd expected someone younger, more in keeping with the third—and fourth-year residents who'd normally been sent to the clinic, not a man who looked as if he'd been practicing medicine for a decade and had early signs of gray sprinkled at his temples to prove it.

He gave a slow nod, his haunting eyes as steady as a surgeon's hands, making her feel edgy. She didn't need any help with that edgy feeling today.

"I'm Jared Finch," he said.

Snap out of it, girl. "Hi, I'm Kasey, and over there is my co-worker, Vincent."

Vincent beamed, more gums than teeth showing. "Hi, thanks for coming."

"Just doing my job," he said, nodding hello to Vincent before turning back to Kasey. "Are you in charge?"

Unable to break away from his gaze, she fought the hitch in her breath and mentally kicked herself for falling apart. He was just a man. A doctor. She'd seen plenty of handsome men in her life, just not here in her clinic. And this man, in ten seconds flat, seemed to have absconded with her composure. She wanted to grab a rubber reflex hammer and pound some sense into her head.

"Yes. I'm the nurse practitioner and I run the clinic. Thanks so much for coming, Dr. Finch." He reached for a quick handshake, though his felt barely alive, and she shook once then let go. Even lackluster, the fraction of a moment's connection had left her off balance. *He came for the patient, give him the information.* Right. She looked through the mess on her desk, found the note, and handed it to him. Clutching the laptop that had Laurette Meranvil's information on it tightly to her chest and feeling fortified, she stood. "Let me show you the patient."

Jared followed the skittish NP down the hall toward the patient examination room. He'd been up all night, moonlighting, and the last thing he'd wanted to do was rush over to a satellite clinic for more work. Part of his commitment to the two-year plastic surgery certification program was volunteering at clinics such as this, all over town. During the month of May, as long as he wasn't doing surgery with his mentors, he'd be at the beck and call of the Everett community clinic, and would be required to put in twenty hours' service. It wasn't a "get" to, it was a "got" to, something he'd have to endure.

The nurse practitioner flipped her dark blonde hair over her shoulder and glanced at him just before opening the door. Since beginning his plastic surgery fellowship, he'd gotten into the habit of looking at women and deciding how he could improve their features. He studied the arch of her brows and the almond-shaped green eyes, the larger-than-average nose with a bump on the bridge, and her lips, small, but nicely padded. Her loose lab coat and scrub pants hid her shape, but he guessed she was at least five feet six.

"Let me show you what we've got," she said, with a polite office smile. It was nice to see she hadn't used Botox, as he preferred expressive eyes.

The corner of his mouth twitched as he followed her inside, and that would have to suffice for a friendly smile these days.

"The patient says she fell against a glass door."

He lifted one brow and shared a knowing look with the nurse practitioner as she opened the computer and brought up the patient's chart. He quickly read over her shoulder, just enough to fill him in.

"Mrs. Meranvil, I'm Dr. Finch. Let's have a look at that cut." After he'd washed his hands and donned gloves, he removed the gauze and examined the depth of the wound and potential tissue damage. "Set up a sterile field," he said to the NP, "and I'll inject some anesthetic. Do you have a tendency to develop keloids?"

The quiet woman's pinched forehead clued him to rephrase his question. "Do you get bumpy scars?"

She shook her head, and he wondered if she'd completely understood him. He glanced over her skin for any evidence of old scars to compare, but her long-sleeved, frayed-at-the-cuffs blouse didn't reveal anything.

The nurse practitioner hustled to set up the pre-sterilized pack, and he switched to sterile gloves from the basic tray then gestured to her. "I'll need five-zero polypropylene sutures."

She rustled through the cupboard until she found exactly what he wanted, opened the sterile pack and dropped it onto the sterile field. He nodded his thanks.

"Let's get started," he said, nodding toward the anesthetic. Using sterile technique, she handed him antiseptic cleanser and the tiny-gauge needle and syringe. He swiped the rubber stopper as she held the bottle upside down, and he withdrew a couple of ccs, then discarded the first needle and switched to the next, which the nurse extended to him from within its sterile wrapper.

"You'll feel a little pinch." He injected into the subcutaneous fat around the laceration as gingerly as possible. Once the effect set in, he'd look more closely for glass slivers or debris in the wound, though the nurse had cleaned it well.

Since he was up close, he gave a tight-lipped, woefully out-of-practice smile. The patient barely responded.

"Are you okay?" the nurse named Kasey asked. The patient nodded.

Right, he should employ some light banter. He cleared his throat. "Need anything?" It came out sterner than he'd meant. The patient shook her head as if afraid to talk to him.

That was the limit of his bedside manner these days, a fact he was gravely aware of and which, considering the field he was going into, needed to change. In his own good time. He took the delicate-toothed forceps and a small curved needle holder and began his meticulous suturing.

Suturing was nothing new to him—he'd been a practicing general surgeon for eight years before making the decision to go into plastic surgery. He almost gave a rueful laugh out loud over that thought as he sank another stitch and tied it off. He'd been forced to go into the big money specialty field after his wife had financially cleaned him out in the divorce two years ago. After all, a doctor of his skill and experience should be able to support his children and ex-wife without going broke.

He needed to think a hell of a lot more pleasant thoughts while treating this patient. She deserved his undivided attention and surgical expertise. The one thing he *was* sure of these days was his ability as a surgeon. Make that plastic surgeon.

Kasey was impressed with Dr. Finch's technique if not his bedside manner, and how he took great care with each stitch. If all went well with the healing process, Laurette would wind up with only a fine pale scar beneath her dark chocolate eye.

After the procedure was finished, she helped Laurette sit up. Vowing never to clean houses like her mother, she'd been a nurse since she was twenty-two, and four years later, when she'd become a nurse practitioner, she'd been initiated by fire when this clinic had opened. Nothing fazed her now. She'd worked with plenty of fussy doctors. Dr. Finch wasn't fussy, just particular about how he wanted things done. Showing a serious lack of bedside manner, he obviously had no intention of sticking around to reassure the patient. Task done, he'd already shoved the surgical tray aside, ripped off his gloves and was halfway to the door without a single word. At least he'd disposed of the trash and the used needles into the sharps container on his way, she'd give him that.

"Thanks, Doc," she said, tongue in cheek.

"Not a problem," he said in a gruff tone. Just before closing the door, he turned toward the patient. "Ms.

Meranvil, we'll need to see you back in four to five days to take out those sutures."

"Yes, Doctor," she whispered. "Thank you."

Slam, bam, thank you, ma'am?

"One more thing…" He popped his head back inside the exam room. "Has she had a tetanus booster?"

"Already taken care of," Kasey said, organizing the dressing. Sheesh, you'd think he could at least try to fake some patient concern! "Ms. Meranvil, I think you'll be pretty as ever after these stitches come out," she said as she lightly bandaged the wound.

After giving an encouraging smile to her patient, Kasey glanced over her shoulder. Jared had paused at the door.

"Agreed," he'd said.

Those unreadable steel-blue eyes almost responded to his flat, partial smile. Or maybe it was just a nod with a grimace? Talk about not putting your heart into it. At least he was a top-notch technician.

Yet those eyes…

Feeling pulled into his stare, she forced herself to look away, back to her task at hand, just as the door closed. "There. I think you're good to go." She patted Laurette on the arm, already planning her revenge on Dr. Finch.

Despite his lack of charm, Jared Finch's haunting eyes reappeared in her mind. There were far too many patients to tend to, so why get swept up in a remote and mysterious doctor's gaze?

There was just no point.

Jared sat at the corner desk in the clinic office, typing his electronic chart entry, when Kasey reappeared. Fortunately, she left him alone to go about his business while she shuffled reports and folders at the adjacent desk. There was nothing worse than being interrupted by a chatty person while trying to concentrate. He cast a furtive glance at her from across the room. Dressed in scrubs and a lab coat, there was no telling what kind of shape she had.

"Since you need to see this patient again next week," she said, ruining his hopes of blessed silence, "why don't we send out a flyer to the neighborhood?"

He stopped typing in mid-word. "A what?"

"A flyer. We can do a one-day surgical clinic."

He leveled her a look similar to that he gave his his son when he got out of line. Apparently it didn't register.

"You know, since you have to come back to follow up with Laurette's stitches?"

His dead stare stopped her for a moment. Ah, peace. He went back to the second half of that word in the report.

She cleared her throat. He tried to ignore it.

"You said yourself she has to come back in four to five days to have the stitches removed. What if there's a problem? Do you want to leave that woman scarred?" He hadn't sustained a dead stare this long since the last time his kids had ganged up on him about flying to a theme park in Florida. "Why not set up an open clinic for the local residents on Tuesday as you'll have to be here anyway?"

He slowly lifted his eyes, sending her another warning glance.

"Did you know there's a huge need for the underserved and minimally insured population in this area?" she said, undeterred. "And also, on the brighter side, you could chip away at some of the required hours for your month-long clinic rotation."

He didn't give a damn how good a saleswoman she

was, he just wanted her to shut up so he could finish his report and get back to the hospital. "Tell you what," he said. "I'll give you one whole day to see your clinic walk-in patients. There. You happy now?" May as well take up her suggestion and get this volunteer time out of the way as quickly as possible. Now maybe she'd be quiet.

She tossed him a don't-do-us-any-favors look before she commenced rushed clicking and clacking on the keyboard.

Yeah, he'd said the words, and they had seriously lacked enthusiasm, but he'd already gathered she was a smart cookie and wasn't about to let an opportunity like this slip by. Now maybe he could finish this consult and head out.

"I'll print up a flyer and hire some of the local boys to distribute them to the houses and on cars in the area."

"Great. Whatever. Now, could you let me finish my report?" That got a rise in her brows, and more speedy typing, as he'd hopelessly lost his train of thought about the wording in the report.

His concentration thrown out of the window, he recalled on his drive through the neighborhood that the boulevard was lined with red-brick and mortar storefronts, and had an eclectic assortment of businesses. Many looked rundown. The place probably could use a day-long walk-in surgery clinic, and the sooner he got his volunteer hours done the sooner he could get back to focusing fully on plastic surgery.

"Maybe you should post flyers in the local business windows, too," he said. "Though you may want to skip all the mortuaries—don't want to send the wrong message."

Quick to forgive, she laughed, and it sounded nice, low and husky. Almost made him smile.

"What's up with that anyway?"

"The overabundance of mortuaries?" she said. "I think it must have something to do with having a hospital in the area since the late eighteen hundreds and the odds of folks making it out alive." Unlike him, she could multitask, and never missed a beat typing and staring at the computer screen. "I guess the morticians went where they were guaranteed business. Though it does seem like overkill these days, pardon the pun."

He nodded, stretching his lips into a straight line rather than a smile, and grudgingly admitted he liked her dry wit and Boston accent. *Pah-din*. "Yeah, so I figure if I'm volunteering time for the month, like you said, I may as well make it worth everyone's while." Code for get it over with ASAP. That's what he was all about these days—meet his obligations as quickly as possible and move on. In another year he'd get his life back and begin his own private practice back home in California. Besides, he hated it when he ran out of things to do, preferring to work until he could pass out and sleep. Then work more. Anything to keep his mind occupied.

He scratched his jaw. "So I'll come at nine and work until seven—that way folks can stop by after they get off work," he said.

"Then why not make it eight p.m.? Would that work? With long commutes, some people don't get home from work until after seven."

Sure, squeeze an extra hour out of me, lady. "Fine," he said, staring at the last dangling sentence in his report.

Truth was, unless he moonlighted, he had nothing better to do with his time most nights. He sublet a basement bachelor apartment near Beacon Hill, with rented furniture and noisy pipes, paid through his nose for the privilege to live there, and after a year had yet to meet a single neighbor.

"That way you'd get half of your required volunteer hours out of the way in one day," she said.

He wanted to protest, say that wasn't the reason he'd agreed to do the all-day clinic, but she'd seen right through his tidy little plan. He cleared his throat. "Good point."

Her fingers clacked over the keyboard again. His concentration shot, he stood, crossed the room and looked over her shoulder at the screen. Within a couple of minutes she'd produced a first-rate flyer, complete with clip art of a stethoscope and all the pertinent information, clear and concise.

"What do you think?" She glanced up, their gazes connected. Up close he was struck by how green her eyes were, and that she was a natural blonde, and he wondered why it registered.

"Looks great," he said, leaning away while she pressed "Print" and stood.

She walked across the small and cluttered office to the antiquated printer to snag the first flyer. Holding the goldenrod paper like a picture for him to see, she smiled. "Not bad."

He looked her up and down before looking at the flyer. Yeah, not bad. "Guess I can't weasel out of it now."

She rewarded his honesty with a smile, a very nice smile. "Nope. I'm going to hold you to your word. We'll put one of these by the receptionist's window right now and start handing them out after lunch."

As she breezed across the room toward the connecting front office in her oversized lab coat and scrubs, he caught a scent of no frills soap and enjoyed the clean smell, then discovered there was something else he favored about her. Unlike so many of his patients— size four with forty-inch chests—she wasn't skinny trim. She was sturdy and healthy looking, not like the lettuce-and-cilantro-eating women he saw in the plastic surgery clinics.

"Look," he said, needing to get away before he discovered anything else he liked about her, or before she bamboozled him into working there the entire month. "I've got to run back to the hospital. I'll see you next Tuesday."

Kasey hopped off the bus on her street, the rich smell of fresh pizza from the corner ma and pa shop making her instantly hungry. She strode briskly against the chill and drizzle toward her house, eager to take off her shoes and relax. In a neighborhood lined with hundred-year-old two-story houses, most divided into two units, she lived amongst an interesting mix of people: the working class; families and seniors; immigrants; and Bostonians who could trace their American heritage back for centuries. She loved her converted first-floor apartment with hardwood floors and mustard-colored walls, and appreciated her quiet neighbors, except for that constantly squawking cockatiel next door. Skipping up her front steps to get out of the drizzle, which had now progressed to rain, she wondered if spring would ever break through the dreary weather.

After grabbing the mail from the box on the porch, she used her key to open the front door, immediately disabling the alarm system. Sadly, living alone in the city, it was a necessary expense, and one that gave her peace of mind. Well worth the cost.

She tossed her mail on the dining table on her way to the kitchen, and the corner of another letter left opened from yesterday caught her eye and brought back a wave of dread. Try as she may to put it out of her head all day, she'd failed. She needed a cool glass of water before she dared read it again. Maybe the words had changed. Maybe she'd misunderstood.

A quiet mew and furry brush against her ankle made her smile. She bent to pick up Daisy, her calico cat, who'd come out of hiding to greet her.

"What's up, Miss Daisy? Did you watch the birds today?" She thought how her cat sat perched on the back bedroom window-sill, twitching her tail for hours on end, most likely imagining leaping into the air to catch a chickadee busy with nest-building. "You want your dinner?"

After she'd fed the cat and drunk a whole glass of water, she went back to the table and picked up the letter from the Department of Health and Welfare.

"It is with great sadness we inform you that your birth father, Jeffrey Morgan McAfee, has passed away from Huntington's disease..."

She tossed the letter on the table, closing her eyes and taking a seat. She hadn't misread it. With elbows planted firmly on the worn walnut surface, she dropped her head into her hands and did something she rarely allowed: she felt sorry for herself.

"We recommend you meet with a genetic counselor and set up a blood test..."

She'd never known her father, her mother had never spoken of him, and this had been one hell of an introduction. She'd called her mother to verify her father's name last night, but had only got her message machine. Then later, Mom had called back to break the bad news. He was, in fact, her father. That's all she'd said, but Kasey intended to get the whole story one day soon.

"Did he leave you anything in his will?" So like Mom. Always looking for a free ride and never coming close to finding one.

"Yeah, Mom, one doozy of an inheritance…"

Kasey wouldn't wish the progressive, degenerative disease on anyone, yet with her birth father having and dying from it, she had a fifty percent chance of developing Huntington's. And once the symptoms began, *if* they began, which was a mind-wrenching thought in itself, there would be a tortured journey of wasting nerve cells, decreased cognition, Parkinson's-type rigidity and myriad other health issues until it took her life.

At least Mom had apologized, but how could a person make up for sleeping with the wrong guy, getting pregnant, and never seeing him again? Actions and consequences had never really figured into her mother's style of living.

She couldn't dwell on the disease. There was no point. While removing her head from her hands, her stomach protested, reminding her it had been hours since she'd eaten. She either carried the marker or she didn't, the ticking clock had already been set or it hadn't. Thinking how her ignorance had been bliss all these years, she had no control over anything, and now her life must go on just as it had before the letter had arrived.

She stood, losing her footing and having to grab the table for balance. Could it be an early symptom? Her throat went dry. Hadn't she been bumping into things more recently? She shook her head, scolding herself.

She'd always been clumsy, especially when she rushed, and she rushed all the time at work. There was no need to second-guess every misstep. She needed to eat, that was all.

And if she wanted peace of mind, all she needed to do was make an appointment and have a blood test and find out, once and for all, if she carried the defective gene. Be done with it or face it head on.

She'd been drawing blood from patients for years, never thought twice about having her own lab work done. Not since a kid had the thought of a laboratory test sent an icy chill of fear down her spine. Until today. What would she do if she had Huntington's? She tightened her jaw and stood straighter. If she had the disease, she'd just have to make the most of each day…until the symptoms began, and even then, she promised to live life to the fullest for as long as she was physically able.

Though her stomach growled a second time, she'd just lost her appetite.

CHAPTER TWO

FRIDAY night, hidden in a booth and lost in the noise of the local Pub, Kasey took another sip of her beer. She'd asked Vincent to join her for dinner, her treat, hoping to work up the nerve to tell him her troubles. So far they'd each had a deli sandwich, hers the chicken breast, his the beef dip, and they'd shared a Caesar salad. Vincent had just ordered a second round of beer, yet she still hadn't broached the subject etched in her genes and squeezing her heart.

"O. M. G., look!" Vincent pointed to the bar with the neck of his low-calorie beer bottle. "It's him, Dr. Tall, Dark, and Gorgeous."

Kasey almost choked on her drink when her eyes focused on the broad shoulders covered in a well-cut jacket, and the trim hips and jeans-clad legs. Though from Vincent's perspective Dr. Finch might be, she wouldn't go so far as to call him tall, but somewhere more in the vicinity of five eleven or so. Why split hairs, when the conclusion was the same? The man was a hunk.

Speaking of hair, and since she was now officially living her life for the moment, waves like those gave her the urge to run her fingers through them, just to see how they felt. She glanced at Vincent and realized he was probably thinking the same thing, and it made her blurt out a laugh. They shared the same taste in men. Where Jared Finch might possess superb physical traits, he sorely lacked both personality and charm, going from the short encounter she'd had with him. Looks could only take a man so far in her opinion. Maybe she wasn't the only person in the world with problems? Kasey continued to glance toward the bar, intrigued.

"I wonder what he's doing here," she said.

"Well, duh, drinking!" Vincent reached across the booth table and patted her hands. "He must be human, just like us. Isn't that sweet?"

Vincent had been teased mercilessly all his life about his carrot-top hair, which he now kept meticulously combed and perfectly spiked, resembling a torch on top. If the red hair didn't set him apart, his alabaster-white skin dotted with free-flowing freckles sealed the deal when combined with his fastidious style of dress and precise mannerisms. He'd survived a tough childhood and now lived life exactly as he pleased. As a result he owned the sweetest content smile on the planet. Right now he shared that smile with Kasey. Sparkles beamed from his eyes—even in the darkened pub Kasey could see them—as he watched Jared standing at the bar, hoisting a mug, taking a swig and watching the Red Sox on the big screen.

"I don't think he's with anyone," Vincent said. "I'm going to invite him over." He shot out of the booth and zigzagged through the crowd before Kasey had a chance to stop him.

"Don't do that!" she said, her voice overpowered by piped-in Irish rock music as he was halfway across the bar. *"I need to talk to you...tell you my horrible news. And that guy's a real pill."*

Biting her lips, she refused to watch Vincent. Instead, she cringed, took another drink of her beer and hoped Dr. Finch had a short memory. Or that he thought Vincent was too forward and invading his privacy and refused to associate with subordinates. That would suit his attitude.

Unable to stand the suspense, she glanced from the corner of her eye toward the bar. Damn, the men were both headed for the booth. She sat straighter and fussed with her bangs, then wished she hadn't left her hair in the French braid tucked under at her nape. They'd come here straight from work, and a whole lot of hair had escaped since that morning, judging by the tendrils tickling her neck. She must look a mess, and what had been completely acceptable for spending time with Vincent would now fail miserably for making an impression on Vincent's Dr. Tall, Dark, and Gorgeous. Why should she care?

Catching an errant strand of hair and tucking it behind her ear, another pang of anxiety got her attention. What the heck was she supposed to talk about? The plan had been to wine and dine Vincent, then tell him her woes, not have a social encounter with an aloof plastic surgeon. She hated it when her plans didn't work out.

When Jared arrived at the booth, his tentative smile made her suspicious he'd had a drink or two already, since friendliness hadn't been his strong suit at the clinic. "Hi," he said. "I was just on my way out when Vinnie caught me."

Vincent preened in the background over his job well done.

"Hi, Dr. Finch, what are you doing here?" she said, ignoring her gloating friend and cringing over the lame question.

"Having a drink—what else?" He pinched his brows together and glanced around the pub just as a group of three waiters broke into song at the booth next to theirs. They sang "Happy birthday" to a young woman who didn't look a day over sixteen, though they served her a fancy umbrella drink with a flaming candle in it, so she had to be at least twenty-one. Yep, by the end of the song they'd sung, "Happy twenty-first birthday to Shauna".

"I feel so old," Jared said, after watching the celebration. "Is there an upper age limit at this bar? No one over thirty allowed?"

"Oh, no. That's not what I meant when I asked what you were doing here. What I meant was I'm just surprised to see you here, that's all." This was more of a locals bar, not a place for doctors, especially future plastic surgeons.

He sat next to her, and she scooted several inches in the other direction, though there wasn't far to go, her hands clutching the glass of pale ale. "And, besides, if the age limit is thirty, I'd be too old, too."

"You're not over thirty, are you?" He sat with a hand on each knee, back to looking stiff and out of his element.

"Thirty-two last January." She didn't care if he knew her age—she wasn't looking for his approval.

"I would have pegged you around twenty-six or -seven."

Well, then. She sat a little straighter. Yes, he was being nice, she knew it, but nevertheless he'd scored a few plus points over the unintentional compliment. His attempt to be kind was a far cry from the standoffish guy she'd met the other day.

"Now I know you've had a couple of pints." She

felt the blush from his compliment as deeply as when she'd been twelve and regularly embarrassed. How silly was that?

He stopped just before he finished off his dark brew. "From these thirty-nine-year-old eyes, you look twenty-six. Trust me."

"How old do I look?" Vincent asked, looking a little desperate to get into the game.

"Vinnie, I'm thinking twenty-four."

Vincent giggled, actually giggled. "Oh, Doctor, you're so funny, I'm thirty. And could you call me Vincent, please?"

"Apologies, Vincent. Then we're all over the hill. Good. I don't relate to the younger generation, anyway. All the face piercings and tattoos, fake boobs."

Kasey took another swallow of beer to help the dry patch in her throat as she thought about the four silver hoops in various sizes in both of her ears, the silver ball in her left tragus, the small rose tattoo hidden on her right hip, and the hummingbird on her left shoulder. Her breasts were her own, though. She sat a little straighter, thinking about it. "But you're going to be a plastic surgeon, so won't you be augmenting a lot of those 'boobs'?"

"I'm depending on it. Lots of cash in breast augmentation. And lipo. Ah, and we can't forget Brazilian butt lifts. Big bucks there, too."

He seemed too caught up with the money side of the job, and it made her subtract some of those points she'd just awarded him. Her thoughts must have shown on her face.

"There's nothing wrong with helping people look the way they want," Vincent said, practically shushing her as if she'd been rude to their guest.

"Within reason." For some crazy reason—maybe the second half of the pale ale—she wasn't ready to back down. "You wouldn't give anyone cat eyes if they asked, would you? Or a doll's nose, or pull someone's face so tight they looked like they'd just hit G-force?"

Surprising her, Jared gave a good-hearted laugh—a deep, really nice-sounding laugh, which suited his urbane appearance and classy charm. "I've often wondered if some plastic surgeons forget their oaths to do no harm." He touched her forearm, sending her focus away from his mesmerizing eyes. "You'd probably think less of me if I said, 'If the price was right', so I won't answer that question."

His dodge disappointed her, and he looked less handsome for it. Then she mentally kicked herself, wondering who was shallower, him for doing what his patients asked or her for getting all caught up in a man with an intriguing face before knowing a single thing about him.

Everyone around the table stared at their drinks. The silence had gone on long enough.

"You're not from Massachusetts, are you?" she said.

He shook his head. "California."

"What brings you out this way?" Vincent asked.

"My kids." He got a distant, almost pained look in his eyes, but quickly snapped out of it. "They go to school out here." He took a long swig of his drink. "My ex-wife insisted on sending them to an exclusive boarding school back east, which meant moving across country and driving two hours in order to see them every other weekend."

"So does your ex live here too?" Vincent asked.

"Nope. Patrice is still back in California."

This earnest dad who'd do anything, including move across the country, to be near his kids, took her by surprise. If she had been keeping tally, he'd moved back up the plus column. "I've heard it's a great school." Meaning it was expensive.

"Oh, yeah, the best." He finished another long drink. "Which is the main reason I chose plastic surgery this time around." He gave an I-don't-give-a-damn-what-you-think glance, meant only for Kasey.

Yes, he came off gruff and uncaring, and maybe a little drunk to be talking about this with near strangers, but Kasey saw through the façade and did the math. He had an ex-wife who got alimony and kids in a private school. The man was upgrading his pay scale by going into plastic surgery. A perfectly respectable specialty in this day and age so she wasn't going to come down hard on him for that.

Her father had never even tried to find her. This guy had moved across the country to be near his kids.

He took a long draw on the last of his beer. Vincent waved his hand to the passing waitress and ordered another round. "You're not driving, are you, Dr. Finch?"

"Call me Jared. Actually, I'm within walking distance of here. What about you guys?"

"The T," Kasey and Vincent answered in unison, then locked pinky fingers. "Jinx, one, two, three, you owe me a beer," they also said in unison.

Jared cocked his head, glancing at Kasey and Vincent. "I keep forgetting I'm not in California any more. We can't live without our cars." Ignoring the pinky locking, he pinned Kasey with an inquisitive look. "Do you feel safe riding the T at night?"

"As a woman, I'm never completely comfortable commuting after dark, but as long as I'm home before midnight, I'm okay with it. Anyway, after the T there's a bus that takes me right to my street corner. It works out pretty well."

Jared glanced across at Vincent. "You're not seeing her home?"

"She's my best friend, but also a big girl, and I'm a big boy in the big city. Besides, I live in Jamaica Plains at the other end of the Orange line, and she lives in Everette. We're okay with that, aren't we, Kase?"

"Yeah." She nodded, just as the waitress delivered their next round of beers. "I'm fine with that. If you can't handle the transportation, get out of the city, I always say."

From across the booth Vincent reached for a high five and she joined him, grateful she wasn't drinking on an empty stomach and wondering what the heck Dr. TD&G thought about their childish antics. Ah, what did she care? After next Tuesday he'd only have another eight to ten hours left to volunteer at the clinic and then she'd never see him again anyway.

By the end of the next beer even Jared had loosened up and the conversation had run the gamut from surviving while going to school to favorite pubs in the area to bad break-ups. And Kasey's head had started to spin with all the details.

"This certain person, who shall rename mainless," Vincent said, and giggled. "I mean shall remain nameless, took all my favorite CDs and DVDs before we broke up. Should've seen it coming, I guess."

"No, no, no." Jared said. "You have no idea what a real break-up is. California style. I've been a doctor for thirteen years and I'm living in a basement apartment with rented furniture, thanks to my ex."

"So that's why you're going into plastic surgery," Vincent said, with a poor-baby gaze in his eyes.

"Absolutely. Plus the fact I believe people should be able to look the way they want. If I can help make them happy with their appearance, I'll be glad to do it."

The man was definitely toeing the line on plastic surgery, and she was beginning to believe his sincerity.

Somewhere during the conversation Kasey had slipped into the shadows of her mind, leaving Vincent to stir up mischief and Jared willingly joining in. She'd heard the retold saga of Vincent's childhood in Kansas and what had brought him to Boston. She'd also gathered some interesting information about Jared's fifteen-year marriage to his college sweetheart, Patrice, and how over the years his ex had changed into a shopaholic, how it had ruined their marriage and caused their divorce two years ago. She also knew one-sided stories were never accurate, and wondered what the rest of that tale was. She suspected he was still hurting about the break-up of his family, and even thought about commenting on that, though didn't get that far.

With all the open conversation, Kasey hadn't managed to share a single thing about herself.

Kasey's mind slipped back to the latest news, the worst news of her life. She'd managed to distract herself the last couple of hours with the male company and pale ale, yet now it tiptoed back into her thoughts and soured her stomach.

"You're awfully quiet," Vincent prodded.

"Yeah, what about you?" Jared said. "Don't you have any dating war stories?"

She laughed and swiped at the air, her idea of feeling cavalier about life's major curve balls. "You guys don't have anything to complain about."

Vincent's cellphone rang. He checked who it was, his eyes going wide. "Speak of the devil."

Kasey faked a grin for Jared, who returned a benign smile, while Vincent took the call. She tore her bar napkin into three soggy parts while mulling over her news. The waitress arrived, and Jared ordered for them, though Vincent shook his head. Jared glanced at Kasey again, one brow raised.

Sure. What the heck. I'm living life moment to moment now, right? She nodded, and Jared ordered for both of them.

Vincent finished his call. "It's been great, but I've got to go." He fished in his pocket for cash for his share of the bar bill.

"You're leaving?" Kasey said, as in was he leaving her there alone with Dr. Finch?

"A certain someone has come to their senses."

"Returning all the CDs and DVDs?" Jared said, surprising Kasey that he'd actually been following along.

Vincent looked startled. "Oh, good point. I'll make sure of it." He flashed his winning smile, kissed Kasey on the cheek, and left.

Wait! I need to talk to you!

What the heck was she supposed to do now?

Jared didn't move to the opposite side of the table, which made a little knot form in her stomach. The waitress brought the drinks and he paid, not giving Kasey a chance to chip in. The tummy knot got tighter. When the server left, he raised his glass to her and took a drink. She joined him.

This socializing business could get long and painful, trying to be polite and having absolutely nothing to talk about. Or he'd finish his drink and get up and leave, and could she blame him Someone had to start a conversation, so it may as well be her.

"What are your kids' names?"

"Chloe and Patrick." His face immediately lit up. "She's ten and he's twelve. Great kids." He got out his smartphone and found their pictures. She admired the bright smiles and happy eyes. Both children had their father's eyes.

"You have kids?" he asked.

"No. I'm not married." Well, that hadn't stopped her mother.

He sat for a few moments, pondering her answer. "So tell me," he said, "what was it like, growing up in Boston?"

Yeah, they really didn't have a thing to talk about.

"Actually, I'm a south shore girl. I grew up in Kingston, which is close to Plymouth. My mom and I lived with my grandmother." She left out the part about her mom cleaning houses for the rich ladies of Duxbury, and how she could never afford to move the two of them out on their own. "I guess it's like growing up any other place."

"What does 'south shore' mean?"

"That I grew up south of Boston. Now, I guess, since I had the opportunity to open the community clinic and move to Everett, you could call me a 'north shore' girl."

He gave her a blank stare. She was failing miserably as a pub buddy.

"In my heart I'll always be a south shore girl, I guess." She wanted to squirm, his lack of interest was so noticeable. What was the first rule of socialization? People loved to talk about themselves. Ask him a question.

"What part of California are you from?"

"L.A."

"Are you the only doctor in your family?"

"Yes. Mom was a teacher and Dad ran a small business in Echo Park. My brother's a fireman."

So he hadn't come from money, like she'd assumed. See, asking questions always helped break the ice.

They chatted about his upbringing, having to yell back and forth in order to be heard over the ever-increasing Friday-night crowd at the pub as they finished their drinks.

"You feel like some coffee?" he said. "The noise is getting to me."

Surprised by his invitation, she nodded. "Sounds good." She wasn't ready to be alone with her morbid thoughts, which had subsided while engaged in small talk with Jared.

Jared watched Kasey as she exited the pub. She'd worn straight-legged jeans rolled up at the ankles, candy-apple red flats, a matching blouse with ruffles down the front, which accentuated her bust, and an oatmeal-colored extra-long sweater with the sleeves pushed up to her elbows. The street lights made all the loose hair around her head look like a halo. He liked the shape of her face, didn't even mind the batch of earrings on both ears or the Boston accent. It was cute and not whiny, like some of the women he'd heard since moving east. Maybe it had to do with the south-shore versus north-shore girl bit, but what did he know?

She was different from most women he'd been around lately, too. After giving it some thought, he decided it was because of a decided lack of pretentiousness. She seemed grounded, wanted to work with the folks who needed her the most, and she wasn't seduced by the almighty dollar like so many people in his life. Hell, like him.

Two doors down he found the local coffee bar, and held the door open for her. She seemed a little unstable on her feet—maybe he shouldn't have bought her that last beer—so he guided her by the elbow to an empty table. "What do you drink?"

She rattled off her latte order, tagging on fat-free milk. He made the order and waited for the drinks while she went to the bathroom. When they met up back at the table, he could tell she'd brushed her hair and put on more lipstick, and wondered if she'd done it for him. The thought, whether true or not, pleased him.

They shared a few sips of coffee in silence. She seemed tense, and he figured it was because she felt stuck with him. He didn't feel the same. In fact, he was glad to have someone to talk to and wished he could make her relax. Truth was, if she couldn't settle down after a couple of beers, there was no helping her.

"I got some pumpkin bread," he said. "Want to share?"

She smiled and took half. "Thanks." She was generous with her smiles, and he liked that.

"Can I get your opinion about something?" he said, just before popping a pinch of bread into his mouth.

She blew over her cup and nodded. "Sure."

"Do you think little girls should be allowed to dress like small adults?"

Obviously, this wasn't the turn she'd expected the conversation to take. She pulled in her chin and thought for a second or two. "No. As a matter of fact, I resent little kids looking better in the latest styles than I do."

"Yeah, well, I'm glad my kids' private school has a dress code, because sometimes I think Chloe's taste in clothes is far beyond her years."

"Sounds like a sore spot."

"Yeah. I don't like to argue with her about it. As long as she dresses within reason, I'm okay, but sometimes she looks like a tiny adult." He grinned. "That's when I pull out the phone and take her picture, text it to my ex and let her weigh in on the outfit. If she approves, I keep my trap shut, but sometimes, well, let's just say I miss my girl in her overalls and flowered T-shirts, you know?"

He wasn't trying to impress Kasey or anything, but he caught a look of longing in her eyes, as if she really dug guys who worried about their daughters. "It wasn't my idea," he said, noticing a touch of confusion in her expressive eyes. "The divorce."

"So you didn't divorce purely on shopaholic grounds?" Her knowing gaze told him he hadn't fooled her for a minute back at the bar.

He offered a humble smile. "Maybe the fact I was never around, always working on developing my private practice, had something to do with her turning to shopping. I guess it filled a void but, damn, practically every penny I made she spent."

"Did you guys seek counseling?"

He nodded. "Too little, too late. I wish my ex well and all, I'd just like to have more say in my kids' lives."

"You *should* have input since you're their dad."

He gave her an earnest smile before he took another drink. She seemed surprised by it, with a quick yet subtle double-take before returning his smile.

"Thanks for being honest," she said, popping another bite of pumpkin bread into her mouth. "We've all got problems. Sometimes we need to get them off our chest. Not that I'm asking you to unload all your gripes about your ex on me or anything."

He laughed. "No-o-o, I wouldn't do that. I'm sure she's got her share of gripes, too."

"Again, thanks." She took a dainty sip and he really liked watching her, making him wonder what was up with that.

"You seem pretty well set up. No husband. No kids. You get to run a busy clinic. Make a differ—" Her laser-sharp stare stopped him in mid-word. "What?"

"I just found out I have a fifty-fifty chance of developing Huntington's," she said, with a defiant, subtly quivering smile.

Why she had let her dark secret slip out to Jared, she had no clue. Maybe it was because he'd opened up about his family and his frustrations as a father. Or because he tried to make her life sound all rosy-toes. From her perspective at least his problems were fixable. Maybe it was because she needed to get the burden of truth off her chest, and Vincent wasn't around, and tonight was the night she'd planned to tell him. Whatever the reason, she'd said it, quite out of the blue, and from the sinking in her stomach, wished she could take it back, or at least stop her eyes from welling up. Darn it. The last thing she wanted to do was go all emotional on him. Not here. Not in public.

His gaze went stone cold, his body rigid. Dead silence ensued. Kasey could have sworn the coffee-bar music, which was quiet compared to the bar, got turned down ten more notches.

She knew the second the words had slipped out of her mouth she'd made a huge mistake. This wasn't how she'd planned to tell someone. She'd wanted to tell Vincent, cry on his shoulder, let him soothe her, not tell a man she'd only just met. She'd never had any intention of telling Dr. Finch!

It was too late to take back the words and, oh, God, the look on his face, his startled gaze, was more than she could bear. She didn't want his sympathy. The truth of the matter was she'd needed to tell someone before she exploded and now that she'd said it she couldn't take it back.

Jared leaned in and looked at her with sad and serious eyes. "Wouldn't you have already known if one of your parents had the disease?"

"Just got word my father died from it. I never knew him. Listen, I didn't mean to say that. I certainly didn't mean to hijack the conversation, but…"

Jared clamped his hand on her forearm. "This is tough news. You should've told me to shut the hell up with all my trivial griping. Have you taken the blood test yet?"

She shook her head.

"You need to have that test. You'll go crazy with worry until you know for sure."

"Tell me about it," she said. "I found out three days ago, and I can barely function."

"I'm surprised you've lasted this long! Listen, we've got a great genetic research department, I'll arrange for you to have the test ASAP."

"I can get it done…"

"Let me help you," Jared said. "Now is no time to flaunt your big-girl panties. I get it that you're an independent, big-city woman raised by a single parent, and you can handle everything by yourself, but just this once why not let someone else help you out?"

Was that what he'd taken away from their conversation tonight? That she was hard-headed and fiercely independent? Right now she felt anything but. Or maybe he saw her as impossibly stubborn. Either way, she was shutting him out with her response.

Hadn't she recently given herself a lecture about needing more than two friends? The man had just offered to help her out. She should take it and be grateful.

"Okay." She glanced at Jared and forced a smile. "Thanks. Let me know when to have the blood drawn and where to go."

"I'll get right on it first thing Monday." He removed his hand from her arm and she immediately missed the warmth. He withdrew his cellphone and entered a note. "Maybe Vincent can go with you for moral support."

She nodded her thanks. "That's a thought." She really didn't want to go through this alone, and having Vincent's support would mean the world to her, that was when she finally had a chance to tell him. Who would have thought she'd first blurt out her news to a near stranger?

"Oh, and another thing," Jared said, putting his phone away.

She looked into his steady, concerned gaze.

"You're not riding the T home by yourself tonight. I'm coming with you."

After a brisk walk a couple of blocks to the station, they entered to the T. She didn't even have to open her wallet to use her magnetic card to open the gate. Being from California, the whole public transportation thing still amused Jared. Seeing him fiddle in his pockets, searching for his Charlie card, she handed him her wallet.

"Here, you can use mine. I've got a bundle on it."

"Thanks." He took it and placed it over the card reader, waiting for the blip and the gate to pop open. Once inside, they rushed towards the red line, heading for Ashmont. She knew what she was doing, had probably ridden this line a thousand times. He followed along, making mental notes to do the reverse when it was time to go home.

She strode along, looking the picture of health and confidence, yet she'd been delivered a blow that would have brought most people to their knees. Huntington's. Man, oh, man.

Granted there was a fifty percent chance she wouldn't have the marker and develop the symptoms, and he hoped that would be the case, but it was still a raw deal. She seemed in her prime and deserved all that life could give her. It simply wasn't fair.

She glanced back as if to make sure he was keeping up, and her soft smile and friendly eyes tugged at his heart. She'd gone from mere business associate to a woman who needed protecting in one evening, and though it was the last thing he wanted to get involved in—he had enough going on already—he felt compelled to be there for her.

Crazy. Absolutely crazy. He hardly knew her. It wasn't his style. He had enough people depending on him already. Surely she had other friends and family around. At least there was Vincent. Yeah, Vincent would be there for her.

She'd never known her father, and didn't seem to be close to her mother. At least that was what he'd gathered from their conversation tonight. She needed a friend, that's all. Was that so much to ask? Yes, as a matter of fact, it was. Relationships of any kind were definitely out for him at this stage as he was still smarting from the divorce. He glanced at her again and felt a firm yank on his heart. Aw, hell, maybe he should make the effort to be a friend before he forgot how it felt. Could he even do "friend" any more?

Did he really want to be a friend? Being a friend meant having a friend. So far, other than medical professionals, he didn't have a single friend in Boston, and it had suited him just fine. Except for when he wanted to go to a Sox game and didn't have anyone to go with, or when he didn't feel like eating alone. Again.

Train fumes invaded his nostrils, a street musician played classical guitar in the corner. A thick crowd of people pushed toward the automatic doors on the train as they opened. He strode in front of her and helped her on board, guiding her at the small of her back. He thought he saw a flicker of surprise in her glance as she boarded. Her eyes were soft and green, and, as hard as he tried not to, he liked them.

Once the doors closed, and they'd both grabbed a pole to hang onto, she looked at him. "What a coincidence, seeing you at the pub tonight."

Should he tell her he couldn't stand the thought of going home to his empty apartment to eat alone on a Friday night? "I heard they had great pastrami sandwiches and I wanted to watch the Sox game because they played the Los Angeles Angels."

She nodded. Maybe she believed him, maybe not. "I love their deli food, too. Do you go there often?"

"Once in a while." Hey, she'd been brutally honest with him, the least he could do was be honest back. With a look of chagrin, he started. "Truth is I hit that pub every other Friday night, same routine. Pastrami. Beer. Ball game. The other weekends I have visitation rights with my kids. Then I head out to the school and stay overnight at a motel so I'll be there bright and early to take my kids for breakfast on Saturday morning."

She looked at him more closely now, as if grateful he'd told the truth. "Very interesting. And to think I thought doctors all hung out in fancy restaurants, having doctorly conversations on Friday nights."

She'd forced a smile out of him, and he shook his head at the upside-down logic. Under the dreary circumstances, *he* should be the one trying to make *her* smile.

At the first stop, a large group of people got off, and they had the option to sit, but Kasey stayed standing so Jared did too.

"Does your mom still live in Boston?" he asked.

"No. She lives in Nevada. Works in one of the casinos." She scratched her nose. "Since my nana died, I don't have any relatives nearby."

No support system whatsoever. That had to hurt.

"But I've got Vincent. He's my best buddy these days."

Vincent was her closest friend, and Jared was glad for that. "That's it?"

"My other best friend, Cherie, moved to New York, so we don't get to hang out as much as we used to."

Something about the matter-of-fact way she'd admitted to being almost completely on her own pulled at him. Made him want to do right by her, which proved he'd had one beer too many, and that was that.

Downtown they got off and headed for the orange line toward Oak Grove. He made another mental note for the trip back home.

Whether she knew it or not, she needed looking after, and against his far better judgment, judgment that would normally have him running in the opposite direction, he saw a person who deserved to have a friend during this tough time. So he made a snap decision to sign on for the job. It wasn't like he had to be her best friend or anything, just keep an eye out for her, make sure she got to the lab and followed up after the results. Hell, the last thing he could handle in his life right now was a new friend with a debilitating disease. Truth was he'd be useless as a friend. He needed to put all his energy into being a good dad. There just wasn't enough left over for anything else.

Aw, what the hell.

Once Kasey and Jared exited the T they were lucky enough to find Kasey's bus waiting out front and hopped right on. She'd grown noticeably quiet, and hoped he didn't interpret it as not wanting him around. She'd been touched by his offer to see her home. Within ten minutes they were at her corner stop and jumped off.

"This is my street. I live five houses down on the right. Mission accomplished." She stepped back and slipped off the curb.

He grabbed her elbow to balance her.

"You don't want me to walk you home?" he said as they crossed the street.

"Thanks. I'm good. Really."

She felt completely out of his league, and it was partially because of his aristocratic air, as if coming from California and riding the T was a big adventure for a guy like him, rubbing elbows with the folks and all. But he'd told her his mother was a teacher and his father a small businessman. Hardly aristocracy. Must be the overly confident surgeon part of his personality coming across.

She'd spilled her guts about the Huntington's so he probably felt obligated to look after her. Well, she didn't need his pity. Not now. Not ever.

He pocketed his hands, waiting.

Maybe she'd been too abrupt, but what was the point? He insisted on following her home, and she was grateful for that, but she didn't need him walking her right to the door.

He couldn't possibly have something like seduction in mind could he? Would he be so crass to take advantage of a woman who'd just admitted she might have Huntington's? Unfortunately, she'd dated a guy or two like that in her life.

She glanced at him, passively waiting for her directions. No. That wasn't it.

They'd reached the other side of the street and Kasey had a decision to make. Let the man walk her to her house and then what? Scurry to pick up the breakfast dishes or discarded clothing from the living room? Feel like she had to offer him something, and not sure she had a single soda in the fridge? Had she left her bra on the sofa?

Or she could stay with him here until the next bus back to the T arrived. Wouldn't that be the practical thing to do?

"Wow, that pizza smells great," he said, leaning back and noticing the Mama's pizza parlor neon sign. "I'd weigh three hundred pounds if I lived this close."

"The novelty wears off as the scale goes up, believe me."

He half smiled, genuine and warm, and it halted her breathing for an instant. Maybe she had pegged him all wrong.

"Doesn't seem to have done any damage to you— you look fine just the way you are."

Ah, a smooth talker. Maybe he did have seduction plans.

Did a girl with a crooked nose, an ordinary face, and

ample hips really look fine just the way she was to a
future plastic surgeon? If her ex, the guy who'd broken
her heart into pieces, hadn't been able to accept her the
way she was, a man like Jared would probably never
waste a minute on someone like her. Didn't he fix people like her? Maybe he did feel sorry for her. Well, no
way would she tolerate someone feeling sorry for her,
even if he did look sexy as hell standing under that neon
sign. Sexy *and* kissable.

What in the world was she thinking, and why did he
cause her to have these thoughts?

Oh, hell, this was too confusing, and the last thing
she needed was to be confused tonight.

She noticed the bus lights coming down the street
with great relief. "There's the bus back to the T station.
You'd better hop on because they come a lot less fre-
quently this time of night."

"I'd rather make sure you made it *all the way* home,"
he said, grabbing her arm and squeezing, making her
wonder what his version of "all the way home" meant.
Did he think she was an easy hit, that he'd be doing her
a favor to seduce her in her time of need?

Though fundamentally wrong, she also saw the upside of grabbing life by the horns and riding it for all
it was worth, especially now, with her future at stake.
But not tonight. Not with Jared. Neither of them had
any business getting involved with each other.

"Really. I'm fine." She pointed down the street.
"Count down five houses and see that big bronze star
on the top floor? That's me. I live downstairs. Got a
guard cat waiting and everything. Go," she said as the
bus pulled up with a screeching of brakes. "You've done
your gentlemanly duty for the night."

He didn't immediately let go of her arm, and gazed

into her eyes so deeply she felt her toes twitch. "I'm calling the lab first thing Monday morning about that blood test. I'll be in touch as soon as I have a date for you."

"Thanks. I really appreciate it." She did, too.

"Which means you'll need to give me your phone number and address."

She rattled off her numbers as he entered it into his phone. "Got it."

He nodded, smiling and watching her, and there was nothing else he could say. Not now. Not until the test was done and the results were in.

The bus door opened.

"I'll see you Tuesday at the clinic," he said, getting on the bus.

She didn't have a chance to respond, but stood and watched as the bus pulled off. Waving briefly, she turned and headed home, seriously hoping he wouldn't forget about making the appointment for the blood tests. After all, she hardly knew the man, so why should he care?

She kept a brisk pace in the cool night, avoiding an overturned trash can and a car in a driveway blocking the sidewalk.

Of all the crazy times to meet a man who intrigued her, a man who turned her on with his dark hair and crystal-blue stare. A man who seemed a little interested in her, too. She shook her head, not believing that part of the equation. At least from the way he'd sat close to her in the bar when there had clearly been room to stretch out, and on the T, how he'd guided her by lightly touching the small of her back when they'd got on and off. Did he have a clue how heady that gesture was?

This was all too confusing. She needed to get a grip, think things through. Jared had changed from an aloof

surgeon into a halfway nice guy tonight, but she didn't
do halfway nice guys any more. That's how she'd gotten her heart ripped out of her chest the last time. She'd
believed her halfway nice guy when he'd told her he
loved her. The problem was, Mr. Halfway-Nice hadn't
convinced himself about love. If love meant sticking
around, being there through the rough patches, he'd
failed miserably. Why would Jared Finch be any different?

She shook her head, remembering her plan B.
Superficial. Keep all future male-female relationships
superficial. But that had been before she'd found out
about her father and Huntington's. Should she think
about any relationships at all until she knew her results?

Jared's handsome face popped into her thoughts
again. He was a man who seemed like he could use
some unattached companionship just as much as she
could. Too bad she wasn't in the mood for an affair.

CHAPTER THREE

TUESDAY morning, Kasey arrived at the free clinic a half-hour early to find a line of people halfway down the block waiting out front.

"Good morning, everyone," she called out. "Please be patient today." She hoped everyone at the end of the line heard her. "We'll work as quickly as we can." She let herself in the door, locking it behind her. The clinic wasn't due to open until nine a.m.

She went to her desk, booted up the computer and went about her morning chores. Dr. Finch hadn't called on Monday as he'd said he would. So much for getting swept up in his promises and dreamy looks. She should have known better since men had a long record of letting her down, beginning with her absent father, her mother's long list of deadbeat boyfriends, and ending with her own string of sour relationships.

With the special clinic today, she'd be too busy to do research on labs that would be able to do special genetic studies, but she promised herself she'd tackle it first thing tomorrow.

What if Dr. Finch didn't show up today? It hadn't exactly been his idea, but he'd agreed. Her stomach tightened at the thought of having to explain to all of

the patients their clinic would have to be cancelled because the future plastic surgeon hadn't kept his promise.

She snapped her fingers. If he did show up, they'd
be short a computer unless he brought his laptop. Why
hadn't she remembered to tell him that? Was it too late
to call him? A sudden blast of nerves had her flitting all
over the nurses' station, searching for his phone number, not even sure she had it.

Vincent arrived through the back door in powder-
blue scrubs, his lab jacket over his arm and hair sculpted
in several directions. "Wow, we'll be here until tomorrow, seeing all of those patients."

"I know," she said, distracted with checking supplies.
"Good thing we set up all the rooms last night. Is Angie
here yet?" Angie, the ready-to-retire receptionist and
medical assistant, was notorious for being late to work.

"She was parking when I got here." Vincent headed
straight for the coffee pot, found a filter and held up
the can of coffee, shaking it to emphasize it was almost
empty as the back door opened. "Do we have a grocery
list going? We need coffee and powdered creamer."

"What we need," she said, "is that doctor to show
up."

"Got it, and present," said a familiar masculine voice.

Kasey glanced up to find Jared standing with a take-
out tray of steaming coffees in one hand and a brown
bag in the other. A mini-cringe made her cheeks warm.
He wore a tan suede jacket over a button-down pin-
striped yellow shirt, pressed denim jeans and brown
loafers. *Who pressed their jeans*? He hadn't forgotten
to bring his laptop either, as a stylish computer case
hung from his shoulder.

"Oh, hi," she said, glancing at his face then her desk,

feeling embarrassed. Even from this distance, his freakishly blue eyes did things to her she wasn't prepared for.

"You're a god," Vincent said, rushing to his aid. "Good morning, and I'll take these, thank you very much."

"Don't thank me, thank Angie."

Vincent grabbed the coffees and passed them out to Kasey and Angie, who'd entered behind Jared. "Thank you, Ms. Angie, and here's one for you." He handed Jared his coffee. "And one for me."

"Yes, thank you, Angie," Kasey said, wondering what had prevented Jared from getting back to her yesterday about the lab appointment.

He handed the brown bag back to Angie.

She held it up. "These bagels were fresh from the oven when I picked them up at the bakery forty minutes ago," Angie said.

"From that line I saw circling around the block, we're going to need carbs and lots of them, so thanks," Jared said, being the first to be offered a bagel.

"How sweet," Vincent said, finding a blueberry bagel and taking a huge bite.

When the cream cheese made an appearance, Kasey sauntered over, though not wanting to get too close to Jared, leery that his sexual gravity might snag her like a magnet. She took a sesame bagel, smearing it with strawberry flavored soft cheese, then savored the fresh-bread smell as she gobbled it down. A simple pleasure on what promised to be a hellishly busy day. From the corner of her eye she noticed Jared watching her as she licked away the cream cheese at the corner of her mouth.

For distraction, Kasey ticked off a list of items for Angie to stock in the patient rooms then sipped her hot, rich coffee. She'd keep today's visit from Dr. Finch strictly business, which it was. Though it had been her idea to run this clinic, he'd be expected to take charge of the lion's share of the patients. At least he'd showed up, that was a start. If all went well, after today she wouldn't have to see him again for the rest of the month.

Grabbing a stack of insurance forms with plans to take them to the receptionist's desk for those in line who might possibly have some additional medical coverage, she turned and almost bumped into Jared. Her pulse, darn it, responded with a quick gallop. She'd remember that citrusy scent in the future, but only so he couldn't sneak up on her again.

He reached into his shirt pocket and pulled out a folded piece of paper. "I was in surgery all day yesterday, so I didn't have a chance to call you. Sorry, but I didn't think you'd appreciate a call after bedtime."

"How do you know my bedtime?"

The corner of his mouth twitched into a reserved smile. "I guessed."

She didn't smile back, refusing to look away. He didn't have a clue how important the test was to her, but why should he? It wasn't his problem. It was just some casual offer he'd made to give the illusion of being nice.

"Again, my apologies."

She saw something there, in his eyes, an earnest appeal? Give the guy a break, she told herself, it's only eight forty-five in the morning. She gave a quick nod.

"Anyway, here you go." He handed her the paper.

Forcing her gaze away, she unfolded it and found a date and time for a genetic marker study at a Massachusetts General hospital. She really needed to quit writing off people so quickly. "Thank you," she said, a little warm bubble rising in her chest. "I'll be there this Saturday."

"Good. Under ideal circumstances you could get the results in a week to ten days, but there's such a demand for this specialty they can't guarantee results that soon. Sorry."

"I understand." Her throat tightened at the thought of having the test done, and her pulse sped up, thinking about the potential results. With a shaky hand she took another sip of coffee. "How much will it cost, do you know?"

"It's all taken care of," he said.

"What do you mean?"

"Professional courtesy."

"Wait. What?"

"The lab extended the courtesy." He gave her a pointed look, and a little voice in the back of her head counseled her to shut up about it and be gracious. Though she didn't believe his explanation for a minute and really wanted to know who'd actually paid for the test, she nodded.

"Well, I guess we better get you signed into our computer system," she said, slipping the paper into her lab-coat pocket. "That line of patients is probably twice as long by now."

Ten minutes later they opened the doors and began processing the ever-expanding crowd. It appeared their little neighborhood had people crawling out of the crevices in need of care. Vincent acted as the triage nurse. Kasey saw the more general-needs patients, such as pap smears, breast exams, flu and vague complaints, and Jared took anyone who needed a surgical consult or onsite care.

Within an hour Jared approached her desk and asked for her assistance. She jotted down a few quick notes on the breast exam she'd just completed then gave him her complete attention.

"I've got a patient who came in for a cyst removal on his shoulder, which I've already done, but I want you to see this." She followed him into exam room two, where she saw a middle-aged man with a bright red complexion and one of his front teeth missing.

"This is Franklin O'Leary," Jared said. "Mr. O'Leary, this is Kasey McGowan, the nurse practitioner who runs this place, and I wanted to have her take a look at your stomach."

The man looked eight months pregnant with a rounded, bulging symmetrical contour. "If you don't mind," Kasey said, warming her hands while he lay flat on the examination table. "I'm going to do a little poking around."

"It's been a while since a lady's poked me anywhere. Go right ahead."

She smiled, then palpated the tightly distended skin and performed percussion, noting tympany over and around the navel, with dullness at his flanks.

"How long has your stomach been distended?" Jared asked.

"Dis—what?"

"Has your stomach been big like this for a while?" Kasey spoke up.

"A few months, I think. Just my beer gut."

Jared marked the level of dullness on the skin with a magic marker.

"Could use a new tattoo." The man glanced at the straight lines. "That's not what I had in mind, but what do you expect for free?"

Kasey smiled again, appreciating his New England humor.

"Lie on your side for a minute or so," Jared said, and waited for the patient to shift his position. The curly-headed man cooperated, though it was awkward to move with his big belly. Kasey helped him, hoping Jared would get the point.

As predicted, the dullness shifted. Kasey knew that meant textbook-wise there was at least five hundred cc of abdominal fluid and, judging from the size of the otherwise malnourished man's abdomen, she suspected a lot more.

"How much beer do you drink?" Jared asked.

"I'm known to have a pint or two whenever I can. Doesn't always work out, though."

Most people underestimated their drinking, and in Franklin's case the "whenever I can" could mean morning, noon and night.

"Roll on your back," Jared said, this time helping him. "Kasey, will you press here for me?"

She placed her hand firmly against the patient's abdomen in the navel area while Jared put the flat of his hand on the left side and tapped with his other hand. Sure enough, this generated a pressure wave indicating ascites.

"Do you have a history of cancer?"

"Not that I'm aware of, Doc. Should I get scared now?"

"I'm just asking questions. No need to worry." Jared gave her a decisive look. "We need to drain him," he said.

She nodded. Normally this procedure was done in an ER, but under the circumstances Franklin needed immediate medical attention. Suspecting he wouldn't follow through on his own if sent to the ER, and the cost of ordering an ambulance to transport him was off the budget, they'd go ahead and do what they could for him right here, right now.

"How would you like to lose a little weight and get your trim waist back?" Jared broached the subject.

"What do you mean?" Franklin said.

Jared explained, though in a rushed manner, that Franklin's liver wasn't functioning as it should, and how the fluid could be removed here in the clinic with an easy procedure, then it would be sent away to a laboratory for studies.

The man licked his lips and stared at the floor for a moment while he thought, then gave the okay. Jared's bedside manner could have been ten times better, but he didn't seem nearly as bad as she'd thought last week. He'd gotten Franklin to agree to an important test. The guy had arranged for the clinic and then shown up. Plus, he'd come through on the lab appointment for her. That said something about his character. A man of his word meant a lot to her these days, so she'd cut him some slack on his under-par bedside manner.

Kasey had Vincent bring in a consent form and she went hunting in the supply closet for an abdominal paracentesis kit. She asked Vincent to assist Dr. Finch, since the waiting room was packed with patients, and all the examination rooms were full.

She entered the next room and found a senior citizen with a swollen cheek and a nasty tooth abscess. In a perfect world this woman would go to her dentist, but from the look of her poorly cared-for teeth, she hadn't seen one in years. All Kasey could do was ask if she was allergic to any medicine and write her a prescription for generic antibiotics, point her to the local discount pharmacist and hope the patient followed her orders about taking the meds until they were finished, instead of stockpiling them for future use.

"Once the infection has calmed down a bit, you'll need to see a dentist."

"Ack, would rather have my cousin pull it."

Before lunch, Laurette Meranvil waited in room one to have her stitches removed. Jared tended to her and, as timing would have it, and admittedly because Kasey was curious, she ran into the patient on the way out. The laceration under Laurette's eye was a thin pink line.

The young woman smiled at Kasey.

"It's healing beautifully," Kasey said.

"I put special ointment from home on it."

"I may have to find out the name of your miracle ointment for our other patients."

"It's Haitian vetiver oil."

"Let me jot that down," Kasey said, making a note to Google it later. The woman walked with her head held high out the door, so different from last week when she'd come in covering her face.

Kasey took a moment to appreciate the much-needed help the clinic brought to the community. She glanced up and found Jared watching her. The usual tension had left his eyes, and she suspected he felt the same sense of pride she did, and wondered if he got that feeling doing cosmetic surgery. He nodded at her then slipped into the next exam room. Kasey might not be sure about the magical powers of Haitian vetiver oil, but she sure as heck knew there was some special voodoo in that man's stare.

And the day continued.

By late afternoon, Kasey couldn't keep track of how many patients she'd seen. Angie approached wearing her usual expression, as if she was in pain, brows knitted, world-weary. Kasey had gotten so used to the expression over the years she hardly took note.

"You've got to see this," Angie said. "It'll break your heart." At second glance, Angie did look more disturbed than usual, shaking her head, first clucking her tongue then pursing her lips.

Kasey followed the medical assistant into exam room three, where a mother and her toddler sat quietly. Angie was right, the pudgy little boy's cleft lip did break her heart. Did the mother think they could sew the lip together in the clinic and all would be well? She tried not to let her sadness show. The child probably had to endure sympathetic glances and an overabundance of pity every day. She didn't want to add to his pain or shame or whatever a two-year-old felt when people looked at him and treated him differently from everyone else.

"Hey, little fella," she said, with a big smile.

She fought an urge to pick him up and hug him tight, and tell him she had a magic pill that would make his sweet little mouth look like all the other children's. Then his big brown eyes would be the feature everyone first noticed, not his lip.

Offering her hand to the mother, Kasey maintained a professional manner. "What can we do for you today?"

The mother explained her son had been born with the problem, which, of course, Kasey already knew. He'd been born in another state, and the family couldn't afford surgery. They'd moved to Massachusetts partially because of the health insurance system. She examined the little boy's mouth and discovered that his palate was intact, and that the congenital deformity was limited to his lip. A good thing. Healthy and round, she realized he had no problem eating. She decided to let Jared take over on this consultation, and excused herself.

"Can you take a look at the toddler in room one?" she said, approaching Jared in the hallway and handing him the intake message. He glanced at Angie's notation then slowly back to Kasey. She hoped the boy's situation would touch his heart as much as it had hers.

"Sure," was all he said as he disappeared behind the exam-room door.

Kasey rubbed her eyes and took a moment to sit down and rest, wishing she had another cup of coffee for false energy.

Pressed for space, and between his triage duties, Vincent had set up a makeshift immunization station in the clean supply closet with no less than fifteen people standing patiently in line. She'd guess they'd seen over sixty patients already, and knew there were at least forty more waiting. At some point, if they wanted to get out of here before midnight, they'd have to cut off the line, and she really didn't want to be the person assigned to do that.

Angie brought another load of messages. Kasey picked the one off the top and before she headed for the next exam room noticed Jared come out from the other room and get on the phone. She overheard him talk to someone just before she entered the other exam room.

"I've got a little boy I'd like to refer for pro bono plastic surgery," he said, and her heart did a little extra pitty-pat of joy. The guy wasn't nearly as uncompassionate as he'd made himself out to be.

At some point, Vincent sent out for burgers and they ate on the run, having turned the day into a medical marathon. By ten o'clock the last patient left the clinic.

Exhausted yet exhilarated, Kasey grinned, hugged Vincent and high fived Angie. "We did it!"

"I think I'm numb," Vincent said.

"I died four hours ago," Angie said.

Jared stood quietly, as if taking in the scene. "You guys are a great team. I'm impressed. It's been an honor working with you."

"Same here, Doc," Vincent said, with a starry-eyed glance.

Kasey nodded and smiled, aware Jared hadn't thrown one single tantrum all day, like so many other doctors she'd worked with were inclined to do. No high drama. No added stress. Just noses to the grindstone, and their little community clinic had turned out to be one mean medical machine.

"Thanks for agreeing to my big idea," she said.

"You're welcome." His gaze met and held hers captive. She was the first to look away.

While Angie tidied up her desk and Vincent put his extra supplies away, Jared approached Kasey in the office. "There's only one thing I'm disappointed about today."

She cocked her head, furrowing her brow. What could he possibly be disappointed about? They'd seen a hundred and twenty-five patients! "You didn't get to see a gunshot wound? Oh, wait, let me guess, you were hoping for a stabbing."

He shook his head and smiled. "It's too late to take you out to dinner."

"Well, that's very kind of you, but I'd fall asleep in my salad if you did."

"So I was right about your bedtime, then."

"Don't get cocky on me, Doc." She grinned.

His gaze languished on her, and a tentative smile creased his lips. "Then we'll have to take a rain-check for when you're more alert."

"That's not necessary, Dr. Finch. Really."

"Jared," he said. "Call me Jared. Let's not take any steps backward, okay?" He took off his doctor's coat and put on his suede jacket, then gathered up his computer case and threw it over his shoulder. "You need a ride home?"

"Angie's dropping me off. Thanks, though."

"I could use a ride to the T," Vincent said, appearing at the door, his normally perfect hair limp and falling in his eyes.

"Sure," Jared said to Vincent, before he turned his attention back to Kasey. "I have the weekend with my kids, but name a day next week. I owe you dinner."

"Really, Jared, it isn't necessary."

He sat in front of her, took her hand, running his thumb over her knuckles. "Kasey, look at me."

She did and could barely take the effect of his solid blue gaze on her, let alone his touch. Spontaneous tingles popped up in unspeakable places.

"I want to. I really want to." He waited sufficiently long for his message to sink in, then released her hand and looked at Vincent. "Are you ready to go?"

Vincent nodded, jaw dropped over what had just transpired. Behind Jared's back, Vincent made eye contact with Kasey and gave her the thumbs-up sign. She wasn't sure if it was on his behalf for finagling a ride with the hot doc, or hers for getting that invitation for dinner. She shook her head. Jared really did feel sorry for her. She'd have to face the fact.

On his way to the door, Jared looked over his shoulder, another quick yet intense glance. It knocked Kasey in the chest like a mini fireworks blast, and left her staring at her desk, trying to catch her breath. Truth was he scared her.

She wondered what in the world "I want to. I really

want to." meant. Did the guy get off feeling sorry for
sick girls or was he really interested in her? Yet how
could he be considering what her future might hold?
And why should she be interested in him other than
because he was so damn gorgeous?

Since she was looking at a fifty-fifty chance in one
area of her life, maybe she should start gambling with
other aspects too. After all, to play it safe she'd come up
with plan B—keep everything superficial. Don't get involved. Take what she could from each day, and enjoy it.

All the possibilities left her mind reeling, with an
excited tickle under her skin, and a definite promise
to herself to find out what Jared's true intentions were.

All she had to do was pick a day.

CHAPTER FOUR

THE clinic felt like a ghost town the next morning, with only a handful of clients wandering in for various ailments. It was a good thing too, as Kasey was dragging from yesterday's manic pace. So were Vincent and Angie, Vincent being more quiet than usual and Angie with less of a scowl and making fewer snide remarks.

Later over lunch with Vincent in a hole-in-the-wall café three doors down, Kasey broached the topic still haunting her mind.

"V., can you go to an appointment with me on Saturday morning?"

"Are you finally getting highlights in your hair, and you want my guidance?" he said, eyes wide with excitement before taking a huge bite of his overstuffed sandwich.

Kasey loved his sense of humor and how he always managed to make her laugh, sometimes even when he wasn't trying to. "No, nerd ball, I've got a special test I need to take and I want you there with me."

All his attention settled on her face. "Is there something I should know?"

"I wanted to tell you on Friday night, but things got waylaid." Kasey gave him every single detail of her circumstances, noticing his eyes soften and well up by the time she'd finished. "So, I'd really like to have some back-up when I go for the test."

"Of course I'll be there, honey. Wouldn't miss it for the world. What time?" He got up, walked behind where she was sitting, leaned over and gave her a hug, his smooth cheek next to hers. He always smelled so good. "This Huntington's business is not going to happen to you. I won't let it. Do you hear me?"

Now she cried, too. She turned and they hugged closer. "Thanks, buddy."

"You bet."

Later, when they walked back to the clinic holding hands, she thought all a person really needed in the world was one good friend, and at the moment she held his hand tight.

Friday turned into another zoo day at the clinic, with patients arriving in groups. The weekend always brought in more folks—those warding off early illness, those making sure their pain medication would stretch through two more days, or those finally finding the time to get to the clinic about something that had been bothering them for weeks.

As the end of the day grew closer, Saturday's lab appointment loomed ahead, and a knot in the pit of Kasey's stomach wound tighter and tighter. She sat hunched over her desk, trying to convert pounds into kilograms and multiplying that by the dose of liquid antibiotics her pediatric patient in room four would need. Her brain as fuzzy as old cheese, she decided to use a calculator, and turned to walk to the cupboard.

Jared stood before her in faded jeans and a form-fitting pale blue sweater with the sleeves pushed up his forearms, which made his eyes so blue they were almost impossible to look at.

"What are you doing here?" she asked, just short of a gasp.

"I'm on my way out of town, decided to take a quick detour." He scratched his jaw. "Wanted to make sure everything was still a go for tomorrow."

"Yes. Vincent's going with me. I'll be at the lab in plenty of time." She forced a glance into his eyes, blinked and looked away as the nerve endings in her chest came alive. "Thanks again."

"Good." He didn't seem ready to leave, hands in his back pockets, glancing at his sports shoes and back at her. "You never got back to me."

Got back to him? She'd thought about him a dozen times since Tuesday. Remembering his almost-smile in between patients and how he'd gobbled down his burger on the run that night just like the rest of them. She'd used her index finger at the corner of her own mouth to let him know he'd had mustard there just before he'd entered a patient room. He'd gratefully licked it away while turning the doorknob, and she'd diverted her eyes because the sight of his tongue had thrown her for a loop. He'd gotten her the lab appointment, had said it was professional courtesy—to the tune of a thousand dollars: she'd researched the cost the next day—and offered her a ride home, and her impression of him had definitely changed for the better, but...

"You were supposed to tell me which day we can do dinner, remember?" His low and sexy voice rumbled through her already heightened nerve-endings, even if he was being pretty persistent.

The thought of Jared asking her to dinner had seemed so absurd that after he'd asked her she'd swept it to the back of her mind and tried to forget about it.

"Oh!" She leveled him with her stare. "You were just kidding, right?"

"Would I be here if I was kidding?"

By the look in his eyes, he wasn't fooling around. He wanted to take her to dinner and the thought of spending an entire evening with him, alone, made her palms tingle. After an awkward beginning, she'd survived Friday night at the bar and the coffee café with him, but this felt different. They'd broken the ice working side by side on Tuesday. He felt more familiar now, plus he knew her big secret.

She swallowed. "Well, in that case, Wednesday?"

"How about Monday? I just got scheduled for an evening Botox clinic on Wednesday that I have to participate in. And Tuesday is back to school night with the kids."

"Right." The thought of stone-faced Jared sticking needles into middle-aged women's faces for an entire evening brought some comic relief, though not nearly enough to help her relax.

Monday was so close. She'd need time to build up her defenses, to talk herself out of how gorgeous she found Jared, even if he was too darned serious and, when she thought about it, far too forward. She'd need time to ward off the self-consciousness of being an ordinary girl hanging out with a man who helped people look like movie stars. Every time he looked at her, the way he was doing right now, she wondered how far short of the mark she fell in his eyes.

He snapped his fingers. "So how about it?" he said.

She zipped out of her trance. "Dinner?"

"That's what I had in mind. Would you prefer dessert?" Something playful danced through his impatient gaze, sending her even more off balance.

She dropped her head. "Jared, I just don't get why—"

"I want to. Would you do me a favor and just say yes? Otherwise I'm gonna be late to get my kids." He looked at his watch.

Flustered and still off kilter, she laughed, and it helped. She unfisted her hand. "Okay. Sure. Thanks for asking. Wouldn't want to upset your ego." She half rolled her eyes, either an obvious sign of insecurity or a pure juvenile reaction, she wasn't sure which. The man had a way of mixing her up with a mere glance.

He approached and cupped her arm, giving it a squeeze. "Good luck tomorrow. I'll make you drink enough Monday night to forget all about waiting for the results. Deal?"

Frozen by the feel of his firm grasp, she found it hard to squeak out an answer. "Deal."

When she finally lifted her gaze, his look delved into her eyes, and more tiny zings of excitement zipped through her. This. Had. To stop.

He smiled. A real smile, not his usual tense excuse for one, and it was friendly, sexy and devious all at once. Way too devious. Kasey wasn't sure if her eyelids fluttered as his warmth rushed into her or if she drooled or what, because once again he'd stunned her to the spot.

"See you then," he said, letting go of her arm and walking off.

"Yeah, see you…" How the heck would she survive being around him if he dared look at her like that again?

On Saturday morning, Vincent sat in on the pre-test genetic counseling and Kasey was glad. Even though she'd studied genetics in science courses, her anxiety level kept her from taking in even one single sentence of information.

The clean, sterile-looking lab, with long white counters and stools, seemed more out of a movie set than a working lab. Behind swing doors with porthole windows she saw the functioning side of the department, with several people in white jackets bustling about, conducting various tests and other functions at their work stations.

After giving a speech about the autosomal dominant inheritance pattern, her fifty percent chance of inheriting it and drawing out a basic graph of stick figures indicating the four parent possibilities and the two child outcomes, the small, dried-apple-faced lab counselor, looked sympathetically through bifocals towards Kasey.

"We'll go ahead and make an appointment for you to see a neurologist, since it can take a few weeks to get a slot. In the meantime, I want you make a list to bring with you of any symptoms you may be experiencing, even if they don't seem related to the disease." He reached into his breast pocket. "Also, you can call this number to make an appointment with a therapist for extra support."

He handed her the business card, then several pieces of paper. "First, fill out this questionnaire, and then we'll draw the blood."

Vincent put his arm around her shoulder while she filled in her key personal information. He offered input when she balked at some of the questions.

"They want to know your recent life stress changes, so mention the main one—your father dropping this bombshell on you!"

"Oh, right," she said, her hand clammy and minutely trembling. She thought it might be due more to clutching the pen too tightly than early symptoms for Huntington's, yet she decided to include it on the questionnaire. *Hand tremors.* "Will you come with me to the neurologist appointment?"

"Of course!"

Having her best friend with her made the nerve-racking experience a bit more tolerable, but her heart thumped in her chest as if she'd taken the stairs instead of the elevator up all five floors. She'd grown up independent and strong, a conscious effort to be the exact opposite of her mother, yet under these circumstances she felt anything but confident.

After the paperwork, she was escorted to the blood draw table. Closing her eyes tight, she didn't watch when the lab tech tightened the tourniquet and took the blood sample. The only thing she could think about was how her entire future rested on this single vial of blood, and whether or not it contained a copy of the defective gene inherited from her father. A man she'd never even known. She hung and shook her head.

Light perspiration beaded above her lip, and the lab tech looked a little startled, as if she'd gone white or something. He reached into his pocket for an ammonia ampoule.

"I'm fine," she said, pulse pounding in her ears. "I didn't even feel the needle."

She took three deep breaths, clutched Vincent's hand, waited several seconds before she stood, then left the building, refusing to drag her feet, determined to enjoy the rest of her day. What was the alternative, go home and pull her bedcovers over her head?

With an appointment with a neurologist in one hand and a tentative follow-up lab appointment in one month to discuss the results in the other, and with Vincent by her side, she pushed through the large glass doors and out onto the loud and busy boulevard.

"Let's have lunch," she said, not feeling the least bit hungry. "My treat."

What her future would bring couldn't be stopped, and she wasn't really sure she wanted to find out, but she could make the rest of the day as pleasant as possible. It was, by far, her best option.

Just before closing on Monday night, Jared arrived at the community clinic through the back door looking gorgeous but distracted. His hair looked as if he'd run his fingers through it more than a few times. Kasey sat at her desk, typing the finishing touches on some nurse's notes. He approached with a grim, preoccupied expression instead of a friendly greeting.

"Are you ready?" he asked.

She swiveled around to face him head on. "You look sick or something. Are you sure you want to go through with this?"

With still no evidence of a smile, he sent a sharp look her way. "We made plans, I'm here, let's go."

Let's go? He sure knew how to make a girl feel special. "What makes you think I want to be stuck with a sourpuss like you for dinner?"

"We'll talk. Come on, grab your purse."

"No."

Surprised, as if he'd never been refused before, he lifted a brow and quit fiddling with his car keys. "No?"

She swiveled her chair back toward the desk. "You can't come in here with that attitude and expect me to jump at the chance of spending an hour with you."

"Two hours for dinner, at least." Her retort had bounced off his armor. "Now, come on, let's go."

"Not even five minutes. No way. I'm not a masochist." Secretly she'd been looking forward all day to seeing Jared tonight, but now she wasn't sure about spending the evening with him in this mood.

"I need to get out of here." He walked up to where she was sitting, took her wrist in his hand, turned and headed for the door. Refusing to stand, she let him pull the office chair on wheels a few feet across the floor. It felt silly, he looked ridiculous, and she needed to take charge or be humiliated. Was that his thing? To treat women like office furniture, to be moved at will, as he saw fit?

Rather than make an even bigger scene, since Vincent and Angie had already stopped what they were doing to watch, Kasey skidded her feet on the floor as brakes, stood, made a big deal about needing to grab her purse from her desk four feet away, and followed him. She'd put an end to their so-called date the minute they hit the street.

He glanced over his shoulder, this time with a grateful look, and there it was, the hint of pain in his eyes. She'd seen it the very first day they'd met, and again at the bar when he'd mentioned his kids. Obviously something was going on, and he wasn't capable of talking about it right now. A twinge of compassion, though against her better judgment, changed her decision to stick it out with him.

"See you guys tomorrow," she said as he tugged her impatiently towards the door.

"Have fun, kids," Vincent said, in an obvious attempt to lighten the atmosphere.

"Yeah, don't do anything I wouldn't do," Angie said in her monotone voice and with the usual pained expression.

Jared ignored both of them.

"Will do," Kasey said, tossing them a perplexed glance.

When they got to the car, Jared glanced at her feet. "Are those shoes okay for walking?"

"Yes. I've walked in them all day."

"Good, because if you don't mind, I'd like to walk awhile before we eat."

"How far are we walking?"

"I'm not sure. I'll know when I start to feel better."

"What's on your mind, Jared?" He opened the passenger door for her. "I thought we were walking?"

"Not here, once we get there."

"Where's there?" She jutted out her hip and placed her hand on it. "You're confusing the heck out of me."

"Where we're having dinner."

He hadn't made eye contact since he'd first arrived and still looked agitated as all hell. Something big was going on. More confused than ever, she got into his nondescript sedan, the questions building with each second.

"We'll talk later," he said, leaning in before shutting the door.

Tension seemed to rise off him like a heat wave over asphalt. She was quite sure it had nothing to do with her, so she sat back and rested her head on the upholstery. Until he was ready to talk, there was no way she'd get anything out of him. But, really, did she need this stress on top of her own problems?

Once he was inside the car, she pinned him with her stare and a surprise attack. "You owe me a lobster dinner for this, buddy."

One corner of his mouth twitched. Zing, she'd chinked his armor. "How about a lobster roll? I'm on a budget."

She shook her head and smiled, grateful he was loosening up. "Whatever."

With that he started the car and headed south on Route 99, the second movement of Beethoven's Seventh Symphony on his CD player perfectly matching his overly dramatic mood. Hmm, she hadn't pegged him as a classical music guy. She glanced around and noticed evidence of his kids in the car with a discarded takeaway bag under her feet and a bag of half-eaten chips left on the dashboard. At least he wasn't obsessive-compulsive clean, like so many other surgeons she'd known.

A little over twenty minutes later they parked in the hospital doctors' lot. Once again without a word, he grabbed her hand, and they walked a few blocks until they hit the meandering Charles River Path from north station Causeway, by Paul Revere Park and the USS Constitution Museum.

"Are you jogging or do you call this walking?" Kasey said, trying to keep up with Jared's determined stride, the constant feel of his hand heating up her arm. It was drizzling and she wished she'd brought her umbrella. He didn't seem to care.

"Sorry," he said, deep in thought, as he slowed down the slightest bit, not letting go of her but pulling her along.

The brisk evening air gave Kasey new energy, but she wasn't ready to run a mile for her dinner. The distraction of being palm to palm with him grew harder to ignore with each step. "So where're we going?"

"The Tavern on the Water."

She'd heard of it, but had never been there. "Good food?"

"Good view. And they've got lobster rolls."

"Better be good." She was out of breath. "You ready to talk yet?"

"Nope." He picked up the pace, and she promised herself not to bring up his talking again unless she felt like breaking into a sprint.

Ten minutes later they arrived at a two-story boat-house with a superb view of the harbor. Due to the drizzle, which hadn't let up and had most assuredly left her hair frizzy and a mess, they headed straight upstairs and inside.

The place was crowded with young professionals from the nearby schools, businesses, and medical facilities. Jared nearly had to elbow his way to the bar.

"Two beers." He named his favorite brand and the pale ale she'd been drinking the other night. Interesting, he'd remembered.

He handed her the bottle and led her to a tall table in the corner that had just opened up.

After she got settled, took a sip of her beer, and sized up Jared's supersized foul mood, she decided to read the menu rather than provoke him with more questions. The cozy harbor view calmed her, and after the energetic walk she was more than ready to eat, even if the company was the worst she'd been around in ages. Actually, not so. She remembered a spectacularly horrible date a couple months back. At least Jared was pretty to look at. Maybe he wasn't so bad after all.

Jared took a long slow draw on his beer. He must have come straight from work because he wore dark slacks and a sports coat and a lilac-colored shirt, accenting his eyes. But then again, what didn't? She noticed how his lashes were so thick they separated into clumps, then she looked quickly away at some ultra-chic apartments right on the waterfront.

After another swallow or two Kasey saw the bunched muscle at the corner of Jared's jaw twitch, then give up as if worn out. He stared hard at the pewter-colored water. All the happy little party lights blinking along the window-frame couldn't change his mood. She knew better than to think she could either. After several drawn-out sighs and another drink of beer, he placed the bottle on the table between his hands and worked at turning it round and round while peeling at the label.

"So, my kids told me they're going to Europe for a month this summer." He tore a big chunk off the label for emphasis. "Four flipping weeks."

He stared at Kasey with furious eyes, and an old saying came to mind: *If looks could kill.* Hey, buddy, I didn't do it!

"Would have been nice to know, as I was planning a camping trip in New Hampshire with them before school started up again." He looked like a man ready to punch a wall. "And here's the real kicker, they miss their friends back home and want to move back to California. Patrice has already found a new school for them, this one's in Malibu. They'll start in the fall."

Kasey noticed he had several scratches across the slightly swollen knuckles of his right hand, and wondered if he'd already punched something.

He was a surgeon. He wouldn't risk hurting his hands…would he? But his ex was playing games with him, even she could see that.

"She knows I'm committed here for another year, and she didn't even consult me on it."

Kasey knew better than to say a word. Her job would be to listen tonight, and seeing Jared's tortured gaze, knowing how much his kids meant to him, she changed her perspective, suddenly willing to listen for as long as it took.

"It's so frustrating to be left out of the loop about something this important, as if I don't count." His gaze lifted to meet hers. "I'm their father, dammit. I'm not going to just give up and go away."

"I think that's great. The world needs more fathers like you."

Her words softened his glare. "Thank you." He looked downright grateful and definitely more handsome when he didn't scowl. He reached for her forearm, his long fingers lightly caressing her skin before they slid south and patted her hand then retreated to his side of the table. "I needed to hear that."

"I meant it. You obviously care a great deal about your kids." She gazed at him long enough to connect with his intense eyes, which sent a tiny shiver through her.

As far as first dates went, this one was a doozy, but how could she be mad at a man so hungry to be involved with his children? Wouldn't she have given anything in the world to know her father when she was a kid? She glanced up and caught him staring at her. He didn't look like he was thinking about his children just then.

If a man could be this passionate about his children, could he be the same about a woman? His touch had heated her skin, and the guy wasn't even trying to come on to her.

Kasey needed another sip of beer to ward off the threatening and highly inappropriate warmth starting in an unmentionable part of her body. That brisk walk had really gotten her blood flowing and right now it had pooled in a spot she shouldn't even be thinking about.

"Patrick has been telling me he misses his soccer

buddies back home, and Chloe texts her best friend back in California every day, but I thought they were okay with this school, and I'm here. Doesn't that count for something?"

"That's what frequent flyer programs are for," she said. "And red-eyes."

He screwed up his face. "Come again?"

"Be the game changer in your relationship with your kids. Be there for them no matter what. You'll just have to fly back to California every other weekend to see the kids. Let them know you will *always* be in their lives, no matter where they live."

The corner of his mouth twitched, tension left his eyes, his brows smoothed. "Good point. I won't take this lying down."

Hearing him say the words *lying down* planted another improper thought in her head. What was her problem?

Meanwhile, he continued to talk and, though she'd temporarily tuned out, she studied him carefully. His dark lashes curtained incredible eyes. The nostrils of his straight nose microscopically flared with emotion while he continued to pour out his heart. Only hearing a word here and there, she watched, thinking inappropriate thoughts. Back at the office he'd been pushy, but now these words about his family came straight from his heart. It touched her in a way that took her by surprise, and, shameful as it was, turned her on.

The guy needed to let off some steam or his head would burst. These days, she could relate to that feeling. Heck, she needed to let off some steam, too. Though she couldn't possibly know his reasons for asking her to dinner, she liked this wicked physical response he drew out of her without even trying. What magic could he spin if he tried?

He'd kept her preoccupied, and she liked it that she hadn't lost a single second to her own worries so far tonight.

Yeah, she'd cut Jared some slack, let him talk all he wanted. Not only because he made her feel horny but because she really wanted him not to hurt so much. Besides, if history really did repeat itself, after tonight she'd probably never see the dude again anyway. So tonight she'd be a team player, help him forget about his worries.

And later, as superficial as it sounded, maybe she'd get lucky.

CHAPTER FIVE

WHAT in the hell was Jared doing, spilling his secrets to a woman he hardly knew? Kasey sat across the table squirming with discomfort and yet he couldn't shut up. Could he help it if she was easy to talk to? Every date guru in the world warned against talking about your last relationship with the new. Relationship? Was that what this was about? He'd only met her a week ago.

And yet. No. Absolutely not. He wasn't in the market for a relationship. It took too much effort, and his ex had cured him of believing in love. From now on he'd keep life uninvolved and uncomplicated where women were concerned.

"Maybe you can take the kids camping at the beginning of summer? You know, before they go to Europe?" She picked up her overflowing-with-lobster roll and took a vigorous bite. Why did he find that sexy? Damn, he needed to get out more.

"I have no choice," he said, digging into his own lobster roll, "but I'll do it, even if it means changing my plans."

"Cuz…love…kids. You…gud fah-fer." It sounded muffled by food, but he got the gist of what she'd said.

He sighed, and chewed without interest in taste or texture. He'd spent enough time working himself up over a situation he couldn't change. He needed to let it go, give himself a break. Hell, he sat across from a young and vibrant woman, a fresh natural breath of air from what he'd dealt with all day. Tonight she seemed to be the game-changer. His eyes were drawn to the neckline of her loose-weave summer sweater, and the pale silver camisole beneath—not a hint of breast on view, yet the fit promised natural curves and fascinated the heck out of him.

It occurred to him how twisted his mind had become. He'd spent the day looking at women's breasts both pre—and post-surgery, and hadn't had one single sexual thought. Quite the contrary. He'd been all business. Yet Kasey, taking a great big bite of lobster roll and wearing a conservatively cut sweater, managed to stir up some purely prurient thoughts. He took it as a healthy breakthrough then wondered what she'd look like with her hair loose and tousled after a night in bed.

Was that the real reason he'd pushed for dinner tonight? Disappointment stopped him in mid-bite. He'd been concerned enough about Kasey to arrange for the genetic testing, genuinely concerned, and worried what her outcome might be, too. More than anything, he was surprised that he had a shred of empathy for anyone these days. She'd come out of nowhere and blindsided him.

He knew she needed a friend. Yet tonight he'd selfishly used her because she was a nurse and a good listener.

Right now, watching her eat, well, his wandering thoughts were anything but appropriate. Again, she'd blindsided him, and he needed to rein himself in.

Kasey lifted her gaze and unselfconsciously gave a bulging, closed-mouthed smile. She covered her mouth with the napkin, those mischievous green eyes peering over the top. "This is delicious."

"I'm glad." He smiled, thinking she was delicious, too. Delicious to look at. He went back to eating, all stirred up. Though feeling guilty about them, he liked the stirred-up feelings. Welcomed them. Great. Just what he needed, more confusion in his life. "For putting up with me, you deserve some dessert."

She smiled, and over the course of dinner he'd looked forward to each smile she shared. "Only if you'll share it with me."

An hour later, uncomfortably full from the chocolate molten cake, and as it had quit drizzling, he suggested they walk a bit more.

"If we stroll, count me in," she said, "but I'm through jogging." Again, she lanced him with those mischievous eyes.

He smiled, enjoying how she always sparked a reaction. "Okay." Realizing his mood had shifted from sour to spicy over the course of the meal, he wasn't ready to call it a night. Not nearly.

This time she beat him to it. She grabbed his hand and, though surprised, he twined his fingers through hers, completely aware of the connection and the hot path winding through his body.

He looked into her gaze. It wasn't his imagination. He saw the dark spark in her eyes, too. "I've been very selfish tonight."

She cocked her head. "You think?"

"I apologize."

"Don't worry about it."

Her easygoing manner enchanted him, but the fit of her sweater and curve of her slacks moved him far beyond enchantment. Hell, where was his head tonight?

The woman was literally waiting for a potential death sentence. A brutally cruel curse of a disease that would alter the course of her life, and he'd griped about not getting his fair share of parenting time through most of dinner. He ought to be dragged into the bay and dunked. But he could fix things. She'd given him several suggestions, too.

Maybe he could help Kasey open up and talk about her fears. He didn't want her to keep things tucked inside on his behalf. She deserved the same freedom he felt with her.

Had some empathetic person snuck in and inhabited his body? This wasn't his style at all, yet…

"Are you going to seek counseling?" he said. "I've heard…"

Kasey stepped in front of him, cupped his jaw with both hands and pulled him closer. "I don't want to talk about anything else tonight," she said, just before planting her mouth on his.

Stopped in his tracks, and not the least bit interested in arguing the point, he kissed her back. Her sweetly padded lips were smooth and warm and she moved them over his with vigor. Wanting more control, he scooped her waist close with one hand and cupped the back of her neck with the other, then shifted his head for a deeper kiss, a slick, silky kiss. She tasted sweet, like chocolate syrup, and his mind scrolled through thoughts of licking that syrup off a thousand different parts of her body. He groaned.

Her hands were now in his hair, and he held her so close his belt buckle pushed into his skin. The soft press of her breasts on his chest was his undoing. His fingertips skimmed from hip to waist to side, stopping at her breast, lifting and pressing the plump softness. He couldn't resist taking her breast into his hand, stroking his thumb over the nipple. This time he was positive the groan came from her side of the embrace.

As their mouths kissed and devoured and plunged, he became aware of two things—her hands had found their way under his shirt, working wonders on his skin, and he had a full, throbbing erection.

Good thing it was dark out.

They broke for air, and her panting breath turned him on even more, if that was possible. Forehead to forehead, he nosed down her cheek then nibbled her ear. Everything he did got a reaction out of her, making the situation below his belt more unbearable. He didn't want to stop, but they were in public, and a nurse and a doctor, well. Weren't they supposed to be practical about such things?

Her hand discovered his bulge, she gently squeezed, and since he couldn't think any more, he moved in for more kisses and full body presses.

The wake of a distant motorboat lapped a bucket worth of water over the harbor deck, and their feet were suddenly drenched.

Jared and Kasey gasped in unison.

Jared had never driven so recklessly in his life. Kasey gave him directions for the back route, and called out the turns. *Left here. Take your next right. Yield to the right. See that brick building? Turn left there. No. There.* He wondered if she'd be a bossy lover, and marveled over the fact he was pretty damn sure he was about to find out, and might even like it.

They made it to her home in less than twenty minutes, though they had to drive around the block once to backtrack for parking on her one-way street.

Still completely turned on, Jared watched as Kasey fiddled with her keys at the side of the house, before bursting through the door. Burning to touch her again, he grabbed her and waltzed her against the kitchen counter for another kiss.

"Wait!" She pushed him away. "I've got to turn off the alarm." He was so focused, he hadn't even heard it.

In a heartbeat she'd done the task, then grabbed him by the hand and tugged him through the kitchen down a short hallway to her bedroom.

The unmade bed looked completely inviting. He'd singlehandedly unbuttoned his shirt and slid out of half of it before he'd even hit the room. Her neck and ears were still red from their makeout session by the harbor, and the hold-onto-your-hats ride home hadn't lessened the sexy sparkle in her eyes.

She pulled the loose-knit sweater and cami over her head and he sucked in his breath at the sight of her lacy-bra-covered breasts. She was deliciously curvy, and he couldn't wait to hold and feel her again. Now both half-undressed, they came together in a tight embrace. He savored her warmth and smooth skin, the impact of her body so close to his, and his hands skated over her, searching for the bra clasp. On the way, he got distracted kissing the curve of her shoulder and just below her ear, and was rewarded with another deep sigh and shiver. Kasey seemed completely in tune with him, every touch and each kiss emitting uninhibited reactions, which turned him on more and more. He removed her bra and felt the heat and weight of her breasts in his palms, wanting nothing more than to bury his face in them. Her pebbled, rosy-pink nipples called out to be kissed. He wanted to do everything at once, all while being buried inside her.

They needed to get completely naked. Fast!

Kasey kicked off her shoes and shimmied out of her slacks and underpants while Jared did the same. God, he was sexy. Not an ounce of excess flesh anywhere, natural muscles rippled and flinched with each move. And, man, oh, man, was he ready for her.

Not thinking. Not thinking. Keep it superficial.

She shooed Miss Daisy off the bed and received a serious warning glance and meow. "Sorry, sweetie." Her cat had gotten used to being the center of her attention, and as Kasey dove on top of Jared, already reclined on the bed and reaching out for her, the cat got the point and took off.

Jared's smooth, hot skin was reward enough, but the hooded, dark-sea stare nearly made her crumple at his feet. *I am not worthy but, boy, am I glad he's here.*

His hands with long surgeon's fingers welcomed every part of her body, soon finding two favorite spots, her right butt cheek and left breast, where his mouth did amazing things. She'd been wet and ready since their world-class kiss in Charlestown, so she straddled his hips and, sweet heaven on earth, he adjusted himself, pressing against and sliding over the pick-me-first nub outside. Several moments passed, doing this heady teasing dance, his erection nudging and massaging her, his hands exploring her breasts, heightening her desire, tension twining ever tighter in her core. Being above and in charge, though feeling completely out of control, she widened her thighs, hoping he'd slide inside.

As though getting a sudden slap in the face, common sense reared its frustrating head. "Wait."

Jared came out of his trance, but barely.

"Condom," she breathed, her breasts skimming his chin when he lifted his head, his eyes looking on fire.

Jared dropped his head on the pillow with a thud and let out a frustrated moan.

"What? No just-in-case-I-get-lucky wrapper in your wallet?"

He shook his head, his lustful look quickly dissolving into disappointment. So he really wasn't a Casanova. Good. "You didn't plan this?"

"I just wanted someone to gripe to tonight, and you were it. Didn't expect you to be so sexy about it."

He was a gentleman after all, hadn't come prepared, hadn't planned on screwing her. The thought turned her on even more.

"Good thing one of us is prepared, then," she said pertly as she reached across the bed for the drawer. She'd been off the dating market for a while, but still probably had some condoms. Somewhere. She sure hoped so, anyway, and if she was lucky, they wouldn't be outdated.

While Kasey balanced on one knee and hand to reach across the bed and pull out the drawer with the other, Jared scooted down and shocked her with a deep kiss and nibble. A reward? Just as she grabbed the condom, when he included his tongue along with another kiss at her entrance, all thoughts left her head, instead pooling between her legs where Jared sent deliciously warm shockwaves throughout her body.

She didn't move and he didn't stop.

A few minutes later, crumpled by her orgasm but determined to stay on top, she sheathed him and guided him inside, and his groan of pleasure matched hers. Looking down into his sex-darkened eyes, his hands moving her hips over his heat and strength, seeing the blissful satisfaction on his face, she powered on as a second release rolled through her.

* * *

Where has this gorgeous, sexy woman been all my life?
Unable to hold back another second, Jared rolled Kasey
onto her back and lifted her hips to meet his quicken-
ing thrusts. Her body melted into his. He hadn't spent
nearly enough time marveling in it, but it was too late
now, they'd moved way past getting acquainted. He'd
take it slower next time.

Hard and harder he took her. Every last bit of energy
in his body focused on their connection, the sheer perfection of it. Her heat and tight feel. Her total response
to him as he realized she'd come again. Her quivering
over and around his erection as he drove deeper. The
power and intensity sent him over the edge, releasing
a mega-force of staggering pleasure, completely losing
himself to the sky dive.

Kasey woke to a quiet room, two eyes staring at her.
Miss Daisy. Miffed from inattention. She sat up. The
other side of the bed was empty. She should have known
better than to expect to see Jared there. They'd given in
to desire. Lust. Pure and simple. He'd made love to her
twice, the first crazy, like scratching an itch, the second much slower and even more amazing. Wow. She'd
lost count of her orgasms.

She sat at the side of the bed. No, she wouldn't let
self-doubt sneak in. This was her plan B. Superficial,
uncomplicated sex. They were adults and had done
exactly what they'd wanted to do. That was all.

She walked to the kitchen to make some coffee and
feed the cat. Her body felt alive and maybe a little achy
but, wow, she liked feeling this way. He'd kept her so
busy and content she hadn't had a single second to
worry about her future. And she'd slept like a rock.

"Maybe I can sign him up for the next month until I

get my results, huh, Daisy?" The cat rubbed her ankle and walked between her legs.

"I'll probably never see him again, you know." She stood straighter, squaring her shoulders before stooping to feed the cat. "I don't need to. What's the point?" She scratched the cat's ears while Daisy ate.

A small piece of paper caught her eye on the kitchen table. *Had an early surgery. Thanks for last night.*

Although there was no mention of calling her, at least it was something. They'd had dinner, then sex. He'd left a note. This was the protocol for a no-strings kind of fling, just what she needed.

Kasey would put on her armor and deal with the consequences of having wildly hot sex with Dr Tall, Dark and Gorgeous, like a grown-up.

She'd done it. It was fantastic. Now it was time to forget him and move on before she invested any feelings in him. There was just one flaw to that logic. It wasn't her style, and she already had.

CHAPTER SIX

WEDNESDAY afternoon at the clinic, with not a single word from Jared since Monday night, Kasey went through a stack of lab results. Franklin O'Leary's lab studies were back, and it wasn't good news. They'd found cancer cells in the paracentesis fluid and he would need further studies, possibly hospitalization, to help discern the primary source of cancer.

Kasey scrolled through the makeshift file she had for him, and found his cellphone number.

She'd tried her best to put Jared out of her mind since Monday night, deciding he was nothing more than a one-hit wonder. Wonder being the perfect word to describe what she'd experienced when making love with him. Now, with the discovery of cancer cells in Franklin's ascites, she felt compelled to tell Jared.

A hard lump formed in the pit of her stomach, followed by a queasy wave. Consequences. Damn it all, she'd acted exactly like her mother, and now had to face the consequences. She'd had sex with a man she hardly knew, a fellow professional, and though they didn't officially work together, she'd crossed the line on her personal rule. Now she'd still have to follow up with Jared on a strictly business level. It wouldn't be easy, but she needed to give him Franklin O'Leary's lab report.

She scrubbed her hands over her face, took a deep breath, and dialed his cellphone number. After four rings, it went to voicemail. Deciding to ignore the phony chirpy social voice, she kept her message all business, gave him the results and asked how he'd like to follow up.

With cancer cells floating around in abdominal fluid, which meant metastases, Mr. O'Leary needed to be seen immediately. She'd give Jared an hour to get back to her then she'd contact Franklin herself and ask him to come in to the community clinic as soon as possible. If necessary, she could request hospital admission for him.

The next chart to cross her desk made her sit up straighter. Bat bite? Did the city of Everett even have bats? Wondering what waited in room number three, she headed down the hall.

A young girl sat sullenly on the examination table, her mother standing next to her wearing a worried expression, biting her lips, fear apparent in the form of constricted pupils.

After introductions, Kasey asked the mother to get right to the story.

"Tessa has nightmares about once a week, and last night she ran down the hall telling me a bird was in her room and it woke her up when it bit her. My husband checked it out and couldn't find anything, but this morning I found this on her."

The mother lifted the six-year-old's long, brown hair to show two tiny pin prick marks on her shoulder. Kasey paused as a rush of possibilities scrolled through her head. The marks didn't look like a scratch, or any spider bite she'd ever seen, unless it was one huge spider.

"Do you own a kitten or puppy?"

The woman shook her head.

"And your husband didn't find anything in Tessa's room?"

She shook her head again. "He turned on the lights and did a quick sweep of her room. I've kept the door closed and haven't gone back in because I think there's a bat in there." Tears welled in the young mother's eyes and the child, picking up on her mother's distress, got restless.

"I want to go. Can we go now?"

"In a minute, honey," the mother said.

"What makes you think it's a bat?" Kasey asked.

"I've read about bats being able to bite people without them feeling it." She scratched her neck, with nervous, quick-moving fingers and whispered, "I'm worried about rabies." She creased her lips tightly to hold back the fear mounting in her eyes.

What the heck was *she* supposed to do? She needed to research bat bites before she could give an educated answer or allay this woman's fears. Only one thought prompted her to answer—what if she was a mother and this was her child?

"Though it is possible, it is highly unlikely that this is a bat bite. And even if it is a bat bite, the odds of that bat having rabies are low. I'd have to look up the incidence of rabies in our bat populations."

"What's rabies?" Tessa asked.

Oh, gosh, Kasey had forgotten how attuned young children were to adult conversations. She'd blown it, and wanted to kick herself for potentially scaring the little girl. "It's like an infection, and if a person has it they need to have medicine to treat it."

Tears, like small waterfalls, splashed over the mother's lower lids. Kasey was treating two patients, one who needed to calm down. But could she blame the mother? Fear of the unknown could start as a spark and spread to a flash fire if not handled properly.

"Like the pink stuff I take sometimes?"

"This medicine is different, but maybe you won't have to take it," Kasey said.

That seemed to satisfy the little one's curiosity.

"Well, here's what I recommend we do. First I'll wash this area for several minutes. Did you wash it with soap and water last night?" The mother nodded. "Good. Is Tessa up to date on her immunizations? Tetanus?"

The mother nodded again.

"Good." Kasey fished through the cabinets for a surgical sponge that already had antiseptic soap infused in it. She popped open the plastic and got it wet then began scrubbing the little girl's shoulder. "Does this hurt?" Tessa shook her head. "Since you haven't opened the bedroom door since last night, maybe you can have a pest-control person come and search the room for evidence of a bat?"

"I'll do whatever you say I should," the mother said.

When Kasey finished up the wash and left tincture of iodine over the two tiny marks they'd agreed as the course of action. Kasey gave Tessa a cherry lollypop and some stickers, though worry made the young one's eyes look even bigger. On the way out, as the child ran ahead, the mother grabbed Kasey's arm. "What if it is a bat bite, and we find it and it does have rabies?"

"We'd have to begin rabies post-exposure prophylaxis within ten days. Don't panic yet. We don't even know if this is a possibility. Please try to stay calm. I know it's hard."

The woman's clutch on Kasey's arm let up. "We've only got ten days to figure this out?"

Kasey gave a solemn nod.

After they left, Kasey didn't know if the mother was delusional or on top of a rare but conceivable possibility. Since the clinic was slow this afternoon, she went directly to her desk and computer to do some research, soon getting lost in the project and losing track of time. At least these days the treatment wasn't as bad as in the past. No more multiple painful injections into the abdomen. These days it would be like receiving a flu shot, five different times over four weeks, along with an initial intradermal immune globulin close to the actual site of the bite.

A shadow darkened her computer screen. Assuming it was Vincent being snoopy, she turned in her swivel chair, ready with a smart-aleck remark. But there stood Jared, dark brown polo shirt, piercing blue eyes, as handsome as ever. All thoughts left her head. The adrenaline pop in her chest couldn't be ignored. She chose irritation as her cover.

"Do you *not* know how to call first?"

"What would be the fun of that?" A slow, sexy smile stretched across his face and she thought she might turn to a puddle of drool right before his eyes, so she kept up her tough-chick act.

"Seriously. You've got to quit showing up out of the blue."

He rolled over Vincent's swivel chair, turned it backwards and threw his leg over like a cowboy mounting a horse. Crossing his elbows over the back, he continued to smile, undaunted by her hardball façade.

"You called. I'm here."

"Don't you have some Botox clinic tonight or something?"

"I asked a first-year fellow to take over." He reached out and touched her shoulder, sending another titillating message in the form of tiny feathers tickling flesh and nerve endings. "So let's see those lab results."

After fishing around her desk for the printed-out labs, she found them and handed them to him. "You'll never guess what I saw today," she said.

"The elephant man?"

She screwed up her face and shook her head. "Where do you get your ideas?"

He shrugged. "You told me to guess."

"You're weird. Never mind. I saw a little girl with a potential bat bite."

"Get out of town!"

"Really. I hope her mother is wrong."

"Me too," he said, now seriously studying the lab results. "Did you call Franklin O'Leary?"

"I was waiting to hear from you." She picked up the phone and dialed, with little hope of actually reaching the patient. Surprise, surprise, he picked up on the first ring.

Kasey gave Franklin the lowdown about his lab reports being back and asked if he could come to the clinic to talk about them. More surprise, he said he'd be right over.

"I was going to come pay you a visit anyway, Ms. McGowan, because my tummy's getting big again, and I'm feeling a bit weird today."

"That's definitely a good reason to come right away, Franklin. We'll see you as soon as you can get here."

After reading the labs, Jared's expression changed. "We need to admit him to the hospital."

"Agreed."

"We'll talk to Mr. O'Leary first, then I'll call in my admission report."

"Vincent can help you with anything you need."

Jared reached over the chair and lightly traced Kasey's jaw with his fingertips. "I don't think he can help me with *everything* I need."

Okay, he'd stopped her cold again, had her at hello, as the movie went. How was she supposed to respond? She wanted to ask why he hadn't called her, but that hardly qualified for relationship-lite status. Besides, she'd turned over a new leaf, hadn't she? Since she had a potential health crisis hanging over her head, the answer to which she wouldn't know for sure for a couple of weeks, shouldn't she live one day at a time and just go for it? Knock him on/off balance by being the no-strings-attached bedroom pal of his dreams?

What about the pep talk that morning? She'd already let her guard down, and some feelings had seeped in for Jared. It wasn't safe to play no-strings starting out with a handicap. But he was there, looking sexy as hell, making all the right moves and saying all the right things.

Damn, she was easy.

She swallowed against a suddenly dry throat, feeling completely out of character from her usual practical and cautious self. "Any time. You name the place." She was quite sure a mischievous gaze accompanied her parry.

After a small but obvious burst of something in his eyes—surprise or turn-on, she wasn't sure which—he glanced around the office with a purposeful gaze.

"Hold on, not here, cowboy," she lifted her hands, steadying the nervous boost.

He lifted his brows and cocked his head. "Was worth a shot."

There was that wicked sexy smile again. The game was on. She shook her head, feigning disgust.

In one week he'd morphed from a standoffish merely obligated surgeon into the sexiest thing she'd seen in a white coat in her entire life. Huntington's be damned, she was going for it, living in the solid present and not going to bother to look back…or forward. At least, not yet.

"Maybe we should lay down some rules with this thing…" she gestured with her hand back and forth between them "…we've got going."

"Such as?"

"No showing up out of the blue."

"What's the fun in that?"

"Okay," she said. "How about you don't have to feel obligated to call me the next day."

"Unless I want to?"

"Unless you want to."

"On this list of rules of yours, is there a limit on how often I can see you?"

"That's a good question."

"Did I tell you I hate lists?"

"We can skip the list, but I feel like we need some ground rules."

"I've lived by ground rules my entire life," he said. "Just once I'd like to wing it."

"You mean, just see how it goes?"

"A novel idea. Let's do that."

"I don't know how that works."

"I don't either, but I like the way it sounds." He grilled her with his dark look. "It sounds sexy. Exciting. Just like you."

If looks could kill, then looks could also make a woman turned on to the point of squirming in her swivel chair. She refused to be the first to look away. Her throat went parchment dry.

Jared unwrapped his leg from the chair, and instead of stealing a kiss he walked across the office to the water cooler. Such a tease. He wasn't the only one needing a cold drink.

Vincent finally discovered him and started a conversation. Shaken by their attempt and subsequent failure to figure out how to handle what apparently was a budding hot-to-the-point-of-nuclear-fusion affair, she rushed back into safe territory, to the bat research.

Kasey looked great in her bright pink scrubs. He even liked the matching clogs and socks with tiny pink hearts around the rim. Not at all the kind of outfit he'd expect a wild and sexy bedroom buddy to wear. How could they put rules on this thing between them? First they'd have to figure out what it was, and he feared if they did that, the label would ruin all the fun. Couldn't they just go with it? Figure things out as they went along? The thought was as new and refreshing as the cooler water.

Jared covertly watched Kasey at her computer while chatting with Vincent near the water cooler. Her hair was parted on the side and pulled up into a loose bun with plenty of straggling strands to make him want to twist them around his finger and pull her close for a kiss. It was the first thought he'd had when he'd seen her today and a continuing image now.

What the hell had he been doing, acting all smooth earlier, as if ready to play a wolf and sex kitten game? Was he ready to pull off an affair? Totally out of character, he admitted he liked the break from his usual responsibilities and cares, and he definitely liked spending down time with Kasey. A quick flash of her naked and on top of him made him refill his paper water cup and take a huge gulp. What was Vincent talking about? Now was not the time or place to give in to a rapidly building desire for her, and the feeling was no doubt the other L word—nothing more than unadulterated lust. Yeah, that was the angle he'd take this time around.

He hadn't called her since Monday because he didn't want to come on too strong, yet that was exactly what he'd just been doing. Vincent was telling him something, but he didn't have a clue what it was.

He had never had an affair when he'd been married, that wasn't part of his honor code, and if he was going to start one now, maybe they should keep to the rules. Yet he'd teased and played with her when she'd tried to make up a rule or two just now. Damn, he was out of his element. All he knew for sure was he wanted what happened Monday night to happen again. And soon. Maybe he should make that rule number one.

"These are all of the admission papers you'll need to fill out for the hospital," Vincent said. "We can do a quick physical here first."

"Sure thing." Jared reminded himself he'd come here for business, but after work he'd give himself permission to enjoy life a little.

As if she knew he was thinking about her, Kasey looked up and their gazes connected. Studying her face, he decided he wouldn't surgically change a thing about her. She had a perfectly fine face and body and didn't need to lift, tighten, plump or slenderize a single feature.

The surprising thought made him smile. She smiled back and a warm itchy trail began in his chest and headed south.

Kasey knew he was only in Boston for another year, that he planned to move back to California to open his own practice as soon as he finished his fellowship in the American College of Surgeons for Plastic Surgery. He also understood she was facing a potentially debilitating diagnosis regarding Huntington's and probably didn't want to start a serious affair with anyone until she knew what her future held. In other words, she wasn't looking for anything permanent any more than he was.

No strings was the phrase of the day, and the more he thought about it, the better it sounded.

Angie approached with her laptop opened, interrupting his thoughts. "Mr. O'Leary's here," she said, her eyes tight as if the fluorescent lights were too bright.

"Thanks," he said, taking the computer. "Send him right in."

Kasey didn't like the way Franklin looked, noticeably thinner and with the abdomen back to protruding as it had before. He was also pale and grimacing as if in pain. She jumped up to help him into the exam room. His skin felt clammy yet cold.

"Are you okay?" she asked.

"Just a bit short of breath today is all," he said, maintaining a charming façade. The thought of what they'd have to tell him later made her heartsick.

"Have a seat on the gurney and I'll take your temperature." She rolled over the stand containing the all-in-one blood-pressure cuff, thermometer, and pulse oximeter, and applied them all. A short time later she saw his temperature and pulse were elevated, and his blood pressure and oxygen were down. She grabbed a nasal cannula and hooked him up to the wall oxygen while they waited for Jared.

Franklin pressed his palm against his sternum and rubbed.

"What's happening?" Kasey asked.

He shook his head, grimacing again. "Feels like I've got heartburn. Felt like it all day."

She should have thought of it the moment he'd

walked in with pale diaphoretic skin and complaints of feeling queasy. The man might be having a heart attack. She opened the exam-room door and called out. "Vincent, can you do an EKG for me, stat?"

That request brought both Jared and Vincent barreling into the room. Vincent pushed the EKG machine with him, and while he set up the procedure, Kasey explained to Jared what she thought was going on, and told Angie to call an ambulance.

Two minutes later, Jared read the twelve-lead EKG and found early ST elevation.

"We're going to admit you to the hospital, Franklin. You're most likely having a heart attack, or you've had a silent MI in the past."

No sooner had Jared said it than Franklin grabbed his chest and groaned. "Ooh, make this stop. The pain. Ooh."

Switching to cardiac-arrest mode, Vincent rushed the crash cart into the room and Angie confirmed the paramedics were on their way. Kasey, Vincent and Jared worked like mad as a team to start an IV, deliver needed medicine, and prevent a full-out arrest. Jared ran the near code with confidence and precision, postponing and possibly preventing more heart damage for Franklin O'Leary.

Fifteen minutes later, having received emergency medication through his IV, and with Franklin stabilized, though nowhere near out of danger, the ambulance arrived. Jared gave a report that was rapid though amazingly thorough. He'd obviously been involved in a number of codes over his career. He also got on the phone and called in a report, speaking directly to the attending ER doc. Under instructions from the nearby emergency department, the paramedics transported a semiconscious Franklin to the hospital. Today, the least of his worries had turned out to be the paracentesis fluid with cancer cells.

Just when Kasey thought she could take a deep breath and relax, she saw Mrs. Nunez in her wheelchair in the waiting room with her caretaker at her side. Carla, the caretaker, had called earlier saying Mrs. Nunez hadn't urinated all day. The eighty-year-old lady's recent stroke had caused her to retain her urine and she needed occasional straight catheterization. This time Kasey had received a phone order from the woman's geriatric doctor to insert a catheter bag and leave it in place.

Kasey met and greeted her patient and rolled her down the hall to the examination room for the procedure.

Twenty minutes later, having given thorough instructions to the caretaker and after typing up her notes, Kasey returned to her desk. Jared was nowhere to be seen, and a blip of disappointment settled over her as she sat.

Her day was over, the surge of adrenaline from Franklin's cardiac emergency had receded and she was left feeling drained yet restless. She straightened her desk and shut down her computer as she rolled her shoulders to fend off the tension. Warm and sturdy hands that definitely didn't belong to Vincent caressed the lower part of her neck and shoulders. They methodically squeezed, strong thumbs running up her cervical spine.

"Where were you?" she asked, sounding as if she'd died and gone to heaven.

"I was in the back, finishing my consult and admitting orders."

Kasey smiled and let her head drop forward as Jared

proved to be a master at upper-body massage. She'd really like to keep him around for awhile.

"How about I take you home and buy you some dinner?" he said.

The invitation seemed out of the blue, but with his soothing finger ministrations on her aching muscles, right about now he could talk her into skateboarding downhill blindfolded, as long as he didn't stop the magic.

"Sounds like a great idea."

Someone cleared their throat. Kasey looked up. It was Vincent with a "gotcha" glance teetering on a smile. "I restocked the crash cart and Angie cleaned the patient rooms, so we'll be going. Have a good night." He emphasized "night".

"Okay, thanks. See you tomorrow."

"Later, guys," Jared chimed in. "Goodnight, Angie."

Once they'd cleared the door and heard the lock click, Jared leaned over and kissed the back of Kasey's neck, releasing a basketload of tiny tingles up and down her spine. She knew it was a bad idea, because she could get used to this, used to Jared's soft lips delivering pure pleasure into her malnourished sex life. Once she let down her guard, she'd be susceptible to more feelings, and feelings led to pain. But he was still kissing her and she really didn't want him to stop. Not now.

When his hands reached beneath her breasts and cupped them, a tiny ragged sigh escaped her lips and her mind gave up every last annoying thought. He nibbled her earlobe while lifting and running his thumbs over her erect nipples. *Listen to your body, not your mind.* Warmth pooled between her legs, soon turning to an impatient burn. She turned her head to meet his lips. His mouth covered hers and she quickly found his tongue, amazed how easily he'd turned her from a diligent, exhausted NP into a sex-starved male fantasy of a naughty nurse. He could do that to her. He worked magic.

Wanting nothing more than her body flush to his, she stood, their lips never breaking contact. His arms enfolded her, and she instantly found his back, pulling him closer. Soon she'd sufficiently raised his polo shirt so she could run her hands over the petal-soft skin of his ribs and back. He found her hips and bottom, first massaging then pulling her tight to his wedge. Knowing he was ready for her, that he wanted her, pushed her longing over the edge. She rubbed against him, sending sparks up her core, stirring up an even stronger desire to be devoured and sated.

At this rate they'd never make it home, and she'd never in her life expected to make love in the clinic. Had never even fantasized about it. Yet here she was. With Jared. Giving nonverbal consent.

In a rush he pulled away and unzipped his jeans, soon tugging at her nursing scrubs, which dropped to the floor in record time. He balanced her hips on the edge of her desk and found her opening with the fingers of one hand, while the other busily dug in his pocket for the foil wrapper. In a flash the protection business got taken care of and, moving her thong out of the way, he entered in a long, smooth thrust. First she expanded to his size as he filled her, then, when she clamped down, an intense shudder rolled through her, long and fathomless. She wrapped her legs around his hips for deeper access and pushed against him, starving for his touch. Each thrust sent a building wave of excitement throughout her body, her heart pounded in her chest, until everything spiraled down to one point of pure pleasure that pulsed and grew until it exploded. With a gasp, her head fell forward onto his shoulder, and she held him tight until he came on a ragged breath and a curse.

"You make me act like a crazy man," he rasped over her ear.

"And I'm as prim as ever," she said, removing her legs from around his waist.

The steamy smile he gave her was genuine and so utterly sexy she had to look away if there was any hope of leaving the office before morning.

CHAPTER SEVEN

FORTY-FIVE minutes after sex on the desk, Kasey and Jared arrived at her apartment with a box of pizza and were ravenously eating. She noticed Jared tickle Daisy's ears when she passed close enough for him to make contact, and a tenderness she hadn't expected settled inside her. She cautioned herself about letting her guard down, about allowing more feelings to mess up whatever this thing was between them.

His cellphone alarm went off.

"Oh," he said, "give me a minute, would you?" He walked to the kitchen and made a call. "Hi, it's Dad. Just checking in to see if you've done your homework. Good. Any tests this week?"

After Jared finished the call to his twelve-year-old son, Patrick—a call more of few words, grunts, and one-word answers than a real conversation, but which ended in a promise to be at a soccer game on one Sunday morning—Jared said goodbye.

After what seemed like a normal father-son conversation, Jared made another call. "Hi, Chloe, just calling to say goodnight."

Not knowing what else to do and trying not to eavesdrop, Kasey ate more pizza. An odd ache started behind her sternum. Had she ever gotten a call like that, growing up? This man might be a California native, but he had roots right here in Massachusetts with his children. And for the record, she was glad he was here.

From the heartfelt tone in his voice, there was no doubt how much he loved his kids, and she'd bet a thousand dollars his daughter and son adored him, too.

"Goodnight, sugarplum. You keep up the good work, and I'll do my best to get to your soccer game this Saturday afternoon, okay?"

Strolling back to the table, he took a seat and ate another bite of pizza. "Any word from the lab yet?" Jared asked.

"Not yet." She didn't intend to ruin their good time by pursuing that topic. "How'd Chloe do on that test the other day?"

"Got a B-plus."

"Great."

"Did Vincent tell you about his big date?"

"Which one?"

For recently having had mind-blowing sex on a desk, their conversation seemed rather mundane, which made it all the more enjoyable.

"Hey, I see you've got my favorite video game."

She glanced across the room to the box connected to her TV. "Really?" Of course, he had kids so why wouldn't he know about the popular games console? "I use the aerobics program." As if that explained why a thirty-something owned a kid's game.

"That explains why you're in good shape," he said, a knowing smile on his lips.

She had the urge to reach across the table and kiss him, but where would that lead? Besides, she had just taken another bite of pizza. "Thank you." She batted her lashes to accentuate the words around her full mouth.

He winked back, and something stirred inside her.

"I like to bowl. Do you have that one?"

"Of course," she said, putting down her pizza. "I'll challenge you."

"You're on!"

"First I'll need to make your avatar." She wiped some pizza grease from her fingers onto a napkin, and headed across the room.

They spent the next ten minutes playing with the game, creating a small round-headed creature with dark hair and incredible blue eyes that looked amazingly like Jared.

"So that's how you see me, huh?"

"I think I captured your inner essence." She hadn't batted her lashes this much since she was thirteen and had declared her love for Mike Murphy to her six closest friends.

"Yeah, especially the scowling brows."

She laughed. He could take what she dished out, and it made him all the more likeable.

"I've got to tell you, your house is so much homier than mine," he said.

"I've been here a few years, so that's an advantage."

"And you don't rent your furniture." He laughed. "My style of décor is functional." He tossed her a humble look. "I just needed some place to flop yet big enough for the kids to come and stay with me." He glanced around her living room. "My place is a one-bedroom apartment, like yours, but the davenport pulls out into a bed," he said, as he rolled the first virtual ball down the virtual bowling lane. "I bet my kids don't even like coming to stay with me."

"I'm sure they want to be wherever you are."

"Not after this summer."

Rather than continue with the touchy subject, she stood to take her turn and scored a strike.

"Well done," he said.

She curtsied.

"Some time I'll have to take you there."

"Where?

"To my basement apartment. You'd be the only person, besides my kids, I've ever brought there."

Putting it into perspective like that, having the honor of being invited into his private world, she looked at the man she'd had sex with on a desk earlier. On the outside he was gorgeous, seemed confident and was definitely accomplished, yet inside he was just like her, a little insecure and very private. "I'd like that." He'd invited her inside, if only to his apartment. Maybe she'd take him up on it. "Thank you," she said as she rolled her second strike in the bowling game.

Forty minutes later, after several games of bowling, with Jared winning the majority, and a couple of tennis matches where Kasey triumphed, they went back to the table. Kasey watched Jared devour two more pieces of pizza while she picked at her crust.

He'd proved to be stellar as a no-strings lover, and she couldn't let feelings mess things up. When he didn't look so serious and earnest his eyes were sweet and friendly. She thoroughly enjoyed playing the video game with him, having him in her house, sharing a meal, keeping her company. She took a bite of pizza and thought what a striking man he was, and how she'd seen every part of him, and nothing had come close to letting her down. Physically.

Again, that caution flag waved in her mind.

Men didn't stick around in her life. She had to remember that. He wouldn't either. She would be nothing

more than a pleasant way station on his journey through
Boston. What could she expect from a man with rented
furniture? That cold, in-your-face fact changed the taste
of the pizza, as it turned from delicious comfort food
into cardboard with sauce.

She got up from the table and went into the kitchen
to gather her thoughts. Who knew what her future held?
She really didn't want to blow this one good thing with
Jared by being needy or afraid. She wanted to take what
she could, for as long as she could. Gulping down some
water at the sink, she straightened her shoulders. She
deserved to enjoy herself with a man, this man. Jared.
She'd enjoy each moment he gave her and be glad
about it. When it ended, that would be it. No strings.
No emotions. In the meantime, they'd have shared good,
thought-free, solid physical contact.

His strong hands cupped her shoulders. The man had
an uncanny knack for sneaking up behind her. She in-
haled the woods and orange peel scent that had quickly
become her favorite aftershave, plus the added touch of
mozzarella and basil.

"You okay?" he asked.

"Fine." She bent her head and brushed her cheek over
his knuckles. He wrapped his hands around her waist
and rested his chin on her shoulder.

"Good. I'm fine, too."

Glancing into the window pane above the sink, she
saw their reflections. To someone passing by they'd appear to be a couple, perhaps in love or married. Little
would anyone know they were nothing more than convenient lovers.

With that she turned into his embrace and they kissed
again, long, slow, lingering kisses, and soon they found

their way into her bed, the pizza forgotten in its cardboard holder and the computer game a distant memory.

Jared watched Kasey stretch like a kitten on the mattress after they'd gotten naked. "We've got to quit meeting like this," she said, falling fall short of coy.

"I'm so glad we have," he said spooning close, nibbling her shoulder, examining her colorful hummingbird tattoo on the back of her shoulder. He wrapped his arms around her and pulled her tight to him. "What do you say we just stay here for ever?"

"Someone would have to bring in the pizza when we got hungry."

He smiled into her hair. "Yeah, and I have a special surgery to scrub in on tomorrow."

"Double stacking implants?"

He tweaked her breast in punishment. "No. I'll have you know, I'm on the surgical team for a certain young boy's cleft lip and palate repair."

She sucked in air and glanced over her shoulder. "Really?"

"Without a doubt."

"That's wonderful."

"I know. I'm wonderful."

She jabbed him with her elbow.

"Ouch. Hey. I'm just being honest."

"So humble."

"You bring out the best in me."

"It's a tough job, but someone has to do it." She snuggled her behind against him, his muscles tensed and the heavy, and hot feeling sprang to life once more.

"Oh, look, you're bringing out the best in me again." With desire pooling in his groin, he positioned himself below her bottom between her upper thighs, close enough to feel her moisture. The damp welcome and heady scent made him shudder with longing. When had a woman turned him on so much?

He moved in tighter then changed her position just enough to give him entrance, and soon the only thoughts in his mind were to please Kasey and satisfy his endless need for her.

Kasey woke in the middle of the night, surprised that Jared was still there. A quick glance at the clock told her it was two in the morning. She got up for a bathroom visit, took one step, but her right leg felt like a tree stump. Falling to the floor, she banged her head on the bedpost. Pain sliced through the side of her head. A brief twinkling of stars appeared behind her eyes. Shaken, she rubbed out the ache.

"Are you okay?" Jared's groggy voice came from over the mattress.

"Leg went to sleep. Tried to walk."

He crawled over the bed and hopped to the floor, pushed his hands under her armpits and helped her stand. Her leg gave early signs of waking up, tingles and pins, burning, and discomfort. He kissed her temple where she'd been rubbing.

"Let me help you," he said. "Bathroom or back to bed?"

She pointed to the bathroom, and he practically carried her as she hopped on her one good leg. "That hasn't happened in years." Yet it had happened last night, too.

"I probably threw my leg over you or something."

Right. But when she'd woken up, their bodies hadn't even been touching. Hummingbird-fast panic shot through her, igniting the nerve endings in her chest. Was this an early sign of Huntington's?

Once she'd made it to the bathroom, she decided to

add this to her surprisingly growing list of things for the dreaded upcoming neurology appointment.

When she returned to her room, the light was on and Jared was dressed and ready to leave. He ran fingers through his hair in an attempt to comb it.

"I need to do some preparation for surgery later today. Guess I'll be going."

He'd clicked into doctor mode, and whatever care and concern he'd shown when he'd helped her up had vanished. The man was the king of compartmentalization.

"Okay, well, let me know how it goes."

He walked toward her, pecked her on the nose. "Without a doubt." Then left.

All the great feelings she'd savored during their time together that night wilted. She tried to buck up under her disappointment, but couldn't quite pull it off.

"Wait!" she said, rushing to the kitchen door.

Surprise changed his sleepy expression as he stopped in mid-reach for the knob.

"I've got to turn off the alarm first."

He nodded in understanding. "Thanks." Clearly, there was no concern about any further conversation on his end. Not even a "Talk soon" or "See you later". Not one further peep from him.

He showed no interest in learning the code to her alarm either.

"Goodnight," she said, trying not to notice so much, fighting off a desire to want more.

"'Night."

The guy had stumbled onto a playmate and could she blame him for allowing for some distraction in his otherwise busy and high-stress schedule? She needed to get used to this no-strings fling. When it was good it was very, very good, but when it felt bad, like now, it stank.

Maybe she wasn't cut out for an affair.

The feeling had slowly and painfully returned to her leg, and only a few needle pricks remained in her foot. She tested her toes by wiggling them and rotating her ankle. As Kasey reset the alarm and walked back to her bedroom, a nagging thought caught hold and wouldn't let her free. What would happen if she turned out to have the Huntington's marker?

On Thursday morning, Kasey received a call at the clinic from the bat-bite mom. The mother's worst fears had come true. There was evidence of bat guano in the child's bedroom. Having done her homework, Kasey told the woman there was only a one percent chance of the bat having rabies in this part of the US, but she still recommended that the mother follow up with her daughter's pediatrician as soon as possible.

Vincent kept eyeing Kasey all morning, a tiny knowing twinkle in his eyes. When he brought her a cup of coffee without being asked, she knew she was in for an interrogation.

"You're banging the doc, aren't you?" His smile was sly and lascivious.

"Is that any of your business?"

"Am I not your closest friend?" He stood before her arms akimbo, with an obvious pout. "I have information rights. You've been withholding breaking news."

She sipped the too-hot coffee, squinted her eyes tightly, then drew in a breath. "Okay. Yes," she whispered, worried Angie might hear. "We've sort of done some things."

"Done some things? Like sex?"

She nodded at his incredulous stare.

"Well blow me away! You little harlot."

"Keep your voice down, would you?"

"I want details. All the details. Oh, my God, Doctor Tall, Dark and Gorgeous is bonking my best friend."

"You say one word to anyone and I'll stitch your mouth shut."

He licked his lips. "Sealed. Promise. But, really, how exciting." He squeezed her shoulder then walked away to pick up a blood-pressure cuff, tossed her an envious glance, then moved on.

The way Kasey felt this morning, all mixed up about what was going on between her and Jared, she wasn't the least bit sure there was anything "exciting" about the predicament she'd found herself in. Now that Vincent knew, he'd keep on her about "Has he called you?" "When are you seeing him again?" and she'd have to be honest and tell him, most likely she'd only been a brief fling. It hadn't meant anything. News she'd rather keep to herself.

It would take diligent practice to start believing the mantra about sex with Jared. *It doesn't mean anything. It doesn't mean anything.*

But, with misplaced feelings beginning to surface, she'd have to try.

Late Thursday afternoon Jared sat down for the first time in hours. He stretched out the aching muscles in his legs and shoulders. The cleft lip and partial palate repair with the pediatric surgical specialist had been fascinating. He wouldn't have missed it for anything, and even felt a little proud that he'd been the person to recommend the child for the pro bono services. Which wouldn't have happened if he hadn't been assigned to the Everett Community Clinic.

He loved being a general surgeon, and plastic surgery seemed like a logical option. He believed in what he did, making people look better, feel better with more self-esteem, no matter how unrealistic some of their goals were. He'd given his new studies his best efforts, because he didn't know how to do anything differently in life, but something had obviously been lacking in the satisfaction department. He hadn't realized how much until now. Today, assisting with the toddler's surgery, it had become painfully apparent. Nothing could compare to the way he felt right now. He'd helped change a child's life.

It felt great, and he wanted to share the revelation with someone special.

Smiling, he fished out his cellphone to give Kasey an update.

"Dr. Finch?" one of the circulating OR nurses said. "Dr. Rheingold wants to see you. He's in the doctors' lounge."

Sliding his cellphone back into his pocket, he walked down the hall.

On Friday morning, Kasey got a call she never expected and was nowhere near prepared for.

A pediatrician for Janie DeHart, the bat-bite child, had decided to take the cautious road and had ordered the treatment for rabies. Kasey understood he was going on the theory of better safe than sorry. Literature suggested that any young child or mentally challenged person suspected of having slept in a room with a bat and having evidence of a bite should be treated. The logic had more to do with the inability to explain exactly what had happened. In Janie's case, she'd thought a bird was flying in her room. Maybe it had been a dream, but the tiny bite marks on her shoulder changed everything.

A large part of her didn't believe it was truly necessary to put that child through the horrendous treatment for rabies, but would she want to risk being wrong? In this case, liability and potential lawsuits may have played a part in the decision by her pediatrician.

The Everett Community Clinic had been chosen to provide the care, since it was close to the patient's house. The unlucky child would receive the treatment. She made an appointment for Janie on Monday, hustled to order the rabies immune globulin and rabies vaccine, then ran back to her computer to study the procedure for giving the medicine to prevent the rabies virus from infecting the patient. She dreaded how hard it would be on the little girl to receive the initial immune globulin followed by four doses of rabies vaccine over fourteen days.

While she had a quiet moment at her desk, she picked up the phone and called the hospital to check up on Franklin O'Leary. Patient confidentiality prevented her from getting a full report, but she'd been assured he'd been stabilized and was now in the acute care ward. Now that they'd resolved his heart attack, they'd have to move on to finding the source of his cancer. She thought of Franklin's weary, craggy, but friendly face. How had he managed to get hit with a double whammy?

In full fret mode, Kasey sat at her desk as the phone rang again. "Everett Community Clinic, how may I help you?"

"May I speak to Kasey McGowan?"

"I'm Kasey."

"Hi. This is the Genetics lab. We have your results and wanted to set up an appointment to discuss them."

The floor seemed to drop out from beneath her feet. A massive influx of adrenaline through her chest, and pulsing into her ears, made her head swim. Her breathing fell out of sync, and she had to remind herself to inhale…exhale.

Was she ready to handle the results? No! Her hands trembled, barely able to hold the phone to her ear. A fist-sized wad in her throat made it hard to respond.

"Ms. McGowan?" the lab voice said.

She swallowed against the dry lump. "Yes. I'm here."

"Are you available to come in tomorrow morning?"

"Yes," she wiped her brow, already clammy with fear. "Of course. What time?"

CHAPTER EIGHT

KASEY grasped at Vincent's arm as he passed her desk in the clinic.

"What's wrong? You look white as a sheet."

"My results are in." Her pulse pounded so loudly in her ears she could hardly hear herself.

"The DNA tests?"

She nodded, unable to draw enough breath to speak.

"Are they negative?"

She shrugged. She'd been told at the original lab appointment that they only gave the results in person.

He hugged her tight, pulled back, grabbed her hands, squeezed, and looked deep into her eyes. "When do you find out?"

"Tomorrow," she whispered.

"Do you need me to stay with you tonight? Then we can go to the appointment together in the morning."

She chewed on her lower lip and shook her head. "Just go with me tomorrow, please."

"Of course. I'll be there. All you have to do is tell me when. Now, let me get you some water."

Her heart swelled with love for Vincent for being there for her. Since she only had two friends, she was grateful he was one of them.

The rest of the day went by in a blur. Kasey hardly

remembered how she got home, but somehow she stood in her kitchen with an attention-starved cat circling her ankles.

After she fed Daisy, and scratched her ears until the cat had slipped into oblivion, she ran a hot bath and slid into the soothing water, hoping it might help unjangle her nerves. Tomorrow held her fate. If she had the Huntington gene, she would eventually get the disease, but wouldn't know when the symptoms would begin. She thought about the recent episodes of her leg going numb at night. Had the symptoms already started? If she didn't have the marker, she could take a deep breath and thank the heavens for saving her heartache, physical pain, and a long and sad demise.

She thought about calling Jared—a fleeting thought, as quick as a drip from the faucet into the bathtub. He had enough going on in his life. Besides, their relationship wasn't like that.

In fact, they didn't *have* a relationship. Beyond sex.

His goofy round-headed avatar popped into her mind, and how earnestly he'd bowled the other night, as if holding an actual bowling ball instead of a video game wand.

What they had was sex. Not friendship. Not a relationship. Sex. Pure and simple. A clench of sadness lodged in her chest. It seemed that life-threatening disease and no-strings sex wasn't such a good mix after all.

Besides, Vincent would be here in a flash if she needed him. He was her true friend. And though right now she felt more afraid and lonely than when she'd been a pre-schooler and her mother had left her alone at night to sneak off and see some man, she refused to burden Vincent until tomorrow.

After the long, warm bath, she got into her pajamas

and poured herself a glass of wine. She'd beaten Jared in video tennis the other night, now she'd leave the ball in his court and wait to see how long it would be before he called her. Yes, it was a test, because her phony no-strings self-esteem could use a little perking up.

Walking to the living room, she slipped a DVD into the player for distraction, and took a long sip of her pinot noir.

Now, if she could only make it through the night, tomorrow she'd find out her future. It all boiled down to a Huntington's disease marker at chromosome four, and that tiny thing made her mad as hell.

On Saturday morning, Jared made early post-surgical rounds for his latest implants, facelifts, lipos, and tummy tucks at the surgi-center recovery, finishing in plenty of time to make it to Chloe's soccer game. Back in his office, on a whim, he dialed Kasey to see if she'd like to come along.

The phone rang and rang, and he admitted being glad, since he wasn't sure if it was a good idea to bring someone to his kids' games. In the two years since the divorce, his children had never seen him with another woman. There had been a few, very few…two, to be exact…and neither woman had stood a chance of having a real relationship with him under the circumstances. His ex, on the other hand, had already moved in with her neurosurgeon boyfriend, and Jared sensed it mixed up the kids, who were still dealing with the split-up of their parents. Why should he add to it?

Okay, bad idea. He didn't need to confuse Chloe by bringing Kasey along, especially if they were only having a fling, and the chances were Chloe might never see her again.

When would it ever be a good time to bring someone else into his kids' lives? He wasn't sure, but Kasey had crept into his mind more and more lately, and he suspected she and his kids would get along just fine. And speaking of getting along just fine, last night he would have given anything to wrap his arms around her and snuggle down for sleep…after a long, thorough love-making session.

The admission startled him. Was he thinking of trading in unattached sex for an actual relationship? He rubbed his temple, cellphone against the other ear. Man, he must be going soft at thirty-nine. Maybe he wasn't ready yet. Kasey was just a woman he enjoyed being around, one who could shake him out of his overly serious moods, one who turned him on like wildfire in weeds. All good, but what would that add up to over the long haul?

The phone continued to ring. Not having to call was supposed to be the beauty of a no-strings affair. So why did he want to talk to Kasey this morning? Simply to hear her voice?

He stared out the second-story window onto the parking lot, not in the least bit sure what to do about Kasey.

Once he heard the voicemail beep on her cellphone he quickly thought about hanging up, but cleared his throat instead. "Hi, it's Jared. I'm heading out for the kids' soccer games and I wanted to touch base. I, uh, just want to wish you a good weekend. I know it's a little tough for you these days, but hang in there, okay?" He hung up, shaking his head. How lame was that? He ought to be embarrassed for such a pitiful pep talk. Some smooth operator he'd turned out to be.

He walked to the elevator and to his car for the two-hour drive by himself, knowing his thoughts would be with Kasey part of the way. Maybe he'd try to call her later, see what she'd been up to all weekend. Could he do that with this no-strings thing? He shook his head and decided to concentrate on his kids instead.

He'd spend the night near the kids' school and stick around for Patrick's game on Sunday morning then head home. He needed a good night's sleep so he could start the mentorship with the head of Pediatric Plastic Surgery for the next two weeks. After the cleft lip and palate surgery the other day, it was a specialty he found surprisingly intriguing, and one more thing he felt compelled to share with Kasey.

Maybe he would call her later.

Kasey rushed into the genetics lab with Vincent by her side. "I'm Kasey McGowan. You have some results for me?"

The receptionist wrote down her name and walked to a cabinet, fingers walking through the files. Soon he found and retrieved a white envelope, returned to the counter, and made a call. While the phone rang he asked, "Do you have a neurology appointment scheduled?"

"Yes," she said, hands noticeably trembling, her mouth drying by the second.

"Hi," the technician said into the phone. "I have Ms. McGowan here for her test results." He hung up the phone. "Ms. Jamal, our genetic counselor, will be with you shortly."

How hard could it be? She either had the genetic marker or she didn't. She didn't need to wait for a special counselor to tell her that.

Kasey wanted to reach for and tear open the envelope with flapping, unruly hands and fingers. She wanted to slide out the report, then open the tri-folded sheets and read the results right that instant. Why did she have to wait?

With her entire body sensing the wildly ragged rhythm from her heart, and her mouth as dry as sand, she did her best to stay calm and patient on the outside.

A tall doctor, with huge brown eyes and a long face and nose, appeared and quietly offered her hand. "I'm Naali Jamal, won't you follow me?" She took the envelope from the technician and led the way to a sequestered corner office.

"I hear you are a medical professional, Ms. McGowan?"

"Yes," Vincent answered for her. "She's a nurse practitioner."

The office was smartly decorated and tastefully furnished, but Kasey couldn't take in details. With Vincent by her side, she sat. He took her hand and squeezed.

The young woman carefully opened the envelope and withdrew the contents. She unfolded the paper and studied the results. Her brows minutely drew together, giving Kasey another rush of adrenaline.

"Hmm," the woman said, before looking up from the report. "Let me show you the results, and explain what they mean."

Both Kasey and Vincent sat forward on their seats to see the report more closely, but she didn't immediately share the test sheet.

"What we look for with this test is the number of CAG repeats. That's cytosine-adenine-guanine. If the repeats are under twenty-eight, you do not have the marker. Between twenty-nine and thirty-four CAG repeats, you won't develop Huntington's disease, but the next generation is still at risk. Between thirty-five and thirty-nine, some individuals will develop HD, and the next generation is also at risk. Equal to or greater than forty, and the individual will definitely get HD. There's just no telling when, and more tests are needed to tell if the symptoms have already begun. That's why we send you to a neurologist."

Lord, could she drag this out any longer? Kasey's foot tapped the air faster than hummingbird wings.

"And what is Kasey's result?"

Ms. Jamal cleared her throat. "Thirty-nine."

Kasey's body went slack in the chair. She'd been tense so long that the borderline result had caught her off guard. "Thirty-nine!" she blurted. "What percentage of people will get Huntington's disease with a result of thirty-nine?"

"Again, it is hard to make this call. More testing will help identify if there is early evidence of the disease. Continued follow-up would be necessary."

"For the rest of my life?"

"Perhaps."

One CAG repeat away from certain disease left her dangling over life's genetic craps shoot. She didn't know whether to be relieved or looking over her shoulder every day for the dark, haunting shadow of Huntington's disease sneaking up on her.

Good heavens. Not knowing if she'd be one of the people in the thirty-five to thirty-nine results range to develop the disease turned out to be worse than knowing for sure that with time she'd succumb to the disorder. The never knowing for sure would drive her crazy, if she let it.

Kasey's hand flew to her mouth. She tried not to whimper, but couldn't stop the sound leaving her throat. "How is a person supposed to live like this?"

"We can make an appointment with a therapist for you."

"A therapist?" She shook her head. "I'm supposed to sit around and talk about my feelings about how horrendous life is and why did I get stuck with this nondiagnosis? No, thanks. That's not for me." Angry about her results, she'd lashed out and immediately regretted it, but she wasn't about to spend the rest of her life worrying. What was the point?

"It's for support, Kasey," Vincent said. "At least think about it."

She sighed, sorry she'd chastised the genetic counselor and her best friend. "I know, you're right, it couldn't hurt to have all the support I can get. If you give me the card, Ms. Jamal, I'll check my schedule and make an appointment as soon as possible."

The woman nodded her approval as she proffered the business card.

"Can we move her neurology appointment up?" Vincent spoke up.

"I'll see what I can do," Ms. Jamal said, glancing over the computer screen. "I'll send the neurologist an e-mail, but I can't guarantee anything."

With her hands cupping her cheeks, Kasey stared at her now perfectly still feet. How could she be so unlucky? They couldn't even tell her for sure if she'd get the disease symptoms. And she sure as hell would never have kids to pass down the curse. She'd never thought that much about having children of her own, but knowing she didn't have an option hurt, like a knife to her chest. She shook her head, knocking over warm tears onto her cheeks from her brimming lids. She'd thought life had sucked yesterday. Today she'd entered a whole new realm of suckiness.

* * *

"I'd like another beer," Kasey said to the server at the harbor-side café. "You know what?" she said to Vincent. "Let's take one of those amphibious tours. I've lived near Boston my whole life and have never taken a tour of the city. What do you say?"

"Sure. I left today completely open for you."

She squeezed his forearm, already feeling the warm fuzzy feeling from the first drink. "I love you, guy."

"Don't go all sappy on me or I'll cut you off the beer."

Kasey dug into her seafood salad, quietly vowing to grab the gusto in life since she didn't have a choice about her health status. A stinking diagnosis with an iffy future was not going to keep her from enjoying the here and now. All things considered, she felt fine today, physically. No aches. No pains. She'd gotten out of bed that morning with everything working fine. She squinted into the sun at Vincent's silhouette, so glad he was there with her.

Riffling through her purse for a tissue, she glanced at her phone—she'd had it turned off all morning, knowing she'd be at the lab. There was a voice message, and she listened as Jared wished her a good weekend. His awkward and businesslike message made her heart clutch the tiniest bit; just knowing he'd thought about her today, well, somehow it mattered. Not good, she reminded herself. She wasn't supposed to care.

"Who was that?" Vincent asked.

"Jared."

Vincent's brows shot up. "Your hot, hunky hero?"

"Knock it off, will you?"

He grinned at her and she took another bite of salad.

"Maybe later we can do the Boston history walk, too," she said, since she had a captive for the day. "I haven't done that since grade school."

Vincent shrugged. "Whatever you want."

"Thanks."

What she really wanted to do was call Jared back and invite him over for some mind-numbing sex, some help-me-forget-about-all-the-bad-luck-in-life lovemaking, but first she needed to figure things out. Should she tell him her results and risk gaining his pity, or keep her diagnosis to herself and take a chance that he'd resent her for it? He'd said himself not to expect results for up to six weeks, so she had time to think things through. He didn't need to know how she'd spent her Saturday morning.

Her second ice-cold beer arrived and she took a sip. "What was the name of that guy you said gives great haircuts?"

"Arturo?"

"Yeah, can you get me an appointment with him? I need some new style or something."

"Of course I can get you in. We're like this." Vincent crossed his fingers.

"Fantastic." She stabbed a plump piece of shrimp from her salad, thinking it was the best-tasting lunch she'd ever had.

One thing was clear—she wasn't going to hole up in her house and waste one second on feeling sorry for herself. From now on, it would be all about living each day as if it were her last. That's what a CAG score of thirty-nine had taught her.

Jared slowed down his car on Sunday night and rolled toward Kasey's house. He'd had the opportunity to go with Patrick's team for a victory lunch after the soccer game and hadn't passed it up. After lunch had come ice-cream treats and a chance to take Chloe along. When the school didn't seem opposed to him being there, he took advantage of more time with his kids. He knew his ex wouldn't mind as he was allowed every other weekend plus one weeknight for visitation per their standard California divorce settlement. Truth was, since Patrice was only able to fly out once a month to visit their kids, she was fine with Jared visiting as often as possible. The problem was, he couldn't make time often enough with his work schedule and his plastic surgery training.

Soon it had been the dinner hour, and again he'd gotten the okay from the school to take the kids out for another meal. It had been a long but enjoyable two days, and he looked forward to doing it all over again next weekend. The thought of his kids not being around after the summer gave him a dull ache in his chest.

The lights at Kasey's house were on, but the blinds were closed. He glanced at his watch. It wasn't that late, nine o'clock. His better judgment told him he should have called before he'd left and that showing up unannounced wouldn't be acceptable no matter how easygoing Kasey was. But, boy, did he want to. She'd awakened a beast inside him, and nothing but her sexy kisses and soft body could tame it.

He sat in his running car, staring at her house. He could make out her silhouette on the blinds. It looked like she was standing and holding something—a guitar? Maybe she was playing that video game again, and she'd like some company. Headlights came up the street behind him. Kicking his inner censor, he pressed on the gas and drove past quickly, hoping she wouldn't happen to notice his schoolboy antics. Some "no-strings" lover he'd turned out to be. Man, he needed to get it together where Kasey was concerned.

* * *

On Monday morning, Kasey went to work dreading facing poor Janie DeHart. Her experience with childhood immunizations reminded her it wouldn't be easy. Kids could freak out and flail about like slippery fish when scared. These shots would be like giving a flu vaccination, they needed to go into deep muscle and the after-effect would feel like someone had punched her in the arm. Once Janie realized how painful the first shot was, her mother would have to drag her into the clinic, kicking and screaming, for the four follow-up appointments. Still, this revised and updated treatment was far, far better than the old twenty-three to thirty injections in the abdomen. The worst side-effect to watch for was the same with any immunization—anaphylaxis. Other than that, the side effects should be mild—headache, nausea, sometimes vomiting. If Janie worked herself into a fit, she might vomit anyway.

Kasey remembered hearing about rabies treatment as a kid, as though it was an urban legend, greatly embellished to scare kids out of their sneakers. In her childhood mind's eye she'd seen evil nurses coming at her with foot-long needles and scowls on their faces. The fear factor had ranked right up there with stepping on a rusty nail and getting "lock jaw." Oh, what her child's mind could do with a little information and a lot of imagination back in her day.

Kasey would do her best not to be that scary nurse for Janie, and to put both the child and mother at ease. She hoped she could make the unfortunate appointment as tolerable as possible.

Angie appeared at her desk. "The DeHarts are here."

Kasey fought back a tiny wave of nervous energy. She'd been a nurse for almost ten years—she'd take control of the situation and make sure nothing got out of hand. In theory, everything should work out fine. In theory.

Kasey stood and called for Vincent. "I'm going to need your help with this. Can you bring in the patient while I prepare the vaccines?"

"Of course."

"Oh, and can you have some epinephrine on hand in case she has an adverse reaction?"

"Gotcha."

"I may need you to hold her down, too."

"I know, I know. Kids love me. I'll make faces at her, get her laughing, then you can slip in with your shots. She won't even know what hit her."

A half-hour later, surprisingly, Vincent's predictions had panned out. Janie got a little antsy while Kasey removed the old dressing to examine the small puncture wounds on her shoulder, but she quickly fell under Vincent's spell.

Now Kasey patted the whimpering child on the head and let her pick the biggest and brightest sticker, plus two lollipops. The relieved Mrs. DeHart looked on with grateful, watery eyes. Kasey nodded at her after a subtle exhalation. "We'll get through this."

"Thank you," Mrs. DeHart mouthed to Kasey, then to Janie she said, "Are you ready for those chocolate-chip pancakes I promised?"

"Yes!" The little girl tugged the air with the fist of her non-shot arm, preferring to hold the other one perfectly still and stiff as if bionic. After waiting twenty minutes, while Vincent did his *Sesame Street* imitations, there had been no signs of adverse reaction.

The bat-bite area was slowly healing, though still red. She'd had Vincent clean the area and put on a new bandage for good measure. Now the little girl was good to go.

Kasey didn't want to push the point, but since the regimen of shots was days one, three, seven, fourteen and twenty-eight, they'd be repeating the process again in three days. Hopefully, all would go just as well as it had today.

CHAPTER NINE

KASEY didn't waste any time grabbing life by the tail. She got off work early Monday evening and took the T to the Chinatown station, took a brisk walk to Boston Public Garden and cut over to Newbury Street to get her hair cut and styled by Vincent's friend Arturo. She never grew tired of the beautiful nineteenth-century brownstones along these tree-lined streets. Her favorite trees were the magnolias down towards the other end of the eclectic European-style shopping area.

She'd eaten before she'd left work, but the rows and rows of outdoor cafés filled to overflowing with customers on this warmer spring evening were inviting, nevertheless. Something on the table she'd just passed was rich with garlic and herbs and made her mouth water.

Skipping down the steps to the lower-level salon, she crossed her fingers Arturo would do well by her. At his this price, he'd better. While she waited for her appointment in the high-tech salon, mildly distracted by strange scents of chemical and hair products, so different from outdoors, she read the local newspaper, wondering if the fumes could be hazardous to her health.

One story caught her eye: "Conjoined Twins Await Delicate Surgery". As she read the story about the twins joined at the head, the article mentioned the children were at the general hospital, where a world-renowned on-staff neurosurgeon had performed a similar surgery several years before.

"Kasey?" A Hollywood pop-goth styled young woman approached. Her edgy multilayered hairdo, including stair-step bangs, and make-up resembling a raccoon, fascinated Kasey. "Arturo is ready for you."

As Kasey followed the click-clicking of the assistant's black stiletto boots toward Arturo's station, Kasey promised she wouldn't get talked into any strange new haircut. Classic was what she had in mind, and if she explained herself well enough, classic was what Arturo should deliver.

Two and a half hours later, Kasey left the hair salon with new lift in her step, probably due to the significantly lighter pocketbook. With hair cut to her shoulders, brilliantly shaped and styled but with just enough edge to stand out, she held her head high, even touching up her usual lip gloss to add to the look. She checked her cellphone to see if anyone had called and kicked herself for hoping Jared might have. No such luck.

As she walked further down the trendy street, she passed a particularly well-manicured spring garden in front and a brightly lit bay window on the first floor. There, on display, was a leopard-patterned sleeveless dress with a Mandarin collar, straight skirt, and a wide black belt. It snagged her attention and held it. Wow, would she dare wear something like that, so different than her usual practical style? She stood beside the pink and white impatiens and spent all of three seconds making her decision.

Her new "why not" attitude was taking hold. If she wasn't careful, she could get used to living like there was no tomorrow. After pushing through the door of the boutique-sized store, she asked for her size in the dress, and then smiled on her way into the fitting room. If Jared had the good sense to call her in the next day or two, she'd model the outfit for him then, if he was lucky, she'd help him remove it.

Wednesday's bat vaccination appointment went similarly to the first, with the exception of Janie being more apprehensive and needing to be bribed into going inside the examination room. Vincent played tic-tac-toe with her while Kasey prepared the shot. Just as she finished with the injection, Angie told her she had a call. Without giving the call a thought, she returned to her desk and answered.

"Hey, good lookin', how've you been?"

"Jared." A pleasant burst of tiny flappy things behind her breastbone made her smile. She couldn't let him know what he did to her. "Long time no hear from," she said in a more modulated tone. She cradled the phone between her ear and shoulder as she shuffled through a pile of messages on her desk, trying to sound businesslike and not to let the migrating nest of jitters in her tummy take over.

"You miss me?"

It sounded like he was smiling. Give him the upper hand? No way would she admit exactly how much she'd missed him since last week. "Maybe."

"Good. Can I take you to dinner tonight?"

She thought of her new dress and how much he'd like it, how he'd give her that lean and hungry look after feasting his eyes on her. Plus the fact that she really wanted to see him. "That would be nice."

"Great. I'll pick you up at seven."

"Sounds good. See you then." For once he'd called

first. Actually asked her out on a date. She hung up, dinner deal all ironed out, beaming.

Of course Vincent caught her with the goofy smile. "Uh-huh," he said, nodding his head as if he were a sleuth solving a case.

At five p.m. Jared finished the rhinoplasty consultation on the fifteen-year-old boy and headed back to his shared office to type up his notes. Wesley Rheingold met him in the corridor.

"I've got some breaking news," he said. "The conjoined twins have been deemed stable enough to undergo surgery and Elwood Fairchild is ready to go."

Dr. Fairchild was the world renowned neurosurgeon who had performed one of the very first conjoined-at-the-head twin surgeries in the United States several years back.

"Fantastic. Any chance I can observe some of the surgery?" Thinking it would be tomorrow before anything got under way.

"Observe? No, my good man. One of the scheduled assisting surgeons is sick and contagious with flu. So I've gone one step further and made you part of team two, plastic surgery. Once Fairchild has completed the head, brain, and great vessels separation, each twin will have their own team to reconstruct their scalps and foreheads. We need all the manpower we can get, and I've watched you work. You'll be a great addition. We'll work in shifts, as this surgery will take anywhere from eighteen to thirty-six hours. Are you willing to help?"

"How can I refuse?" Just thinking about the major opportunity gave Jared goose-bumps. He'd never dreamed of being a part of something like this, something great and life-altering. "Of course I want to!"

"Great. Then grab your stuff, it's time to scrub in."

Jared jumped at the chance to make history. With all thoughts focused on the twins and the surgery, he followed Dr. Rheingold down the hall toward the OR. Totally stoked, as he'd said back home in California when he'd been a teenager. Then it hit him: he needed to let Kasey know he couldn't make their date tonight. He rushed to keep in pace with his colleague as he fished out his cellphone. Deep in the heart of the solidly built hospital there wasn't a signal. He grimaced, knowing he'd have a lot of explaining to do to Kasey later, but opportunity and history called, and he followed Dr. Rheingold into the OR.

Kasey checked her watch for the third time. It was now nine o'clock. Jared's cell went directly to voicemail. She shook her head. All dressed up and with no one to see her, she felt foolish. And angry.

To hell with it.

To hell with him!

She picked up her rock musician video guitar and switched on the TV monitor with plans to get lost with her second-favorite pastime after making love with Jared, playing lead fake guitar in seventies rock classics.

It felt far too familiar to be left dangling by a man without the common courtesy of a call. With her last break-up, her boyfriend had taken off with another woman and had gotten in touch with Kasey as an afterthought three weeks later. She'd never allow that feeling again. Not if she could help it. Smack in the middle of a Pink Floyd classic, things got blurry and she started missing notes, which knocked her expert status back toward novice. She gave up, sliding the strap for the mock guitar from her shoulder and turning off the game.

She marched down the hall, took off her new dress and put on a baggy T-shirt and flannel PJ bottoms. She didn't have time for this any more. Her last boyfriend had called her clingy and insecure. Well, she'd never give a man the chance to say that about her again. As far as she was concerned, Jared Finch had just severed the non-existent strings of their superficial relationship.

Thirty-six hours after the opening incision, two sedated and separated toddlers lay in their own cribs, each whole. The team of two dozen neuro and plastic surgeons, and nearly as many OR nurses, all equal parts exhausted and elated, congratulated themselves on a job well done.

With the monitoring equipment, heart and breathing machines pushed aside in an obstacle-course manner, discarded sheets and blankets cast off in piles, overflowing hampers, and bloodied basins and surgical instruments filling the stainless-steel sinks, the OR looked like a war zone.

Jared rubbed his neck and checked his watch. It was five a.m. Friday morning. There was only one person he wanted to talk to. The surgery had been a game changer, to use Kasey's term. It had revived his love of the intricate, helpful, healing art of surgery. Yes, he'd understood what cosmetic procedures could do for patients, but it didn't put the fire in his belly like this type of surgery did. The experience had convinced him to change his plastic surgery focus from strictly cosmetic to a more intense specialty, pediatric repair. Kasey had figured out he wasn't really happy with his chosen course before he'd even admitted it to himself. He couldn't wait to share the news with her.

Kasey!

He'd stood her up, would have to face her certain disdain, yet he still wanted to see her. He strode toward the doctors' lounge for a quick shower, after which he planned to head over to her house to see her before she left for work. If he was lucky, he'd be early enough and she'd still be in bed.

Kasey came out of a deep sleep and heard what sounded like ice cubes clinking in a glass. She shook her head, listened, and heard it again. Was it raining? Or hailing? That didn't make sense. The sound came in spurts. What the heck was going on?

"Kasey!" She heard a muffled version of her name from outside the window. "Kasey!" This time it was more like a strained whisper.

More ice tinkling.

She sat bolt upright, pushing her hair out of her eyes, and leaned toward the window near the bed. Lifting the blind, she peeked beneath. Jared! In the bushes under her bedroom window, he stood looking disheveled and super-tired. Had he been on a binge for two days? More importantly, what was he doing here now?

He saw her and waved, pointed to his chest, then to the other side of her house. The door. "Let me in," he mouthed.

Was he crazy? Stand her up on Wednesday night without the courtesy of a call, no word the next day, then show up at her house at stupid o'clock on Friday and expect to be let in?

Oh, gosh, he was bending to grab more pebbles. She tapped on the window and waved her hands back and forth in the international sign for "Enough. Please stop that".

He pointed toward the back door again, looking earnest. Oh, hell. She dropped the blind and scrubbed her face, walking—more like stumbling as if half-asleep, which she was—to the kitchen entrance. It was six o'clock, and there he was, standing on the steps, sports jacket open and shirt tails hanging beneath, his hair finger-combed at best. There were deep, dark circles beneath his eyes, like the sign of a madman, yet the blue velvet shone through the thick outline of his lashes as if a beacon. She had to be crazy to let him in. Yet she wanted to.

Once she'd punched in the release code on the alarm system she opened the door.

He burst through, eyes bright, cheeks flushed, face animated. "You won't believe what I've been doing the last two days."

In no mood to play guessing games, she gave him Ms. Daisy's favorite cat-eye glare. "Were you in jail for public drunkenness?" Her deadpan reply fell flat. "Because that's what you look like."

He bent his head, chin to chest, looking at himself. "Sorry." Suddenly distracted by her, he gave a probing gaze from head to fuzzy slippers, then back to her face. "Your hair's longer on one side than the other."

She screwed up her face. "It's supposed to be that way. Now, are you going to tell me where you've been the last two days or are we going to discuss my latest hair fashion?"

He leaned one elbow on her countertop. "I was part of the conjoined twins surgery! You know, the little girls who've been plastered all over the news the last six weeks? Them!"

She'd heard of them, joined at the forehead, sharing part of each other's brain.

"I was on one of the plastic surgery teams," he said, standing tall.

"Wait a second. I'm not awake yet. You were what?"

"I got to be part of the team of surgeons. It was fantastic." He practically danced around the room while telling her about his good fortune. "I haven't slept in two days, but I'm high as a kite about this. I finally figured out what I want to do with my plastic surgery fellowship. Sure, I was committed to be the best cosmetic surgeon I could be, making people look their best, giving them a new lease on life…but something kept nagging at me, that maybe this wasn't what I really wanted or needed to do. You noticed that, too, didn't you? It didn't grab me by the soul and say, hey, this is what you were made for, but this type of surgery sure as hell did. It was like a huge breakthrough, and—" He stopped long enough to take her all in again. "It was my game changer, and you're the first person I wanted to tell."

He let her stare at him, a long, sober stare as she digested the significance of that remark. In return, he grinned at her, waiting.

"I'm the first person you wanted to tell?"

He nodded, stepping closer. She backed up, leaving no room between her and the kitchen sink. He'd finished a cut-and-dried monologue on professional fulfillment, changing from cosmetic leaning to a reconstructive slant, and he'd still somehow managed to break into her heart and do a different kind of repair. The kind of game change that helped a girl, this girl, open up to new and exciting possibilities. She couldn't dare let him know what was running through her mind.

"But you stood me up Wednesday night. You didn't even call."

He shook his head, his eyes begging for understanding. "No, no, no. I was at work, getting ready to leave for our date, when they grabbed me. Well, Dr. Rheingold grabbed me at the last minute. I tried to call but couldn't get a signal. Time was of the essence. It wasn't like I could run outside and make the call first."

"Really?"

"Honestly. If I could've, I would've."

This was either the biggest and best excuse she'd ever heard for being stood up, or Jared really meant it. She didn't live with her head under a rock. She'd read the newspaper headlines yesterday about the dramatic surgery in progress. He looked totally sincere, and since his life-changing soliloquy had touched her so deeply, she decided to give him the benefit of the doubt. "Are you freaking pulling my leg, or are you serious about all of this life-changing stuff?"

"Serious as a heart attack." It really was obvious. Of course he was telling the truth. Of course he'd made a major decision about the direction of his career. He'd even used her term, a game changer. Of course he'd wanted to tell her first. All she had to do was look into his captivating blue eyes to know that.

He opened his arms to welcome her in. It seemed like the right thing to do—come on, the guy was practically a hero—so she stepped into his embrace, immediately amazed by how right he felt. And how great—solid chest, heat radiating from beneath his shirt, all lean muscle and strength.

"So what are you waiting for? Tell me all about the surgery."

"Put on some coffee and I will." She could tell he didn't want to let go, but he did.

Jared watched Kasey move purposefully around the kitchen, opening a cupboard here and a drawer there as she gathered the coffee, a filter, and two mugs. She wore a slinky wraparound daisy yellow robe that tied at the waist and accentuated her curves, and he thought he might like to see her in it on a regular basis. The thought made his mouth go dry. "May I have a drink of water?"

"Of course, help yourself to anything," she said, filling the coffee maker with water.

He moved behind her and put his free hand on her hip as he filled his glass with the other and drank from the tap water. Damn she felt fantastic. "You realize that's a loaded invitation."

Help himself to anything.

She glanced over her shoulder and smiled. He put down his glass, lifted her hair and kissed the side of her neck. "For the record, I like the new uneven look. Makes me want to put my fingers in your hair and mess it all up."

She held perfectly still as he placed light kisses up and down her long neck, as her silken skin beneath his lips rose in tiny bumps. He wrapped his arms around her center and pulled her close to his arousal, then nuzzled her ear with his nose, wanting nothing more than to plant himself inside her. Drained from two days without sleep, yet still mightily turned on by Kasey, he asked the question front and center in his mind.

"Will you go back to bed with me?" he said, his voice raspy with desire.

Her head came up, her shoulders back. He felt her inhale and her spine go board stiff. Disappointed by the change in body language, he waited for a rejection. But he was being honest, as honest as it got. He wanted her, with all his heart. Her denying him would hurt to the core.

How bold could he be and still expect results? Could

he blame her for kicking him out of her kitchen? He'd stood her up, shown up at the crack of dawn, and now wanted to take her to bed. He held his breath, preparing for the worst.

"Yes," she whispered.

Jared made long, slow love to Kasey, and if she wasn't careful she'd interpret it as committed lover sex. Through his fingers and lips he'd told a tale of deep attraction, admiration, and wonder. His thighs and pelvis followed up with bold, uninhibited desire on a mission for satisfaction. As always, her body responded to each touch, slowly building tension, sometimes unbearably so, and longing for release, fighting for it with every fiber in her body. Though he seemed to have read her mind on so many levels, he hadn't been afraid to ask what she'd wanted, meeting whatever need she'd had— Do you want me to touch you there? Like this? Is that good?—until he'd brought her to the limit and she'd shuddered beneath him.

No man could make love like this without caring. Could he? With his head above hers, his eyes probing deeply into hers, his heated, hooded look went beyond sex—it spoke of connection and broken-down barriers. Intimacy. Of that she was certain.

It sent shivers through her, and she saw the satisfaction on his face when he noticed as she delved into those inviting blue eyes and soon got lost in the sensations.

Her release was so strong it opened a gate she'd been guarding with all her heart. With each spasm of climax tears welled in her eyes. Stripped down to the rawest of feelings, through Jared's meticulous lovemaking, Kasey couldn't control her crying.

"What's wrong? Did I hurt you?" He rolled off her and came back up on his elbow.

She shook her head, pulling the sheet to her face to wipe away the tears.

"Sweetheart, what's up?"

She pulled away from him, embarrassed by being so obvious. He spooned behind her, his hand and fingers splayed across her stomach. He hooked his chin over her shoulder.

"Tell me," he whispered.

After hesitating, not wanting his pity, she changed her mind about keeping the information to herself. The weight had become unbearable. "I got the results."

His hand tightened over her waist. "And?"

"I'm as close as you can get to being positive for Huntington's without getting complete confirmation."

"Come again?" He pulled her onto her back so he could look at her face. A shadow of sadness and confusion covered his eyes.

She explained everything the genetic counselor had told her. How she might or might not develop the symptoms of Huntington's over her lifetime, and how her offspring could also develop the disease.

"I never really thought about having children, but now that I've been told I shouldn't." More tears brimmed. She shook her head. "I hate not having options. I hate wondering if I'm going to get sick and lose everything I've worked for my whole life."

He kissed her forehead. "Sweetheart, you're only thirty-two. You'll have your whole life ahead of you."

"How do you know that? Are you God? I could develop this vile disease next week, tomorrow even."

He enveloped her in his embrace, rocked her gently, and kissed her hair.

Pain sliced through her core. She'd been given a damning diagnosis, or non-diagnosis, depending on how she interpreted it, and she'd fallen in love with a man, a most unlikely man, all in the same week.

That's why what she was about to tell him would be the hardest thing she'd ever had to do in her life.

CHAPTER TEN

"TELL me what you need." Jared wrapped Kasey tight against his body, and she almost succumbed to feeling safe. "I'm here for you," he said.

"I don't want your pity." She pushed away from his chest, trying to roll away.

"I'm not pitying you, I'm consoling you." He wouldn't let her go. "That's what friends do."

She quit fighting him. He admitted he was her friend. That was something, but was it enough? And what about that look she'd glimpsed in his eyes when they'd made love? Truth was, she couldn't deal with her diagnosis and confused heart, and Jared offering his friendship when what she really wanted, if she was being honest, was so much more. Their simple, no-strings relationship was tainted now. She'd never know if he'd stuck around because he felt sorry for her or if he really cared. It was all too confusing. She had to put a stop to it. "Will you do anything I ask?"

"Yes."

"Then leave. Please. Leave and never come back or call."

As if the words had hit him like a sucker punch, it took a moment for him to answer. "You don't mean that." He tried to pull her close again, but she wouldn't let him.

"Yes, I do."

"Come on, you're just all shook up." He held her by the shoulders and tried to make eye contact. She didn't cooperate, afraid of what she might see, of being convinced too easily her plan was full of holes. "You're not thinking straight. You need me now more than ever."

"I don't want to need anyone. I hardly know you."

He gave her a gentle shake. She still refused to look into his eyes. "You know me better than any person in my life right now. And I think I can say the same of you."

"In the bedroom, Jared. Only in the bedroom." She tried not to watch his mouth tighten into a straight line of disapproval, tried not to think of how it would be to never see him again. "You're just someone I happened to know for a couple of weeks. Someone I screwed. That's pitiful. Isn't it?" Finally, she glanced at his eyes, saw the hurt and disbelief there, then flicked her gaze away because it hurt so much. Hit and run. She couldn't get sucked into emotion.

"Not from where I'm standing. I think what we've got is pretty damn great."

"Please go, Jared. Just go." She squirmed like a child in trouble, needing to do something drastic.

"I won't do it."

Houdini quick, she disengaged from his grasp, jumped out of bed, and hit him with her pillow. "Go!" she yelled, hitting him over and over again, letting all the pent-up frustration and anger at her circumstances take over. "Go away."

He crossed his arms to cover his face, ducking with

each pelt of the pillow. "You're being unreasonable. Hysterical." He rolled off the bed and stood. "Calm down."

She couldn't let him close again. "No! Go away. Leave me alone!" she said, ready to hit him with the pillow again. "I don't want you here."

He raised his hands in surrender, an odd, unidentifiable expression on his face. Defeat? "Is that what you really want?"

Steeling herself against whirling emotions and a deep pain in her sternum, she drew a calming breath. "Yes. Please leave."

The muscle at his jaw bunched as he pressed his mouth into a thin line of disbelief. His eyes probed with surgical precision, yet he didn't utter a sound. She didn't think she could bear another second of his scrutiny, wanting to take the pillow and cover her face. He must have sensed her desperation. He swallowed, bent to pick up his clothes, got dressed, and left without another word.

Once he'd cleared the house she dropped to her knees and let the tornado of feelings overcome her, tearing her apart, thrashing her against the walls until she surrendered. Sobbing, curled into the fetal position, she stayed on the wooden planks of her floor letting time slip by one heartbeat at a time.

She couldn't control the disease that toyed with her wellbeing, but she could control who and what came into and out of her life. Jared had found the key to a satisfying profession, he had two children he adored, and a future bright with possibilities. He was a California native and would move home as soon as his fellowship ended. There was no future for the two of them.

Did she even have a future?

The last thing he needed in his life was to be shackled to a wildcard like her.

Kasey had been the second woman in his life to kick him out. Jared slammed the car door and started the engine. His wife had done it because he'd quit caring. Kasey had just given him the boot because he *did* care. Would he ever figure women out? He shifted the car into gear but had the good sense to wait until he calmed down to pull into traffic.

He'd just made love to her in a way he'd never made love to his wife in thirteen years of marriage. He'd never wanted to please anyone more in his life. Since when had caring and consideration become a bad thing?

Well, to hell with her. He'd been kicked in the teeth enough and he'd had it. From now on it was all going to be about his kids and his profession. And getting back to California as soon as possible.

He pulled onto the road and immediately got honked at when he cut off a car. Not giving a damn, he cupped the crook of one elbow with his other hand and shoved his fist in the air when the other car swung wide around him. The guy gave a reciprocal gesture.

He'd had it with love.

Halfway down the street, the thought finally sank in. The word stopped him cold. Love?

He got another honk and remembered to put his foot back on the gas to enter the freeway.

Was that this crazy feeling he'd been carrying around with him lately, the odd sensation that nagged at him and kept him awake at night? The constant and unsettling feeling that there was so much more to take out of life, that he'd been squandering good solid feelings by shoving them deep down inside until they backed up and made him one miserable guy?

He shook his head. If this was love, who needed it? He changed lanes and got another horn toot for his efforts. What was up with his driving today?

Nowhere near ready to call what he was feeling for Kasey right this moment anything but being mad as hell, he stepped on the gas and headed for his exit.

Somehow Kasey managed to get through work. An onslaught of patients helped keep her mind focused on the job and not her troubles.

As she called in the ultrasound request for one of the regular Everett Clinic patients and waited on hold, she explained her reasoning.

"We've been putting this off long enough, Mrs. Driscoll. It's time to get an ultrasound of your gallbladder. You've been coming here complaining of dyspepsia for a couple of months, and last week we drew some blood. The lab results show an elevation of bilirubin, alkaline phosphatase, AST and ALT. These indicate something is going on beyond an upset stomach."

"What if it's gallstones?"

"First we see what the ultrasound shows. If there are gallstones, the radiologist will contact me and we can arrange for a surgeon to examine you. Oh, excuse me." The radiology department receptionist picked up the phone, abruptly ending Vivaldi's *Four Seasons* smack in the middle of the movement that sounded like rain. "Yes, this is the Everett Community Clinic and I need to schedule an ultrasound to rule out cholelithiasis." Kasey gave all the pertinent information then waited, once again put on hold, while the appointment date got worked out.

"These days, having your gallbladder removed is much easier," she said to the sixty-five-year-old woman. "They do it as day surgery, go through your navel, collapse the gallbladder, pull it out through a tiny opening, put in a few stitches, and send you home with a little drain in place."

"My goodness. That doesn't sound so bad."

"It really isn't. Of course, if there are complications, they'd remove the gallbladder the old way, and you might have to spend a day or two in the hospital."

"I'd rather have it the easy way," Mrs. Driscoll said, a pyramid of lines on her forehead.

Kasey smiled at her. "That would get my vote, too." The woman came back on the phone and gave the appointment date and time. "Great. Thank you."

Kasey jotted down the information, pulled one of her low-fat diet sheets from the file in the cabinet, and faced Mrs. Driscoll. "I've made an appointment at the radiology department for next week. Here's the date and time." Kasey handed the appointment sheet to her. "Notice there are instructions to follow down below there." She gestured towards the sheet of paper. "Stay on the low-fat diet from now on, and have nothing by mouth after midnight the night before the examination."

Kasey finished up with patient education, reassuring Mrs. Driscoll they'd take this process one step at a time. It made her think of her own circumstances, and how she'd have to take the rest of her life one step, one day at a time. After seeing her patient out the door, she quickly became distracted by her worries again, and wandered toward her desk.

Vincent must have sensed that something was up as he hung around the area, finding this and that to fiddle with. "Want to talk about anything?" he asked, avoiding eye contact.

"I'm fine."

He turned his head and stared. "You look like hell."

"Blame it on Arturo."

"Whatever, girlfriend." He brushed her off with a loose wave. "Yesterday you loved the cut."

"That was yesterday."

He shook his head. "When you're ready to talk, I'm all ears." He walked off in a huff, grabbing his laptop on his way.

Was her plan to alienate everyone she cared about? Dropping her head into her hands, she leaned her elbows on the desk, holding her breath and squinting to stave off the tears. It wouldn't work. Eventually she'd have to come up for air from fighting the steadily mounting sobs.

Jared made surgical rounds with the conjoined twins team on Friday afternoon. Amazingly, he'd managed a couple hours' nap after leaving Kasey's house, and almost felt human again. A team of neurologists was exiting the patient rooms when they arrived.

"Jared," Dick Ortega said. "I got that referral you sent me, and made an appointment for next week."

It didn't register. "Referral?

The neurologist must have read his blank stare. "The one for the nurse with Huntington's. I got your e-mail and expedited her appointment—plan to see her Monday afternoon."

"Hey, great. Thanks for that."

"It's the least I could do after the way you made my wife look fifteen years younger." The silver-haired doctor smiled with a knowing twinkle in his dark eyes.

Face lift? Tummy tuck? Oh, snap, both.

"What time's the appointment?"

"Four-thirty."

His surgical team had moved into Twin A's room, the girl named Estrella, so he thanked the good doctor. After all the headlines across the globe about their surgical success, her name couldn't be more appropriate. She was definitely a star. He rushed to catch up, not wanting to miss out on the first day's progress post-op, which gave all the signs of being phenomenal. Even with the historical ramifications of this surgery, the excitement of a dozen surgeons beating their chests with success, his mind had drifted somewhere else.

Surrounded by no less than thirty people, it occurred to Jared that Kasey had to face her future alone, and the thought sat like a boulder in his gut. He knew what it was like to be alone, how a person scarred up and lost the gift of feelings. She was too vibrant and full of life to allow herself to become one of the walking dead. Kasey had challenged him, debrided his thickened hide, and welcomed him back to life. Just like the cleft palate surgery had given him the clue that he wasn't content to be a cosmetic surgeon. She'd reached him through no-strings sex, sex that had turned into a surprisingly easygoing friendship, and much, much more.

Jared exited the hospital room along with his colleagues, smiling over the patient progress yet lost in his own thoughts. The "much, much, more" part of knowing Kasey was what worried him. How had it happened?

The answer didn't matter, because he was well beyond reason and logic. He was desperate. He'd hooked up with a nurse for some fun, had gotten in over his head, and had fallen in love instead. Didn't that beat all?

* * *

All Kasey wanted to do was sleep through the weekend. She knew it was the coward's way out, but at the moment the wounds she bore were too tender for everyday life. She also knew she'd toughen up eventually, but right now she wanted to baby herself. Didn't she deserve it? She'd allow herself this one weekend to wallow in her cares, and then she'd do what she always did when life kicked her in the gut, she'd stand back up and get on with it.

On Saturday morning she hugged the pillow to her stomach and curled around it on the bed. *Stop thinking. Go back to sleep.*

Who the heck was knocking at her front door? She'd paid the rent. She'd also warned Vincent to leave her alone all weekend. He wouldn't dare stop by, unless he wanted to chance her wrath.

The doorbell rang. Three. Annoying. Times.

Kasey curled tighter, humming to drown out the sound, determined to let whoever the rude person was think she wasn't home.

It got quiet. Phew, they'd left.

New rapping came from what sounded like the back door. Was someone trying to break into her house?

Don't get up. Ignore everything. The alarm is set. This is your weekend off. Besides, it was probably Vincent being a PIA, even though she'd told him to leave her alone, and the last thing she needed today was a pain in the ass hanging around.

After another few seconds of silence, the damn front doorbell rang again. Could anyone on earth *be* this rude?

Tossing the pillow aside, she strode to the living room and looked out the peephole, soon needing to catch her breath.

Jared was at her front door, looking through the peephole back at her. All she could see was one huge blue eye.

"Go away."

"I want to talk to you."

"Our fling is over."

"Daddy, what's a fling?"

Kasey moved from the peephole and lifted a corner of the curtain. A spider-thin, preadolescent girl stood beside Jared. She wore straight-legged jeans and a fuzzy fake fur jacket with a hood, had wavy hair like her father, which was pulled back into a ponytail, and, well, she'd seen the girl's picture before. She had her father's eyes.

"It's what people who like each other do. We call it dating." Jared glared at her through the window. "Are you going to open up?"

It was his weekend to have his kids and, knowing Jared, he wouldn't miss it for the world. She noticed a healthy-looking boy on the sidewalk, playing Hacky Sack—the spitting image of his dad in baggy shorts and a bright red T-shirt. His dark brown hair was on the long side.

"You brought your kids here?"

"What else was I supposed to do? Desperate men do desperate things. Besides, this can't wait. Now open the door."

"Go away."

"You're going to turn me down in front of my kids? That's cold, lady."

"You're not fighting fair."

"I'm not fighting. I said I'm desperate. I want to make up with you. Now."

"Why do you want to make up, Daddy?"

Kasey grimaced. What was she supposed to do? Jared had brought the subject back up, and regardless of what went on between them the kids didn't need to be dragged into it. Why did he have to be so reckless?

"Because Kasey is my friend, and she's mad at me, and I don't want her to be." He said it so fast Kasey could hardly follow.

They hadn't had a fight. What she'd had was a rare moment of common sense regarding Jared. Could the little girl understand that?

"This is totally inappropriate. You shouldn't have brought your children here."

"Desperate times take drastic measures."

If desperate times meant that a man who only got to see his kids every other weekend might do something crazy like bring them along when he needed to make things right with her, he certainly had taken drastic measures. It was almost touching, but she couldn't let him sway her.

She opened the door a couple of inches. "I'm not dressed for company. Can you come back later?"

"I've made plans with my kids, and you're going to come along," he said, hands on hips, looking beyond manly. The word rakish came to mind. The tight polo shirt accentuating naturally developed deltoids, and narrow hips in snug jeans didn't help.

"I don't think she likes you, Daddy," the little one at his side said. Chloe. That's right. Kasey remembered her name.

"Trust me, she does. She's just playing hard to get."

"Am not!" How dared he make her out to be the stubborn one?

"Yes. You are."

"Hard to get?" Chloe repeated.

"She knows I like her. A lot. The same way Mommy likes Bradley, and she isn't making it easy for me."

"Is she your girlfriend?"

"Yes."

By now, Patrick had heard the ruckus, stopped playing Hacky Sack long enough to look up at the entertainment on the front porch. Chloe shrugged towards her brother, skipped down the steps to join in with Patrick's game. "Daddy's got a girlfriend!"

"As I recall, I was pretty easy to get," Kasey said in a strained whisper, once Chloe was out of earshot.

"That was before."

"Before what?"

"Before we got serious."

Was he serious? "When did we ever get serious?"

"Yesterday morning."

So he'd felt it too. Dear Lord, the man looked crestfallen standing on her porch, admitting he'd gotten serious with her, with his kids looking on. He really was desperate, and it drove his brows together as he stared at her with those dangerously blue eyes. This could be terrible for his ego, and mess up his kids for life. What was he thinking!

Desperate men often had poor judgement.

No one in her entire life had ever been despairing over her before. Desperate enough to drag their kids into the fray.

She was not going to give in and let him run roughshod over her just because he'd brought his kids as a lever. Cheap shot, if you asked her, regardless of whether or not he could find child care. She had no intention of letting the man, who was obviously out of his mind, get stuck with a health risk like her. She'd hold him back in life, and she cared about him too much to do that.

Oh, hell. She did care about him. Loved him. He wasn't about to take no for an answer, even though it was the best thing to do to just forget the whole damn affair.

She glanced at the children by the curb, tossing the Hacky Sack back and forth, then she looked back at Jared, who had fire in his eyes, and an air of determination rolling off his skin. How would they work this out?

"Okay. You wait on the porch, because I've got to put on some clothes," she said as she headed down the hall hell-bent on not letting his little ploy change her mind about the bigger picture. She'd be civil to him and kind to his children, and patiently wait for the afternoon to be over.

Two hours later, they'd finished a trip around the Boston Public Garden Lake on one of the pedaled swan-styled boats. Both children had watched her closely the entire ride. She wondered if she measured up. The children had been shy at first in the car on the drive over, but once they'd gotten to the park they'd opened up and asked her questions as they'd walked. She'd done her best to stay engaged with them, while being pulled by Jared's audacious vibes. He had no intention of making things easy for her.

Once they got off the boat, the kids ran ahead to a street vendor, looking for iced lemonade and a churro. In an odd change of dreary May weather, the sun was out and glistening off the water.

"I don't know what you have up your sleeve, but I distinctly remember asking you to leave me alone."

"I did."

"For one day?"

"That's longer than I wanted to, believe me." He reached for her hand, but she moved away.

"Why?"

"Because I care about you. I don't want you to go through this mess alone."

She quit walking, and squared off in front of him. "For how long? How long will it be before you get tired of doing that? Before we realize we should have cut our losses a long time ago?"

"Friends shouldn't think like that."

"So are you saying we're not hot sex partners any more, but now we're just friends?"

He wore a pained expression, eyes and lips turning downward. "Don't be that way."

"I've got to think like that. I can't let myself fall for someone who plans to leave in another year. Where will I be then?"

He offered a dead stare. She'd heard about his apartment with the can't-wait-to-get-out-of-town feel and the rented furniture.

"Look," she said, "I'm not trying to be contrary, but we've got to be realistic. We signed on for a fling and wound up with all kinds of extra junk thrown in. We didn't see that in the package deal when we bought it, you know?"

"Do you give a damn about me?" he asked.

"What has that got to do with what I'm trying to explain?"

He took her hand. "Something changed between us yesterday morning. I know you felt it too. I can't walk away from that just because you tell me to."

She couldn't let him hijack her plan. The guy didn't deserve one more tether in his life. His kids looked up

to him and he'd just done something crazy on her behalf by dragging them along for the confrontation. He
was embarking on a new direction in reconstructive surgery, and he needed to be free of any constraints. She
wouldn't—wouldn't!—let him get involved with her.

No matter how much she wanted to.

With the kids busy buying treats from the vendor
three hundred feet away, she gave him a rueful smile.
Damn if her lower lip didn't tremble. "Look, I gotta go."
She couldn't let him see her tear up. "This isn't going to
work out. Let's face it now." Before it hurt even more
than it already did. She turned and rushed toward the
passing crowd.

"Kasey." He called her name, but she'd started with
a slow jog and stepped it up to a lope in the opposite
direction from his kids. She knew he wouldn't come
after her and leave them unattended. "I'm not giving
up!" he called out.

That's what she was afraid of. She ran as fast as she
could out of the park, toward the Chinatown T entrance,
away from Jared and all the hopes and dreams to which
she couldn't let herself fall prey.

On Monday afternoon, after Kasey had given the third
rabies vaccination to Janie, she clutched the paperwork
in her hand and left the clinic early for her four-thirty
appointment with the neurologist in Boston. Vincent
had volunteered to go with her, but she'd decided to
take this examination alone.

The high-rise medical office was typical of many
such buildings with cold tile floors that made footsteps echo off the granite walls. A chrome and mirrored elevator took her to the seventh floor. The hall
felt compact, claustrophobic even, and quiet, thanks

to thick brown carpet. The narrow corridor was lined with framed prints and posters by famous artists she recognized. Miro, Picasso, Modigliani. Rather than enjoying the art, she looked straight ahead to the office at the end of the hall, wondering what she'd find out today. Maybe, just maybe, Dr. Ortega would be the one to tell her not to worry. Maybe he'd laugh and say, *Oh, for crying out loud, you got yourself all worked up over this? It's nothing. Absolutely nothing.*

A girl could hope, couldn't she?

She swallowed and opened the door to the waiting room then stopped abruptly. Jared sat in a chrome and wine-colored leather chair, watching her. His piercing eyes were determined yet questioning when he looked up. The usual effervescent feeling she got in her chest whenever she saw him still happened, and it surprised her. She should be angry. What on earth was he doing there?

She'd asked him to leave her alone, had run away from him at the park. Why couldn't she get the point through to him? They didn't belong together. Ever. Regardless of her feelings for him.

She couldn't make a scene. Not here. What was he trying to do, out-stubborn her and force his way back into her life?

He jumped to his feet and rushed to take her hands. "Don't get upset. I just want to be here when you're done with your appointment. Then we'll talk about anything you'd like."

Right now the only thing she wanted to do was pound his chest with her fists. He was driving her crazy with this "being there" for her business. Couldn't he let her suffer in silence as she was used to doing?

She bit her tongue rather than tell him to leave. A

wiser part of her conscience stopped her from overreacting. "Okay," she said.

Jared didn't want to drive her crazy—he wanted to offer her support. She'd humor him. Let him stay. But there was no way she'd take him into the appointment. This was her business. Hers and hers alone. And afterwards she'd search for a rear exit.

After checking in with the receptionist, she sat in a matching chair against the opposite wall. She'd let him stay—did she have a choice?—but in the meantime she'd do her best to make him suffer. She covered her mouth with her hand and stared at the plush coffee-brown carpet in silence until the nurse opened the door and invited her inside.

As she looked up, without meaning to, her eyes connected with Jared's. He nodded. She glanced away, refusing to admit it felt reassuring, and followed the nurse through the door.

How different it felt to be the one in the gown with the opening to the back, sitting on the exam table lined with a tissue-paper-thin barrier, having her blood pressure taken. She waited with her bare feet dangling over the edge of the table as she thumbed through a surprisingly recent design magazine from the wall rack. Try as she may, her pulse quickened with every movement outside the door. What if she already showed signs of Huntington's, had been compensating for physical changes, and hadn't even known it?

After a couple of taps on the door, a silver haired doctor entered and introduced himself. "I'm Dr. Ortega, and you must be Ms. McGowan."

She nodded. "Call me Kasey."

His inviting smile helped her relax a tiny bit.

After going through her list, he glanced up. "We usually recommend having someone with you during this examination to help you remember what we've talked about."

"No, thank you. I'm a nurse practitioner. I'll remember what we talk about."

"Okay."

"Have you noticed any personality changes such as irritability, anger, depression or loss of interest?"

She'd certainly been irritable and angry lately, but that had been for a good reason. Depressed? Who wouldn't be? Yup, she'd lain around in bed all day on Sunday, tuning out the world. Oh, hell, it all seemed circumstantial. "Not really."

"Have you recently had difficulty making decisions, learning new information, answering questions?"

She shook her head. Except for making decisions, she seemed to be waffling back and forth where Jared was concerned. And she'd pay a thousand dollars to answer the big question occupying her heart today—just because she loved Jared, did that make it okay to mess up his life?

"Any problems with remembering important information?"

She shook her head in double time.

"Balance problems?"

She remembered feeling clumsier than usual lately. "Maybe."

"Anyone notice you making involuntary facial movements?"

She screwed up her face, definitely a voluntary movement, and shook her head again.

"Slurred speech?" *Only when I've had too much to drink.* "Or difficulty swallowing?" *Only when she had a huge lump in her throat when crying.*

"No." Her reply came out breathy.

"Let's begin with a neuro examination, then."

She'd given enough abbreviated neuro exams at the clinic to know the doctor was not only assessing her nerve function, motor system and reflexes with his thorough investigation but her mental status and speech as well.

The extensive test would take over half an hour, beginning with her head and ending with her toes. He had her smell things, distinguish between hot and cold, make faces at him, show her teeth, smile, frown, puff out her cheeks, raise her eyebrows, stick out her tongue, shrug, walk heel to toe.

He had her hop in place, first on one foot and then on the other, and she flexed and extended just about everything that could bend. He measured her muscle strength with various tasks of resistance, while standing and lying down. Then he moved on to the sensory system, using various items to test her reactions to pain, temperature, light touch, and vibration. Finally, using his rubber hammer, he tested all the usual reflexes she knew about from her own training, and several more she'd never have thought of, ending at the soles of her feet.

Once he'd finished the examination, after writing in a chart for what seemed like eternity, he glanced up. "You seem perfectly normal, but due to your family history and recent genetic tests, I'll order a CT scan and an MRI. This will give us a baseline for future reference. My nurse will call you with the appointment dates."

Kasey let out her breath, unaware she'd been holding it for the last few seconds. "Okay. Whatever you suggest."

After he left the room, she got dressed, thankful to know that nothing, so far, was abnormal. Kasey didn't expect that to change overnight either. She'd cleared the first hurdle, but would have to go for the CT and MRI to see what they showed, if anything. Dared she think things were looking up?

Once she was dressed she headed back to the hall-way, searching for a back exit. No such luck. A tiny flutter of nerves winged through her center at the thought of seeing Jared again or, worse yet, that he wouldn't be there.

The only remaining test for today was the one sitting in the waiting room.

Jared.

CHAPTER ELEVEN

KASEY stepped into the waiting room to find Jared sitting exactly where she'd left him. She let out her breath. Those big blues peered up at her from beneath tented brows. He couldn't feign the look of concern, and it made the butterfly flutters go double time in her stomach.

What was she supposed to do about Jared?

"How'd it go?" he asked.

"Fine. He says I'm fine."

His brows smoothed, relief washing away the tension in his eyes as he stood and reached for her. "Fantastic."

Kasey believed him. He was on her side. He'd proved it on Saturday, rashly doing whatever he needed to do to make her understand, even to the point of dragging his kids along, and he'd shown up here today in support without being asked. How much more proof did she need? He cared about her, and right now that meant more than anything else in the world.

She let him enfold her and draw her to his chest. Man, oh, man, she'd missed being held by Jared. His usual citrus-woodsy scent welcomed her, and even the scratchy tweed of his jacket felt fantastic against her cheek. She sighed, relaxing for the first time in days.

"Dr. Ortega wants me to get a CT scan and an MRI."

She felt him nod. His hands rubbed her back, soothing her even more. She could get used to this, but knew she shouldn't. If she let go of her resistance, he'd entice her back into bed, and she knew in Jared's case food hadn't been the only way into his heart. In fact, she'd never even cooked for him. What would happen if he found out she was a great cook…when she wanted to be. No, she shouldn't even go there with him.

Her mind spun with confusing thoughts about Jared—how she should keep him at arm's length, banish him from her world, from her heart. But he was here, and he made her feel safe, and maybe just one more day with him was okay, just for emotional support. Suddenly amidst all the jumbled ideas she wanted to prepare him dinner for being here today, for forgiving her stubbornness on Saturday. For refusing to let her push him away.

Only a good guy with nerves of steel would show up here and wait, and that gutsy guy deserved to be fed.

"Are you hungry?" she asked.

"Sure. Where do you want to go?"

"I thought I'd cook us something. Is that okay?"

He pulled back to look at her. "You cook?"

Showing the first sign of spunk in what seemed like ages, she cocked a brow. "You don't know what you've been missing."

His mouth twitched, his eyes dancing from concern to bring it on. "Oh, yes, I do." He lightly swatted then caressed her hip.

She'd meant it about her cooking, but he'd obviously taken it the wrong way. "Hey, I'm only offering dinner. Friend. Because you've been so annoyingly nice lately, in a desperate kind of way."

The mouth twitch stretched into a wide smile and,

coupled with his afternoon stubble, he looked far too appealing. "Whatever. I'm there."

"Then let's get going." She stepped out of his embrace and immediately missed his warmth.

As they drove home in Jared's car, he quizzed her about the examination. She opened up about it, even made light of some of the ridiculous poses she'd been in. "I felt like I was taking a sobriety test."

His deep, healthy laugh put a full smile on her face. Her expression may have been involuntary, but it sure had nothing to do with Huntington's.

She glanced across the car at him, his noble profile, the way his thick, dark hair curled on his collar. What the heck was she supposed to do about Jared?

Jared and Kasey walked the aisles of the supermarket together. He couldn't remember the last time he'd shopped for groceries with a woman. She wore black slacks with low-heeled boots, a bright green cowlneck sweater that made her eyes pop, and a dark gray blazer. The new haircut gave her a sophisticated air, but that bright-eyed stare she gave while picking over the zucchinis and yellow squash looked nothing short of playful.

"Chloe said she thought you were pretty," he said, pretending to examine a tomato.

"She did?" She slid him a sideways glance while her fingers tested more vegetables.

"Yup."

He followed her to the next stand. "And Patrick thought you were weird for running off like that."

Her head dropped back. She sighed. "I can see why he'd think that. What a lousy first impression to make on them, but you forced me into it."

"He thought you were pretty, too, by the way."

She tossed her head and snorted. "Get out of town."

He couldn't resist, so he kissed her cheek. "Not without you." She didn't push him away. Progress.

Kasey was a breath of fresh spring air after a long New England winter, and a welcome change in his life. He was definitely ready for a change.

After she chose a red bell pepper, she assigned him the job of choosing the crimini mushrooms, as she'd moved on to the fingerling potatoes. On the way to the butcher counter, he grabbed a bottle of white wine, a pinot grigio, as she picked out some chicken cutlets. His mouth was already watering and, watching her, the Pavlovian reaction wasn't all from food. She shopped with confidence, sure of what she wanted. If only she could feel the same about him.

It wouldn't be easy, but he was determined to convince her to give him a chance. He wouldn't be like the other men in her life.

Would he?

Back at her apartment, he was banished to the living room while she prepared dinner. The aroma emitting from the kitchen piqued his appetite. He nibbled a pretzel or two from the dish on the coffee table by the sofa, took an occasional drink of the not great but very drinkable wine, and scratched behind Miss Daisy's ears while watching the news on TV. From the loud purring, and insistence about his continuing on with the petting, he gathered the cat liked it.

He needed to come up with a plan to make Kasey purr tonight.

"Dinner's almost ready," she said. He sure hoped so because the combination of garlic, parmesan, olive oil, and pan-seared chicken was driving him crazy with hunger. So was she.

"At least let me set the table," he said, jumping up and disturbing Daisy, who'd settled in his lap. The cat protested with a protracted meow.

After Jared washed his hands and set the table, Kasey brought out the dinner on a single large platter. The chicken cutlets were lightly breaded and browned to perfection drizzled with a thickened lemon sauce and placed in a row down the middle. The sautéed veggies were on one side, and the golden brown buttered and herbed roasted fingerling potatoes lined the opposite side.

"I think I need to take a picture of this," he said, smiling.

"You going to post it on your social network page?"

He made a goofy face. "I might." Never occurred to him. He didn't even have a social network page.

As beautiful as the food looked, it tasted even better. "You've been holding out on me," he said, using the stabbed potato on his fork for emphasis. "This is delicious. And the chicken, wow, great, just great."

"There's so much you don't know about me," she said, teasing him with a flighty expression while sipping her wine.

She'd fed him an opening line, and he needed to take advantage of it. "I'd like to know everything about you," he said, feeling as earnest as all hell, wrists resting on the table as he leaned toward her.

She paused and gazed at him.

"I'm serious," he said.

"You'll be leaving next year, Jared. What's the point?"

He was well aware that she didn't need a lecture on taking it one day at a time and seeing where it led when she could very well be the one left behind. That had happened once too often to her, and though he couldn't predict what the future held for them, beyond what he wanted it to, nothing was certain in life. "So you can read the future? Are you a fortune teller?"

In mid-bite she stopped to give him an annoyed glance.

"I'm just saying," he continued, "we don't know what the future holds for us. All we can do is enjoy what we can of it."

"Is this the part where you try to talk me back into our no-strings fling?" She cut off a piece of chicken with extra vigor. The suspicious stare wounded him. He hadn't made any headway in the trust department with Kasey.

He should have waited until after dinner, because the conversation was affecting his sense of taste. Great dinner or not, he needed to get some things off his chest. Before she kicked him out of here tonight he needed to make sure Kasey knew where she stood with him. "No. This is the part where I tell you exactly how I feel."

He glimpsed an alarmed look in her eyes as she rapidly chewed her food. He refilled his wine glass and topped off hers, then took a long drink as he'd suddenly developed a deep thirst.

"We've done everything backwards, Kasey. We hopped right into bed without getting to know each other, discovered we really dug each other in there…" he pointed through the dining-room wall to where her bedroom was "…and we, I at least, realized how much I liked you. How I admire your dedication to your job and how you'd pulled yourself up by your own bootstraps and made something of yourself. Hell, I discovered that the first day I'd met you." He watched her pushing her food around her plate instead of eating, listening to every word. "At the coffee bar that night, when you'd let slip how you'd been handed a lousy diagnosis from a father you'd never even met, I knew you weren't any ordinary lady. Yet you still held your head high and refused to let it get you down. That was amazing." Their gazes met and fused. "You're amazing."

She quickly glanced away. He took another bite of food and drank more wine, waiting for his words to sink in. "The thing is, you're my game changer, Kasey."

Her head shot up, she nailed him with her stare. For someone who didn't usually hold back her thoughts, she'd gone eerily quiet. If he could only read her mind.

"Remember," he said, "you told me to be the game changer in my relationship with my ex-wife. You told me to fight for what I wanted with my kids." He pushed out his chair, stood, and walked behind her, resting his hands on her shoulders, then whispered, "You're my game changer. I didn't think I wanted another relationship for as long as I lived. Now I understand I'll never be truly alive if I don't have another relationship. And I want that relationship to be with you." He squeezed her shoulders, hoping she'd understand. "I want to be with you, Kasey. I want to find out what happens when you and I quit hiding behind our walls and instead start pulling them down brick by brick." He knelt beside her so he could look into her eyes, which were welling up. "I know what may happen with you, Kasey, and I'm dead serious about seeing you through it." Big, fat tears brimmed in her eyes and some dropped over the lids. "Give me the chance to prove myself, sweetheart. I love you."

Her fork clinked onto her plate. She shook with emotion. He thumbed her tears away and hugged her close, then kissed her hair.

"I do love you. Even though I don't totally know you yet, I already know enough about you to fall in love." He kissed her cheek. "You've got to believe me, because I'm not a liar."

Kasey let go a ferocious cry, flinging herself into his open embrace. He'd risked it all, and reaped an amazing result.

"I love you, too, Jared," she said, burying her face in his shoulder.

He'd finally heard the sweetest words on earth, and it made him feel as though he was floating in the air.

Kasey used the cloth napkin to wipe her face and eyes. Smiling, and refreshed from a long-overdue cry, she shook her head. "I must look frightening."

"You look beautiful."

Her knees turned to butter, seeing the sexiest man on earth with eyes only for her. Her fingers trembled as she gave one last swipe under her eyes.

Her body had just gone through the entire list of life's emotions and now a warm pooling between her legs added another. Lust. She wanted him. "What do you say we clear the table and have dessert in bed?" she said.

Every cell in her body was marked to want Jared. He looked longingly at her—so long and sexily she could count it as foreplay. Jared held out his hand, she took it, accepting the warmth and electricity of his touch, and together they walked to her bedroom.

The instant they passed the threshold he grabbed her shoulders, held her still and kissed her yielding lips. His tongue soon made love to hers as they held each other so tight she could already feel his arousal. Could anyone else's body ever feel as right next to hers as Jared's? He kissed her again. Easy answer. No.

She caressed his hips and pushed him tighter. Why

did they have to have clothes on? Pulling away, she tried to unbutton his shirt, but he stopped her. His firm stare communicated without a doubt that he planned to take charge of this party.

She'd never surrendered completely to anyone, couldn't trust enough to let it all go, but this was Jared. The man had just told her he loved her, and she knew he'd meant it. There was something else she knew without a doubt. She loved him back.

With her breathing steadily mounting as he delicately removed her sweater and slacks, and with tingles and shivers rushing over her skin from the dome of her head to her nearly curling toes, she let him undress her garment by garment until she was naked and positioned on her bed.

Jared was fully clothed when he leaned over the bed and started applying butterfly kisses to every erogenous zone she possessed, beginning at her neck. Her breasts tightened and pebbled as his mouth found each one, teasing the nipple with his feathery tongue lashes. With each kiss and suckle, she gave in to him, riding the beautiful wave of excitement from a whole new perspective. She wanted to close her eyes to enjoy it more deeply, but didn't want to stop watching him. His kisses moved to her stomach, playfully nipping at her navel, making her squirm, before he continued south to her core.

The sweet torture went on until she twisted and writhed on the sheets, fisting them tightly, while he kissed her most sensitive spot as thoroughly as he'd kissed her mouth.

Not usually one to beg, she pleaded with him, called his name as if it was all she had left to hold onto now that he'd taken complete control of her body. Tension built steadily, the sensation so delectable she selfishly never wanted it to end. She indulged in the exquisite pleasure, her body coiling tighter and tighter, until she couldn't bear it any more. Jared took her to the tipping point with his loving tongue, and she dove into the releasing waves as they rolled from gentle to tsunami in strength.

"Now," she said, "I need you now."

Jared removed his clothes in lightning-quick time, and while she still rocked with the climax he'd given her he climbed onto the bed and thrust inside, immediately heightening the already amazing sensation. She wrapped her legs around his hips and he filled her, finally satisfying the missing link to her total satisfaction. He continued to take complete control as he held her hips tilted just so and they rocked together at his pace, a hard and driving tempo. The deeper touches awakened new points of awareness that heated up, spilled over, and traveled her body like rogue waves of pleasure. Her head frantically moved from side to side as he pushed her against the mattress time and time again.

Nothing had ever been like this, giving in completely to her man—the man who loved her. He worked her and drove her ever closer until the sublime moment where she felt him turn rod solid, throb, and with a wild groan spill inside her yet never let up on the piston pace. His massive climax swept her over the edge as she tightened in deep blissful spasms around him and let herself go to a place she'd never been before. Complete abandon. Completely at one with him. Completely his.

It was midnight before they ventured out for dessert. Famished from their nonstop lovemaking, they ate leftovers from dinner instead. Kasey had never felt happier in her life.

"So what happens now?" she asked, mouth full of chicken cutlet.

"You let yourself trust me as much outside the bedroom as you just did in there, and I promise I won't let you down."

She got up and nuzzled his shoulder. "I'm beginning to realize that."

"Then I'll just have to help you figure it out the rest of the way, too." He kissed her cheek, a greasy kiss from the potatoes. "What do you think about living together for a while before we make the big move?"

"What big move?"

"The one that takes vows and official papers and all that kind of thing."

"Hold on. This is moving way too fast for me."

"You're the one who just asked what's next. I'm only being honest with you. Like I promised. Remember?"

She shook her head. "You're blowing my mind."

"I thought I already did that in the bedroom. Let's see, about three times as I recall, give or take a whimper."

Kasey pummeled him with her palm, and he faked being hurt. "You're brutal when you're satisfied, you know that?"

"Are you kidding?" she said. "I can hardly lift my head."

They laughed and delicately danced away from the commitment conversation, and when they'd eaten their fill, they went back to bed. This time, since both had to be at work in the morning, to cuddle and sleep.

Kasey and Jared strolled into the Everett Community Clinic the next morning holding hands. Vincent shot up from his desk, his look of interest so obvious his mouth was open.

"Well, well," he said.

"That's only half of it," Kasey said.

Vincent's eyes bugged out and Jared laughed.

"Yes, we are," Jared said.

"Are what?" Vincent seemed to have trouble forming words.

"A couple," Jared said. "I finally convinced her about the shallowness of superficial sex."

Vincent clapped his hands, eyes sparkling. "Congratulations. And would you mind talking to my steady guy about that shallowness bit, too?" Vincent asked.

"Sure thing. Bring him to the bar on Friday when we celebrate. I'll clue him in."

Jared kissed Kasey lightly on the lips. "I'll be here tonight to pick you up."

"You will?" she asked, still amazed by the change in her circumstances.

He nodded and smiled as he backed toward the clinic exit. "And tomorrow night, and the night after that, and the night after that, and…"

CHAPTER TWELVE

Ten years later...

JARED pushed Kasey in the wheelchair up the incline towards the car.

"What a beautiful graduation, Jared. Weren't you proud of Patrick?"

"Couldn't be prouder. Pre-med is a huge undertaking, but since he's interested in getting both an M.D. and a Ph.D. in research, that near free ride for medical school will help us out a lot."

"You would have been thrilled to pay every penny for him to go to med school, you know it." She smiled over her shoulder at him and he leaned forward so he could give her a quick kiss. "You need to let up on Chloe a little, though."

He shook his head. "She isn't even trying, Kase."

"By your assessment maybe, but not everyone is cut out for higher education."

"If she'd just applied herself a little more in high school, she could have gone to a four-year school instead of junior college."

"There's nothing wrong with junior college. That's how I started my nursing education."

"I'm not saying there's anything wrong with it, it's—"

"She's pursuing her interests, so get over it. Chloe needs to find out who she is, and that won't happen if you push her in a direction she doesn't want to go. You need to get it through your head that she wants to be a hairstylist and not a chemist."

Jared sighed. "Why do you always have to be the voice of reason?"

Kasey offered another bright-eyed smile. He still lived for those looks.

"One of us has to," she said.

He feigned shock. "If I'd listened to the voice of reason, I never would've ignored you asking me to leave you alone and not come back. I never would have asked you to marry me on the spur of the moment."

"And under different circumstances, I might have taken life for granted and decided you were like every other guy and blown you off, too."

"Sometimes bad things happen to great people, and good things come from it," he said, wheeling her over a particularly bumpy patch of parking-lot pavement.

"Going all philosophical on me, are you?"

"Just trying to put this Chloe business in perspective," he said.

"Give her time, darling. She's coming off a bad relationship. Her heart is broken. She's trying to stretch her wings and be independent. Give her time. That's what it took for you to get used to living in Boston, right? Time?"

"Time and the right lady. Heck, if a south shore girl like you could move to the north shore and get used to it, the least I could do was handle leaving the west coast for Bean Town."

He sighed, then spotted their car and rolled her to the handicapped spot for easy access.

"Before I met you," she said, "all I wanted to do was

run my little clinic in Everett. If you'd told me back then that one day I'd be in charge of six community clinics, I would have laughed in your face. Hell, I could hardly handle one."

"You laughed in my face a lot back then, remember?"

"Only when you deserved it, dear."

When he bent over and reached down to put the brake on the wheelchair, Kasey grabbed his hand and squeezed. "If I hadn't been diagnosed with the Huntington's marker I might never have opened up to life or hung on for this wild ride with you. I've loved you fearlessly since you took the risk of telling me how you felt, and for asking me to marry you when you didn't have a clue what the future held for me, Jared. For us."

He hugged her and kissed her again. "And I'm incredibly grateful you took the gamble." He helped her stand. "Think of what we would have missed out on if you'd let pride win."

"I can't bear to think about it. I'd be a sad and lonely person who'd missed her chance of a lifetime." She hugged him with all her might. "And I would have missed watching Patrick and Chloe grow up, graduate from college. Well, one of them anyway. Didn't he look handsome today? Just like you did, I bet, at that age. Tall. Dark. Gorgeous. Some poor unsuspecting girl's worst nightmare." She looked wistfully at him. "Or dream."

He covered her mouth with a kiss, which, if he didn't put a stop to it soon, could get out of control for a parking lot. "And you would have missed all of Chloe's teenage angst," he said, after breaking off the kiss.

"How true. Maybe that part would have been okay to miss." She laughed and he joined her. "I love you so much."

"I love you, too."

He gazed into her eyes, now more beautiful than ever with a few creases around them from years well spent grabbing life by the horns and shaking it for all it was worth. With him.

Kasey hopped to stand alone while he removed the wheelchair. "How am I supposed to get everything ready for Patrick and our guests with this blasted cast on my foot?"

He opened the car door for her to slide in. "You'll manage, you always do. And I'll help."

"Why did you let me try snowboarding again?"

He bent and kissed her again. Smiled. "Because I've been married to you long enough to know that once you put your mind to something, there's no talking you out of it."

"Like loving you," she said. "There's been no talking me out of that either."

He stopped, love swelling in his chest, and grinned at the pride of his life—after his children, of course. "You know I love you, but promise me one thing."

"What's that?"

"You can sky dive, zip line, learn to ride a motorcycle if you insist, but from now on snowboarding is not negotiable."

"Yes, darling, whatever you say. You're the famous pediatric reconstructive surgeon."

"Since when has my professional title ever won me an argument with you?"

"Since right now, simply because you're taking such great care of me since I broke my ankle on our vacation. And since I've categorically decided that when I married you, nine years, seven months and twenty-five days ago, I officially became the luckiest woman in the world."

* * * * *

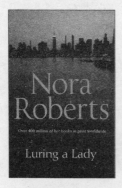